D0752884

WITHOUT A HITCH

AVERY MAXWELL

Dear Cinthia,
Chase Dreams 'e.
HEAS!
♡ Avery Maxwell

That's What She Said Publishing,Inc.

Cover Design: Kari March Designs

Cover Photo: AdobeStock image

Editing and Proofing: Jessica Snyder Edits

www.AveryMaxwellBooks.com

ISBN: 979-8-88643-970-0 (ebook)

ISBN: 979-8-88643-971-7 (paperback)

090722

This book is dedicated to you, my amazing readers who have followed, LUVed, and supported me on this journey! It's also for anyone who has had to deal with a Christine. Their issues are not yours, don't take them on. Trust me, they're not worth it, but your mental health is!
You do you, boo!
XOXO,
Avery

AUTHOR NOTE

In this story:

When Tilly was a child, she lost her mother to mental illness. This is as in-depth as the storyline goes with her mother, and I understand that can be triggering for some readers.

If you or someone you know struggles with mental health, please reach out below:

https://www.nami.org/help

National Suicide Prevention Lifeline: 1.800.273.TALK (8255)

https://findtreatment.samhsa.gov/

LOCHLANISMS

Dear Reader,

The hero in this book, Lochlan, has a lot of quirks. Here are some of my favorite Lochlanisms:

Bloody fucket: Lochlan's favorite curse word. Part British, part his father's colorful influence.

Dachoobie: This refers to a man who is both a douche and a dirtbag.

Skittle scuz: The film you get on your teeth from too much candy.

Floating bed of doom: A hammock.

My favorite thing about writing books like Lochlan's is being able to explore different family dynamics. The family you choose, the family that chooses you, and the family you blend to make one. Lochlan's parents are a perfect example of creating a family by blood, by choice, and by chance.

However you find your family, love them hard.

Luvs,

Avery

PLAYLIST

WITHOUT A HITCH

1. Raise Your Glass, Pink
2. Wildest Dreams, Taylor Swift
3. Renegade, Big Red Machine
4. I Need My Girl, The National
5. What Have I Done, Dermot Kennedy
6. New York, Snow Patrol
7. Flaws, Bastille
8. Welcome To New York, Taylor Swift
9. Demons, The National
10. Steal My Sunshine, LEN
11. Distorted Light Beam, Bastille
12. You Oughta Know, Alanis Morissette
13. Things You Do for Love, Thomas Rhett
14. I Can't Be With You, The Cranberries
15. Gaslighter, The Chicks
16. Something Just Like This, The Chainsmokers & Coldplay
17. Semi-Charmed Life, Third Eye Blind
18. Outnumbered, Dermot Kennedy
19. Mo Money Mo Problems, The Notorious B.I.G.

20. Another Place, Bastille
21. One Week, Barenaked Ladies
22. Power Over Me, Dermot Kennedy
23. Good Riddance, Green Day
24. Lover, Taylor Swift
25. Unforgettable, Thomas Rhett
26. Father and Son, Cat Stevens

Spotify: https://geni.us/WOAHplaylist

PROLOGUE

TILLY CAMDEN

Without A Hitch!

They say behind every good man is a great woman. They say a hospital is only as good as its nurses. They say a hotel is only as good as its employees. They say behind every good wedding is a bridesmaid who gets shit done.

Okay, so maybe that last one isn't quite true, but as I stand here, arms spread wide, yelling at one bridesmaid to put down the ice bucket and another to drop the hairspray while I'm wearing a sherbet orange dress and my hair is teased to within an inch of its life, I'm going to say it's true.

Why, might you ask, am I playing referee in a wedding where I don't know a single soul? Not even the bride or groom?

Well... That's a funny story. One I'm happy to tell, but it started a few years ago while I was working for my brother-in-law's brother (Did you follow that?), traveling the world, and staying in some of the fanciest hotels I'd only ever dreamed about.

I was just a girl with a dream. A dream of starting my own

1

wedding planning business (because weddings are my happy place!), writing my own blog (to keep my sanity in the insanity that's life), and to not, under any circumstances, fall in love with my boss's best friend (because that's always a bad idea).

Okay, that last one came later. Much later. Much, much later, after I learned why he had that slightly British lilt to his voice. Or why he could be so charming to those he cared about but the devil incarnate to everyone else. Or why, why, why he would do the sweetest things but never admit to them.

This is my story of business, sex, and love. Buckle up, buttercup—it's going to be a bumpy ride!

CHAPTER 1

TILLY

Six Months Ago

"You got penis whipped. Pe-nis whipped!" My childhood best friend, Delaney, gasps as our roommate, Hadley, stares on in wide-eyed horror.

Eli, my only sister in attendance, documents our reactions with photos on her cell phone as any good sister would. Her long legs are on display tonight, and the dirty blond hair she got from our father falls in loose curls that frame her face. She's beautiful, even if she is annoying.

She holds the phone out for another photo op, and I let out a low groan. "I—I think I'm going to kill Sloane."

Sloane! My youngest sister, an award-winning romance novelist who, since marrying her super-spy husband, has veered off into the erotica category. I don't even want to think about how she comes up with her story ideas, but it's probably why she's now six months pregnant and home on bedrest while we're at a male strip club in Myrtle Beach at her request. Research, she'd called it.

I'm vaguely aware of Hadley digging around in her purse

and then coming at me with a tiny spray bottle. "Hads, I love you, but if you're about to spray my face with hand sanitizer, I might lose my shit."

"But germs," Hadley whispers, glancing over her shoulder like she might offend the male stripper. She adjusts her glasses but lowers her spray bottle.

"Please," I say with a slow exhale. "Can we please go somewhere else? *Anywhere* else. I'm positive we have enough ammunition for Sloane." My skin crawls as strangers' eyes still laugh in my direction. I sink even deeper into my chair, wishing it would just swallow me whole already. A fire drill would be my dream come true right now.

"Who knew schlongs could even rotate like that?" Delaney whispers. Her bright pink lips remind me of cotton candy as she licks the sugared rim of whatever sickly-sweet cocktail she just sucked down.

An involuntary shiver runs down my spine. It doesn't seem fair that my longest dry spell since I started having sex ended ten seconds ago with a ten-inch torpedo bitch-slapping not one, but both cheeks.

If it weren't for my darker complexion, I'd have a penis-sized bruise on my right cheek. That fucker hurt. My mother's tiny percentage of Asian-American heritage shows in my bronzed skin. All three of my sisters and I look eerily similar. Considering we all have different mothers, I suppose it's a testament to my father's Irish genes.

My complexion is a part of my identity I've always struggled with. I have my mother's silky dark hair and tawny skin, but my features are all my father's. My eye shape, bone structure, even the slant and size of my teeth, match my sisters, who are all spitting images of our father. I've never truly felt Asian or Irish. I'm just me. I blend in where my sisters and gorgeous friends are destined to stand out. That's why we were all shocked when it was my chair that Brawny Barry spun away from the table for the impromptu chair dance.

Eli leans in, roping her arms around my neck and dragging the other girls in close for a selfie. The extra two inches she has on me shows as she reaches around us to take the picture. "Yup. Let's go! I'm in the mood to dance."

I barely contain a groan. I want to go home, crawl into bed, and watch *How To Lose A Guy In 10 Days* until I fall asleep, but I'll never ruin their fun. When Delaney gives a little whoop of glee, I know she's feeling good, and I nod in agreement.

None of us know our way around, but we pile out into the street anyway. We're on the strip and bound to find a club in either direction, so turning to the right, I lead the way. I'm thankful when, less than a block away, Pink's "Raise Your Glass" filters out of a club. I grin, knowing we've found our place.

Even Hadley does a little dance that has her strawberry blond hair bouncing in her always efficient ponytail, so I step forward and offer the security guard my ID. The girls follow closely behind as I open the door and wait for each of my friends to pass.

Two steps in, Eli grabs my hand, which sets off a chain reaction. I grab onto Delaney, who takes hold of Hadley. Our single-file train pushes and slides to the dance floor of the dimly lit club. The beat of the music vibrates through my lungs like a tremor I can't control.

Staring at my girls, I can't help but grin. Their bodies are engulfed by the music the second we step onto the floor that's sticky with spilled drinks. Our bodies shimmy and sway to song after song as flashing lights turn our skin all the colors of the rainbow. It doesn't take long for our group to be encircled by random guys, and with a heavy sigh, I watch as they each pair off.

I always seem to be the odd man out. I think I give off some sort of *don't fuck with me* vibe or something. I don't know. But I have spent many hours in front of the mirror trying to figure it out. I don't appear to have a resting bitch face. I'm generally smiling and friendly. I just seem to be…invisible.

After years of practice, I'm used to it, so I stand and sway awkwardly because Hadley is a head counter. She could meet the love of her life on the dance floor, but the second she can't see all our heads, she panics. So, instead of slinking off to find a table, I dance alone and let her have her fun.

Sure enough, I catch her eye a second later. She gives me a worried glance, but I give her a goofy thumbs-up and pretend I'm dancing with someone to my left. When she finally looks away, my shoulders droop. My skin is still crawling from the penis massage my face took, and now my makeup is melting under the sheer heat radiating from the dance floor.

Snaking my way to Hadley, I lean in but still shout to be heard over the hip-hop song that's playing. "I'm running to the restroom. I'll be right back." She nods and kisses my cheek, then splutters, spitting her tongue out in disgust, obviously remembering where my cheek has been tonight.

It makes me chuckle as I scan the crowd. I find Eli and Delaney and give them the hand sign for the restroom. They both nod happily, and I make a beeline for the edge of the dance floor. People shift and let me through, but no one pays me much attention. Being invisible is a blessing and a curse, I guess.

Eventually, I make it to the door with a triangular-shaped woman on it and am shocked there isn't a line. Pushing through the swinging door, I find out why.

"Seriously, Sybil. You can't keep doing this every time we go out." Two women rush past me with a huff, leaving a girl leaning against the sink with mascara streaming down her face.

Why do I always make friends with the drunk girls?

Unable to help myself, I cross the black-tiled floor. "Are you okay?" My face scrunches up as I ask. Obviously, she isn't okay, or she wouldn't be in here crying.

"I-My-She…" A hiccup escapes before she tries again. "I think my fiancé is cheating on me. With…with my friend." Her glassy eyes follow the trail of the two women who just left.

Well, shit.

"Have you asked them about it?"

She nods. "He denies it. B-But I have this feeling and a text message." Her toned body deflates like a sad balloon animal.

"Oh, honey. I'm sorry." I grab a wad of tissues and hand them to her.

"I don't know what to do," she admits, and I realize she isn't as drunk as I originally thought. She's hurt. Who knew the optics of those two things could be so similar?

"I don't want to tell you what to do, but I would follow my gut. If something feels off, it usually is. And truthfully? If he's cheating with your friend, she isn't your friend. You don't owe either of them anything."

Her shoulders straighten as she contemplates my words. "You're right. What would you do?"

That startles a laugh from me. "Well, I'm a hopeless romantic, but I'm also detail-oriented. I'd want proof. I'd get proof, then I'd burn their world to the ground." The admission shocks us both, but she's nodding with wide eyes in agreement. Crossing my arms, I tell her my truth. "Marriage is important to me. It's a promise made between two people, and if one of those people is in it for the wrong reasons, they make a mockery of something I hold dear to my heart. So, I'd probably hack their phones and then put them on blast. Then, I'd cry. A lot. But I'd eventually pick myself up because I truly believe there's a happily ever after out there for all of us. If this guy isn't yours, don't waste your time crying in bathrooms. He doesn't deserve you, and you deserve a hell of a lot better."

The bathroom door opens, and Delaney slips inside.

Turning toward her, she offers a kind smile. This isn't the first time she's found me making friends in the bathroom. She says it's so I can hide, and maybe that's partly true, but I've never been able to walk away from someone in need.

"You're right." My new friend sways slightly. Maybe she is at least a little buzzed. "You ready for a show?"

"Uh…yes?"

She uses her fingertips to angrily wipe away the mascara marring her cheeks. "Good. I'm about to set off some fireworks in there."

Oh, shit. "I didn't mean right now." Holy Hades, what did I just do?

The stranger grabs my biceps with more strength than I'd given her credit for. "This has been a long time coming. I'm either going to put two shitty people on blast, or I'm going to wake up and apologize for my drunken debauchery." She winks, and my jaw drops. "Thank you. You're amazing."

She's gone a second later, and I'm left staring at Delaney, who shakes her head at me.

"Your collection of drunken admirers is growing."

Rolling my eyes, I head into a stall. "As one of four girls, I just know how to handle overzealous emotions."

Hovering over an absolutely disgusting toilet I barely contain a groan. I should have stayed home tonight.

Delaney is leaning against the sink, waiting for me, when I leave the stall. "Someday, you'll find your Prince Charming, and it's going to be one hell of a ride."

"I know," I mumble. Emotions clog my throat, so I clear it as I wash my hands. My friends have always been able to see through me when they look hard enough.

"And he'll find you were hiding in plain sight," she continues. "I know you prefer to be on the sidelines, behind the scenes. Blend into the crowd. But you're a bright light waiting to shine. You know that, right?"

"God, Del. How drunk are you?"

She sighs as she bumps my shoulder. "Not enough. I saw your face on the dance floor. I'm sorry you felt left out."

"I didn't…" She raises her brow, and I let all pretenses go. "It's not that I felt left out. I just didn't feel like I fit in. There's a difference."

"I know," she says, hooking her arm through mine. "Ready to go home? Kate Hudson and Matthew McConaughey are waiting for us!"

I give her arm a squeeze as we exit the foul-smelling room. Remembering my drunken friend, I seek her out in the crowd and find her just in time to see her jam a phone screen in her friend's face.

My heart splinters for the girl I don't know. Betrayal of that magnitude rocks me to my core, and I've never been so thankful for the built-in friendship and loyalty that came with having three sisters and no parents to count on. I hit the jackpot with Hadley and Delaney. I've kept my circle small my entire life. And watching the drama unfurl in front of me, I'm thankful.

"Jesus," Delaney whispers. "That's going to hurt tomorrow."

No punches are thrown. Just verbal sparring, but Delaney knows better than most that words can cut deeper than a knife.

"Come on," I say, dragging her behind me. "Let's make sure she has a place to go."

I don't make it a habit of opening my home to strangers, but if ever there were a time, this is it. If her friend is sleeping with her fiancé, there's no way her other friend didn't know about it.

Hadley and Eli join ranks a second later. "We heard it go down. By the look on your face, you made another friend?" Eli guesses.

I'm not in the mood for a lecture, so I ignore her. "Just help me make sure she's okay and has a safe place to stay, all right?"

Eli, who is always on the go with a plan and a purpose, hugs me close. "This kind heart of yours is why we love you, sis. Let's go save our damsel."

Two hours later, I crawl into bed with Kate Hudson's voice in the background. Turns out, my new friend was staying at her parents' house tonight anyway, but I haven't been able to shake the hurt I saw in her eyes. Before we left the bar, Sybil and I exchanged numbers, and I know I'll be checking in with her often. I won't allow the betrayal she experienced to turn her off from love.

I only fall asleep after convincing myself that everything happens for a reason, and her Prince Charming is still out there searching for her.

CHAPTER 2

LOCHLAN BRYER-BLAINE

Four Months Ago

*B*itter cold assaults my eyeballs the second I peel myself away from the plush leather seat of the hunter-green Range Rover I've rented. It's colder than a witch's tit, and the wind is pure evil. Point Judith, Rhode Island, holds a fondness for me, but there's a reason I don't visit this part of the country in winter.

It's fucking bloody cold.

Fortunately, I'm propelled forward by revenge.

In the summer months, nearby Wickford holds an annual art festival that my stepsister, Nova, has loved for as long as I can remember, so I make the trip north each season. There isn't much I wouldn't do for my annoyingly perfect little sister. But summer is when everything is green. Lovely. Alive. Today, I realize they call it the dead of winter for a reason. Everywhere you look is gray. Cold. Dead.

Fitting, I suppose, since it's rage that has me here in the first place. It's been months of preparation. Years, really, but I won't dwell on that. I'm here to meet my old friend, the one person who will understand my need for vengeance.

Blake Kingston is the only man I know who understands loss in quite the same way. His grief has turned him into a recluse, but he won't turn me away. Not when I'm coming to him for help. That's the thing about true friends—even in our darkest times, we're there for each other.

I'd like to say I'm an asshole—dead inside without feelings or remorse. And most people in my life would say that's the God's honest truth. Now. They didn't always see me this way though. At one point I believed in happily ever after. I believed in the love my parents still had for one another after their divorce, even if I didn't understand it. Those beliefs were shattered with one wedding that nearly ruined me. I used to allow people to see the vulnerable man behind an empire. I used to allow them to see me. But now I keep the world at bay with my carefully curated dickhead persona.

I need revenge, but the tiny piece of my heart that wasn't broken by betrayal won't allow me to proceed with my plan if innocent people are harmed. Even financially. So, I need Blake to come through for me. I'll even appeal to his grief to get him on board if I have to. He can protect the thousands while I destroy the two.

Pulling my wool pea coat tighter, I join the queue for the ferry that will take me the short distance to Block Island. Blake doesn't make it easy to see him these days, but that's fine by me.

Icy rain pelts my head, and I curse myself for not being better prepared. Each time the frozen rain licks my face, silent rage fills my lungs.

"Ticket?" an older woman asks with a thick New England accent.

I flash my phone, and she smiles as if she isn't freezing.

Liar, my head screams, but of course, I rein it in.

"Have a nice trip. We'll be taking off in a few. Just waiting on three more tickets." She babbles at me like we're friends, and I barely manage a growl. Niceties are saved for my family and a few select friends these days. The more bastardly I behave, the less likely I am to get roped into any more lies.

"Three tickets?" I finally mutter because I'm also holding the other three tickets.

"Yes, sir. There will be eight of you tonight. Busy night for a winter ride to The Block."

Removing my phone from my pocket again, I hold it out for her. "I have the other three tickets."

"You waitin' on friends?"

"No."

"Family?"

"No one is coming. I merely bought the tickets."

"You bought three extras?"

"Yes." She stares at me like she's owed an explanation, and I blame the cold for why I give one. "Your bloody system would only give odd-numbered tickets. I had to buy four before I got an even one."

She blinks slowly. I can't tell if she's processing what I've said or if the sleet has frozen her eyelashes in place. "You bought four tickets for one trip so you could have an even-numbered ticket?"

"Yes," I say through a locked jaw.

She studies me for an uncomfortably long time before finally shrugging. "I gave up trying to figure people out a long time ago, handsome. Whatever floats your boat." She chuckles at her inane joke and ushers me aboard.

Relieved to be able to move away from her, I stalk onto the small vessel like a villain in a Bond movie. I choose the bench that's second from the back and ease onto the hard surface. Bench number two. Even. I wish I could say the same for the ship.

The ferry ride to Block Island's shore is choppy at best.

Motion sickness is a nasty bitch and three people hurl around me as the ship sways. My growing frustration comes to a boiling point when the small vessel shifts, sending us all sprawling to one side.

I catch myself, but my neighbor does not.

"S-sorry," she whispers. When she looks up, I see the instant her shame turns to interest, and my stomach revolts.

There was a time when I may have found this young woman interesting. Not anymore. I gently shove her back to her side without saying a word.

Twenty minutes later, the ferry docks with an announcement that all trips have been canceled until the storm passes.

Looks like Blake will have a house guest tonight.

The island itself is small, maybe ten square miles, and it's essentially a ghost town in the winter months. Scanning the near-empty parking lot, I'm relieved to see the black sedan waiting. My name is printed on a worn sheet of paper that sits on the dashboard.

I cross the parking lot, wrench the door open and cram my large body into the back seat. Removing a folder from my coat pocket, I toss it on the seat next to me. At least the damn thing stayed dry.

"Welcome to Block Island," the cheery teen in the driver's seat says with a grin.

I frown. *Is this kid even old enough to drive?*

He shifts the car into gear, and we lurch forward. Jesus Christ.

"Sorry." He shrugs while glancing in the rearview mirror. "I haven't driven this car before. Got my license last month, though, so you're good."

"Three Dodger Lane," I say. "Keep your eyes on the road."

The flustered kid nods, and I pinch the bridge of my nose to keep from yelling at him. He could very well hold my life in his hands. I Googled it earlier. It's less than a five-minute drive. Surely he can get me there in one piece.

"First time to the Block?" His voice cracks, and I grind my teeth.

"No." It's the best I can do. Asshole is my default now, but even I can't be a prick to the smiling, pimple-faced kid.

"Oh, you friends with Mr. Kingston? He's growly like you, but he's nicer. He pretends to be a jerk, but mostly just to tourists."

I tighten my lips to hold back a grin.

When the kid's brain catches up to his mouth, his eyes go wide with fear.

I give him a semblance of a smile in the mirror. "Mr. Kingston pretends. I'm the real deal." Even my voice sounds like a villain. Part of me hates that this is who they've turned me into, and the other part is grateful. I'll never again be put in a position where love blinds me to the realities of life.

The car jostles as he turns onto a grass driveway. It's difficult to see through the sleet coming down like a thick blanket, but the faint glow from the small home up ahead tells me Blake isn't living like royalty out here.

My driver pulls as close to the house as he can get, and I hand him a hundred-dollar bill.

"Holy crap! I don't have change for this, mister."

"Keep it," I grumble. I'm out of the car and up the steps a second later, pounding on Blake's front door. Reluctantly, I turn to watch the kid as I wait. He's attempting to turn the car around in the small drive, and a four-point turn quickly becomes a twelve-point turn. It reminds me of the time I taught Nova to drive, and a genuine smile surprises me.

I return to Blake's front door with a shrug and knock harder this time. Then I do it again. The prick thinks he can ignore me. Hell, he probably does ignore most unannounced visitors, but not me.

The door is ripped open with so much force I feel the breeze it creates across my palm. "What?" Blake hisses with all the dominance of a mountain lion, which is fitting considering his current appearance.

"If you want people to leave you alone, you'll need to work on your delivery. It's not scary at all." I clap him on the shoulder and muscle my way past.

"Blaine? What the fuck?"

I unbutton my coat as I walk farther into his space. When I notice the yoga mat in the middle of the family room and a workout video my sister would probably enjoy on the large screen above the fireplace, I freeze mid-step.

"Are you…are you doing bloody yoga?"

Blake bumps my shoulder and points a remote at the screen on his way by. "It's supposed to be good for meditating or some shit."

My eyebrows must be near my hairline, and I feel my face transform. I can't decide if I should give him shit about this or not. He makes the decision for me with his next breath.

"I'm trying to learn how to let go of the hate. It's insidious and it's rotting me from the inside out."

Pure shock swamps me as I shrug out of my coat. "You're going to forgive your father?" His father is single-handedly responsible for the car accident that took Blake's family.

My friend's expression goes cold. His face is a murderous mask. "Never." His voice is lethal. "I hope hell shows him no mercy, but I need to learn to forgive myself. Shannon wouldn't like me much these days."

Fuck. How will he take the information I'm about to drop in his lap?

He crosses his arms over his broad chest and stares at me like he knows I have something to say. We grew up together. Went to the same summer camps and ran in the same circles, but you'd never know it looking at us now. Blake has a full beard that's in desperate need of a trim, and if he put on a flannel shirt, he could pass for a full-blown lumberjack. I'm still dressed in my standard three-piece suit.

"What are you doing here, Loch?"

"I need your help."

He lifts a brow but says nothing. After an eternity of scowling at each other, he sweeps his arms toward the small table between the kitchen and family room. "Take a seat."

Relief washes through me, even if I don't show it. I'm confident enough in my plan, but it would be harder to proceed without Blake's help. My body drops heavily into the wooden chair. I feel much older than my thirty-two years.

"I'm not going to like this, am I?"

He moves about the kitchen as I lay out my plan but doesn't say a word until I'm done. Slipping a cup of coffee my way, he takes the chair opposite me.

"You're motivated by revenge."

"Yes."

"That's not healthy."

"I didn't come here for a counseling session," I growl. "They targeted us. First my mother, then me."

"I don't disagree with you, but this...this has teeth and a reach far beyond anything I would have expected from you. I don't even want to know how you found out he's leveraged all his properties or how you know it all hinges on this winery."

"It's not just the winery. It's the property that comes with it."

"Okay, but are you sure you want this on your hands?"

"Blake, he married my mother. Gaslit her for two years. Mentally tried to break her down, and when that didn't work, he sent his girlfriend to do it to me. Christine fucking pretended to be pregnant for five damn months and then faked a miscarriage, which she blamed me for! I spent a year mourning a loss that never existed while she infiltrated my company for his gain. If I hadn't found the falsified ultrasounds after she moved out, I'd still be mourning that loss. Pretty sure that justifies my petty revenge."

His sigh is heavy, and I can feel his pain as he runs a hand over his beard. "Doing something like this changes a man. Are you sure you're ready for those consequences?"

"I'll take whatever comes at me."

"But...there's something else. A reason you came to me. What?"

I hand him the folder I've had tucked under my arm and watch as he scans it. "There are a lot of employees this will affect."

"Yeah." I wish I didn't care. I wish I didn't have a conscience.

"What do you want me to do?"

"They'll only have two options when this goes down. One, use all their resources to keep things afloat for a month, three tops, or find a quick sale for all his properties."

"I don't run Kingston Corp. anymore, Loch. You know that." His voice takes on a graveled tone and I feel the tension building within my friend. "You should talk to Nate. He's in charge now."

"I can't be involved in that conversation. I know what I'm asking, Blake. I know that you're not part of the company anymore, but Nate is your brother—he'll listen to you. He'll take it on if you ask him to."

"He'll just as easily take it on if you ask him. It's a good deal for Kingston Corp. It could be a good deal for you too. Why won't you take them on yourself?"

"I want the properties shut down. Dismantled. Destroyed. Incorporating them into Bryer-Blaine would keep his legacy alive. I won't do that."

"You want to shut them down immediately?" he asks.

"Yes."

He scans the document in front of him again. "What about

all the events they'll have scheduled? Weddings? Bat mitzvahs? Sweet sixteens? You'll be coming up on the money-making season. The one in Santa Barbara alone books years in advance."

"I don't give a shit about weddings." I don't mean to snarl at him, but that's what weddings do to me these days.

He shakes his head sadly. "This isn't you, Loch."

"It is now."

He's quiet as he stares past me. Blake walked away from his family and their business, but I know he still has love for his granny and his brother. Hopefully, that love is enough to concede to my plea. "You're sure this is the way you want to go?"

"It's the only thing I want."

"Revenge is a tricky thing, Loch. You may think it'll make you feel better, but what if it doesn't? What then? Hanging on to hate only ensures there's no room left for love."

"Exactly."

He lets out a harsh breath, then shakes his head. "If you go through with it, I'll talk to Nate." Relief floods my veins. "But you're a better man than you're allowing yourself to be, or you wouldn't be so worried about the three thousand, four hundred and twenty-two employees."

This is why I came to Blake. His family, other than during his father's short reign as head of Kingston Corp, has always made sure the damage to unsuspecting employees is minimal. If they can't immediately absorb them into another position, they give the best severance packages of any company I know.

"I want revenge, but I'm not a monster."

"Sometimes, that's a fine line. Hopefully, you'll remember which side of it you belong on." He shakes his head but closes the folder. "I take it you're here for the night."

"Ferry's closed." I chuckle. "It'll be like summer camp all over again."

"If you sit your naked ass on my pillow and fart, I will kill you this time." Blake says it so gruffly, so straight-faced, that I nearly miss the mischief in his gaze.

"Did the curmudgeon make a joke?"

"Whatever, asshole. Go change. There's a Celtics game on."

"Why would I change?" I ask, glancing at my trousers and button-down. I straighten my vest, then unbutton it. It's as relaxed as I get. "I hate basketball."

Blake grins for the first time since I've been here. "I know."

Clapping him on the shoulder, I can almost believe we're not two broken, heartless souls floundering through life.

Almost.

I'm just standing up when an alarm goes off on my phone and I fall back into my seat like the weight of the world has knocked me on my ass. That sound coming from my phone only means one thing.

Someone is in my apartment. Again. With a low growl that has Blake leaning forward, I wake up my phone and open the security app.

The screen comes to life, and I flip room to room until I find the culprit in my bedroom.

"What the hell? Do you have cameras in your bedroom?"

I wish I didn't have to, but when you live and work in a hotel, an abnormal number of people have access to everything.

"This is my new assistant-in-training, Kerry," I say flatly. "She asked me out for drinks last week, fell into my lap yesterday, and now she's poking around in my private suite."

"Jesus, Loch. I knew you got hit on a lot, but this is…this is a lot."

"It happens way too bloody often. Everyone wants something *from* me."

"Growing up the way we did, it's hard to know who wants you, and who just wants to use you."

I grunt, unable to form words. That's it exactly. It's also why I thought Christine was different. I've never been more wrong.

Closing out of the live feed, I call my private security at the hotel.

"Mr. Blaine," Antonio answers on the first ring. "We're aware of the, er, situation. It's being taken care of as we speak. How would you like to proceed with HR?"

"Have Natalie meet you to conduct the exit interview. Now. I don't want this woman allowed on my property again."

"I'll see to it. Have a goo—"

I hang up and pinch the bridge of my nose.

"It can be tough not to lose sight of what matters in this world, Loch. But not everyone is out to get you. Not everyone wants you for your bank account."

Bile rises in my throat. "If someone like that exists, I haven't met them yet." The words are harsh and painful in my chest.

Understanding hits as I realize Blake had found his person, and she was taken from him. My cold heart cracks like a first thaw. But it's just another reason to stick to my plan. Love and feelings fuck up everything.

"Where should I drop my stuff?"

"There's a guest room down the hall to the left."

I march past Blake but pause just before he's out of sight. "Thank you," I mutter sincerely. He might be the only one keeping my soul from burning to ash while I fight the devil.

CHAPTER 3

TILLY

Present Day

"You've got this, Tilly. You've been through all the training, even more than most, and I know you can handle it." Colton's praise has me fidgeting with the cocktail napkin on the bar just as a glass of wine is slid my way by an attractive bartender.

I want to roll my eyes at my boss. But I don't, because he's right. I'm just scared out of my mind. Plus, Colton Westbrook is an amazing boss. He's also Preston Westbrook's brother, which makes him sort of my brother-in-law?

"I know," I say instead, staring into the FaceTime screen of my MacBook Pro. It was a graduation present from my sister Emory and Preston a few years ago. It's probably still the most expensive thing I own.

"What are your biggest concerns, Till?"

After I finished an internship with The Westbrook Group, Colton became my boss and I fell in love with marketing and PR. I'm getting to experience everything firsthand, but sometimes I wonder if he's placing too much trust in me.

"Ah, that I'm going to blow it? How much money will you lose if you don't win this bid?"

He laughs. It's light and fun, much like the man himself. I know everyone in the office considers him a practical joker, but I see the work he does. I did a short stint with each Westbrook brother during my internship, and I can confidently say Colton puts in more hours on a regular basis than any of his brothers.

"Tilly, this is just recon. You're collecting information. You've done this a thousand times by my side. I have full confidence in you." He speaks to me like I'm a little sister about to head off to summer camp for the first time.

"Thanks," I grumble.

"Hey." He waits until I peer up at the screen again. "I wouldn't send you out alone if I didn't know you could do it, so believe in yourself. Until we get this mess sorted out, you're the only one I trust to get things done. I'm heading to my brother's place in Vermont, but I'll be available 24/7 via phone."

"I know. I still can't believe this is happening."

"When you're successful, Tilly, people will always try to hit you where it hurts. I got caught with my pants down. Literally." He rolls his eyes, but I see pain there too. "And now we have to sift through this PR nightmare. Maybe I should be more of an asshole like Lochlan. At least no one bothers him."

Ah, yes. His mysterious friend, Lochlan. Hotelier and rumored curmudgeon. I don't understand how they're friends if the rumors are true.

"What's that look for?" Colton asks with a smirk that could rival any of my teenage obsession's posters that lined my childhood bedroom.

"I just don't get it. Assistants talk, you know? Your friend has a reputation for being a miserable jerk." I clamp my lips shut. Colton and I may have a different kind of relationship, but he's still my boss.

His hearty laughter revives my heartbeat to a steady rhythm again.

"He does. And he is, but he's a good friend. It might be different if I had a vagina, but he's a good guy at heart."

"Why would it be different if you had a vagina?" I can't help it. I laugh.

"Lochlan lives his life like Cupid is the boogeyman. Women are drawn to him. He's a wealthy, pretty face, but he views love and marriage as a prison sentence. If you have a vagina, he's either going to screw you or shut you down." I scrunch my nose up, and he laughs again. "I didn't say his thinking was right, but Loch doesn't believe in fairytales. Not anymore anyway. As long as I've known him, he's been a skeptical, broody bastard. But he's become nearly unbearable in the last couple of years."

"That's really sad."

He nods at the screen. "It is, but maybe if I were more like him, there wouldn't be photographs of my naked ass all over the tabloids right now."

Poor Colton. I do feel bad for him. He doesn't have a malicious bone in his body, but someone has been selling stories to every gossip column in the world, and he's had to go on administrative leave to protect their company.

"What are you doing tonight?"

I frown because I know he's digging for information. Ever since I let it slip that I was making my dream of running my own business a reality, he's been relentless. I haven't given him or Preston any details because it's just a dream right now. My blog is taking off, but it's not a business per se. Plus, the second I tell either of them, they'll step in to make my dreams a reality I didn't work for. I need to work for it. Emory gave up so much to make sure my other two sisters and I had everything we needed. It's my turn to prove to her and myself that I can stand on my own.

Dropping my chin into my palms, I stare at him. "I'm in the bar right now. I'll have dinner, work on my business plan, then go to bed."

"And where are you on your business plan? What steps have you taken?"

"The right ones," I hedge with a smile.

"Jesus, Tilly. You're so stubborn. We've always known you won't be my assistant forever. You're too talented for that, but why must you venture out on your own? We just want to help, you know?"

"I do know, and I appreciate it. But when you grow up learning how to survive, not thrive, at some point, you have to stop simply surviving and make your own path."

Colton grins, causing his kind eyes to crinkle at the corners.

I don't want to admit to these billionaires that I'm scared to make the leap. Everyone in my life is so dedicated, so motivated. It's embarrassing to admit I feel lost. I've always been better at existing in the background, helping everyone else find their dreams. Chasing my own is terrifying.

"Okay, well, you know where to find me if you change your mind. While I'm out on leave, you won't have much to do unless assignments like this one come up. Take this time to really figure out what you need. If you can't make it happen on your own, there's no shame in asking us for help. Even if it's just for advice. We're family, and family helps one another."

"I know. Thanks, Colt."

"No worries. Tomorrow, just stick to the outline I gave you, and you'll do great. Oh, and if you mess up, it's only ten million we'll lose out on."

My drink sprays from my nose. "Ten million?" I splutter, trying to wipe the burning sensation from my nostrils.

He smirks like he did it on purpose. "Yup, just ten million. It's a drop in the bucket to us."

"Right. Billionaires and all." I can't contain my eye roll, and he chuckles.

"That's right. Don't put so much pressure on yourself. I believe in you. You should try it sometime." His signature grin is on full display.

"Okay, boss man. Anything else?"

"Yes. Have some fun while you're there. California is amazing this time of year and you have to head into San Francisco proper too."

Fun. Right. I sometimes forget that my boss is the emperor of fun. "I'll try."

"Are you heading back to the office before you go to Charlotte?" The way he asks has me smiling like a loon. Colton may work hard, but he also makes sure everyone around him remembers to live, laugh, and love.

"I wasn't planning to. Why?" I lean in closer to the screen to examine his reaction.

"Lochlan is being a pain in the ass. I think he needs a little sparkle in his life."

Colton has an affinity for glitter bombs, and no one in his life is immune.

"You know, for the longest time, I wondered if you had any friends. Now I wonder how you keep them. I've yet to meet anyone in your circle who likes being doused in glitter. Even if it is your love language."

His laughter sounds rich even through my AirPods. "Why would you think I have no friends?"

"Because how long have I worked for you? Not once, in all that time, has anyone visited you besides your family, and no one ever calls unless it's business-related."

"It's not the nineties, Till. We have cell phones, remember? No one calls anymore, especially not people who are busy running their own empires all over the world."

"I guess," I grumble. Would it hurt for some of his hot

friends to pop by once in a while, though? Geesh. "Fine, what color this time?"

"Pink, of course."

"You want me to send it from the same place? Ruindays.-com? Or did you need me to send it personally from the office?"

"The online one is fine." He chuckles like a ten-year-old. "Bye, Tilly."

"Bye, Colt."

Shaking my head, I click out of FaceTime and pull up my current blog post. I'd never had the urge to blog until I started traveling so often. I'm not a writer like my sister Sloane, but after an experience at a hotel in Arizona with an overworked housekeeper, I knew it would be all about the services that make the business—the helpers. With a side of love thrown in because it's me.

Love in the Lobby was born out of a need to stay connected to how I grew up, even if I'm living in the land of excess that someone else funds. For now, anyway. I wasn't expecting it to take off so suddenly, but I had a hundred thousand subscribers by my third post, and it's growing every day.

The bartender places a glass of water in front of me, so I remove my earbuds. "Thank you."

"Anytime." He winks. He's a shameless flirt and has the dimples to get away with it. He might be a perfect person to interview for my next post.

I'm about to ask him when my thoughts are interrupted by a screeching banshee to my left. "You're telling me *now* that my boyfriend can't come to your wedding? It's tomorrow, Jenna. To-mor-row! He's already here. What am I supposed to tell him?"

"O-liv-ia!" someone else says dramatically. "If you'd told us who your boyfriend was months ago, Jenna would have told you then. But you didn't because you obviously knew it would be an issue."

Angling myself on the barstool so I can spy on the action, I try really hard not to make it obvious that I'm watching the show, but they're so close I could easily pass for a member of their party. I think Olivia is the one with her back to me, but there are four women huddled together facing her.

"It isn't my fault he didn't want you, Melinda," the maybe-Olivia hisses.

Ouch. Olivia's bite is as ruthless as her bark.

"Do you even hear yourself?" another woman, presumably another bridesmaid, chimes in. "You slept with Melinda's fiancé, and now you think it's okay for him to attend her sister's wedding? You can't be that dense."

Oooh, the drama! Where's the popcorn when you need it?

The maybe-Olivia stands with a drink in her hand, and in slow motion, I see what she's about to do. Without thinking, I reach up just in time to stop her forward motion and remove the drink from her hand. I'm pretty sure it was headed toward the bride-to-be.

"You probably don't want to do that. Olivia, is it? If the wedding is happening in this hotel, one or both of the betrothed have money. This can only end badly for you."

"Who are you?" She scowls as the bridal party watches, some in shock and some with bemused expressions that would concern me if I thought I'd ever see them again.

"I'm just a friend watching out for everyone's best interests. I work in PR, and I can promise you, this would be a disaster of epic proportions. My advice? Fulfill your duties to the bride, then skip out on the reception if you *must* be with your boyfriend. But"—I lean in conspiratorially—"in my experience, once a cheater, always a cheater, so make this decision carefully."

They all stare at me, wide-eyed and shell-shocked. I

covertly check my wine glass. *How many have I had? Am I drunk?* I try really hard not to get involved in other people's drama without their permission! Most of the time. Ugh! *What have I done?* But of course, I know that answer. I'm a sucker for brides, weddings, and all things happily ever after.

Because your biggest, deepest wish is to be loved for who you are. Scars and all. My sister's voice rings in my head. Unfortunately, it may sound like her, but it's my fear of never being enough that has the words lancing my heart.

Olivia steps away from the bar. "Fine. I'll see you all tomorrow, but don't expect me to be happy about it." She glares at me, then back at the group. "And I wouldn't be caught dead at the reception anyway."

As soon as she's out of sight, the maybe-bride closes in on me, her eyes unblinking, and she doesn't speak right away. She watches me with an intensity that has my cheeks heating.

"Ah, are you the bride?" I'm suddenly nervous that Bridezilla will show her teeth because I definitely overstepped. I grab my wineglass for liquid courage and take a giant gulp.

Shit. Shit. Shit.

"I am." She nods emphatically, but a huge grin appears on her face. "I'm Jenna. You just handled my stepsister in a way I never could. How did you do it? And more importantly, will you do it again?"

"Ah, sorry." I giggle nervously. "I'm not in the habit of interrupting sibling rivalries. Plus, I doubt she's coming back tonight. She was pretty pissed."

"No, you don't understand." Her eyes plead with the girl on her right. The two of them have a silent conversation I recognize can only happen between sisters. Their expressions go through a myriad of feelings, then they turn on me with so much excitement I fear they'll explode. "I want to hire you for the rest of the weekend."

I laugh nervously and place my wineglass on the bar. I'm

going to need both hands to hold me up for this. "Hire me for what, exactly?"

"Whatever you want to call it, but I need a bridesmaid babysitter. I'll pay ten thousand dollars for you to be in my wedding, all expenses paid, and all you have to do is attend the rehearsal dinner tomorrow night and the wedding on Saturday. I'll literally pay you to keep Olivia in check."

I gape at Jenna. Surely, she's joking, but as I stare at the bride's hopeful smile and kind eyes, I know she's one hundred percent serious.

"I'll pay you in cash if that helps."

"Jenna, you don't even know me. Why on Earth would you want me in your wedding?"

"Because Olivia is a bitch who has ruined every good thing I've had in my life since my father married her mother when I was six years old. I can't let her ruin my wedding too." Her lip quivers, and my arguments fade.

Lifting both hands, I rub small circles around the migraine that's trying to form in my temples. I sneak a glance at their table, expecting it to be littered with champagne bottles, but it's not. It's empty.

"Have you been drinking?" There must be a reasonable explanation for her outrageous offer.

"I don't drink. Please..." She cuts off with a slight frown. "Oh, what's your name?"

I answer with a heavy sigh that promises a long night ahead. "Tilly. My name is Tilly."

"Tilly. I like that. Please be my wedding fixer. I really, really need you."

"I don't know..."

"Fifteen thousand."

"No, it's not..." *Am I breathing loudly? It sounds like I'm breathing loudly.*

"Twenty thousand."

Is this girl insane? Who just has twenty grand lying around? But as I sit in the swanky Dorrety Hotel bar, memories of the West-brooks fill my head. *People who stay in these kinds of hotels have that kind of money, Till.* I swallow painfully.

"You want to pay me twenty thousand dollars for two days of bridesmaid-sitting?"

"Yes. I do. My stepdad is a lawyer. He can draw up a contract for you tonight. I'll even make sure he doesn't use too many lawyer-y words, so it'll be just a straight-up agreement we can both sign."

Oh my God. Am I really contemplating this? My computer screen flashes with my blog header, and Jenna doesn't miss it. Her eyes gleam with excitement.

"Is that your blog? *Love in the Lobby*?"

I try to hide the flinch. My blog is successful because I remain anonymous. "Do you know it?" I ask cautiously.

"I do. I freaking love it. I wish you'd done a post on this hotel before we booked it. OMG! Is that why you're here? Never mind." She answers her own questions, talking so fast my head spins and I can't keep up. Or reply. "I'll tell you what. Twenty thousand dollars, and I'll promote your website on all my social media accounts for an entire month after my honey-moon. I have over two million followers."

Holy shit.

"Wow. Okay, let me think a minute." She offers me a radiant smile. "My blog is completely anonymous. It needs to stay that way for me to get the inside scoop." I'm whispering now, but no one around us is paying any attention.

"Done. We'll give you a fake name." She gives me a once-over. "We'll call you, hmm… We'll call you Abby Chambers for the wedding. How's that?"

A pseudonym. A wedding. And a crazy bridesmaid with a potentially crazier bride? Sign me up. Twenty grand would be a huge jumpstart for my—my what? A career that shall remain nameless for now, I guess. But this could also help launch my blog to the next level too.

A wedding! My literal happy place! And twenty thousand dollars.

When I think about it in blog terms, it's a no-brainer.

Reaching out, I shake Jenna's hand. "What about a dress, shoes, all of that?"

"I'll get my wedding planner on it now. Give me your sizes, and it'll be here by morning."

Shaking my head, I smile. You truly can make anything happen if you have enough money   ay. Jenna. You have yourself a deal. Anything else I sho   my charge for the weekend?"

She launches herself the last fe   e us and wraps me in a giant hug. "You, Abby   ifesaver. All you need to know is to keep Oli   my big day. She's sneaky, and I wouldn't put an   r. Oh, and keep Jacob from crashing."

"Jacob is the boyfriend?" I ask g   nda's reaction.

She nods, but it's Jenna who ans   vas engaged to Lindy when Olivia got her claws in

"Jesus. Not that it's any of my business, but w   n in your wedding?"

"Ugh," she scoffs, hurt and anger flickering   ross her features. "My father made me. He's kind of an asshole, and she has had him wrapped around her big, sticky fingers ever since he married her mother."

The two women share another look that has me missing my sisters terribly.

Melinda turns to me with affection written all over her pretty face. "At least mom remarried someone with a heart. Our father might be a troll, but our stepdad is a hero straight out of a fairytale."

I stare at Melinda, and my heart hurts for her. What a

betrayal that must have been. And from her own stepsister? My gaze returns to Jenna, and I really wish I had my glass of wine in my hands as they begin to shake. "Okay. Keep Olivia in line. Keep Jacob out. Got it."

"Gah! Give me your room number. I'll have my stepdad write up a contract and wire the cash to you. I'll come by your room in a couple of hours?"

"Ah, sure. I'm in room 1219."

Jenna scrunches up her nose. "Oh, no. That won't work. Pack up your stuff. We'll get you an upgrade."

"That's really not necessary." Judging by the horrified eyes of the girls around me, I just made a serious faux pas.

"Oh, it is. All the bridesmaids are staying on the twentieth floor. It'll seem weird if you're not with us."

I nod because what the hell did I just get myself into?

Two hours later, I'm standing inside a suite better suited for royalty than a poor girl from Camden Crossing, with twenty thousand dollars in cash, still wondering how I ended up in the wedding of a woman whose last name I don't even know.

Par for the course for you, Tilly. Par for the course.

LOVE IN THE LOBBY

Hello, lovely readers,

Gah! Full disclosure. I'm two glasses of wine in, and I'm feeling a little sad today.

Or lonely.

Or sad that I'm lonely. I guess that really comes down to the same thing, doesn't it? But I love love. Rom-com? Yes, please. Pop songs about heart-stopping love? Hello, Swiftie for life, right here! Pinterest board chock-full of my dream wedding? Check. Check. Check.

I'm not desperate. I'm waiting patiently for my turn because we all deserve the fairy tale. Someday I'll find that special someone who loves me for who I am today and who I'll be tomorrow.

I've dreamt of my wedding day since I was a little girl. Not because I need a man to take care of me, but because I want a partner who chooses to love me at the end of the day, even if it's hard. Even if I'm a raging lunatic or a crying mess. A partner to stand by my side in good times and bad.

Is that so much to ask?

I'm sure you're reading this and thinking I have a giant

flashing *daddy issues* sign on my forehead. But you'd be wrong. It says parent issues. Plural.

Growing up, my dad loved whiskey more than his girls. My mom had demons who won the battle of life. They couldn't choose me. I know that now, but I also know that there's a man who will choose me every day. Because that love I'm waiting for? I know it exists. I feel it all around me. And even if it's not my turn to find it yet (YET, you hear that universe?), I'll do everything in my power to make sure other people get their HEA until my turn comes.

That's why, tonight, as I sit here in The Regency by Hollands in Scottsdale, Arizona, I'm looking for the couple in love. Haven't you ever walked into a place and thought, *this is it*? This is where my meet-cute will happen? Or see a couple and just know they're destined for a lifetime of love?

I know I'm not the only one who still believes in ever afters. So, as I sip my wine and glance around, I zero in on the happy couple snuggling together on the same side of the booth. Am I doing a karaoke lip-sync version of their conversation?

You bet your ass I am. But the question remains, will they get their happily ever after in this hotel?

At first look, yes! The Regency is everything you could hope for when planning a wedding. The elegance. The grandeur. It's magnificent.

But like many things, after the shine wears off, you're left with the underappreciated cogs that make the world turn. In this case, the employees. The bartenders. The housekeepers. The service industry workers who keep up The Regency's appearances.

Watching my couple, whom I've named Tammy and Timmy, I chat with my bartender. She's exhausted, having worked her fifth double in a row. Something that is unfortunately common for this understaffed establishment.

As the couple laughs together, my bartender, we'll call her

Amber for privacy's sake, gives me the inside scoop on The Regency and her coworkers. I'm sad to say, it's an abysmal letdown.

If The Regency invested a quarter of what they pay their CEO (I Googled him) into their employees, their turnover rate and employee satisfaction would improve immeasurably. But more on that in my rating.

I've decided my couple were on a first date. He was more into it than she was, but he slowly won her over.

Will they go home together? Bartender Amber thought so. I wasn't convinced, but I'm confident a second date will be in their future by the time they leave.

So, can The Regency deliver a Happily Ever After?

Here's my Five-Diamond-Rings Rating:

Cleanliness - Five Diamond Rings: (Make sure you tip housekeeping!) This morning, the lovely lady I met was so sweet and exceeded all expectations.

Friendliness - Two Diamond Rings: I don't believe this is necessarily the employees' fault, but exhausted staff will yield lackluster results.

Location - Five Diamond Rings: Luckily for The Regency, the location has nothing to do with them.

Amenities - Three Diamond Rings: It just goes to show, money can't buy class.

Last Call: So much potential, but until they learn to treat their employees with respect, the customer experience will suffer. The bottom line is, do your research before booking your big day!

4,320 likes. 226 Comments.

Barback92: Cheers for shitty parents.

Barback92: Also, thank you for reminding people to tip!

HappyEndings: You sure you're not desperate? Reads a little desperate to me.

TessaJane: I am so happy I found this! I was planning to have my wedding there! Now I'll be doing more research before committing!

CHAPTER 4

TILLY

The Frye/Grant Rehearsal Dinner

Tilly: I got all the pictures. I've uploaded them to Dropbox.

Colton: Got them! They're great. Good work.

Tilly: Thanks. Would it be possible to take the afternoon off?

Colton: No problem. Are you going to play tourist?

Tilly: Something like that. I'm actually thinking about changing my flight home to Sunday if that's okay.

Colton: Have fun! You deserve a break. I'll have Jill in travel change your flight. Sunday afternoon good?

Tilly: Are you sure? I can do it.

Colton: Already sending her a message. Afternoon good?

Tilly: Yeah, thanks, Colton.

Colton: No worries. Have a great weekend.

I wouldn't say it'll be great, but it will be an adventure. Closing my computer, I put away all my work files, then head to the closet where I put the four dresses and coordinating shoes that showed up this morning.

Tilly: Hi, Jenna.

Tilly: **Any dress in particular I'm supposed to wear tonight?**

Jenna: **The navy dress is for tomorrow. You can choose from the others for tonight. Whatever you feel most comfortable in.**

Jenna: **Choose one, then come to my room for hair and makeup.**

Tilly: **I'll be there soon.**

Jenna: **Great. Olivia is throwing a tantrum.**

Ugh. Scanning the dresses, I select the least scandalous. And that's saying something because the little black dress in my hand is cut down to my navel and probably hits just below my ass.

Twenty thousand dollars, Till. Twenty grand. As I toss the garment over my arm and grab the silver strappy heels, that becomes my mantra.

I take a few minutes to scan the notes Jenna sent me last night. I have them mostly memorized. Parents' names, the groom's name, even pictures of Jacob, the cheating ex. She left nothing out in her synopsis, and I'm eternally grateful.

Jenna's room is three doors down from mine. I lift my hand to knock, but Melinda yanks the door open before I get the chance. "She hid one of my shoes," she hisses.

"What?" I swear I'm slow blinking.

"She hid one of my shoes. I know she did. She's trying to ruin things already."

"Oh, geez. Okay. I won't let her out of my sight until the wedding is over."

Melinda takes my dress and ushers me inside. Olivia is easy to spot. She's stewing in the corner with an annoyed expression on her face. I cross the room and hug Jenna like we've been friends for years.

"What is *she* doing here?" Oh, Olivia. Such a pain in the ass already?

"This is Abby. She's a friend from yoga. Her dad has been sick, so we weren't sure if she could make it, but surprise! Here she is."

Wow. The lies fly from Jenna's mouth with such ease. I'm seriously going to have to up my game. And yoga? I might be the least coordinated person on the planet.

"Who is she supposed to walk down the aisle with?"

"Oh, don't worry about details, Liv. That's what the wedding planner is for," Jenna replies with false sweetness dripping from every word. "Abby? Why don't you go first? I know you have some stuff to do. We can keep each other busy while they do your hair and makeup." Jenna points to a chair set up by the window.

"Ah, sure." I follow her directions and take a seat. Two women descend on me like flies to shit. "Okay, so we're missing a shoe?" I ask innocently. "Anything else?"

You could hear a pin drop. "I don't think so. Not yet anyway," Melinda huffs.

"I've got it." I'm about to tell them my plan when the makeup artist shushes me, and I automatically snap my lips closed. They paint my face and pull my hair into a high, sleek ponytail for the next twenty minutes. I'd be lying if I said I didn't love how it swishes when I walk.

"Perfect," Jenna exclaims. Grabbing my arm, she leans in and whispers in my ear. "Lindy had both shoes when she walked in. We went into my bedroom for a few minutes, and when we came out, Olivia was here, but the shoe was gone. She's such a bitch."

"Okay, so we think it's in the suite?"

"I think so?" That doesn't sound promising.

I glance around. "I'll find it. My sister Sloane used to hide and refuse to come out. I'm a great seeker."

Jenna grins. "You just might be the best investment I've made for this wedding."

I laugh because what the hell do you say to that? The fact that she has twenty grand in disposable income still shocks me, even after spending so much time with the Westbrook billionaires lately.

With my hands on my hips, I scan the suite. When my gaze lands on Olivia, the faintest hint of remorse flits across her face before she dons a mask of indifference. She's definitely attempting to sabotage this wedding, but I don't have the time or the expertise to go all Dr. Phil on her ass. She sits perched on a windowsill beside a large armoire and watches me from the corner of her eye. While everyone else shuffles about the room, she's the only one that hasn't moved.

Narrowing my eyes, I search for something to prop me up high enough to search the top of that armoire. My gaze darts from the giant maple furniture to the chair sitting at the desk and then to Olivia. I see the nervous twitch of her eye and know I'm right.

Without preamble, I drag the chair over to where she sits. It's much heavier than I was expecting, but I muscle the damn thing across the carpet. I give her a *gotcha* look when she doesn't move out of my way. The room around us goes silent, and when I peek over my shoulder at Jenna, she stands with a satisfied smile.

Removing my shoes, I step onto the chair's seat and try to climb up high enough to see, but I'm still a good six inches short. I hop down, turn the chair around, and call for Melinda. "Hey, Melinda? Can you come hold this chair for me?"

Melinda literally skips across the room. Her gleeful face shines brighter than diamonds. "Of course," she sings.

"Seriously. What do you think you're doing? There's nothing but four inches of dust up there," Oliva mutters.

I give her the side-eye. "I guess we'll see, won't we?"

Climbing back onto the chair that now has its back propped up against the door of the armoire, I gingerly step onto the backrest. When I know it will hold me, I push off and hook my arms on the dusty top. "Well, you're right about one thing, Olivia. There is about four inches of dust up here. But, huh? Looky here." Pressing onto my tiptoes, I lean forward and hook my finger around the heel of Melinda's shoe.

"Huh," Jenna scoffs. "I *wonder* how that ended up there?" Her tone drips with sarcasm as everyone in the room turns to Olivia.

"Who knows? If Melinda could take care of her shit, she wouldn't keep losing things. Would you, Lindy?" Even I know she's referring to Jacob.

I hop down from the chair and accidentally lose my balance, making sure to catch her drink with my arm on the way down.

"Oopsies," I singsong as I plow into Olivia, knocking her drink all down the front of her.

"Hey! You idiot. What the hell is wrong with you? Look what you did to my dress!"

"Gosh. I'm so sorry. I was up much higher than I thought. I never in a million years would have thought I'd run into you when I jumped down." I flash my best *aw-shucks* expression.

"What am I supposed to do now?" she wails. "I didn't bring another dress, and we have to be downstairs in an hour."

"Oh, geez. You know what?" Jenna makes a cutthroat motion behind Olivia, and I give her the most serene smile. "I saw a strip mall about five miles away. Surely you can find something there. But"—I check my watch dramatically—"you'd better hurry. I've heard Daddy doesn't like you girls to be late."

Melinda chokes on her mimosa, and I keep my plastic smile in place.

"Jenna. Give me one of your dresses."

Jenna's face turns beet red. "I don't have an extra. Sorry. As the bride, I need to keep my backups. You know, just in case someone acts up."

"Ugh. You're all assholes." Olivia slams her empty glass down and storms out of the suite.

When the door clicks shut behind her, I'm tackle-hugged from all sides.

"I knew you'd be amazing," Jenna cries. "Now, let's get ready for this party! I'm getting married, biatches!"

Quietly, I slip back into my shoes as they all down a shocking amount of champagne. Crap. Now I'm going to be babysitting more than just Oliva.

Twenty thousand dollars, Till. Twenty grand. Glancing around at the women before me, I know I will earn every cent.

* * *

THE REHEARSAL DINNER has been blessedly uneventful. Olivia showed up a half-hour late, so she was seated in the back of the room. She also seemed to have gotten an earful from her step-father. She's barely moved from her seat, but that doesn't stop her from glaring at every bridesmaid at the head table.

Luckily, my knack for blending in has allowed me to go mostly unnoticed by Jenna's guests. From my post next to Melinda, I'm able to scan the crowd, thankful I haven't laid eyes on Jacob. Until I do. Yuck. He even looks like a weasel. He skirts the back of the room, partially hidden in shadows.

What the hell is his deal? Leaning over Melinda, I tap Jenna's shoulder. "Hey. Psst. Jenna?" She turns to me with a worried expression. "How do you feel about a toast that may embarrass a certain cheating ex?" When I nod toward the back of the room, her expression goes from worried to furious.

"I think it will piss off my father and thrill my stepdad. Go for it, Abby. Also, you're officially my hero."

Leaning back, I search Melinda's eyes.

She shakes her head with a forced smile in place. "You don't need my permission. Every single person here was witness to my humiliation. I have nothing left to hide."

Gah! My heart nearly explodes from the pain I see in her eyes.

I squeeze Melinda's arm and stand slowly because my knees are knocking together so hard that I'm afraid I'll keel over. What am I doing? This isn't me. I'm the shy one. The one built to blend in. *Just think of the money, Tilly.* I lift my spoon to the glass in my hand with trembling fingers and tap it three times. Then three more until the guests settle into a hushed silence. Every eye is on me, and I pray I don't pass out.

Clearing my throat, I focus on my fingers until I'm able to find my words.

"Hi, everyone. Most of you don't know me. I'm Abby, Jenna's friend, but I guess you already know that." An awkward half-giggle escapes, and I panic. Melinda takes pity on me and encourages me to continue with a gentle nudge. "Um, I'm so happy to be here celebrating the love that she and Tyler share. It's rare to see a love like theirs, and I'm so lucky to have a friend like Jenna." My gaze darts around the room, making sure Jacob stays in my sights, and I feel my confidence grow when the weasel stands tall like he's proud to be here. Asshole.

"She brought me into her world and never once made me feel like an outsider. Over time, I've gotten to experience the bond she has with her sister, Lindy, and I quickly realized that Jenna loves with her whole heart. She loves her friends like she loves her sister, which is something special.

"There have been a few frogs in her journey to find Tyler. Luckily, they weren't like some of the snakes out there. Just ask Lindy. She sure dodged a bullet with Jacob. Was that his name?" I glance over at Melinda and see a huge smile as she nods. "Gah. What a nightmare that would have been. Luckily, Jenna doesn't have to worry about Tyler cheating on *her*." I lean forward so Tyler can see me and give him the hand gesture for *I'm watching you* with my fingers. Everyone laughs.

Okay, this isn't so bad. And the best part is, Jacob has slipped out the door while Olivia stews in her chair.

"Tyler has proved time and again what an amazing partner he'll be for Jenna, and I can only hope we'll all find that someday. We all deserve a love that honest and real. Thank you, Jenna and Tyler, for being a shining example of what a happily ever after can look like.

"To Jenna and Tyler. May you have years of happiness and love to last a lifetime."

Everyone raises their glasses. Everyone except Olivia and Jenna's father, I notice. As the room congratulates the happy couple, I lean into Melinda. "Why is your dad so pissed off?"

"Jacob works for him," she whispers. "He tried to hide that he cheated on me with his stepdaughter."

"Oh, shit." My stomach plummets, and uncomfortable heat fills my chest. "I just made an enemy for life, didn't I?"

"Well." She smirks and I get the feeling I won't like her next words. "Abby did. Tilly is free and clear after tomorrow night."

I stiffen as a large head drops between us. "What the fuck was that?" Jenna's father hisses with his face down so no one can see him.

"What was what?" I ask innocently while clasping my hands so he can't see them tremble.

"Don't play games with me, young lady. It will not end well for you."

Ah yes, the threats. This is something I know how to handle.

I stand abruptly, forcing him back and pitch my voice low. "I was standing up for both of your daughters. Something you should have done years ago. Lindy's ex-fiancé is here to hurt her, and your psycho stepdaughter is trying to ruin Jenna's wedding. I suggest, *sir*, that you get your head out of your ass and get your priorities straight."

Melinda gasps, just as another gentleman I recognize as their stepfather slides in beside me. "Great speech, Abby. It's about time someone had Jenna's back."

My entire body trembles watching these two men discuss my actions. The whole exchange is like an out-of-body experience. I barely recognize myself. Where the heck has Tilly Camden gone?

"This doesn't concern you, Michael."

"Doesn't it? Considering I've spent a lifetime with your daughters, while you spent a few measly weekends, I think it is my concern. I suggest you take a seat before you cause a scene."

Jenna's father gives a jerky nod as he notices we've drawn the attention of most of the guests. "Don't pull this shit again," he warns a few inches from my face with a menacing smile.

Jenna's stepfather pulls me in for a hug and thankfully forces me to retreat from the other man who looks like he wants to rip my head off. "Keep it up, sweetheart. You're making Jenna's wedding everything she wanted." He pats me on the shoulder a couple of times, then heads to the other side of the table.

I plop down with a heavy sigh, only to have Jenna reach for my hand with a happy squeal.

"Best wedding investment ever!"

It's hard not to share her enthusiasm. I just need to make it through twenty-four more hours with the bridesmaid from hell.

CHAPTER 5

TILLY

The Frye/Grant Wedding

"*E*xplain to me again how you ended up in a wedding?" My sister Eli is slightly hysterical. I'm closest to her of all my sisters, but I can't blame her for the panicked screeching. My situation is straight out of a fucked-up romcom.

"This girl, Jenna, paid me twenty grand to babysit a loose cannon of a bridesmaid." I smile at the phone screen.

Eli leans back in her chair. She's a coordinator for an after-school program funded by the Westbrooks. I find it hard to believe it was always in their plan and didn't magically appear after she told them about her dream job, but I appreciate that they were looking out for her.

"Maybe this is it," she says. Her eyes gleam, and I can almost see the wheels turning, cogs clicking into place, in her beautiful hazel irises.

"It? What's it?"

"Maybe this is the jumpstart you need for your event planning company," Delaney cuts in. I'm pretty sure she shits rainbows and glitter, and I wouldn't have her any other way.

"Admit it, you've been planning weddings since you were old enough to know what a wedding was. For the love of happy, you used to make us take turns dressing up as the groom when we were little. Maybe you have a niche business. Part wedding coordinator, part bridal party wrangler." The image on the screen shakes, and I can tell she's bouncing on her toes with excitement.

I laugh at her absurdity. "I don't think so, Del. This is definitely a one-off. Who in their right mind will pay me to keep bridesmaids from cutting each other off at the knees?"

"Have you learned nothing from Preston or Colton these last few years?" Eli wrenches the phone from Delaney's grasp. "While those two are mostly normal, the people they associate with are freaking nuts! One of Preston's friends spent forty-five thousand dollars on a vase. A vase, Tilly. You don't think they'd shell out big bucks to make sure the most important day of their lives is perfect?"

"No, I don—" The alarm goes off on my phone. "Shit, E. I have to go. I'm supposed to be in Jenna's suite in ten minutes."

"Okay. Love you. Go get those bridal baddies," Delaney cheers.

"You're both ridiculous." I can't help but laugh though.

"Would you prefer malicious maids? Oh, oh, or maybe mismannered maids? Gah! You can name your company The I Do Crew!"

"I'm hanging up now."

"No, Till. I'm serious. Just hear me out."

"I really have to go. I'm late. Love you both." I hang up before she can add anything else.

Grabbing my dress, shoes, and anything else I think I'll need, I hurry to Jenna's suite. I unlock the door with the key card she gave me and am immediately assaulted by a shouting match.

"I know you did this, Olivia. I know you did."

What the hell did she do now? I hurry to hang up my dress, then round the corner just in time to find Melinda holding up her dress with a slice down the center.

"Holy hell. What happened?"

"This crazy psycho bitch shredded my dress. I saw her putting the scissors in her purse."

I glare at Olivia. *What the fuck is wrong with this girl?* She has the gall to shrug like we're wasting her time. All right, Olivia. Game fucking on. No one is going to ruin a wedding on my watch. Not when they're so magical and special. It's your one day to be *the* princess.

"Not today, Olivia," I mutter under my breath and cross the room wearing my best angry face. Granted, my sisters have always told me I'm the least scary person alive, but I put as much venom into my expression as I can muster.

"Remember how I told you I work in PR?" She rolls her eyes. "Well, I also run a blog. A very successful blog that routinely goes viral, and since I owe you nothing, I have no qualms about blasting this to the world."

"My father would sue you for everything you have," she replies flippantly.

"Stepfather," Melinda mutters.

"Funny thing about that. I have a contract with Jenna that says I can use any piece of her wedding for publicity purposes." I'm totally bluffing, but Melinda cuts in to bail me out.

"And since we all signed a similar disclosure, granting Jenna and Tyler permission to post, share, and publish our involvement in the wedding, you included, your behavior is fodder for a lot of stories."

Jesus. Did they really? Rich people are nuts!

Olivia pales but says nothing.

"So, this is what you're going to do," I say. She turns a hate-filled glare my way, but I don't back down. "You're going to go to your room and get ready. You will follow whatever guidelines Jenna requested for hair and makeup. You'll do it with a smile on your face and without uttering a single word. Then you'll meet us in the ballroom ten minutes before the ceremony starts, and not a second before. I will start the media blast if I even catch a whiff of you trying to cause trouble. Do I make myself clear?"

Holy geez! Who the heck am I? If I could high-five myself right now, I totally would.

"Who are you?" she hisses.

That's a great question. I'm miles away from my comfort zone, and my insides are trembling from nerves. The only explanation I can come up with for my behavior is that my love for weddings outweighs my instinct to hide. "Just call me a baddie bridal wrangler."

Jenna chokes on something behind me, but Olivia storms off, slamming the door on her way.

"The baddie bridal wrangler?" Melinda gasps through a fit of full-body laughter. "Where did you come from?"

A wretched flush heats my cheeks, and I'm sure the embarrassment is clear even through my darker complexion. *Freaking Delaney*.

"No, Tilly, no," Jenna jumps in when she sees my expression. "We're in awe. No need to be embarrassed. You're amazing. Seriously."

"Do we think Jacob will make an appearance today?" Audra, another bridesmaid, asks. She's the sweet one who has been following Jenna around, trying to keep her calm.

Scanning the room, I realize each bridesmaid has a function. This will make a fantastic blog post.

"Probably." Melinda groans. "He has FOMO worse than any teenage girl."

"Okay, well, it'll be fine. I'll stay on top of everything. Plus, Liability Liv said she won't stay for the reception anyway, right?" I ask.

Peals of laughter fill the room. "Do you give everyone nicknames?"

Do I? I stop and think about it. "Hmm. I guess if I have a strong enough reaction to them, I do."

"Priceless. But what are we going to do about this dress?" Melinda's tone is stressed.

Taking it from her, I scan the material. I haven't sewn anything since high school when I helped make my sister Sloane's graduation dress, but I think I can do something with this. "Okay, Audra? I need you to go to the front desk and get a needle and as much navy thread as they'll give you."

"On it," she chirps like the happy little bird she is.

"Jenna? How would you feel about your maid of honor having a slightly different dress than the rest of us?"

"You sew too?" Her eyes light up like the Fourth of July.

"Not in a long time, but I can fix this." *I hope.* "She cut right up the seam, so we can give Melinda a sexy little slit up her left leg. Well, it won't actually be little. You're going to show a lot of leg." I look over my shoulder and see the two sisters grin at each other.

"Olivia will hate that." Jenna giggles. "I think it's perfect. Can you do it in time?"

"Yup. You ladies get ready. I can do my own hair and makeup if I need to. No one will be looking at me, anyway. I promise. Your wedding will be perfect."

* * *

"Oн, my gosh, Til—ah, I mean Abby. How did you pull this off?"

I watch with a satisfied smile as Melinda twirls in the mirror. We're doing final dress, hair, and makeup checks in the bridal suite adjacent to the ballroom where the ceremony and reception will take place.

"A side effect of growing up with nothing," I reply. "You learn to be very resourceful."

"Honest to God. Best money spent for this entire wedding is Abby Chambers." The grin hasn't left Jenna's face since I booted Olivia from the room.

"Well, I appreciate that, but you should prepare yourself. Olivia will be here any minute."

A collective groan escapes from the entire bridal party.

Michelle, the wedding planner, pokes her head in the door. "Five minutes, ladies."

The women squeal with excitement. It makes me sad that Olivia has been ruining this for them. It also makes me miss my sisters and friends. I've loved all the places I get to travel to, but I'm away more than I'm home these days.

"Excuse me," sniffs that snotty voice that could make your ears bleed.

Olivia stands just behind Michelle with her arms crossed.

"Am I not allowed to enter?"

Geez, she sounds like a rude version of Cher from the movie *Clueless*.

Michelle takes a very deep breath but doesn't roll her eyes. She has the self-restraint the rest of us are lacking.

"Come in." I wave to Olivia. "There's been a change in the lineup. You're going down after Jess, Audra, and Amy. I'll be right behind you," I say sweetly.

The wedding planner raises a brow in Jenna's direction, but the bride smiles and nods. "Okay then. Line up. The music will start soon."

"Why did the lineup change?" Olivia whines as she steps in front of me.

I lean in so only she can hear me. "So I can keep an eye on you." I pull my phone from my bouquet and wave it in front of her. "It's on silent, but it's set to live-stream at a click of a button. I sure hope no one ends up as a blooper or a meme."

Olivia's eyes rage as she tosses her hair over her shoulder. The fear of strangers judging her works to keep her from making any snarky remarks.

The doors open, and Jess starts the processional, followed by Amy, Audra, and then Olivia, who stops after only a few steps. I keep walking until I'm beside her and flash my phone as I hook arms with her.

"Move your ass," I hiss through a plastic smile. Shrugging to the guests on either side, I say, "Nerves. Gets the best of us sometimes." Sensing Melinda behind me, I drag Oliva the rest of the way.

When we get into place at the end of the aisle, I scan the room, frantically searching for Jacob. My shoulders relax when I don't spot him, but my body heats uncomfortably when I make eye contact with a sexy stranger near the back.

His piercing blue gaze stays locked on mine and doesn't even flinch when I catch him staring. Ever so slightly, I raise my brow in challenge just as the string quartet starts the bridal march. I watch in amusement as he rises from his chair but doesn't turn to see the bride like everyone else. No, this guy openly examines every inch of me with the faintest hint of a smirk on his very kissable lips.

It's like he can only see me. The thought makes my palms sweaty, but I tear my gaze away when I feel Olivia sway beside me. As inconspicuously as possible, I place my flowers on the floor behind me and take her arm.

When I'm sure she's steady, I hiss through gritted teeth and a picture-perfect smile, "Don't even think about pulling a fainting act right now. I will use every muscle in my body to keep you upright."

She yanks her arm away from me. "Whatever. Don't touch me," she seethes loud enough for the people in the front row to hear. Jenna falters in the aisle, but I give her my broadest smile and flash a big, cheesy thumbs-up. "I've got this," I mouth silently and am grateful that Jenna relaxes and continues on her way.

And I do have this. So help me, this wedding will go off without a hitch if it's the last thing I do.

When Jenna stands at the altar with Tyler, my skin prickles with the uncomfortable sensation of being watched. My gaze involuntarily snaps to the audience. To him. *He* is studying me like a final exam, and I'm pretty sure I want to pass his test.

CHAPTER 6

LOCHLAN

"*T*ell me again why I must go to this thing?" I bark at Angie, my sixty-two-year-old assistant. She started out working for my mother, but I brought her to my team after my last four hires flirted with, alluded to, or flat-out propositioned me.

I'm still not recovered from Tom, the assistant who chained himself to my bed and live-streamed for over an hour before I was alerted. Unlike everyone else, Angie doesn't take my shit, but she's also made it clear that she's a temp.

"Because, *Mr. Blaine*." I wipe my mouth with the back of my hand to hide the grin her teasing causes but she continues without missing a beat. "You've been friends with Tyler since grade school. You declined to be *in* the wedding party. The least you can do is attend with a smile on your face and a big fat check in your pocket."

"Fine. Hold my calls for one hour only. I'll be out of there before they cut the cake."

Angie sighs but agrees. "Fine, Lochlan. You know, it wouldn't hurt you to have a little fun."

"I do have fun, Miss Angie. A bloody ton of fun." I scoff. "Weddings are the exact opposite of *fun*."

"Weddings are the perfect place to meet the love of your life."

"Not happening. Love is a myth. An illusion. A fairy tale for disillusioned people searching for happiness in someone else. It isn't real. Happiness doesn't come from anyone but yourself or your bank account." The very last thing I need is love. I've seen how it ends.

My parents divorced when I was eight. A few years later my father married Lila and adopted my stepsister, Nova. Lila was the love of his life, and he has never recovered from her death. My mother has chased love, evidenced by her seven failed marriages.

Seven! And she kept my father's last name through each of them. She must have known they wouldn't last, but she married them anyway. At least she saved herself some paperwork by remaining a Blaine.

Her last marriage set me on my current path though. Her marriage and mine. The connection between the two still makes acid rise high in my throat if I think about it too long.

Nova thinks I should be thankful that my parents have remained friends all this time. She wants me to be grateful that they've had dinner together nearly every Friday night since their divorce. Before Lila passed away, she would join them. My mother's husbands were less involved, but whichever man she happened to be married to at the time would often tag along too.

It's bloody strange as fuck.

"Someone's going to kiss that bitter toad right out of you. In the meantime, Brittney will be starting on Monday." I swear Angie's taunting me.

"Brittney? Really?" I know I'm being a judgmental prick, but Brittney?

"Yes, *Lochlan*." Now I know she's taunting me. "And I expect you to be on your best behavior. I am only a temp, remember?"

A temp who has been with me for eighteen months and through twelve assistants-in-training, but yes, still a temp.

"I'll raise your salary." This is a game we've played more times than I can count.

"I'm sixty-two years old, Mr. Blaine. I will not work forever, so I suggest you make an effort with Brittney. Her resume is impeccable, and she's very motivated."

"Yes, ma'am. I'm walking into the ballroom. I'll check in as soon as it's done."

"Put a smile on your face and your phone in your pocket," she orders. It makes me chuckle. No one speaks to me the way she does and keeps their job. Angie is different, and she never hesitates to tell me what to do.

"Smile, pasted in place. Phone? Never. Good-bye, Miss Angie."

She huffs, then clicks her tongue like she wants to scold me. I pause just outside the door to see if she will. A genuine smile worms its way onto my face as she says, "Good-bye, Mr. Blaine."

Disconnecting the call, I palm my phone and enter the god-awful ballroom. This is exactly why I don't allow weddings at my properties.

That and the small detail of the event coordinator trying to ruin me.

"Bride or groom?" someone vaguely familiar asks the second I step inside, but I don't pay him any more attention.

"Groom."

"Right this way." He points to the right side of the aisle and intends to lead me toward the front.

"This is fine, thank you." Without waiting for his reply, I slip into an aisle near the back.

Am I bloody early? The rows are filling up quickly, but

they're not nearly as full as I'd hoped. With a shake of my head, I bring my phone to life and respond to as many emails as possible before the music starts.

I get glimpses of navy in my periphery as it drifts past me, but I continue with my email. The faint scent of citrus triggers a distant memory and has my thumbs halting, but it's when I hear her that I pause altogether.

"Move your ass," the woman to my left hisses under her breath, and that voice glides over my skin like butterfly kisses. If she wasn't standing directly beside me, I would have missed her words completely. My gaze jumps to her, and the hand holding my phone drops into my lap. An uncomfortable pinch hits my chest. I can't take my eyes off her.

"Nerves." She shrugs to no one in particular. "Gets the best of us sometimes."

I watch her closely as she hooks arms with the trouble-maker beside her. Something in her tone tells me they've tasked her with babysitting the scowling bridesmaid to her left, and it makes me irrationally invested.

I'm intrigued. I shift in my seat as my anatomy attempts a resurrection. Since the last disaster I let into my bed, he's been on lockdown.

My gaze follows her ass as she strolls down the aisle, and my cock twitches against my zipper again. *Well, I guess the little fucker isn't dead after all.* It's not that I don't get turned on by beautiful women, but I've found them to be more trouble than they're worth lately, so I've resorted to my fist most nights.

Fiery. Dazzling. Goddess. All three words could describe this woman, and yet they don't encapsulate her. I have an uncomfortable feeling that she could harness the sun and bring me to my knees in one fell swoop.

Where in the bloody hell did those thoughts come from? Harness the sun? That's dangerously close to fairy tale territory, so I adjust my thinking to something more realistic.

She'll be a good, quick fuck.

Or she could bring you to your knees.

She probably sounds like the annoying girlfriend on Friends.

I shiver, remembering the mind-numbing sound Nova used to laugh at while binge-watching the series when she was a teenager.

Maybe she has genital warts.

My head snaps up to scan her again. No, my Pepper does not have genital warts, and even thinking about genital warts does nothing to tamp down the sorcery this woman has done on my cock without even touching me.

Her gaze darts around the room like she's searching for someone. *Who are you looking for, Pepper?* My phone buzzes in my hand, but I ignore it. I stare intently as she does a sweep of the room with her eyes, and another before her posture relaxes.

Then, in slow motion, her chocolate brown eyes land on mine, freezing me in place. I'm breathless as she quirks an eyebrow but doesn't glance away. Time stands still. The connection I feel with this woman makes my palms sweat. The insane need to know her has me tugging on my vest uncomfortably.

She stands perfectly still at the altar, and I feel a sudden loss when she finally averts her gaze to deal with the woman beside her. I grin maniacally as her lips start to move. I learned to read lips when my sister was a sulky teen, and I watch with interest as she sets her flowers down, grabs the troublemaker's arm, and tells her, "Don't even think about fainting."

The music changes, and everyone around me turns to watch the bride walk down the aisle, but my gaze never strays from the dazzling sprite before me. I'm the last to sit once the bride's father hands her off to Tyler, and I only remember to sit when Pepper flashes a sexy, questioning smirk my way.

Pepper? Yeah, she's Pepper all right. Spicy, sassy, and sexy as hell. If I were a different man, she would certainly ruin me. But that doesn't mean I can't let her ruin me for the night.

Perhaps that's all I need to get out of my head. A hard, fast fuck.

I send Angie a quick text as the wedding proceeds with words I don't hear.

Lochlan: Cancel my calls for the night.

Angie: Cancel them? All?

Lochlan: Yes. I'll be staying at the reception after all.

Angie: Uh-huh. What's her name?

Lochlan: No name. Just trying to have some fun…at your suggestion, I'll remind you.

Angie: Right. Meetings canceled. You're free until 11 AM tomorrow. (winky face emoji)

Did she seriously just use an emoji? I've never seen her use one before, and it confounds me momentarily. Glancing up, I find Pepper's gaze on me with that amused expression that makes me want to lick every inch of her, and I'm disarmed for an entirely different reason.

I don't hear the rest of the ceremony. I don't acknowledge the well-wishers sitting to my right. I don't see anyone but Pepper.

As the bridal procession exits down the aisle, I wait for her to glance up as she passes, but her gaze stays singularly focused on the woman in front of her.

Did she just snub me?

I've never been snubbed in my life.

Why the hell does that make me like her that much more?

No! Not like. I'm intrigued, that's all. Liking her indicates I want more than a one-night stand, and that's not what I want. Not at all. I scowl. Even I don't believe the bullshit forming in my head. But one night is all I'll allow.

My determination is stronger than my hormones.

Maybe her breath will smell like sweaty armpits. Or maybe

she'll talk with her mouth full. Something about her is sure to extinguish this instant fascination. It always does. With a slightly heavier heart, I follow the other guests to the cocktail hour to find out what it is about Pepper that I'll hate.

* * *

"Loch! I can't believe you're still here. I expected you to cut out as soon as the ceremony ended."

I take my martini from the bartender and turn to find my friend Tyler standing with his new bride. For the life of me, I can't remember her name.

"Tyler, come now. Would I skip out on your big day?"

"Yes." He laughs, clapping me on the back. "In all the years I've known you, I've never seen you stay for a reception. Not even your mother's." I nearly flinch, but I hold a fake smile in place after years of practice. "Loch, this is Jenna. I can't believe you two haven't met before now."

Holding out my hand, I gently shake hers. "That's probably my fault," I admit. "I work all the time."

"So I've heard." She smiles. When she peers up at Tyler, I see it in her gaze. Love. *For now,* my inner asshole adds. "Well, I'm really glad you could make it."

"It was a wonderful ceremony," I redirect. "You have a very attractive wedding party. I'm sorry I was unable to participate." Tyler laughs. I do not. "Are all the ladies friends of yours?"

Jenna's grin turns mischievous. "Most of them, yes. Anyone in particular you were interested in, Lochlan?"

"No, no. Nothing like that," I say smoothly. "One of them looks familiar. I believe she was fourth in line. Long, dark hair?"

Jenna and Tyler share an uncomfortable expression before Jenna turns back. "Yes, that's my friend Abby. Abby Chambers. She's amazing."

Abby? My gaze darts around the room as I frown. Abby is much too plain for her. Who the fuck named her Abby? I immediately hate it.

"I can see that," I say neutrally. And truly, I can. I wouldn't be standing here if she were anything less than mesmerizing. "She seemed to have her hands full with another bridesmaid." I take a slow sip of my cocktail and watch Jenna's reaction. She doesn't have a great game face.

"Ah, yeah. She's been…"

"That's Jenna's stepsister, Olivia. She's been a real pain in the ass. Abby has been a lifesaver at keeping her in check," Tyler explains.

Huh. That's interesting. I surreptitiously glance around, searching again for the infamous *Abby*, but can't find her. Even thinking the name causes a scowl, and I mentally replace it with Pepper.

Jenna giggles beside me. "Are you smitten, Lochlan?"

She catches me off guard this time, and I choke on my drink. "No," I almost hiss. "Smitten"—the word sounds dirty coming from my mouth—"is not in my genetic makeup."

"Well, if you were, I'd probably tell you that she's in the restroom making sure Olivia doesn't try to throw a bucket of paint on me or something equally as evil."

"So, she's a babysitter?"

Tyler shifts and doesn't quite meet my gaze.

"She's my friend, doing what good friends do. She's making sure my day goes off without a hitch. That's what *friends* are for, Lochlan."

"Of course. Congratulations to you both. I wish you a lifetime of happiness." *Chumps.*

Love doesn't last a lifetime. A night, a month, possibly a year, but never a lifetime.

"Thanks, Loch. We need to make our rounds. I'll catch up with you in a bit?"

"Absolutely. I'll be here."

Jenna leans in for a hug. "You know," she whispers, "we're not doing a head table. I scattered the bridesmaids throughout the reception. For instance, if someone happened to switch your place setting with Theodore Ackers at table two, I wouldn't be the wiser." She pulls away and winks.

When they move to the next guest, I take off to the table settings to search for Theodore Ackers. Once I've traded the name tags, I take my seat and wait for Pepper to find me.

Another new one for me. I don't believe I've ever stalked a woman at a wedding before. In fact, I've never chased a woman before. I don't know what it is about Miss Abby Pepper, but I'll have a bloody good time finding out.

CHAPTER 7

TILLY

*O*livia exits the bathroom stall with a huff when she sees me washing my hands. "What do you think I'm going to do, Abby? Sneak Jacob in under my skirt?"

"It must be exhausting," I say.

"What is?" she snips.

"Carrying around so much hate. You know, two of my sisters married into a family who values their chosen members just as much as their blood ones, but not one of them balks when a new person enters the fold. They literally open their arms and make them one of their own. Wouldn't it be better to be part of a family rather than trying to tear it apart?"

"You have no idea what you're talking about," she hisses. "I'll never be part of their family. Jenna and Melinda have always made sure of that." There's an edge and a sadness to her words, and I almost feel sorry for her. Then she opens her mouth again. "My wedding will make this one look like trailer trash."

I see red. I didn't grow up in a trailer, but close enough. Camden Crossing is the armpit of North Carolina, and only by the grace of God and my sister Emory did we have a roof over our heads. Being raised in a town that also held our name did nothing for our lot in life.

She storms off before I can lay into her. I take a few calming breaths, then follow her into the ballroom. She's standing across from a man with his back to me, and she has an odd expression as she speaks to him. By every indication, he's relaxed, exuding a confidence I can feel from here.

I move quickly toward the table, knowing I'm seated next to her, and I nearly stumble in my stilettos when she coos, "Maybe we could get out of here," in a sickeningly sweet voice.

I'm not sure who the man is, but I can tell by his suit and shiny watch that he's wealthy. You pick up on these things after working for a few billionaires. God, she's disgusting.

"Wouldn't your boyfriend object to that?" I ask, crossing my arms. "You know, the boyfriend you slept with while he was still your stepsister's fiancé? I can't imagine he'd take too kindly to your advances here."

Her face goes volcanic. She downs her drink and then slams the glass on the table. Before she can spew any more hate, I place my palms on the table and lean in.

"Do not make a scene here, Olivia," I warn her in a deadly calm voice that's equally aggressive. "Remember how much appearances mean to Daddy dearest."

"You're such a cunt."

Air stills in my lungs as shock registers. I've never been called the c-word before, but I refuse to react in kind. "Sit. Down. Olivia."

She calls for a server and orders two more cocktails. *Shit.* This is going to be a long night.

With a heavy sigh, I straighten and pull out the chair in front of me. Only then do I remember the stranger to my left. Easing myself down, I chance a peek at him and instantly wish I hadn't. He's the stranger from the ceremony, with a smirk I'll dream about and sparkling blue eyes that turn my insides to liquid. But it's his troublemaking expression that has me so nervous I nearly miss my chair. He reaches out with one hand to steady me, and I feel his touch everywhere.

My face flushes, and for once, I'm thankful for my darker complexion. My sisters would be fire-engine red right now. When I'm seated, the sexy stranger gives a slow clap, and Olivia scoffs.

"Hello, Pepper. It's nice to meet you. You've had quite the job here today." His low baritone causes my skin to pebble with goosebumps.

"Oh, I'm…"

"Blaine? I'll be damned. I thought that was you." We're interrupted by a fast-talking, slimy-looking, middle-aged balding man.

"Adam," the man apparently named Blaine replies. His tone has gone cold though, and he's shielding me from Adam's view. It's oddly protective, and even more strangely, my body reacts as if it likes it.

"I told Roger I thought that was you, but he disagreed. Said you never socialize with peasants." He gives a throaty laugh that's much too phlegmy and makes me want to gag.

"I socialize plenty with people deserving of my time. You, Adam, are not one of them. If you'll excuse me, I was in the middle of a conversation."

I hear Adam balk, even though I can't see past the wall of a man beside me. But Blaine doesn't give him another breath and instead turns his attention back to me.

"Well, that was kind of rude, wasn't it, *Blaine*?" I say. What the heck kind of name is Blaine, anyway? It sounds like knock-off-Barbie's Ken doll.

He shrugs as if he hasn't a care in the world. "I told the truth. My time is valuable. I give it freely to those who deserve it. He mistreats his employees and puts them in dangerous situations without a second thought. *He* is not deserving of my time." His focus is intense as he regards me. The way his gaze slowly grazes down my body gives me the impression he thinks I am worthy of his most valuable time.

So, Blaine has standards. *That* I can stand behind, even if he does go about it arrogantly, with no regard for other people's feelings. "A-And I'm deserving of your time?"

That wicked, wicked grin transforms his face as he draws closer. "You, Pepper, can have all my time. Today," he adds, almost as an afterthought.

It's not like I have time for a relationship. Today is truly all I can give anyway since tomorrow I go back to being Tilly. I hold up my finger to pause our conversation and peek across the table at Olivia, who is now on her second drink, at least. Then, I pull out my phone and open the text chain between my friends and sister.

Tilly: How do we feel about one-night stands?

Eli: Get it girrrrl! (Fire emoji, salsa dancer emoji)

Delaney: Whoa. I just sprayed iced coffee all over our couch.

Hadley: Time out.

Hadley: Where are you? How do you know he's safe? Do you have an out in case he tries to tie you to a bed in the red room of pain?

That's what I love about these girls. Eli is full steam ahead all the time, Delaney is the planner, and Hadley is scared of her own shadow. Hadley also has an affinity for dark romance novels.

I chance a peek at Blaine to find him watching me with a bemused grin. Oh, shit. Can he read my messages? Covertly, I angle my phone away from him, and he chuckles. It's a rich sound that shakes his entire body, and my spine tingles with awareness when his shoulder rubs up against mine.

Tilly: He's wearing a Cartier watch and a suit that costs more than our rent.

Hadley: So? He could be a rich Dom who wants to own your body!

Eli: Is he hot? If he owned your body, would you like it?

Hadley: Eli! Not helpful!

Eli: If you're into him, go for it. Men do it all the time. Be a boss bitch of your body, baby!

Tilly: I'm going to do it.

Hadley: Don't you dare.

Eli: If you get more than two orgasms, he's a keeper.

Delaney: Eli!

Eli: If you don't get any, run as fast as you can.

"Pepper?" His close proximity and breath on my ear cause me to jump in my seat and I bobble my phone.

"Jesus, Blaine. What the hell. Warn a girl! And my name is not Pepper."

"I know. It's Abby, but tonight? You're my Pepper. Want to know why?"

Desperately! I want to scream, but force myself to swallow the word since my mouth is unhealthily dry.

"You're fiery, Pepper. Sprightly. A sassy little pixie who gets shit done, and I find that sexy as fuck."

It's like he's seen past the façade I present to the world in a misguided attempt at protecting myself. I'm not sure how to feel about that. No one ever sees me, not really anyway. I also think I might whimper a little when he says the word fuck. My lady bits are one thousand percent dancing a jig. He has a lilt to his voice that reminds me of London but is mostly Americanized, and I cross my legs to ease the tingling it causes in my panties.

"I'm curious," he drawls. "How did you draw the short stick?"

The low rumble of his voice shakes the cobwebs from my brain. "Excuse me?"

"Well, it seems like someone's trying to take a piss out of the wedding, and they tasked you with babysitting her." He raises his brow toward Olivia, and I flinch.

Crap. No one's supposed to know I'm babysitting the baddie!

"You hide it well, Pepper. But I'm paying attention."

"To what?" I gasp. My heart speeds up like it's the lead car in a NASCAR race, and I feel slightly lightheaded.

"You."

Amusement and heat shine from those knowing blue eyes. This man sets me on edge and sets me free at the same time. It's a heady combination, and for the first time in my life, I'm feeling truly confident in my own skin.

"If you were paying attention, you would have noticed that I'm just a good friend who intends to make sure this wedding is perfect."

"Why?"

Why? Is he serious? It's like he lit a fire under me, and I'm about to give him the happily-ever-after education of his life!

"Why, what?" I nearly spit. I blink a few times at the vehemence in my tone while straightening in my chair to collect myself. He sits calmly and waits for me to continue, and I have the ridiculous urge to ruffle him. *What would it take to make a man like this lose his cool?* My cheeks burn, and I force myself back on track.

"It's a wedding, Blaine. The most magical day in a girl's life. Literally what all our fantasies are made of since the time we're ten. Okay, maybe since I was ten, but most girls have a dream wedding, and my friend paid a lot of money to be a princess for a day. I'm just making sure nothing messes it up."

"Because you want your friend to have the best day?"

"Because I think everyone deserves to have their happily ever after and not worry about a spoiled brat ruining it," I say with a huff.

"Do you believe in all that?" His tone has gone soft, almost uneasy, like he's disturbed by my answer.

"All what?"

"The happily ever after? Are you a romantic, Pepper?"

"I am." Did he just groan? "Why? Do you not believe in finding your one true love?"

He stares for so long my fingers fidget under the uncomfortable weight of his gaze.

"I want to believe in love, but it's a fickle bastard." He's so quiet I have to lean in to hear. "So, you probably have a plan for your perfect first date too?"

His words feel like an attack, but it's his sad tone that has me answering. "I'm a planner, but some things should be spontaneous. Like first dates. Coffee or sushi? It depends on how we meet. The vibe you get from someone."

"What would our first date be?"

"Explosive." It slips from my lips, and both hands fly to my mouth. I stare at him, unable to blink as I watch the fire catch in his gaze.

"I could get on board with this kind of planning, Pepper," he growls, and that tingling in my belly wakes with a vengeance.

"Er, what would be your perfect first date?"

He's saved from answering when I hear an amplified voice that douses the heat between us like a bucket of ice water.

Olivia stands in the front of the room with a goddamn microphone. How much has she drunk?

I'm out of my seat without a second thought. I ignore the strange looks I get as I sprint toward the back of the room where the sound system is housed. Glancing over my shoulder, I see her swaying as she speaks. I also don't miss that Blaine has risen from his chair and is coming after me.

Gah! I don't have time for Sexy-McSexerson right now.

Tearing back the curtain, I find a tech nerd eating a sandwich.

"I—I was s-s-supposed to be today," Olivia slurs. "But Jenna's ah, ah bitch."

"Turn her microphone off," I demand. "And get me a new one. Right now."

The tech nerd drops his sandwich, and I feel a twinge of guilt, right before I detect the heat and masculine scent that can only be Blaine. Pinching the bridge of my nose, I ignore him and take the mic the tech hands me.

There's a squeak as he turns Olivia's mic off and mine on.

"But really…" I begin in a voice as similar to Olivia's as I can manage. I push past Blaine. Olivia is still talking wildly into her unplugged mic. It's like a version of bad lip-synching, but it's the best way to avoid disaster, so I continue. "What I meant to say is that Jenna's a bad bitch who knows what she wants and goes after it. I've always admired that about her." Olivia's face goes crimson, and I know I have to make this quick. "I've actually admired a lot about my stepsister, but I don't always know how to show it."

"Olivia is going to blow a gasket," Blaine whispers in my ear, sending a shiver across my skin.

"Jenna is truly one of the best people I know. I hope one day I can be as caring, honest, and forgiving as she has been with me. I may not have chosen a boyfriend quite as good as Tyler, but I'm young. There's still hope, right?"

Everyone laughs, thank God. I scan the crowd for Jenna and breathe a sigh of relief to find her laughing with Tyler.

"So, if you could all turn your attention to the happy couple and help me wish them a lifetime of love and happiness. To Jenna and Tyler!" I toss the mic to Blaine and sprint back into the ballroom. Grabbing Olivia's purse on our table, I head straight for her, but Jenna's father beats me to her.

"What the fuck was that?"

"Sorry, Mr. Frye," I say, slipping between them, which is no small feat considering he's a bulging man invading her space. "I believe they overserved her. I'll escort her to her room."

He glares at me with barely-concealed rage before turning back to his stepdaughter. "Don't let me see your face at this reception again, Olivia. Do you hear me?"

Her lip quivers, and guilt hits me full force.

"Come on, Liv. I'll help you to your room."

"I—I don't need your help." She hiccups. "I don't need any of you."

"Okay. But it's never safe to wander around hotels at night by yourself. I'll just walk beside you. Come on."

I catch the scent of citrus and ocean breezes before I feel his gaze on my back like a lover's caress. Blaine doesn't say a word as he follows us into the hallway. Or when we get on the elevator. Or when I leave him at the door and walk Olivia into her room. She passes out cold the second her head hits the pillow. I remove her shoes and tuck her in, then go to the bathroom to get her a bottle of water and two Advil that I place beside her bed. I debate leaving a note but figure it's best if she hears it from me.

Dear Olivia,

I think the cocktails won last night. I walked you back to your room without incident, but you did cause a tiny scene making a toast at the reception. Mr. Frye requested you not return to the reception or brunch tomorrow. Give him a little time to cool down, then I'm sure you'll be able to mend bridges.

Take care,

Abby

I'm exiting the bedroom when Jacob walks in with Blaine on his heels. Geez! This night will never end.

"Jacob," I acknowledge tersely.

"What are you doing in my room?" he slurs.

Oh, wonderful. He's drunk too.

"Mr. Frye sent me up here to make sure you both stay in

your room for the rest of the night. If he sees you anywhere near the wedding, you won't have a job when you return home. Is that clear?"

"Whatever," he hisses. As he stalks past me, he nudges my shoulder just enough with his to make me wobble on my heels.

Blaine has him pinned to the wall a second later. "Touch her again, and it will be the last thing you do."

Recognition and possibly fear are the only expressions I can read on Jacob's reddening face when he finally focuses on Blaine. "Mr.—Mr." He makes a gurgling sound in the back of his throat and Blaine eases his grip slightly. "Blaine, I'm s-sorry. I…"

"Shut up, you fucking cack. Go to bed. And don't ever let me catch you treating a lady like that again. You won't like the consequences. Got it?"

Jacob nods frantically and stumbles when Blaine lets him go. He doesn't look back as he enters the bedroom and closes the door.

I stand slack-jawed as Blaine turns toward me, a predatory smile replacing his pissed-off expression. "Am I correct in guessing you're off duty now?"

I nod, unblinking, and he takes my hand in his. "I want to kiss you, Pepper. But not in this jackhole's room, so you have three options. One, you can say no, and I'll walk away, no hard feelings. Two, we'll go back to the reception, and I'll kiss the living hell out of you with witnesses. Or three, you can come to my room, and I'll kiss you in private. Everywhere."

"Holy geez!"

His grin is blinding. "I'm not a patient person, Pepper. What's your choice?"

I mean, is there really a choice here? My epic dry spell has had me in a funk for months. This man seems to actually see me. Wants *me*. And my body is doing the tango, propelling me forward.

"P-P-Private." It's the best I can manage as my heart thunders in my chest and blood rushes in my ears, making me dizzy.

Holy geez. Holy geez! I'm about to have a one-night stand with Sexy McSexerson.

Blaine grins wickedly. *Oh, no. Did I say that out loud?* I don't have time to ponder because he's dragging me out of the room, down the hall, into the elevator, and the second the doors close, his lips cover mine. His tongue doesn't ask for entry. It demands it.

Oh, Mylanta. If he can kiss like this, I know his sex will destroy me. And I'm here for it. I do a mental inventory of my panties. It's quick because I couldn't wear any with this dress, and luckily, I got waxed right before this trip.

Hip hip hooray, my pussy's here to play! It's the last coherent thought I have because Blaine, not sure of his last name, takes full control of my body, and I happily go along for the ride.

CHAPTER 8

LOCHLAN

*P*ossessive. That's the only word to describe what I'm feeling as I crash through my hotel room door with my hands gliding over every inch of her I can reach.

My Pepper.

Truthfully, I'm not sure how to process these uncontrollable feelings, so I don't. Instead, I focus on how good she feels under my outstretched palm. And how her body molds into mine as I press her against the wall. And I most definitely pay attention to how she moans when my thumbs caress her nipples.

Tonight is about carnal desires and nothing more. End of story.

I take Pepper's hands in one of mine and hold them above her head. Her eyes sparkle with anticipation, and knowing she wants this as badly as I do has my cock begging for release.

"Let's see how well you listen, shall we? Keep your hands here and don't move them, or I'll stop."

"Not even if I want to do this?" The little minx wiggles her wrist free to fist my hard-on through my trousers.

"Not until I say so," I growl. It's authoritative. It's a

command, a demand, and everything in between, but she just grins and squeezes harder.

Fuck me. My little Pepper is more than a spitfire. She's a seductress. A siren. A goddess that could bring me to my knees. She unzips me and slips a hand inside to rub her thumb around my crown.

"You don't listen very well," I groan through clenched teeth.

"I never have. You don't seriously expect me to start now, do you?" she asks as she slowly lowers herself to her knees. The image of her like this will be my fantasy for years to come.

"I told you to keep your hands above your head." Either I'm losing control, or she's taking it. I'm not even sure I care.

She undoes my trousers and drops them to the floor with quick but graceful movements. If the lack of undergarments shocks her, she doesn't show it. My painfully hard dick dances before her, and she licks her lips.

"Yes, sir." She looks up at me through long lashes, and two things happen at once. She crosses her wrists, lifting them to my chest, and her lips close over my raging erection. Pure. Fucking. Ecstasy.

I'm so hard that the throbbing vein on my shaft's underside aches.

Then she licks it better.

Holy Christ.

My fingers close around her delicate wrists. I push them back against the wall, bowing her body toward me. It's a delicious sight. Her nipples pebble behind the thin silk of her dress, and I long to have them between my teeth.

Then, she swallows around me, humming a most beautiful tune, and I see stars. I pride myself on my stamina, but my little Pepper has me ready to blow my load in less than five minutes. And that will just not do.

"Stand," I command while lifting her by her wrists. I'm not rough, but I'm certainly not gentle. It scares me that she can unarm me so completely, but my need for her outweighs any concerns trying to form in my head.

She releases me with an audible pop, then licks her lips like she knows it makes me want her even more. When I have her on her feet, I crash my face to hers, licking her lips and grasping the back of her neck to hold her to me. I need this woman with me. Tonight. I need her tonight.

"You're a bad, bad girl, Pepper."

I lower my lips to her jaw and make my way down her slender neck, pausing only briefly to nip the pulse point, beating an unsteady rhythm.

"Yes," she breathes, still attempting to free her wrists from my grasp, but I hold tighter. She tried to undo me. Now it's my turn.

"Hold still," I warn as I run my fingers beneath the strap of her dress. I follow it all the way down to the swell of her breast and back up. Her chest heaves under my touch, and my hips try to thrust forward, try to make contact with this beautiful devil before me, but I refrain.

When she whimpers, I move my hands to her ass and slowly skim up her perfect body that smells like lilacs and rain until I find the closure of her dress.

It takes all my restraint to go slow as I lower the zipper and watch with hooded eyes when her dress gaps in the front. I lower one of her arms, then the other, and finally the dress. When she stands before me in a sheer strapless bra, *come fuck me* heels, and nothing else, my chest rumbles with a growling sound of appreciation that's never escaped my body before.

"See something you like?" she asks saucily, shimmying her shoulders so her tits rub against my dress shirt.

I don't answer her, but I take half a step back and stare at her with unadulterated lust. I take my time in my perusal too. I watch how her stomach tightens as my gaze lingers on her tits. Most men wouldn't notice how her thighs clench with need.

And good God, I can smell her arousal. Spicy and floral and so perfectly *her* that my mouth waters in anticipation. Actually, fucking waters like a dog in heat.

"Are you uncomfortable, Pepper?"

"Not at all," she fires back, but her legs rub together, causing the friction I know she needs. "You can ogle as long as you like, but I'll warn you. I feel even better than I look."

Fucking. Sassy. Mouth. Is she always like this? Or just with me? Why do I want it to be just me more than anything I've wanted in a very long time? I've never been this out of control before. Not even with...

I snap. Thinking of my ex and the vendetta against her will not interfere with what's happening here and now. Not tonight, fuckers.

I roughly rip Pepper's bra away, and my teeth pluck her left nipple before moving onto her right. I lick and lap and savor every inch of her perfectly swollen breasts.

"You taste even better than you feel," I groan against her ribcage in my quest to move south.

She lifts her leg the second my knees hit the floor and rests it over my shoulder. She's completely open to me. My watering mouth is inches from her slick heat, but I make her squirm as I stare and inhale. I want to bottle her spicy scent and mark her with mine. But not yet. First, she needs to beg. I rub my nose up the inside of her thigh, stopping just short of where she wants me.

"Tell me what you want," I demand, taking back some of the control.

"I want to come." Her words are direct. Honest. And I fucking love it.

I waste no more time diving in. Opening her slit with my left hand, I run my tongue up and down her slick folds a few times before plunging into her depths. Her taste is unique and addictive. I want to coat my entire body in it.

"Oh, God," she wails.

She's loud, but I want her louder. I won't be satisfied until this entire floor hears her screaming my name.

My tongue circles her clit before I flatten it and flick relentlessly at the tiny bundle of nerves. Her hips move up and down, riding my face, and I put my dick in a choke hold before I pop off prematurely. Her leg slips off my shoulder and she rolls her hips as both feet find purchase on the floor. I tug myself with slow strokes as I take my time learning Pepper's body. When I insert two fingers into her slippery channel, I release myself so I can use both hands to hold her to me.

I can't help the groan that escapes when she clamps down on my fingers. She might squeeze the life out of my cock when I finally enter her. *Wouldn't that be the way to go though?*

"Lift your hips toward the ceiling," I whisper against her pussy, and she complies.

Removing my fingers, I use her juices to rub tight circles around her clit as my mouth moves lower.

"Blaine," she shouts, and I pause. An overwhelming urge for her to know me sits heavy on my chest. The real me. Not the Blaine persona I present to the world, but Lochlan. Then she pushes her hips forward, urging me on, and I forget everything but making her come.

Lifting up on my knees, I grasp her hips and flip her around so her chest and face rest against the wall. She starts to speak, but I press her forward, grip her ass, then dive back in. Licking her from behind, I slip one hand around her hips to attack her clit again.

She writhes beneath my touch, and I can't ever remember being this turned on. I place both hands on her ass and spread her cheeks as I lick from her clit to her puckered hole and back again. She gasps and shoots forward to the wall, but I pull her back to me.

"Hold still," I repeat. Then lift my hand and massage her left ass cheek, gratified when her pussy tries to clamp down on my tongue. "You liked that, you naughty girl."

She howls her consent as my tongue rims her ass again, and somehow I know that no one else has ever touched her here. It makes me that much greedier. My fingers on her clit speed up to keep pace with my pounding heart.

"I. Blaine? I. Holy shit."

I grin evilly against her ass, then bring my other hand between her legs and enter her pussy without warning. My fingers work on overloading her senses, and it doesn't take long before her legs quiver and shake.

Precome seeps from my engorged cock. The sounds she's making alone could cause my release.

Standing quickly, I detach myself just long enough to push her back down a little more, remove my shirt, and grab a condom. Once I'm sheathed, I lift her hips so she's standing on her tiptoes. She's completely open to me like this. Her arousal is dripping down her legs, and I can't wait any longer. I enter her in one forceful thrust.

She cries out. I see stars, and it takes me a minute to get hold of myself. A minute she doesn't give me as she lifts even higher onto her toes and pushes back against me. I stand completely still as she moves up and down on my shaft. It's reverse cowgirl standing up, and I fucking love how her tits slap against the wall, but this is my rodeo.

Wrapping one arm around her waist and another around her shoulders, I hold her to my chest, lifting her off the floor, and back us up to the bed in one sweeping motion.

When my knees hit the mattress, I lower us down, never once losing the connection, and when I'm resting comfortably against the headboard, I release her. Pepper drops forward onto her hands and knees, and I've never seen a fucking sexier sight.

Scrambling to keep our connection, I nearly cry out when

I slip from her pussy. I've never been this desperate to get deep inside a girl again, but that's what I am. A desperate, desperate man, and I can't take another breath until I slam back into her.

Pepper pants below me, arching her back, begging for me. And bloody hell, do I give it to her. Grasping her hips, I thrust harder and harder until I bottom out. Her walls quiver again, and I know she's close, but I can't let this end. I don't want it to end. *I may never want it to end.*

"Tell me how you like it, darling. Fast and hard? Slow and sweet? Or maybe you want it a little rough?" I demand as I continue to pound into her.

She's breathless as she pants her answer in time with the punch of my hips. "Hard. Rough. Dirty," she gasps.

Christ. She might be the perfect woman. If that's what I was searching for.

I growl. It's a feral sound that echoes off the walls. "If you want it dirty, sweetheart, I'd better hear you. Every sound. Every thrust. Every slap. I want to hear your reaction. Do. You. Understand?" I punctuate each word with a deeper thrust than the time before.

"Yes. Yes. Please, yes!" she shouts. Her knuckles turn white as she clutches the bedding.

Leaning forward, I place a hand over her throat and pull her to me before running my thumb along her lips. "Suck it." Pepper doesn't hesitate. She pulls my thumb into her mouth and tongue-fucks it like she did my cock. It makes me impossibly harder. I allow her a few moments with my thumb, then yank it from her lips and gently lower her down to the bed.

"Take a deep breath."

I wait for her chest to expand with air, then breach her ass with my thumb, slippery from her own saliva.

"Gah. Bl-Blaine. I. Ugh."

Her legs shake, and her skin slicks with perspiration, but

she doesn't stop pushing back into me. In fact, she speeds up like she's chasing her orgasm now, making me double down.

I pump in and out of her with my cock and thumb. Rotating my hips when I'm fully seated, I match the movements of my thumb. She comes in a violent torrent of screams and spasms that drag on for long minutes. But I don't let up. As her spent body falls forward, so do I.

Pushing her legs together, I lift her just enough to get a pillow under her hips, and then I rut into her. I push and pillage and thrust until I'm out of breath, but I can't stop. Keeping my hips against her ass, I grind into her so deeply that I hit the end of her.

Her moans begin again, and I slip a hand between her and the pillow. "You will come again for me before I explode."

She shakes her head, but I lower my front to her back and pin her down so I can whisper hoarsely into her ear. "You can, and you will, darling. Then we'll do it all over again. This will be a night you never forget."

Or maybe I'm making sure this memory brands me.

"Blaine. Blaine. Blaine." It's a chorus, a love song, a prayer, and it's intoxicating.

One hand speeds up on her clit, and the other bears down on her hip. I need to be deeper. I need to feel all of her.

"Do you know what you taste like, darling? How sweet you are? When you come this time, I'm going to roll you over and drink every drop of your arousal until you come again all over my face."

"Fu-uck." she groans, and I feel the fire at the base of my spine. I won't hold out much longer.

"Did you like my tongue on your ass, baby? Would you let my cock fuck you there too? I'll open you up with my tongue and my fingers. I'll get you so wet you'll think you're swimming. Then I'll ram into that virgin hole over and over again until you come so hard you forget to breathe. Is that…"

She comes with the force of the Royal Navy, and I clench my teeth as she shudders around me. When her tremors begin to subside, I pull out, rip off the condom and jerk off until my load coats her back and ass. Rope after creamy rope marks her as mine.

For the night. Mine for the night. But it's a beautiful sight. As the last stream exits, I roll her over and find startled eyes staring back at me.

With a wicked smile, I make good on my promise. I torture her clit until she's panting, pleading, and begging for mercy. I lick her until she coats my face, and her scent and taste are committed to memory. I lick her until my tongue rebels, and she passes out in my arms.

LOVE IN THE LOBBY

Hello, lovely readers,

How do we feel about one-night stands? For ages, it's been a pseudo-acceptable pastime for men, so I'll start by saying I'm not interested in your approval, hate, or condemnation. Cool? Good. Let's dig in…

By definition, a one-night stand is not a relationship to build a future on. But what if…

What if you meet "the one" at, let's say, a wedding, and one night of passion ruins you for all other men? What then?

Sigh. Sometimes, one night is all it will ever be.

This week's *Love in the Lobby* takes place at The Dorrety in San Francisco, California.

The Dorrety is a truly magnificent shell. I'm sad to say that it falls into the average category everywhere else. Could you have a perfectly acceptable wedding here? Absolutely. But why settle for acceptable when you can have extraordinary?

Let's talk about weddings for a minute, shall we?

Nothing makes my rage-o-meter fly into orbit faster than someone intentionally trying to ruin a special day. Nothing.

At this particular wedding, the bride had contingency plans

in place. And the event planner at The Dorrety did an excellent job of making sure everything within her power went precisely as planned. She's the only reason for the higher ranking though.

So, can The Dorrety deliver a Happily Ever After?

Here's my Five-Diamond-Rings Rating:

Cleanliness - Five Diamond Rings: (As always, don't forget to tip!) My suite was very clean, and housekeeping did a great job of checking in during my entire stay.

Friendliness - Four Diamond Rings: The staff I interacted with went above and beyond. They lost a star because finding the staff was sometimes an issue.

Location - Two Diamond Rings: Once you're here, plan to stay put or rent a car. There is no easy access to anything outside of the resort.

Amenities - Three Diamond Rings: It had everything you could need but not enough staff to cover all services.

Last Call: With a few improvements, The Dorrety could be a contender. Make sure you specify your service needs ahead of time, and your wedding just might go off without a hitch!

17K likes. 2K Comments.

BanBB: How do you fact-check your information?

BanBB: Sometimes, one-night stands are too memorable.

Exeter432: Slut.

Momager69: Ignore the idiots. One-night stands are a healthy part of growing up. Experimentation is the spice of life!

Girlwomanfree: You are the owner of your body! YOU make the decision. Get it, girl!

CHAPTER 9

TILLY

"*W*hat do you mean, you snuck out of his room? After all those orgasms, you didn't stay to get his number, or at the very least, another orgasm? Are you insane?" My sister Eli scolds while Delaney watches on, her anxiety draining all the color from her face. Hadley paces behind us.

"I mean, it was a one-night stand. Why would I want to experience the walk of shame in front of him? *I wouldn't!* So, I snuck out before the sun came up."

"How were you even walking after that?" Delaney gasps.

Eli and I try to hold it together, but the second we make eye contact, laughter bursts from our bellies.

"Take a sitz bath if your kitty's sore," Mable, our seventy-year-old neighbor, calls through the vent in the floor.

We all freeze.

Her kitchen table sits directly below our family room, and she can hear everything through the grate on our floor. We've become real-life versions of her daytime dramas she calls out of the senior center to watch.

How can you call out of the senior center like you're calling out of work? We're not sure, but she seems to do it more times than not so she can stay home and sip her sweet wine.

"Mable! Isn't it past your bedtime?" Eli yells down at the grate.

"Not when I've finally got some gossip to hear, *Eliza*," she calls back up. "Y'all have been boring me to tears lately. I've had to go to Fiddle the Bean four times this week just to hear anything interesting."

Only our neighbor would own a chain of coffee shops called "Fiddle the Bean."

"You're a dirty old bird, you know that, Mable?" Eli laughs.

"Pfft. If it ain't dirty, it ain't worth doin', and it sounds like little miss fairy tale up there has the dirt on the dirty. I'm not missing this," she says with her thick southern drawl.

"Mable, do you want to just come up here and join us?" Delaney asks. Delaney's default is people pleaser, and she never wants to leave anyone out.

Mable coughs like she's on her twentieth cigarette of the hour. "No, I don't want to join you. Why would I want to hang out with a bunch of gossip girls who walked out on a perfectly good opportunity to get another orgasm?"

"You'd rather just eavesdrop?" Hadley's curious question has Mable laughing again.

"It's not eavesdropping if you know I'm doing it. Now get on with it. I need my beauty sleep."

Mable has skin like a fake crocodile purse, mischievous eyes that sag with age, and yet, she is truly still beautiful.

"Ah, okay."

We all stare at each other.

"You were about to tell Delaney she needs to get laid," Mable supplies helpfully.

"I've had sex before," Delaney huffs.

"Yes. You have. With Micropenis Mike. That doesn't count," Hadley deadpans.

Delaney's face turns an uncomfortable shade of red, and I can't tell if she's angry or embarrassed, but her freckles appear purple.

Eli jumps in to redirect the conversation back to me. "You met an amazing man at a wedding, and you walked away before he could reject you."

"Well…"

"Titty, that's exactly what you did," Mable interrupts.

"No, it's not," I protest. "You don't understand. It was one of those lightning strike moments. He saw me, and I—I don't know—it's like I wasn't myself. I was flirtatious and forward. I mean, the sex was otherworldly. But I felt like a different person around him. Like his energy infiltrated my soul and turned me into this confident version of myself that takes charge and gets shit done."

There's a long silence while everyone stares at me.

"Oh, honey," Eli says. "Don't you see? That *is* you. You make sure everyone is taken care of. You do get shit done—you've just never wanted the parade announcing it to the universe." She stares me down, daring me to argue with her.

"You guys are missing the point. Blaine was a one-night stand that will live rent-free in my head for the rest of my life. But, two weeks ago, I was at a wedding, babysitting an unruly bridesmaid, and I made twenty thousand dollars!"

"You lucky bitch." Hadley smiles. "I still don't understand how that happened or why we're just hearing the details now."

"I've been traveling. You guys have been working. Need I remind you it's the first time we've all been together in weeks? Again, twenty grand, Hades! Can we focus here?"

"How do you claim that on your taxes?" Delaney asks, full of wide-eyed innocence.

I turn to stare at her.

"Only you would be worried about the taxes." Eli laughs.

It's not that my best friend is necessarily naïve, but she is a rule-follower to her very core.

"Death, sex, and taxes." Mable chuckles. We've learned sometimes it's best to just ignore her.

"Well." Delaney sniffs. "It's an important thing to worry about. The IRS doesn't mess around with taxes."

I'm about to tell her that I'll look into it first thing Monday morning when my phone rings. Glancing down, I see it's Jenna Frye calling, and my nerves get the better of me.

"Holy crap. It's Jenna!" I hiss. "The bride!"

"Oh, God. What if she's calling to ask for a refund or something?" Hadley squeaks, then chews on her nails while humming low in her throat. It's a habit that's both endearing and devastating at the same time. A side effect of losing her parents in college.

I reassure her with a soft smile. "No, Hades. I don't think she'd do that. But she *is* supposed to still be on her honeymoon…"

"Just answer the damn thing already," Eli barks, snapping me out of my haze.

"Right. Okay." Pressing the green button, I clear my throat before answering. "Hello?"

"Abby Tilly Chambers, how are you, my amazing wedding-saving friend?"

"Ah, I'm good." I laugh, raising an eyebrow at the girls, then I pick up where Hadley left off pacing earlier. "How are you? Aren't you still on your honeymoon?"

"I am, but I have a job offer for you."

I stare at the girls, flabbergasted, and put my phone on speaker. "Ah, a job offer? I already have a job."

"Will it pay you 30K for a few days of work?"

"Wh-What?" I choke. Eli jumps to her feet, waving wildly, while Delaney gently pushes me into a chair, and Hadley stands frozen in our small family room.

"Yes. Audra, remember her? She was one of my brides-maids. One of the nice ones. Anyway, she's getting married, and her best friend and her cousin are at war. She wants to hire you to micromanage her cousin because the bachelorette party was a disaster of epic proportions. And, her parents are loaded, so I told her it would cost thirty thousand instead of twenty. See, good things come to those who stick their noses in bitchy bridesmaids' business."

"Holy shit," Eli hisses. "Say yes. *Say*. Yes!"

"Umm." I flash a panicked look at the girls, shaking my head while my heart kickboxes my chest.

"It's a no-brainer, Til-Abby. You have a gift for taming the bitch brigades. Take advantage of it while you can. So, is that a yes?"

"I. Well…"

"Great. I'll forward your number then. She knows you go by Abby Chambers. That's how she'll list you on the wedding website and introduce you. But prepare yourself, lady. This wedding will be unlike anything you've ever seen. The event of the decade, for sure. No pressure though. Anything you can stop will be better than what will happen without you. You'll be great! Okay, gotta go! Talk soon."

I lower my phone in slow motion. Hadley might actually faint, but my doer sister is taping a piece of posterboard to the wall.

"A-Are you okay, Tilly?"

My gaze cuts to Delaney. "What the hell just happened?"

"What happened is, you just got handed a business proposition."

"Titty Camden just got paaaaid," Mable wheezes, and if she were here, I'd slap her back to make sure she's not choking. "Well, sounds like all the sexy talk is over. I'm heading to bed."

We all shout goodnight to our nutty neighbor. With worried eyes, I turn my attention back to my sister. "I don't know what kind of business this is. I'm not like you guys, or Emory, or even Sloane. I'm just kind of…"

"Procrastinating."

"Eli!" Delaney hisses. "That isn't nice."

"I don't mean it in a bad way, Till. But you never do anything until you know you'll do it perfectly. It's why you interned for an extra year. It's why you practiced softball in our backyard for a year and a half before trying out for the team. You want to own something. Something you created, right? Well, this opportunity just got dumped in your lap and is offering you a chance to make a boatload of money. Even if this isn't exactly what you want to do in the long run, it gives you capital to get started. Let's turn this opportunity into something. Let's make a plan."

"Eli, this is glorified babysitting. I can't turn this into a business."

"Actually," Hadley squeaks, "I read an article last year about dates for hire."

"I'm not an escort, Hadley." Oh, God! I think my throat is closing up.

"No!" Her face goes crimson. "They weren't either." Her words tumble from her lips at a frenetic pace. "It's like getting invited to a wedding but not wanting to show up alone. Or wanting to attend with someone super-hot to piss off an ex."

"Yes." Eli claps then adds more tape to the posterboard on the wall. "You'll offer that in bridesmaid form. Except you're keeping shitty people from making shittier choices and ruining someone's big day. And you, of all people, can appreciate the magic of weddings."

"This isn't a business plan though, E."

"But it can be," Hadley whispers, crossing the room and pushing her bright blue glasses up.

Delaney claps her hands. She's like Business Barbie with her blond hair, bright outfits, and a smile that could melt glaciers. "Let me get my sticky notes!" She dashes from the room, returning a second later with every neon piece of paper she could find and colored pens spilling out over her arms. She's leaving a trail from her bedroom, Hansel-and-Gretel style. "Let's just think about it for a minute, Till. It is a lot of money."

"Delaney Marie Daniels. You cannot seriously be on board with this?"

"Tilly Elaine Camden," she mocks. "It's thirty thousand dollars."

Inhaling through my nose, I raise my hands to my temples and rub small circles around the migraine forming. When the three of them start murmuring and agreeing, their hands moving a mile a minute, I sink into the sofa and put an arm over my eyes.

"Okay, Hades, what kinds of bridesmaids are there?" Eli asks.

"Ah, I mean, I've never been one."

This has me moving my arm to peek at her. Hadley has the heart of a giant, but she's also painfully shy. She's the most genuine person I've ever met, and it's always made her an easy target for mean girls. She's the reason I know that even at almost thirty years old, some girls never left high school.

"You'll be in all our weddings, Hades," Delaney promises.

Hadley rolls her eyes, but her cheeks turn pink, and she adjusts her glasses.

"I've only been in my sisters' weddings," Eli commiserates. "But we've all watched every movie with a happy ever after known to man, and Delaney has been in at least ten weddings this year alone. So, let's compile a list."

"A list?"

"Yes. If we list every type of potential disastrous bridesmaid, we can make a plan for handling them."

Hadley nods. "Yes." She waves her hands excitedly. "This is

good. She'll have a game plan heading in before she even talks to the bride."

Delaney dumps all her supplies on the end table, then reaches up on her tiptoes and writes *bridal baddies* in magenta, her favorite color, on the posterboard.

Peeling myself off the couch, I walk to the corner and grab her stepstool. The rest of us are average height, but Del is on the other side of five feet and fights for every quarter inch. I place it by her feet. She shrugs and hops on with a sunshiny grin so sweet it could make your teeth ache.

"Okay. We can do this. What type of relationship did the last two baddies have?"

"I don't know. Frenemies," I tell them, standing with my arms crossed as I watch the controlled chaos unfold around me.

Hadley takes the marker from Delaney and writes *frenemies* on the posterboard.

"You know, we have computers for this," I tease.

"Nah, I'm with Del. I like the colors, and it'll help us work out a plan of attack together," Hadley states. She pushes her glasses up. Again. It's a habit she's had as long as I've known her. It allows her to break eye contact without feeling so insecure. "I've got one." Underneath *frenemies*, she writes *the one-upper*.

"Ooh, good one, Hades. The rapacious one." Eli smirks.

Delaney turns her head over her shoulder. "Greedy," she whispers.

"Thanks." I roll my eyes. "How about the insensitive one?"

"Oh, that's totally one."

I'm getting into it now as we list off every possible type of baddie. Most come from personal experience, unfortunately, but Eli's right. With our combined experiences, we'll know how to handle them all.

"The unreliable one."

"Macy Jones." Delaney laughs.

"Talebearer," Eli says with an eyebrow raised to the sky.

"Ugh. Mary Ward. She could spread gossip faster than the internet."

"The pessimist."

"The superficial."

"The bullheaded." We all pause and stare at each other.

"Sissy Stewart," we say in unison.

"Gah. She was the worst. You could never be right with her in the room."

"Stingy."

"The liability." I wait for them to look at me.

"Jessica Flint. The second alcohol got involved, all bets were off."

We spend another twenty minutes making a list, and when we finish, there are at least twenty different types of baddies.

"Okay, so we have a list of questionable personality traits. How does this turn into a business?"

"With careful consideration and meticulous planning," Delaney croons. "First, we need a mission statement. Then a company description and market analysis." She's in full-on business mode right now, and her numbers-loving, graph-making heart is probably ready to explode.

"Market analysis, D? I can't imagine there's market analysis readily available for this type of thing."

She furrows her brow and taps her chin. "You're probably right, but we can use Jenna's wedding as a guide since you're not looking for funding right now."

"This is good," Eli says from her perch on the arm of the sofa. Even with her dirty blond hair falling out of her ponytail, she still manages to appear chic. "Next, we'll need a list of services you can offer and price points for each."

"Oh my God. Are we really doing this?" I stare at my sister

and best friends. They're wearing identical expressions of determination.

"We're doing it, Tilly. You're doing it. We're just giving you a little push."

Eli rushes past me and opens my computer on the coffee table, urging Delaney over. "Delaney and I can set up an LLC online. So," she asks as her fingers fly across the keyboard, "what are we going to name your company?"

My brain goes blank. "I have no idea."

But I do. Ever since Delaney said "The I Do Crew" when I was in California, it's been rattling around my head like a bad pop song.

The girls shout out suggestions until Eli comes back to it. "I still like 'The I Do Crew.'"

"Holy meatballs! I do love that," Delaney cries.

My gaze cuts to theirs, and they have my answer.

"The I Do Crew it is! Let's see if it's available."

Delaney, Hadley, and I crowd in on either side of Eli to watch the screen. The circle spins around and around on the name. After an eternity, we get a giant green check mark next to it.

"Yes!" Eli shouts. "The I Do Crew LLC is available in North Carolina." She presses a few buttons. "I need a credit card. Hurry before someone takes our name."

As I'm running in circles like a chicken with my head cut off, Delaney starts spouting off numbers.

"What are you doing?" I ask when she stops talking.

"Your credit card is probably in your purse, and we could spend forty-five minutes searching for it, again, and possibly lose this name, or I can give you $79 and get the name now."

"Done," Eli squeals over Delaney's shoulder. "It's all done. They'll send you an email, and then you'll get all your paperwork. You'll have to download it, but you'll officially be a business owner as soon as they file this on your behalf."

"What?" I choke out. "In less than five minutes, I have a business?"

"You have an LLC in the works, and you have the start of a business plan that you can adapt for all event planning later on," Delaney corrects.

Hadley takes the computer into her lap. "Eli? Go grab my computer and start looking into logos while I type up the business plan."

Eli scurries into Hadley's room while I sit there watching it all happen. "What do I do?" I ask when I finally find my voice again.

Delaney is in her element, and she wastes no time putting a plan into action. "You, my friend, start researching the best ways to handle the baddies. I think if you do an Enneagram for each personality, it will give you best practices. It's a good place to start at least."

"Enneagram? You mean the personality tests Sloane uses to create the characters in her books?"

"Yes! That's basically what we're doing here, right? Except, we're not creating them. We just need to know how best to disarm them."

"Right," I reply, absently grabbing my iPad from the kitchen table.

By the time the weekend is over, we have my business plan typed up with my new logo front and center. An LLC is in the works, and a business banking account is ready to go as soon as I get the paperwork declaring The I Do Crew an official business.

And when Audra calls on Wednesday night, I'm ready for this new challenge.

CHAPTER 10

LOCHLAN

"*W*hy isn't there a new blog post?" I bark, walking past Angie and soon-to-be-fired Brittney on my way into my office.

"Does he ever say hello?" Brittney whispers, but not so quietly that I don't hear. I pause mid-stride, ready to lay into her, but Angie jumps in.

"Mr. Blaine is very efficient with his time, Miss Wallace. He says what he means when he means it, but he's also very deliberate. I suggest you watch your tone and learn to manage expectations."

Satisfied that Angie has handled things, I slam my door with enough force that papers flutter on my desk thirty feet away. It felt good. Really good. Rolling my neck, I'm just settling into my chair when Brittney teeters in on heels far too high to be efficient in my office.

Angie enters next, shaking her head. She knows I'm not here for the rubbish people keep dishing my way. Perhaps there's something in the Manhattan water?

Brittney walks straight to my desk, moves a candy dish

aside, and places her palms on the freshly polished glass surface. All I can focus on is how she moved the bowl of red candies to do it. My fingers twitch with the need to adjust it, but with her standing there, it's impossible. I stare at the damn candy, trying to give her a hint that she shouldn't touch my shit, but she doesn't take it.

Instead, she leans over my desk, her blouse unbuttoned so low that her breast actually pops out. She lifts her gaze, attempting to appear sheepish, but I keep my eyes on my bloody fucket candy bowl. When I don't acknowledge her, she licks her lips and shrugs unnaturally as she straightens herself out.

I tap my forehead with my index and middle fingers. Grinding my teeth to sawdust, I take a deep breath to prevent myself from saying something that will get me sued.

"Miss Wallace," I fume. "Go see Natalie in HR. Now."

"Oh." She pouts. "I'm terribly sorry, Mr. Blaine." She sounds like an animated version of Marilyn Monroe, and she's lucky that Angie interrupts her when she does.

"That's all, Brittney. Natalie will be waiting for you."

"But if I could just explain…"

"Now, Miss Wallace." Thank God for Angie Moore.

I turn my chair to face the floor-to-ceiling windows looking out over Manhattan as Brittney click-clacks out of my office. The view of the city is spectacular, but I rarely enjoy it. I sit with my back to it to remain as productive as possible. I don't allow myself distractions. Of any kind. Ever.

Pepper's face flashes like the perfectly haunting memory she is, and I scowl.

"Perhaps we need to try a new agency," Angie says, dragging me back to the present. I hear her behind me, adjusting the mini sake cups I sort my candies into. "This one does seem to attract the same type of person every time."

"Or," I say, swiveling my chair back to face her, "you could just stay."

"Or," she challenges, "you could try to be less charming for the next applicant."

"Charming?" I scoff. "I haven't said two words to that girl the entire time she's been here."

"Some women do like a bad boy, Mr. Blaine."

My eyes roll so hard they ache from the effort.

"Now, what is it you were bellowing on about when you walked in?"

I hold up a finger. "First, you must have noticed her attire change over the last few days, Angie. Right? Why did you let her strut in here like that?"

"One of these days, someone will grab your attention and shake some sense into you. Who am I to say it's not an employee?" she muses.

"I'm to say. You're my executive assistant who knows I have a firm no-fraternization policy."

"Yes, but I can't help it if men and women alike want to be the one to lure you in, Lochlan. You're quite the catch when you're not barking orders, you know?"

I smile when she uses my name. Most people in my life call me Blaine. A couple of friends and my sister are the only exceptions. Even my parents call me Banny, for Christ's sake.

"I'm not fishing, Angie. You know this. Perhaps we should try a male assistant again."

Her laughter lifts some of the weight that's settled in my chest. "Not that it will stop them. Remember the last two men who applied for this job?"

"How could I forget? Reggie asked me to marry him in his second week, and Jordan tried to punch me."

"Yes." She giggles. "Jordan couldn't quite handle being bossed around in the charming way you have. And Reggie? Well, that boy will make some man very happy someday."

"No doubt. He would have been great." I sigh because he truly had the makings of a perfect assistant.

"You know what the problem is, don't you?"

"No, but I'm sure you'll tell me." I don't bother taming my grin.

"You're sickeningly handsome, wealthy, and have a heart of gold when you allow people to see it. You're what we call in my book club a cinnamon roll."

I arch a brow with a full-blown smile. "A cinnamon roll? Explain. Please. I'm intrigued."

"Yes. A cinnamon roll. You're crusty and a bit rough on the outside, but all ooey and gooey sweetness on the inside."

My mouth drops open in horrified amusement. "I am not ooey and gooey, Mrs. Moore. And just what types of books are you reading in this book club of yours?"

"The good kind." She winks. "Now, what had your knickers in a knot earlier?"

She might be one of the few people in my life that can make me smile like this.

"There hasn't been a new blog post in almost a week."

"Ah, yes. *The Love Lobby*."

I narrow my eyes at her goading. "*Love in the Lobby*, Angie. She always posts on Monday mornings, and she didn't post this week. It's Thursday."

"I'm aware of what day it is, Lochlan."

"Have we found out who is behind this rubbish?" I can't ignore the needling at the base of my spine that worries this is another attack from Christine.

"I've said it before, and I'll say it again. I don't believe it's rubbish. Just because they're anonymous posts doesn't mean they haven't done their research."

"I know. She's taking a human approach to dragging these hotels. The ones who pass her test have an overly romantic element to them. The waitress that worked a wedding. The bartender at the bachelorette party. She's getting to know the staff at each one. Know them enough that they confide in her. She's been to some of the best hotels in the world, yet she hasn't been to one of mine, and I want to know why," I growl, flattening my tie and pulling down my vest to compose myself.

"They're only dragging the hotels that deserve to be called out for poor behavior. Think about it, Lochlan. The Roper in Boston? The Montlake in The Village? How about The Dorrety in San Francisco?"

My mind wanders to Pepper and The Dorrety again. The blog author couldn't have known how close to home she hit with her post about one-night stands.

Could she? Paranoia creeps into my gut.

Angie flashes an expression of concern but continues. "You were there recently and came home complaining about the standards you witnessed. But you're right. The ones who get glowing reviews are the ones who cater to weddings, and you don't allow weddings at your hotels. Perhaps your mystery author is a wedding planner. That would explain why they have not visited your hotels."

A fantastical dreamer. Fucking awesome.

"She hasn't visited yet, Angie. But I have thousands of employees. It would only take her speaking to one bad apple to tarnish my reputation."

"You're known in this industry for your standards and how you take care of your employees. Even if you do hide behind a gruff exterior to keep them at bay, you offer some of the highest wages, and don't forget the incentive plans, bonuses, and benefit opportunities you supply each and every employee." She scans my face. "Are you upset that they haven't found fault with your hotel or that you're being left out on purpose?"

She knows me too well.

"Of course, I'm not worried about either of those things. I

just want to make certain that however she's getting her information, it's accurate and substantiated."

"You know the hotels they've featured, Lochlan. Do you believe anything they've said to be untrue?"

"No," I concede. "But it's an attack on my industry. I must be vigilant in protecting my legacy."

Angie stands, then pats my shoulder. "Your legacy is in fine hands, Lochlan. I'm sure your mystery blogger will have a new post for you soon. Until then, perhaps you can focus on some people that actually *add* value to your life."

I groan because I fucking hate the sound of that. "What now?"

"Well, your parents want to know if they'll be seeing you at the Foundry wedding…"

"No."

"Lochlan. Your parents have been friends with the Foundrys for years. You went to school with their daughter."

"No."

"Fine. I'll let them know."

"What else?" I can see her wheels turning.

"Well, Mr. Grant called the office because you haven't returned his call yet. Your friends never call the office so I'm assuming you're avoiding him for some reason?"

"He's a needy bastard." I laugh. Tyler Grant, Blake Kingston, and Colton Westbrook are the entirety of my inner circle, but with the exception of Blake, who no longer talks to anyone, they're much too chatty for my liking. "I'll call him back. Anything else?"

"That's it for now. But you really should reconsider the wedding. You never know who you'll meet there."

My mind instantly drifts to Pepper. Not that she's been far from my thoughts lately anyway. The damn girl ghosted me. Sure, I would usually plan a quick escape, but I fell asleep that night knowing I wasn't done with her. When I woke up the next morning, she was gone. No trace of her. I'm not sure if I'm pissed that I didn't get to experience her again or that she didn't give me a say in things, and it has made me a right surly prick ever since.

I shake my head, realizing Angie is still speaking. "Didn't you have fun at Mr. Grant's wedding? You stayed for the reception, so you must have found *something* to fill your time."

I'm nodding along but not really listening because I did find something. *Someone*, rather. Someone I would very much like to see again. Just one more time. It's unusual for me to want a repeat, so it must be the chase with Pepper. She left, so I want more?

I've refrained from reaching out to Tyler because I'll only sound like a lovesick puppy by asking, but as more days pass, I realize I won't simply forget her.

"Yes, Angie. I did have a good time at Tyler's wedding." I grin. "A very good time."

She huffs and storms out to her desk. Perhaps I missed part of her conversation, but I'm already lifting my mobile phone.

Tyler answers on the first ring. "Lochlan? This is a surprise. I thought for sure I wouldn't hear from you until I kicked down your office door." He chuckles. "Is everything all right?"

"Of course, of course. How was your holiday?"

"We're still here, actually. Heading to the Greek isles next."

"Very good. Very good. Give…" Shit. *What's his wife's name?* "Give the missus my best."

"Jenna, Lochlan. Her name is Jenna."

"Right, yes. I know that. Give her my best."

"Did you need something?" he asks, but I hear the teasing tone. He's not about to make this easy on me.

"You called me first, arsehole," I remind him, then shake my head. I always sound more British when my emotions are out of whack. "But actually, I did need something. I have a, uh, job opportunity for one of Jenna's bridesmaids. I believe her name was Abby Chambers. She and I had a lovely chat at the reception, and I think—"

"I think you're full of shite, mate," he mocks.

"Bugger off. Seriously, I just need her number."

"Jenna? Lochlan's on the phone. He's looking for Abby."

I hear their murmurs but can't make out their words. Then his voice is back. "Okay, I'll meet you over there. Sorry, Loch. Abby apparently has a rule about giving out her contact information. You're shit out of luck."

"Bloody fucket," I bite out.

"Whoa. Someone's gotten under your skin."

"Whatever, Tyler. Have a great trip. We'll catch up when you get home."

"You know," he drawls. "I was calling to tell you that Audra Foundry has a wedding next week."

"Have fun. I don't do—"

"You might want to take a look at their wedding website, especially at the wedding party. I think you'll find it interesting. Talk soon." He hangs up.

I toss my phone away in my hurry to Google the Foundry wedding.

It takes only a moment, which isn't surprising. The only family with more money than the Foundrys might be the Westbrooks. I scan the header, searching for the wedding party. When I find it, I click it so many times my computer freezes. Not cool, Loch. Not cool at all. Slowly, the page loads, and I scroll down with as much patience as I can muster until my gaze lands on the wedding party.

Abby Chambers, Bridesmaid

"Angie?" I bellow and hear her drop something just outside my door.

She remembers herself and uses the old-school intercom she insisted I install when she came to work for me. "Yes, Mr. Blaine?" She asks, not bothering to hide the snark in her tone.

"I changed my mind. Tell my parents I'll meet them at the Foundry wedding. And please RSVP for me."

"May I ask what changed your mind?"

"No."

I swear I hear her laughter through the thick wall.

Okay, Pepper. This time I won't let you escape so easily.

CHAPTER 11

LOCHLAN

The Foundry/Bamford Wedding

The music starts, and I feel her before I see her. I turn my head just enough to see the women walking down the aisle, but my body zings in anticipation for only her.

Pepper is more beautiful than I remembered, and her face has been at the forefront of my thoughts for weeks. Her dark hair cascades over one shoulder in waves so shiny the light reflects off them like diamonds.

She hasn't noticed me yet because she's too busy whispering orders as she marches down the long path of the old Catholic church we're in. She wears a lavender slip dress designed by my sister. It hugs every curve and dips low between breasts that taste like salty wildflowers. My mouth waters when I remember the freckle on her sternum like she's a mirage in the desert of my desire. I mentally slap myself. I would kick the shit out of my mates for having thoughts like this.

I chance a peek at my overly sentimental father, who always seems to read my mind, but his teary-eyed gaze roams over the wedding processional. For once, he isn't focused on me, so I turn my attention back to Pepper.

I feel it the second she recognizes me. As her gaze locks on mine, her sharp intake of air might as well have been sucked straight from my lungs. Her long, slow exhale caresses an uncomfortable pang I haven't wanted to address, and I smile when she lifts her chin and marches forward.

When she's close enough, I whisper a greeting. "Pepper. I look forward to picking up where we left off."

Her eyes go wide, and she wobbles slightly but catches herself before continuing without a word.

"Who is she?" My father murmurs at my side, glee seeping from his pores. When I don't answer, he pinches my side.

"Ouch! She's just a friend," I mutter but don't give him the satisfaction of searching my eyes. I'm afraid of what he might find there.

"Oh, a friend," he croons in sheer delight. "I'll be sure to introduce myself."

My gaze snaps to his, and he gives me a knowing wink.

I'm screwed. But when I turn my attention back to Pepper, his whispered words fade away. Her gaze is cursing me, and this time, I'm front and center, not hidden away in the back. I'm so close that I can scan her full body over and over again. She keeps the forced smile in place as she nudges a bridesmaid to her left and taps the one on her right with her toe.

So, she's babysitting again? My Pepper seems to be a very trusted friend. My estimation of her just improved tenfold. There are few trustworthy people in the world, yet this is the second time someone in my orbit has depended on her, and it has me infinitely more curious.

When she chances a peek in my direction again, I give her a small salute and mouth, "I'm not done with you." Through the thin material of her dress, I watch her thighs wiggle and her tummy tighten. Her brain may be fighting this reaction to me, but her body doesn't lie.

It seems my Pepper is ready for round two, and I'm more than happy to oblige.

* * *

I ENTER the great hall of the New York Public Library with my parents on each arm. Lanterns illuminate a path up the stone stairs and lead us to our destination. It's truly a magnificent sight, but my parents miss it all as they talk to each other around me. My head is on a swivel, searching for Pepper.

My mother's hand clamps onto my forearm, forcing my attention to her. "Who are you looking for, Banny?" Kitty Bryer-Blaine is an elegant woman who has never followed a rule in her life. Her silver hair shines even in its sleek updo.

"My money is on a certain dark-haired bridesmaid." My father, Oliver Blaine, chuckles on my left. His signature bright pastel pocket square matches his cummerbund and stands out in a sea of black-tie tuxedos.

Mum stops walking, forcing the men in her life to halt as well. "What bridesmaid? You know, Ollie, it's a little disheartening that you can still read our boy better than his own mother."

"You know you're the brains of this friendship," my father assures her. "I'm the heart. It's always been that way—it's why we get along so well." He leans forward and squeezes her hand on my arm affectionately. Looking at them now you'd never know they've been divorced for over half my life.

He's right, of course. My father may have been the face of our company for years, but she was the one running things behind the scenes. And my father? Let's just say he could give Prince Charming a run for his money in what my sister calls the "swoon department."

"All right, you two. I don't know what either of you is droning on about. I'm a benefactor of this library. I'm merely making sure their events staff is up to snuff."

My father snorts on my left while my mother very demurely giggles behind her hand. I let out an exasperated sigh and drag them both forward.

"I spoke to Mrs. Moore yesterday." My mother has never minced words or had any tact for timing.

"Yes. And?"

"She's still planning to retire, but you're going through assistants faster than a used car salesman can say hello," my father interrupts. His bright blue eyes are so like my own. But his dance and sparkle with pure joy. Mine do not.

"It's nice to see the two of you haven't slowed down in retirement. You still spend your days gossiping about me." It's annoying, but I don't fault my parents. Even if they have an unconventional friendship, their love and commitment to Nova, me, and each other have never wavered.

"Oh, Banny. It's not just you. We talk about Nova too," my mother says absentmindedly, like that will help.

"Speaking of Nova, where is our girl?" my father asks.

"Considering she designed the wedding gown, I'm going to assume she's with the bride." I also make a mental note to ask her about Abby.

"I am so proud of our girl," my mother coos, and I smile at her fondly. In a world notorious for women tearing other women down, my mother always accepted Nova, and her mother, as part of our unit. Even when Nova's mother was alive, the three of them worked hard to make us a cohesive family by taking co-parenting to new extremes. Our family blended seamlessly and because of it, Nova has never been an outsider; she's never been a step-anything. She's always just been ours.

"Me too," I say wistfully. "She's truly making her own way in this world."

"But you're keeping a handle on her Bryer-Blaine affairs, correct?"

I give my mother an incredulous glance. "Mother, I'm offended. I tried to get Nova to take her inheritance in Bryer-Blaine 50/50, you know that. The only way I could get her to even agree to stay on the board was to buy out five percent of her shares. She wanted me to take it all. We negotiated down to thirty, but I only took over five." I flash her a dimpled grin. "But we'll keep that on a need-to-know basis."

"I'll never understand why she's so stubborn. She's as much a part of this family as I am," my mother tuts. "Oh well, I'm proud of you, Banny. Let's go find our table and get me a Manhattan. Since neither of my children are giving me a wedding anytime soon, I'll have to live vicariously through Sonia Foundry." The bitter tone is clear. Sonia isn't known for being overly friendly. It always shocked me she could produce a child as kind as Audra.

Leading the way, I escort my parents into the Celeste Bartos Forum. They've truly transformed the space into one of the most elegant venues I've ever seen. If I allowed weddings at any of the Bryer-Blaine establishments, this is exactly the kind of affair we would host. Covertly, I slip my arm from my father's grasp to duck around a corner and take pictures. For research. Just in case.

Long banquet tables shimmer under the elegant drop chandeliers with bouquets of flowers in all shapes and sizes running down the center. The flicker of candles and fairy lights accentuates the dim lighting and tastefully adorns the table and large flowering trees that were brought in. Match with the domed ceiling bathed in blue with twinkling lights that mimic the stars, and it has a very distinct fairy tale vibe. It all surrounds a dance floor that reflects the magical glow from above.

Tucking away my phone, I rejoin my parents and I'm not at all surprised to find my mother is still discussing the wedding.

"Well, I'm glad Sonia didn't ruin this for Audra. That child has wanted to get married in this library since she could walk." She sniffs.

"Whoever decorated in here outdid themselves, don't you agree, Banny?" My father is baiting me. He's not a fan of the embargo I've placed on weddings in our venues.

"They did. I'm sure Audra will be very happy with the outcome. I'll leave you two here while I find our table assignment, then I'll grab your drinks."

My father pats my cheek as he has done since I was small. "You have a sparkle in your eyes tonight, my boy. It looks good on you." For an aristocratic Brit, Oliver Blaine is overly affectionate.

I nod, tug at my collar, and pull away. "I'll be back."

Their eyes burn into my back as I retreat, and I know they'll have a mouthful to talk about, so I take my time scanning the place settings. It seems there's a head table at this wedding, and I feel an uncomfortable pang of disappointment that I can't get Pepper at my side. What I can do is make sure my seat faces the head table and, as luck would have it, we're positioned so I have a direct line of sight straight to my girl—er... My Pepper. I have a great view of the bridesmaids.

Bloody fucket.

"What has that V forming between your eyes tonight, Loch?"

I turn at the sound of my sister's voice. Nova is eight years younger than me, and I've always been a protective prick when it comes to her. When my parents divorced, they remained close, so nothing really changed for me. Then my father married Nova's mother, and brother bear tendencies I'd never known developed overnight for the three-year-old girl with a mischievous grin.

"I was just wondering where you had run off to." I wrap her in a hug. "Were you with the bride?"

"I was. Fluffing her dress and making sure all the ladies were ready for their big entrance," she explains while handing me a tumbler of amber liquid.

"Oh, yeah? Did you get to know them all well?" I hope my interest isn't too obvious.

"Mostly, except the latest addition. She joined late, and I had to scramble to get her dress fitted in time, but she's lovely and is absolutely keeping Audra's best friend and cousin from killing each other."

"Hmm…"

"What's hmm? Why do you have a funny expression on your face? Come to think of it, why are you here? Weddings are synonymous with funerals for you."

"Come now, Nova. You made the dresses. Of course, I came to support you." I offer her my most chivalrous smile.

"It might have something to do with the beautiful brunette too," my father unhelpfully supplies from behind.

Nova's eyes go wide. "Is that right?" She leans in and hugs him, then stands between my parents to form a wall of solidarity pointed directly at me.

Here we go. No one can give shit like a little sister with intel.

"I don't know what they're talking about," I tell her, but my hand trembles as I bring my whiskey to my lips.

That can't be a good sign.

"The bridesmaid." My father nudges my elbow like I've forgotten who he's referring to. "The pretty one, with the hair and the smile?" He talks with his hands like a native New Yorker and not a posh Brit from Knightsbridge.

When I quirk an eyebrow toward his hands, he chuckles.

"You can be such a snob, Banny. I haven't lived in London in years. I'm as New York as they come, son."

Nova laughs and kisses him on the cheek. "New York with a thick side of Britishisms, papa." Then she turns on me.

Bloody fucket. Here it comes.

"You just said bloody fucket in your head, didn't you?" Nova's laughter draws the attention of the small group of men to our left, and I scowl fiercely until they avert their gazes.

"Banny, you must stop scaring away the young men. How is Nova supposed to find a match?"

"Mother, Nova has no trouble finding dates. Trust me. I live right next door to her."

"Hold up. Stop right there. We're talking about you and a bridesmaid, not me and my love life."

We glare at each other with no heat, accustomed to throwing each other under the bus and waiting for our parents to choose who is in the line of fire. The second my father takes a breath to speak, I know I've lost this round.

"Just wait," I mouth so only Nova can see.

"I'm here for it," she mouths back.

"Nova, you must know her name," my father continues. "The beautiful one with long dark hair?"

"Abby," we say in unison.

Nova narrows her eyes. "So, you've got a thing for Abby? I'll have to see what I can find out."

"Leave it. I've got it covered," I warn.

Music begins to play, and people are starting to mill about our table. I nearly take out a server in my quest to claim my chair. The douche that had his hand on its back will just have to move along.

Setting my tumbler on the table, I slip into the seat as if I didn't see him, and attempt to shake out the strange sensation affixed to my spine.

"Smooth, Loch. Real smooth," Nova whispers, sliding into

the seat beside me. "Sorry about that." She nods to the stranger at my back. "He's very territorial, it seems."

I hear him speak but pay no attention to the words. My gaze and my focus are on the door. Things are about to get spicy.

CHAPTER 12

TILLY

The Foundry/Bamford Reception

"I'm not sure how it happened," Bailey, Audra's best friend, whispers. Tears pool around her eyes.

Bailey is what we labeled in my business plan as the guardian. She has made it her job to ensure everything goes perfectly for her best friend and bride, Audra. Unfortunately, Audra's cousin, Katrina, is a one-upper and has spent every waking moment trying to outdo her cousin.

That included the wedding photos we took during the cocktail hour. The photographer wanted one of Audra pretending to throw her bouquet over her shoulder with bridesmaids flanking either side. Katrina shoved her out of the way to ensure she was fully facing the camera instead of peering over her shoulder like the rest of us. Bailey, who was on Audra's other side, dove forward to keep the bride from falling down the stairs.

"It's okay, Bailey. It wasn't your fault."

"It was absolutely her fault," Katrina hisses.

Squaring my shoulders, I transform into the bridal baddie

bitch. "Listen to me," I snap. "What is wrong with you? Seriously. This is your cousin's wedding. The one day in her entire life where she gets to have everything be about her, and you have pissed, moaned, and one-upped her every move."

Audra's mother enters the room with a scowl that matches Katrina's. "Well, what are we supposed to do now?"

All eyes turn to me, but I lean into Katrina even more. "Do not fuck around with me. Wedding days are magical. Fucking magical for the bride and the bride only. Do you hear me?"

She sucks in a breath but doesn't fight me, so I give her a lingering glare before turning back to Audra. "Okay, this is what we're going to do. Bailey, you're going to take Audra into the bridal room. I'll run out to the reception and tell them to extend the cocktail hour a few more minutes while I find the girl who was fixing our dresses."

Audra holds her broken heel in her hands. "Maybe I can just go barefoot?"

"Not on your life," her mother rolls her eyes. "Audra, that dress was made to the exact length so you would float into the reception. *Float*! Without those shoes, you'll look like an over-iced cupcake."

Audra's lip trembles.

"Just as a backup, what size shoe are you?" I ask, ignoring the wicked witch of a mother.

"A f-five."

Of course, this little peanut of a woman would have a child-sized foot.

"This is absurd. You know that, right?" Jefferson, the groom, growls in Katrina's direction.

She just shrugs.

"Okay, Bailey, Jefferson, and Audra, go to the bridal suite. I'll be there soon."

Jefferson gives me a grateful nod and shoots a look full of

hate at his mother-in-law. Eesh. Family dynamics are tough among the one percent.

Snagging the broken shoe from Audra, I hike up my gown and hurry out into the reception. There must be close to five hundred people here. How the hell am I going to find this woman? I'm searching for the proverbial needle in a haystack when my breath catches in my throat.

He's found me.

My heartbeat thunders inside my ribcage when I meet Blaine's gaze. His eyes darken at first, but then his head tilts with intrigue, and that one tiny gesture causes a hive of hungry bees to riot around my heart. I can't begin to imagine how I look, but I don't have time for Sexy McSexerson.

I scan the room once more and almost immediately end up back at Blaine's side. Nova sits with her hand on his forearm.

Oh, crud. Is he married? My eyes grow hot as I watch them. Am I cursed? Closing my eyes, I count to five because I don't have ten seconds to get my shit together, then force my feet to move toward them.

When I'm within speaking distance, I keep my gaze trained on Nova. If I stare into his eyes, I know I might crumble. I promised myself I would never be that girl, but I have a sickening feeling that's exactly who he turned me into. The homewrecker.

"Excuse me?" My voice falters, and my hands clench into fists. "Nova?" I try again.

Her smile makes my stomach drop. I feel dirty and sick.

"Abby, right?" She stands, and I'm at a loss because the entire table stands with her. Including McSexerson. I nod because I've forgotten how to speak. "Is everything okay?" she asks gently.

No! I want to scream. I think I had the best sex of my life with your man, and it turned me into his dirty little secret. I see him in my periphery, but he doesn't appear distressed. What the hell? I could blow up his world right now. Why is he smiling at me like that?

"Abby?" Nova tries again, and it shakes me from my panic.

I shrug and hold up Audra's shoe. "Any chance you know how to fix this? Momzilla won't let Audra enjoy her party until she can wear these exact shoes."

My body shivers. I'm not sure if it's from the blazing heat in Blaine's eyes or because I'm suddenly worried. What if I can't pull through for Audra?

Nova inspects the shoe and offers me an apologetic frown.

"Okay. That's okay. I—shit. I don't know this city. Where the hell do you get a"—I peer down to see what kind of shoe it is and roll my eyes—"a Manolo at 7 PM?"

An older man with a kind smile steps up beside me. "Poor Audra. Banny? Call Monica at Saks." Returning his attention to me, he grasps my shoulders and forces me to look at him. "We've got it. What else do you have to do?"

I stare in silent horror at these people with features so similar to Blaine's. The older couple is obviously Blaine's parents, and the way the older woman holds Nova's hand makes my stomach curdle. They're trying to help a home-wrecker.

"Abby?" Blaine's voice cuts through the crowd.

"Ah, I need to extend this cocktail hour. How far away is the shoe store?"

"Nice to meet you, Abby. I'm Ollie, Banny's dad. Saks is about eight blocks. We can get a car…"

So that's where Blaine gets his almost-accent from. "Oh, that's okay. It'll be faster if I run."

"Run?" Blaine chokes. "In that dress?"

Nova watches him with a curious expression, and I turn on my heel before he outs our indiscretion.

"We'll take care of the reception," Ollie calls to my back. "We know the manager."

I offer a halfhearted wave and push through the crowd, only to be yanked back by my arm and fall into a wall of man.

"Pepper," he commands. "Wait."

I rip my arm free and shake it violently as if bugs were swarming up it. He holds his hands up at my aggressive behavior. "Go back to your family. I'm sure your wife, or girlfriend, or whoever she is, will be horrified that you chased down a one-night stand. How exactly will you explain that anyway?"

A troubling grin slides over his decidedly unhandsome face. "My wife?"

I turn on my heel again and head toward the door. "I don't have time for games, Blaine." Every ounce of vitriol I can manage is spat in my words.

I burst through the doors and am assaulted by a bitter wind. Jesus. It's flipping cold. I glance left, then right, and realize I don't have my phone, any money, or a sense of direction.

"Ugh!" I yelp as something warm and silky slips over my shoulder. I can tell by the scent wafting from the fabric that it belongs to Blaine. Turning toward him, I'm struck momentarily speechless as he stands in a tuxedo vest and closes his jacket around my shoulders. His fingers work the buttons and skim my ribcage.

"Come on. We'd better hurry."

"We? What about Nova?" I try to pull myself from his grasp, but he holds tighter to my arm.

"Nova? My sister?" My jaw officially comes unhinged, and he smiles devilishly. "I'm a lot of things, Pepper, but a cheater isn't one of them. Now, come on. I know Mrs. Foundry. She can be a real bitch. My car is just…"

He scans the street. It's gridlock. Car horns beep, people yell and curse, but no one moves. Bending down, he lifts the hem of my dress, and I swat his hands away.

"Now is not the time to get frisky," I snip.

He lifts his gaze but stays bent over, staring up at me with hooded eyes. "Does that mean there's a time to get frisky later?"

"Seriously, Blaine. I need this shoe. Which way do I go? Gah! What do you think you're doing?" I gasp as he scoops me up in a wedding hold and starts jogging down the street.

"We have to go almost eight blocks. You cannot run in those heels."

"Put me down, you idiot. You don't even know me."

"Pepper? I know what you taste like. I know what sounds you make when you come, and I know how my name sounds on your lips as you do. I know you well enough to get you this damn shoe so the mum from hell can have her perfect wedding."

"Blaine!" I screech. "I don't even have any money on me. Put me down. I…"

"I'm not worried about it." He doesn't slow down and doesn't seem to lose his breath as he continues to barrel down 5th Avenue, barking orders. With a hand around my back and one under my thighs, I have no choice but to curl into his chest so I don't bounce wildly against him.

"Put me down, Blaine. Seriously. I can run just fine. Plus, I need to get my wallet." He blows past city block after city block but never releases me. "Do you have any idea how much these shoes will cost?"

"We're about to find out," he growls, drawing my gaze to his lips. Shouldn't he be out of breath by now? Geez! "I know Audra is a sweet girl, but you seem very invested in making sure these weddings are perfect. Are you a wedding planner or something?"

I tense, and he glances down at me. I stare over his shoulder. "Something like that. But it's a wedding, Blaine. The one day where you get to be the princess in your life story. That means something." He grunts, and I peer into his eyes, swirling pools of emotion that he quickly shuts down. "You don't believe in love?"

"I believe in love, Pepper. I think I do, anyway. I love my parents and my sister. I've been in love before," he admits bitterly. "But I know what weddings can do. How that single piece of paper can ruin people."

"You're a commitment-phobe," I say in understanding.

"On the contrary. I very much believe in commitment. I don't believe you need a big, flashy show of it or a piece of paper declaring it."

I have an inexplicable pain in my chest at his words. "Th-That's so sad."

"Prince Charming is for fairy tales, Pepper. I fully believe in monogamy, but putting the pressure of forever on something that can never be just destines it for failure."

His words foolishly cause tears to spring to my eyes.

"Love, in its purest form, is a choice. Love is the commitment. The paper? As you say, and the flashy show? Those are just expressions of it."

"You can have commitment, Pepper. But every commitment, contract, and choice comes to an end eventually. Even if it has a better outcome by ending, it always ends."

Just as I'm about to start kicking so he'll put me down, he nods to a doorman and places me on the sidewalk. The doors open soundlessly, and with a hand at the small of my back, he guides me inside.

"Mr. Blaine!" A saleswoman coos the instant we step inside the store. "How lovely to see you again! Your sister said to expect you. I believe we have just what you're looking for."

Blaine grips my wrist and holds up the shoe. "What size?"

"Um, a five."

"Come right this way." We follow the woman deeper into the store. "I'll see what we have in the back."

She leaves us alone, and I can't bring myself to meet

Blaine's gaze, so I wander through the displays. My chest feels like an elephant is sitting on me, and it's so unreasonable I want to yell at myself. My eyes catch on a pair of sparkling, strappy heels, and I run one finger along the thin ankle clasp. When I catch sight of the price, my hand snaps back like it's on fire. They cost more than my rent and car payments combined.

"I want to see you in those and nothing else." The heat from Blaine's words caresses my skin like a kiss and a promise of all things naughty.

"I have more responsible uses for that amount of money," I mutter.

I feel his gaze on me, but he says nothing more. The sales associate comes back with a box in her hand and dollar signs in her eyes. Blaine takes the box from her and removes the shoes.

"Put them on my bill," he orders, taking my hand in his and dragging me behind him.

"Mr. Blaine?" the doorman calls as we hurry outside. Blaine pauses with an irritated expression.

"Miss Nova called. She said you may need this." He holds out something that looks like a ten-year-old's scooter.

"What in bloody hell is that?"

"An electric scooter, sir." The doorman appears to be holding in laughter, but I don't. I laugh out loud as if I don't have a momager waiting to cut me down to size. Blaine stares between the two of us. He's a horrified Adonis, and it makes him even sexier.

"Yes, I see what it is. What am I supposed to do with it?"

"We ride it," I say with as much seriousness as I can muster.

"We what?"

"Come on, pretty boy. Hop on." Before he can argue, I hook the shoes—that are probably going to do serious damage to my bank account—on the handlebars and stare at him over my shoulder. "I'm driving." I add a saucy wink that causes his eyes to dilate. He likes it when I take control, and it gives me that jolt of confidence I'd never realized I was missing.

"Abby. We are not riding on this thing. Get off."

"Hmm…the last time you said that, I was dressed a wee bit differently, don't you think?" I press the accelerator, and I jolt forward a few feet. Holy geez, does this thing pack a punch! I wobble in my heels on the narrow floorboard, and I'm nearly positive Blaine just let out a rather undignified shriek.

Glancing over my shoulder, I find him racing toward me, white as a ghost. It makes me laugh even more, and because I sometimes revert to being a toddler, just as he reaches me, I press the accelerator again, this time prepared for the jerky take-off.

His resounding growl has my core clenching.

"Come on, Blaine. I don't have all night. Audra is counting on me, and five hundred people are waiting for her." I force my tone to sound exasperated, but a grin ekes its way out too.

"Pepper," he rumbles through clenched teeth.

When I feel his heat getting close, I scoot forward again, not even attempting to rein in my laughter.

I'm just coming to a stop when his hands clasp my waist. "I'm going to smack your ass for that. Tonight. Possibly before the reception is over as punishment. You'll finally be forced to hold in that sass so no one hears."

My breath catches in my chest, and my eyes get hot. I blink feverishly. "There's no way," I object, just as he steps on behind me. I'm forced to turn one foot sideways so we can both fit.

"Never underestimate me, Pepper." He leans in so his front is plastered to my back. Then he places a hand over mine on the handlebar. "I'll steer the ship from here on out, darling." The endearment drips with sexy innuendo. I'm fairly certain my knees knock together, and not from the bumpy ride our scooter is giving us.

"You left me." His voice is raspy and so quiet that I barely hear it over the wind whipping around my face. "I was beginning to believe you were a memory meant to haunt my dreams for eternity."

I crane my neck to scan his face, but he's wearing a mask of indifference. *Had I imagined his vulnerable tone?* He maneuvers the scooter around pedestrians while I'm stuck in my thoughts.

"You've thought about me? I—I mean, it was one night."

"Yes. And now it will be another."

The feminist side of me wants to stomp my foot at the presumptuous nature of this bossy jerk, but every other part of my body is doing the macarena.

"That's a bold statement." That's it. Obviously, my body and mind go on vacation when this man is around, leaving an outspoken, sassy, take-no-prisoners version of myself. And I'm shocked by how much I like this version of me too.

"I only tell the truth."

We come to a halt, and my heart skitters like it did the first time I saw the library lit up like a fairy garden. "It's so magical."

CHAPTER 13

LOCHLAN

"It's so magical," she gasps as she hops off the wretched scooter. I'm going to have a word with Nova about that. But as I stare at Abby, all I can think is she's the magical one. The damn organ in my chest flutters at the realization, but internally, I tell it to calm the fuck down.

I offer my hand as we climb the steps, and something I can't place settles over my entire body. A sense of calm, of belonging. A rightness. Like my world has been running on a treadmill in a dark room, and she just showed me all the wide-open spaces I've missed out on.

My throat feels itchy, and as she withdraws her palm from mine, my chest hollows out like it's trying to follow her.

She slips out of my jacket and hands it to me. "I have to get these to Audra. Thank you for your help, Blaine."

She disappears through the hidden double doors to our right, and I stand there feeling empty and clutching my chest.

Bloody hell. Instead of entering the reception right away, I slink into the shadows and remove my phone from my pocket. A while ago, my friend Colton asked me if I believed in love at first sight. At four in the fucking morning. I'm not prone to such fantasies, but my father is, and I'd told Colton that.

I'm unsettled as I stand here, staring at the closed door Abby just entered. So, against my better judgment, I message my friend.

Lochlan: Why did you ask me about love at first sight?

Colton: Holy shit. Did you get bit by the love bug?

Colton: Or are you sick?

Lochlan: I'm just asking.

Colton: For no reason?

Lochlan: Nothing concrete.

Colton: Because when love hit me, it hit hard. When she walked away, I felt as if my soul had gone with her.

Colton: I spent months walking around clutching an invisible ache in my chest that hurt worse than any physical pain I've ever experienced.

I nearly drop my phone when I glance down to find my fist clutching my dress shirt above my heart.

Lochlan: What if it doesn't last forever?

Colton: I'm going to assume you're going through some sort of crisis, so I don't have to find you and kill you for insinuating my love isn't forever.

Colton: But to answer your question, I would rather have experienced her love and lost it than never live in her light. We could get hit by a bus tomorrow. I'm not willing to hibernate indoors because of it.

Colton: Listen, Loch. I know you have a wealth of love to give, but I also know your views on marriage and why you think the way you do. Don't let the fear of where it will end keep you from a magical beginning.

There's that damn word again.

Lochlan: Thanks, mate. You good?

Colton: Better than you're doing, I'd say.

Lochlan: (middle finger emoji)

Lochlan: I'm at the Foundry wedding. Let's get a pint soon.

Colton: Done.

Pocketing my phone, I almost feel worse than before I texted my friend, but I square my shoulders and enter the reception anyway. Somehow, the bridal party has already made their entrance, and as I walk toward my family, my gaze never leaves Abby. My fire.

I don't dwell on the fact that I keep referring to her as mine. For tonight, and maybe tonight only, that's exactly what she'll be.

* * *

I'VE SAT THROUGH A MEAL, four dances, and a fucking cake cutting that required no less than six helpers because it stood at least five feet tall. Now there are speeches I'll never remember, and I've stared, glowered, and ogled Abby the entire time while shooting daggers from my eye sockets at the men who have touched, talked, or laughed with her.

To say I've hit my limit with this wedding bullshit is the understatement of the fucking century. I'm done. So, when my girl excuses herself from the grasp of lecherous man number five, I track her movements to the restrooms.

When did I start stalking women headed to the loo? Tugging on my earlobe, I sit back in my seat and attempt to fake a relaxed position.

"You like her," Nova whispers to my right.

"Oh, he likes her all right." The glee in my father's voice makes a smirk lift at the corners of my lips. I don't give into the smile entirely because I will not give him false hope. One-night stands do not mean love.

"Why are you glowering at her then, dear?" my mother asks

through a smirk of her own. She is truly diabolical. Kitty Bryer-Blaine is as shrewd as I am.

"My guess is because of all the dances she's had with other men as part of her wedding party duties." Nova stresses each word.

Logically, I know she's correct. But I still hate it.

"Nonsense," I say instead. "We simply have unfinished business. That's all."

"Unfinished business, Banny? Like slime the banana?" My father wiggles his eyebrows with a suggestive expression.

I choke on my old-fashioned. "Jesus, Dad."

"Check the oil," my mother adds.

"Feed the kitty? Knocking boots? Bumping uglies?"

I glare at Nova. "The last thing I need to think about is all the euphemisms my family can come up with for having sex."

"The no-pants dance? Two-person push-ups? Stuff the taco?" My sister is thoroughly enjoying herself now.

"Test the humidity?" my father barks out.

"Burping the worm in the mole hole?"

"Bloody hell, Mother! The mole hole? Are you serious?"

I feel my face flame, but my family is on a roll, and laughter rings out loud, proud, and happy. They're nothing if not thorough.

I precisely fold my napkin, taking a moment to count to ten before I storm off like a... what is it Colton calls it? Ah, yes, a juiced-up nut monkey. Lovely. Now I'm quoting my most immature friend.

Perhaps I am having a midlife crisis? Yes! Can thirty-two be considered midlife?

I've had enough of my own shit. My thoughts are rampant and unnerving, and no matter what I do, I cannot get them under control.

"Ride the skin bus to tuna town." My father guffaws so

loudly at his addition to this insanity that it snaps me from my wayward thoughts, and I stand quickly.

"I have to take a piss."

"Right," Nova sings. "It's cheeky that your bladder is on the same schedule as our beautiful new friend, Abby. Don't you think, Kitty?"

"Very," my mother agrees.

Tossing my napkin onto the table, I turn on my heels and stalk off in Abby's direction.

Finding a bench in the hall, directly between the men's and women's restrooms, I take a seat and pretend to scroll my phone. It doesn't take long before sounds filter out through the women's room.

It's loud.

Not loud enough to be considered yelling, or for me to clearly make out all the words, but loud enough that someone sounds slightly hysterical. I lean closer, straining to ensure it's not Abby's voice.

Once I'm reasonably confident it's not Abby, I relax against the wall.

I'm content replying to work emails until the door to my left flies open and a wave of activity filters out into the hall.

"Katrina! You cannot be serious right now. It's your cousin's day! Her wedding day! You need to be here."

"Whatever," Katrina scoffs. I know this woman too. She's the bride's evil cousin, and I'm seriously beginning to believe that Audra was adopted. "And don't be ridiculous. Knowing those two, she'll get a chance to be a bride again in three years, tops."

A collective gasp rings out behind her. Then the voice I crave fills the space as Abby moves into the restroom doorway. "You listen to me, you nasty little she-devil. If you're leaving this wedding, you're going out the back door, without making a scene. Without speaking to Audra. Without showing anyone else what a horrid bitch you are. Do I make myself clear?"

Well, well, well. My Pepper is spicier than I realized.

Katrina moves forward into Abby's space and, leaning in, I can see that she doesn't back down. "Do you have any idea who I am?"

Now it's Abby's turn to step forward, and she carries the threat Katrina couldn't pull off. Katrina arches her body back as Abby crowds her space. "Yes, you're a twat, and I hope to God you never need Audra for anything. You may think her good nature will always have her running to your side, but after tonight, all her friends will make sure she knows exactly where her loyalty should lie. Spoiler, it's not with a selfish asshole. What. Is. Your. Choice? Stay and plaster a smile on that vicious face of yours or slip out the back with whatever manwhore caught your attention?"

"How dare you," Katrina snarls. I choose this moment to make myself known and rise to my full height.

It's not that I approve of weddings, but if anyone can pull off a forever, it's Audra Foundry.

Katrina is the only one facing me, and her gaze goes wide and unblinking when she sees me. "Actually," she fumbles, "I'm not feeling well. I'm heading home." She sniffs the air in a pretentious way I know well.

She's about to say something snotty because she just can't help herself, but I intervene. "Sounds like a wise plan. I mean, I've heard weddings can be downright *magical*—isn't that right, Abby?" Abby spins quickly on her heels, and I register shock before a mask I can't read returns to her beautiful face. "The last thing we'd want is anyone ruining the lovely Audra's sparkle. Don't you agree, Katrina?"

"Hmph." She sighs and stomps toward the exit.

"Bailey," Pepper says, "you go back to the reception. Let Audra know that Katrina is ill. I'll walk her to the door and meet you in there. We only have about an hour left anyway." There's a gentleness to her voice I like. It's not the bossy tone she sometimes uses. It's not the commanding one either. It's something almost vulnerable, soft. Something real that I like so much but can't put into words.

"Okay. Done. Thanks, Abby." Bailey passes by me, appearing much more relaxed than she did moments ago. Abby did that.

I nod in Abby's direction as she leads Katrina to the door. I stand back and let her take care of her charge. After a few minutes, she walks back to me slowly, almost cautiously, like I make her nervous, and I give her an easy smile.

"Pepper," I groan when she's close enough to smell.

She lets out a heavy sigh. "Man, rich people can be exhausting." She mumbles it under her breath, but I hear every word. Is she not wealthy herself? If that's the case, how has she become friends with all these people that clearly trust her? She's a mystery I enjoy finding all the clues to.

Hooking an arm around her waist, I pull her to my side. "Move with me."

"What?" she gasps, glancing up, horrified. "You mean dance with you? Not move in with you, right?"

I did mean dance, but the idea of seeing her every morning doesn't send me running for the hills as it should.

"No, Pepper, I mean move with me." Leaning down, I whisper in her ear as I lead her back to the dance floor. "Move with me so I can feel your body glide against mine and remember what it felt like when you were naked. Move with me so I can hear those sexy mewls in the back of your throat. Move with me so when I pull your body tight against my hips, you feel just how much I've thought about you every day for weeks." I pause, willing her to peer up at me. "See? So much more than dancing, my sweet Pepper. And with my arms wrapped around you, I can make sure you don't run from me again."

Jesus, Loch. Put a cork in it. You're about to cock up everything here. The last thing Pepper needs to know is that she's infiltrated my mind.

"So, what you're saying is, you've thought about my body, huh? Just my body?"

A legitimate grunt escapes me, causing the couple in front of us to shift quickly to their left. "And your gobby, sexy mouth."

"Gobby?" She laughs until she notices my expression.

It's all I can do not to ravish her right here, but true to form, the second I glance up, my family is standing at the edge of the dance floor, watching. I'm almost surprised Nova doesn't pass out popcorn.

I move quickly, turn my back on the peanut gallery, and take Abby into my arms.

I don't fight the sensation that she fits. Or the way my heart flutters when she's nearby. No, I bask in it all while we move as one. It's one of those songs that's not particularly slow or fast. It's a strange beat that allows us to bend and flow in a way that feels like we've always done it.

As a general rule, I hate music. It's a distraction I don't have time for, but as she sings against my chest, I know I'll be reliving this moment for a long time.

I don't hear the band anymore. Not when I have her this close. The words coming out of her mouth sound sad, and while they match the song, it just doesn't sound right coming from her.

"What are you singing?"

She stares up at me with a frown, and I prepare for something snarky. But then she tilts her head, and her tone is soft, careful, and full of patience when she speaks—even if she does lace it with a teasing wink.

I realize I've been holding my breath, waiting for a confrontation that never comes—because that's how it was with my ex—and I let it out slowly. Pepper is nothing like I expect and it makes me like her that much more.

"It's Taylor Swift. You do know who Taylor Swift is, right?"

"Yes." I sigh. "I recognize the name. What does she have to do with anything?"

She glares at me like I just kicked a puppy. "First of all, she's one of the best songwriters of our generation."

"I don't listen to music."

She stops moving and drops her arms from my shoulders, taking all her warmth with her. "Ever?"

"It's a distraction," I say with a shrug.

"This song is called 'Wildest Dreams.' I would have thought you'd like it. It seems to fit your *love doesn't last forever* mantra."

"Why would they play this at a wedding then?"

She shrugs as if it's obvious. "It's classic Taylor. Audra is a big fan, and when you're a big fan, you play all the songs. Even songs about love that leaves you in the end."

I'm physically incapable of handling the sadness that washes over her, so I react. I'm doing that a lot around her, and I don't know what to make of it.

"Memories can last forever," I tell her. "And I'd very much like to make another with you. Right. Now."

CHAPTER 14

TILLY

"What do you mean, right now?"

"Are you finished with…" He watches the wedding that's carrying on in all its enchanting glory. "With whatever it is you do at these things?"

Irritation rankles my spine, and I plant my hands firmly on my hips. "Being a good friend and making sure the most magical day in my friend's life goes off without a hitch? Is that what you mean?"

"Yes." He huffs like he's the one with the right to be annoyed.

I narrow my eyes and lean in, ready to give him a piece of my mind, but he grasps my wrist and hauls it to his chest. The movement catches me off guard, and I teeter on my heels. "Hey! Do not manhandle me." I aim for pissed off, but it comes out breathy and maybe a little wanton.

"Pepper." His tone is low and controlled, like he's working extra hard at keeping himself in check, and it makes me want to push him. Shove him, actually, until that long-practiced control he holds on to snaps like a twig. But I don't get a chance.

"I'm going to own that sass tonight. Then I'm going to spank you so when I reach around to that *magical* little pussy of yours, I find it sopping. I'm going to fuck you so hard you'll remember me with every step you take for a week. Do you want me to do it right here, or are you finished?" The last three words come in a harsh staccato.

"You speak as if I'm going to follow orders, lover." His gaze widens, and I smile. What is it about him that makes me want to shred the traits that have always made me invisible and push all of his buttons? "You keep calling me Pepper, well, guess what? You've made it very clear you don't do happily ever after, and I do nothing else. So, that makes you my lover until I say otherwise. You're not boyfriend material because we can have no future. Lover it is."

His jaw ticks, and I almost laugh, but then I see his hands twitch at his side. Holy hot pockets, does he really intend to spank me? *Would I like it?* Hot tamale, hell on a cracker, *yes*, you idiot. *Yes*, you'd like it. My mind flitters to all those naughty books my sister writes. Wanting to act out dirty scenes your sister writes must be a new level of kink I'm not prepared for. Or maybe I can pretend she didn't write them?

"I am boyfriend material, Abby."

Gah! Blaine's voice hurtles me into the present.

The anger in his voice has a shiver running down my arms. "I'm just not wedding material."

"Same thing, Blaine. Same freaking thing." Sidestepping, I ease out of his grasp and leave him on the dance floor. I weave through the maze of people in my search for Audra. I'm so tempted to peek over my shoulder, but by the inferno at my back, I know he's followed me.

"A committed relationship, love, and marriage can happen independently of one another."

"Not in my world, lover. In my world, you meet a guy, fall in love, commit to them and only them, then you get

135

married," I call over my shoulder and catch his sister watching us.

"But why?" he growls at my ear.

I turn slowly, carefully choosing my words. I'm hit by a wall of emotion when my gaze locks on his, but I swallow it down.

"Because, Blaine…" A heavy, painful sigh escapes my lips. Much too painful to be directed at a one-night stand, that's for sure. Staring into his bewildered blue eyes, I open my heart to him. "I've been searching for the fairy tale my whole life. I need the happily ever after. I deserve the happily ever after, and I won't settle for anything less. Why are you even pushing this when it's clear all you want is one more night?"

His mouth opens and shuts. Then he does it again, but he speaks no words.

"Abby!" Audra's angelic voice sings out excitedly, giving me a reprieve from Blaine's intense scrutiny. "You did it again! You're truly amazing. You saved my wedding, even if my mother is a rocky turd sometimes."

"Oh, Audra. I'm so happy for you. This entire evening has been stunning. Um, so Katrina wasn't feeling well and went home. Did Bailey tell you?"

"She did." Audra smiles ear to ear.

"Audra," Blaine's cantankerous baritone says at my side.

"Oh my goodness, I cannot believe you're here! You never come to weddings," she screeches, launching herself into Blaine's arms. "Can you believe I've known this grump since we were both in diapers?" He holds her like a two-by-four and pats her like he's tapping out of a wrestling match. It's so at odds with the way he is with me. My nose scrunches up as I watch.

"Really." I take a step closer to her. Maybe Audra will know why he's such a dark cloud sucking all the light and love from my happy places. But, in true Blaine fashion, he doesn't give me a chance.

"Do you need Abby for anything else tonight? Or is she free to join me on a private tour of the library?"

"Ooh, I thought you two had hit it off at Jenna's wedding. It's so nice to see you pursuing someone again."

Here's the thing about Audra. She's like a mix of Snow White and Bambi. It's impossible to dislike her, and even if her words grate on Blaine's last nerve, he can't be rude to her.

"You're sweet, Audra, but Banny here doesn't believe in love."

"I believe in love, Pepper. Just not mar—" He cuts himself off when he realizes he's about to offend our host.

"Pepper? Banny? Eek! You guys are so cute! Maybe I'll get to save the day at your wedding soon." Audra claps her hands while bouncing up and down. She lifts her gown to flash her shoeless toes with a wicked grin. "My mother can't always win." Her smile never falters while studying the two of us. "Isn't it just the most amazing feeling?"

"What feeling?" Blaine's voice cracks. If I knew him better, I might think Audra's words are getting to him.

"Love, silly. I didn't realize you two knew each other so well, but you do look amazing together."

"Oh, we don't really know each other," I blurt, just as Blaine drags me closer to his side.

"Are you done with Abby?"

"Yes. You know," she whispers conspiratorially, "Jefferson and I had our first kiss in the old Romantics section."

"I'll see if I can top it," Blaine murmurs to my neck, then lifts his head to speak to Audra. "That's very...*dreamy*." He's so condescending! I elbow him in the gut, and he adjusts his attitude for Audra's benefit. "Congratulations again, Audra. If you'll excuse us, I'll be stealing Abby away for a bit."

"Have fun." She wiggles her fingers, and Blaine wraps an arm around my back. His hand falls on my opposite hip, and he uses it to guide me.

"You know, you could have asked if I wanted a tour." I'm poking the beast, but I can't stop myself.

He doesn't reply with words, but he squeezes my hip before releasing it to take my hand instead. Lacing our fingers together, he's leading me out of the ballroom when we're interrupted.

"Mr. Blaine."

Blaine stiffens almost imperceptibly, but I feel it because he's attached to my hip. He turns us slowly. "John Ross," he says with a practiced smile. His demeanor has changed, but he hasn't let go of my hand. "How are you? I didn't realize you knew the Foundrys."

The older man smiles but gives nothing away. "For years. I went to prep school back in the day with Audra's father. She's my goddaughter. I can say I'm surprised to see you here, though I have heard wonderful things about your date from Audra."

I smile pleasantly at the uncomfortable exchange.

"Ross, this is Abby." Blaine stares at me just long enough to convey *something*, then returns his gaze to Ross. "My girlfriend."

Oh, he is going to pay for this! I smile serenely even as a fire ignites in my core.

Ross's eyebrows raise a fraction. "Girlfriend?"

"We've been together almost two years," Blaine continues to lie. "But you know how it is to be in the public eye. We try to keep a low profile whenever possible."

I should interrupt him. I should call him on this farce, but watching Blaine in action is too much fun. How far will he take this fib of his?

"Well, isn't that...lovely." Ross casts a questioning gaze my way. "Audra truly has said magnificent things about you and your...work, *Abby*."

Oh, shit. John Ross knows my secret.

Now it's Blaine's turn to stare at me. So many lies. The skin on my neck prickles, and I feel my cheeks flush. I'd fan myself if they weren't both watching me so closely.

"I'll let you two get on with your night." Ross turns to Blaine, but his gaze darts to mine every few seconds. "Why don't you give me a call next week. I…" He hesitates, eyeing me like a Rubik's Cube. He thinks he can solve me, but there's always that one pesky color. It makes me want to laugh. I'm not that interesting, Mr. Ross. "Perhaps we can discuss your proposal in the coming months," he finally settles on.

Now Blaine appears to be truly baffled, but I'm impressed with his quick recovery. "I'll do that. Thank you. I think you'll be pleased with what I can offer."

"We'll see. You two do make a very handsome couple. I'm pleased to see it. Have a great night, *Abby*."

"You too, sir." When he's out of earshot, I turn on Blaine. "What the hell was that? Your girlfriend? One quick fuck, and you grew feelings?"

"I don't fuck quick," he bites out. "And I'm incapable of feelings, remember? But thank you for going along with that. You may have just saved my ass with a deal I've worked on for two years."

Blaine tugs his earlobe and then pulls on the bottom of his vest. I notice he's always straightening his appearance. What would happen if I just…messed him up a little? His eyes narrow like he can read my thoughts, and my body preens like a peacock.

"Huh. I guess I should be rewarded, now, shouldn't I?"

His eyes turn molten, and he pulls me deeper into the room until we're standing in front of a security guard.

Blaine nods. "I'll be taking a private tour tonight. We're not to be disturbed. Understood?"

"Perfectly."

Blaine rubs circles on the top of my hand as he leads me

behind a tall velvet curtain. The gentle movement is at odds with his harsh words and cold interaction with the poor guard.

"Aren't you going to say thank you?"

"I'll tip him well."

I stop and tear my hand from his. He halts abruptly, appearing confused and possibly amused, as I stomp back through the curtain.

The nerve of this guy!

"Hello, sir. What's your name?" I ask the security guard.

"It's Matt, miss." He eyes me like I'll bite. Having had the displeasure of dealing with two assholes tonight, I can understand why.

"Hello, Matt. Thank you very much. I'm sorry my friend was so rude."

Poor Matt tries to hold in a smile but fails miserably.

"Part of the job, miss."

"Dealing with prickly asshats?" I stage whisper.

Matt wisely keeps his lips pursed tight. I catch movement in the corner of my eye and find Blaine watching me with a curious smile.

"Enjoy your evening, miss."

"Thank you, Matt. I will. I hope you have a great night too."

"Thank you, miss." He schools his grin as I sashay back to Blaine.

"Was that so hard, lover?"

"I'm going to show you hard. Come."

"I plan to if you're up to the task later." Jesus. Why do my lips write checks my heart can't cash?

"Not later, Pepper. Now."

I whimper as he climbs the stairs, tugging me behind him. You can smell the history in these walls, and my romantic heart squeezes, knowing this is a once-in-a-lifetime experience.

As a child, the library was a haven of hope. A place we could go when the weather was iffy and hide while our father drank our lives away. And a place where all our childhood fantasies were researched and developed. I can't tell you how many times I fell in and out of love in the library. Each page brought new adventures and added goals to the story of my life.

My heart races as we climb. I can't wait to see where this story will lead.

CHAPTER 15

TILLY

"They just let you have the run of the place?" I ask in between pants. Blaine's long strides are not easy to keep up with, and I add going back to the gym to my to-do list.

"When you donate as much as I do, yes. For the most part, anyway." He doesn't peer over his shoulder. He doesn't slow down. He's a man on a mission, and it appears that mission is me.

He pauses at the landing long enough to retrieve his phone and turn on the flashlight. My eyes have had a difficult time adjusting to all the lighting changes the twists and turns have created, and I'm thankful when he illuminates our way. Walking like he's done this a hundred times, he moves with purpose until we stop outside a door. I have no idea where we are, but I shiver in anticipation.

The scent of old books, history, and a million stories waiting to find homes in the hearts and minds of readers amps up my excitement.

There's a faint clicking sound in the empty hall after he presses a code into the keypad. With a hand at the small of my back, he ushers me into the darkened room.

"It's probably not safe to enter a dark room with a stranger," I tease.

"It's a good thing I'm not a stranger then."

He has me up against the wall a moment later, hands in my hair, hips pressing into my belly, and dear lord, that thick, magnificent cock is ready for me.

"It's infuriating that you occupy as much space in my mind as you do," he mutters between licks at the base of my neck.

Good God, this man knows how to use that muscle. His tongue swirls and laps along my skin, and my body comes alive.

"Careful there, lover. You're awfully close to being confused for a romantic."

The words have barely left my mouth when he hitches my dress over my hips and turns me around. My belly hits a table in front of us before my brain can comprehend all the movements.

He leans over me, holding me to the table, and my harsh breaths leave a cloud of mist against the black marble surface I'm pressed against. I flex my fingers and see my handprint left behind on the shiny surface. My body is on fire. The table is cold. The fear of being caught is overwhelming. The juxtaposition of all these senses intensifies the anticipation of what's to come.

"Do you want me, Pepper?"

I wiggle my ass against his engorged crotch and feel his entire body tense. "If you don't fuck me soon, I'm going back to the party," I say hoarsely.

Slap!

The sound catches my attention before any other sense kicks in. My eyes go wide, and I attempt to arch off the table, but he has me caged in. Then the fire begins to form on the skin of my right ass cheek.

Motherfucker, this prick just spanked me.

My throat feels like I've been sucking on cotton balls, and my heart is beating erratically, causing the puffs of air to leave more condensation on the table. It's all I can focus on. It's an odd sensation as he rubs and massages my ass. Not at all unpleasant, causing my head to war with every other organ in my body.

"Your damn mouth," he whispers, and I realize he's no longer pressing me to the table, but his presence at my back holds me still just the same. His words caress my back, then I feel him between my legs. "Do you want me?" he repeats, the vulnerability in his words unnerving.

I can't reconcile the uncertainty of his words with the domineering man that just gave me my first ever spanking. *What's troubling your heart, Blaine?* But that's a question for a boyfriend, not a lover, so instead, I focus on pieces of him. His scent. His fingers on my skin. Anything but the feelings he conjures.

"Yes, I want you. C-Can anyone see us in here?" Awareness of our surroundings crashes into me and pulls me from the sexy scene that will most definitely live rent-free in my brain for the rest of my life.

"Not in here. I would never do that to you, Abby."

A lump forms painfully in my throat, and my eyes burn like lava. If he were relationship material, those words could lead to forever.

He hooks his hands into the waistband of my thong and slides it down my legs, then stands. Leaning over me once more, he gently takes my right hand, then my left, and laces them behind my back.

I'm unable to crane my neck far enough to see what he's doing, but then I feel the soft lace that can only be my panties wrap around my wrists until it goes taut. *He's bound me with my own flipping underwear.*

"You're v-very kinky tonight, lover."

His lips land between my shoulder blades, and it sends a jolt of longing straight to my core. He takes his time tasting and exploring before answering. "I have to make sure you don't leave me again."

A breath hisses between my teeth. "I...Blaine?" I shift and wiggle, trying to make eye contact, but he continues his leisurely exploration of my body. "Blaine? Did I hurt you by leaving that night?"

I feel him lift his head from my back as his five o'clock shadow scrapes up my spine. "Well, Pepper, that would imply that I have feelings, now wouldn't it?"

"I never said you didn't."

Slap!

This time it's my left ass cheek, and I still wasn't prepared. Moisture drips between my legs, and my pussy clamps tight.

Well, that's not the reaction I was expecting.

Just as I open my mouth to protest, he puts two large palms on my thighs and spreads them wider. I adjust my stance, and he tugs my body down on the table a few inches. Then he's on the floor, under the table, with his mouth sucking on my pussy. His grasp on my thighs strengthens and holds me to his face so tightly I'm afraid I'll suffocate him.

My hips undulate shamelessly as I ride his face. I grind and moan, and he does wicked things with his tongue. When he takes my clit between his teeth and slaps both ass cheeks, I come in a riot of feelings and sensations I can't begin to explain. Bright lights and shooting stars don't do it justice.

Every muscle in my body tenses and quivers while he continues his attack on my clit. Just as the tremors ease, he slips two long fingers inside me. Scissoring them, opening me, and the tightening begins at my core again.

My knees tremble with the effort of holding myself up, and when he sucks me right to the edge, he slides out from between my legs. With my body plastered to the table, my shoulders still manage to sag at the loss of contact. But it doesn't last long.

The crinkling sounds of a condom wrapper have me spreading my legs as wide as possible.

"You're so damn beautiful." He says it like a curse and I hear him stalk toward me like a hunter. My dress is still pooled around my waist, and he clutches it along with my bound palms and pulls me up, turning me to face him. "Are your wrists okay like this?"

I nod. Words, even snarky ones, are lost to the moment. His breath tickles my forehead as he searches my eyes, and I nod again.

"I need to see you. I need to see your eyes when I enter you and when you come."

"Yes," I whimper.

He smiles, but it doesn't reach his eyes. There's a sadness hidden behind his mask that makes my chest ache. He steps forward, placing both hands on my hips, and lifts me onto the table.

"Use your hands to hold yourself up." I place my hands on the warmed surface behind me, and he places my feet on the edge of the table. My knees naturally drop open. It's not the most comfortable position, but as he stares with pure lust in his expression, I fight my body to hold still.

He drops his pants to the floor and unbuttons his shirt. When we're done, my dress will be a wrinkled mess, but as I watch his chest rise and fall, I realize I just don't care. His fist wraps around his thick length as he steps forward, then runs the tip up and down my slit.

Bound, awareness of our situation hits me like a tidal wave, and a sense of sadness washes over me. I can't touch him like this, and suddenly, I feel claustrophobic. "Release my arms." His tip pushes into me, and my eyes close at the sensation, but my chest still feels heavy.

"Blaine! Undo me," I order.

His worried gaze cuts to mine, and he immediately leans forward, wrapping his arms around my back to undo the panties holding my wrists hostage. His cock thrusts deep inside me as he does, and we both freeze. That ache of rightness riots in my chest, becoming nearly unbearable.

"Bloody fucking fuck, Pepper." He comes to his senses before I do, and he continues to work my hands free. The second he drops my panties to the table, I lift my hands to his chest, just above his heart. I've never felt one beat so hard against my palm, but I hold it there, with him buried to the hilt inside me.

We speak no words as he begins to move. I wrap my legs around his waist to hold him to me, as close as I can get him. The sense that this is more than either of us can handle threatens to break the spell, and I think he feels it too as we both keep quiet. We fill the room with sounds of slick skin and moans of pleasure. Pleas and grunts. And as his thrusts pick up speed, we never glance away from each other. Our connection is so intense that even the world crumbling around us couldn't break it.

His eyes are piercingly blue in the dimly lit room, and they flicker back and forth between mine like they're searching for an answer to a question I didn't hear.

Sweat coats his skin, and mine pebbles with awareness when he leans down to press his forehead to mine. He rotates his hips as he grinds into me with the precision of a maestro. Yet we still don't utter a word.

We don't need them. We hear everything we want to say in the touch of our skin, in the way we move to become one, and in the way our gazes lock as if we're noticing the only thing we're ever meant to see.

I come in an explosion of sounds that echo in our magical room.

Whispers of "beautiful," "lovely," and "mine" leave Blaine's lips as he breaks our visual connection to watch our physical one. He comes silently, with a pain-filled expression that causes tears to prick the corners of my eyes.

When he finally lifts his gaze to mine, I see the same anguish in his pools of blue.

I don't know how to explain what just happened. Or why my heart feels like it's being shredded in a meat grinder. Or why, when he pulls away to deal with the condom, I feel the need to flee. But it doesn't ease when he returns and silently helps me clean up. Or when he messes with a machine at my back that illuminates the wall opposite us.

He remains silent as he sits on the edge of the table and stares at two works of art displayed on the screen before me.

I turn a quizzical gaze toward him, but his remains focused on the portraits, so I study them also. After a long while, he speaks. "My father is a romantic, you know?" That lump in my throat grows to the size of his forearm. "He loves love. And art, music, theater. He just truly loves the idea of love."

I feel him staring at me, but I don't turn my head. I'm too scared of what I'll find.

He continues. "I took an art class in college. Have you seen these before?" He nods to the screen.

"N-No," I whisper, barely containing a sob. I don't understand the empty feeling or why I'm on the verge of tears.

"They're digital copies of James Gillray's etchings of *Harmony Before Matrimony* and *Matrimonial-Harmonics*."

I glance from the wall to Blaine and back again before slipping from the table and walking closer to study them. "They look so happy," I say after I take in all the details of the first etching.

"At first sight, yes. But when you really study the details, Pepper…"

"Cupid's holding a gun," I gasp.

"Among other things."

I chance a peek over my shoulder, but Blaine stares at his shoes, so I move to the second etching.

Matrimonial-Harmonics causes the tears I've been holding back to fall free. It appears to be the same couple, but there's no happiness to be found anywhere. It's sad and tragic. And how Blaine views marriage.

"You think this is what marriage does to people?" I ask, turning to face him because the image before me hurts my heart in a way I've never felt before.

"No, I think forcing love to last forever does this to people."

"That's so sad," I rasp.

"It's not your magical fairy tale anyway." He shakes his head. "I'm sorry. I don't know why I showed you these. I didn't mean to ruin your night. Our time together."

"They obviously haunt you for some reason."

He stares at me thoughtfully. "Maybe." He nods, then drops his gaze to his watch. "The party is probably just wrapping up, but this is the city that never sleeps. Can I take you out somewhere?"

He's trying so hard to get that glimmer back in his eyes, but I know there will be no hiding my emotions now, which seems silly considering he can only ever be a fling. I don't even know his last name, and as I focus my attention back at the screen, I realize that's for the best. This man has the power to destroy my heart.

He already has.

My sisters and I didn't have an easy upbringing. We didn't have shining examples of love—but the idea of it? Of ever-lasting love? That's what got me through all those hard times. I can't give up the one wish I've ever had for myself for a man who, at his very core, doesn't believe in the one thing that has gotten me through life.

Pulling on all my reserves, I flash him what I hope is a

fetching smile and hold out my hand. "Actually, I can't commit until I've gone to the restroom and grabbed my purse from the bridal suite downstairs. I also need to check in with work to see where I'm heading tomorrow."

He stands with a skeptical expression but places his hand in mine. My heart clenches, knowing this will be the last time we touch.

"What do you do for work, my sweet Pepper?"

"I'm an assistant." With a parting glance around the room, we shut the door, he locks it, then he leads me down the stairs and back to the party. "I'm going to grab my stuff."

"I'm not going to see you again, am I?" His voice is quiet. Almost strangled. *Is he feeling this same sadness? The loss?*

The plastic smile melts from my face, and the lump in my throat bobbles with the effort of words.

"No," I say softly with a quiver I can't hide. "But the memory will be magical."

He swoops down and kisses me gently. Once, twice, three times before I pull away and run to the safety of the bridal suite.

CHAPTER 16

LOCHLAN

"*A*ngie!" I bellow. My voice is scratchy with a hoarseness that comes from being pissed off at the world.

"Lochlan, I swear to the lord above that I'll quit, right here and now, if you yell for me like that again." Angie's voice cuts through the intercom. "What do you need? And if you're going to complain about a certain blog post, you can forget it. You know The Firethorne is not even in the same league as Bryer-Blaine and that they deserved every word that was written."

She's right about the blog post, but I couldn't give a flying fuck about it today.

It's been three weeks since I walked away from Pepper, and every intelligent bit of my brain tells me it's for the best. She lives in a fantasyland where weddings are magical and the key to all her happiness. Even if I am a bastard, I can't ruin that for her. It doesn't keep me from obsessing over her though. Every goddamn minute of the day.

It also doesn't help that Ross refuses to meet with me without her by my side.

My office door crashes open, and Nova floats into the

room. She smirks, and I cut her off before she can pull any of her little sister teasing bullshit.

"I'm not in the mood."

Her grin grows wider. She often reminds me of the woodland fairies she used to adore as a young girl, and if ever there were a time I thought she'd throw pixie dust at me, it's now. The mischievous gleam in her eyes is unsettling, but I rise from my chair and greet her properly.

"What can I do for you, Nova?" She's the only one I always keep my temper in check for, even when she's trying to push me out of my comfort zone. Shove me kicking and screaming is probably more accurate. So, when I lean in to kiss her cheek, I'm not even all that surprised when she attempts to give me a titty twister.

"Jesus, Nova. What the bloody hell?"

"Angie, your *temporary* assistant, just told me you've gone through six replacement assistants in three weeks. Seven, by the look of the girl sitting beside her out there."

"What can I do for you, Nova?" I repeat, though my tone is growing icy against my will.

She burrows into my chest, wrapping me in an embrace that makes me go stiff with worry. "Are you okay?" I ask, attempting to pull her from my body.

"Geez, Lochness, I'm fine. I just thought you could use a hug." Sometimes I swear she should have been born into my friend Colton's family. I'm confident that he is the only one on the planet who hugs more than my sister.

I pat her head uncomfortably. "Why would I need a hug, Nono?" Her childhood nickname always slips when she appears vulnerable.

"Because you're sad, and you're taking it out on everyone like an asshole."

Now I do push her away. "I'm not sad," I mutter, putting some space between us by returning to my desk. She flops sideways into the chair opposite me, her legs swinging over the armrest.

"You are sad. What's going on with Abby?" Her eyebrows raise, and her dimples cause her entire face to light up.

"Nothing."

I shake the mouse on my desk to wake up my computer and am glad the screen faces away from her. I quickly close out of one wedding website after another.

"You know what's funny about dreary days in New York?"

I don't like that tone.

"What?" I almost shout, but because she's Nova, my pain in the ass little sister, it only comes out slightly irritated.

"It causes the windows behind you to become reflective." She laughs. She giggles so hard she snorts, then laughs harder. "How's The Knot treating you these days? Lots of research for weddings you don't allow in your hotels?"

"Our hotels," I grumble as I click out of The Wedding Wire website with lightning speed.

"Your hotels," she counters. "Tell me again why nothing is going on between you and Abby?"

"It was a one- or two-night thing. That's it."

"So, you wouldn't want to get in touch with her then?" She messes with her nails like she's bored, and my jaw clicks with the effort to remain calm.

How do I tell her *yes, I want her number more than my last breath* without admitting that Abby is, in fact, the reason I'm a growling maniac who cursed so loudly in the gym this morning they asked me to leave?

"Abby's a funny character, that one," Nova says. "All these weddings. She's like a fixer, and I'm so intrigued."

She just gave me an in and doesn't even realize it. "Two weddings do not make her a 'fixer,' Nova."

"No, but the Cartwright wedding in Boston this weekend

might." She purses her lips, obviously pissed I tricked her. I feel marginally better. "Damnit, Loch."

My thumb drums the desk before me with impatience. I love my sister dearly, but the sooner she gets out of here, the sooner I can Google the Cartwright wedding. I need Abby now more than ever. The thought does funny things to my stomach. Funny things I don't bloody like.

"I'm guessing she didn't show up in your searches because they only have her listed as AC on the wedding website," she says, rolling her eyes. "Does Abby have a reason to hide from you, Loch? What did you do?"

Nova swings her short legs impatiently over the arm of my chair like a pendulum. Back and forth. Tick tock. *Sisters.*

"I didn't do anything. I can't help it if she wants something that isn't real."

Her gaze softens as she takes in my expression. "What's that, Loch?"

"Nothing. It's nothing, Nono. I have a lot of work to get done. Is everything okay?"

"With me? Everything's great. Sam has been an amazing help. I hate to admit you were right. A personal assistant has helped everything run more smoothly."

I knew it would. After I had him thoroughly vetted by a security firm, I put him through six rounds of interviews myself.

"I'm glad to hear it. Are you going to dinner with Mum and Dad tonight?"

"Of course. I'll be over at six so we can ride together."

"Oh, I've got—"

"You've got nothing. I already checked Angie's calendar. See you at six, big brother." She stands and sprints around my desk, enveloping me in another hug. Nova truly has an energy like no other. "If you ruined things with Abby because of your beliefs about weddings, maybe try to take things day by day.

You never know what you'd be willing to change for the right person."

"Not that, Nova." Her lip quivers, and I glance away, hating that I hurt her feelings with my jilted beliefs. It wasn't that long ago we both wanted the same thing. A happy life with a partner who made the bad days better. I have to remember that just because my world spun out of control, it doesn't mean Nova's has to follow suit.

"So, what? If I find the love of my life, you won't celebrate my wedding wholeheartedly?" She's like a dog with a bone, but this time, something feels off. My throat is itchy, and I wonder if I'm developing an allergy to her shampoo or something.

"You know I will always celebrate your happiness, Nono. However it comes."

"God, you're such an ass." She punches my side like she did when she was little, but I don't miss the sadness in her expression.

I watch her leave, then cross the room quickly to shut the door. As I do, I find the new assistant, Brooke, I think her name is, staring at me wide-eyed and hungry. I slam it in her face, then text Angie to fire her on my way back to my desk.

Opening Google, I search for the Cartwright wedding in Boston.

Jonas Cartwright. I know him. *Was I invited?* I scan through the website, finally landing on a page about the bridal party. It's loaded with pictures, and the very last one is a photo of Abby with a group of people at Audra's wedding. She's the only one without an individual photo or some sort of selfie taken with the bride.

Who are you, Abby Chambers?

I do a quick search in my email but find nothing from Jonas after an emailed invite to go golfing. Three years ago. Fucking wanker. Pressing the button on the intercom, I don't wait for Angie to answer. "Was I invited to the Cartwright wedding?"

My door cracks open, and Nova's laughter filters in. Bloody fucket. Was she just sitting out there waiting?

"I knew it," she screams, and I envision her high-fiving the air while her toes tap against the floor. I don't have to wait long for the confirmation. She bounces back into the room with her fist raised like she just won the New York City Marathon.

"You, my dear brother, were not invited to the wedding. But I was. Would you like to be my date?"

Was that my tooth? I'm reasonably certain I just cracked a molar. "You were invited, and I wasn't? I went to school with the prick. Wait, why don't you have a date already?"

"You weren't invited because you don't know how to keep a friendship that doesn't revolve around work."

"That's not true. I have plenty of friends," I say bitterly. "It's about quality, not quantity."

"Loch, you're friends with Colton, Blake, and Tyler because they don't let you dick around."

Blah. "Could you not say dick? It's not right coming from my sister's mouth."

She leans forward so fast I don't anticipate her next move, but she grabs a handful of Skittles off my desk and throws them at my head.

"Dammit, Nova. Those were all sorted."

She grabs another handful and throws them too. "You're so weird," she screeches. "Why do you have to eat five Skittles at a time? Five!"

"I don't know," I yell back, and suddenly, I'm not a distinguished hotelier anymore. I'm a fourteen-year-old in a fight with his pesky little sister. "Five is just the right number. One of each color."

She reaches for another candy bowl, a gift from Angie, and I catch her hand before she can toss my special treat again.

"You have to loosen up, Lochlan. Seriously. Life is unpredictable." She demonstrates this by climbing onto the desk one-handed. Using the other hand, she shoves my candy down my dress shirt.

"Jesus, Nova. We're not ten years old," I bellow. Just as I'm removing her from my desk, my father walks in and laughs. Long, loud, and happy. My mother walks in behind him, gaping at her two children in the middle of a wrestling match.

"And to answer your other question," Nova huffs, sliding off my desk like she wasn't just behaving like a raging lunatic. "No, I don't have a date. I was going to make Sam go with me. Dating has been…interesting lately. It wasn't worth the hassle."

My big brother instincts take over, and I lean forward across my desk. Throwing her my most menacing expression, I wait for her to speak. She winks and sticks out her tongue.

"What's going on with dating, Nova?"

"Oh, for crying out loud. Nothing, brother bear. I just haven't found my Abby yet."

My scoff, sounding like a mixture of a cough and a belch, surprises us both. Nova giggles, but I force my scowl to stay in place. While she laughs, I pull down my vest, making sure the buttons are perfectly aligned with the zipper on my trousers.

"I've met Abby twice. That's it. I'm intrigued by her, sure. But fundamentally, we want very different things."

"She wants the fairy tale." My father doesn't miss a beat of this conversation as he takes a seat on the small sofa in the corner.

"Don't they all?" I growl, unable to keep my ruffled feathers straight under this sudden interrogation by my entire family.

Nova stares out the window to my right, and sweat forms on my spine as the silence becomes uncomfortable.

"You know," she finally says without making eye contact, "life is full of shitty things, Loch. Without something to look forward to and strive for, wouldn't we all live a bleak, depressing existence? Yeah, I think we're all, in some way, searching for our happy. It's human nature, but happiness looks different for everyone." She lowers her eyes, and I feel her words like a punch to the throat. "Not everyone is like Christine."

Fucking Christine. My ex-wife.

"This has nothing to do with her," I mutter, but it lacks the vitriol I usually save for conversations about Christine. "The thing with Abby is just different." I toss my pen onto my desk and drop back in my chair to stare at the ceiling. "Abby is the first woman to interest me in a…different way in a very long time." Even with Christine, the relationship was mostly physical. That's what got me into trouble, if I'm being honest.

"More than sex, you mean."

"Yes, Mother. Can we not talk about sex though? I've already told you that's too close, even for us."

"You need to grow up." Nova laughs.

"It doesn't matter, Nova. Abby told me she's been searching for the fairy tale her entire life. For her, that means a wedding, forever."

My family exchanges a look I choose to ignore. They know where I stand on love and marriage.

"Our hopes and dreams change, Lochlan," my father says. "They grow and expand. They readjust as our circumstances change. Get to know her. Let her know you. Really know you, and then reevaluate. You never know. She could end up driving you insane, or one of you, if not both, could decide that your future isn't the ideals you've set in stone."

He chooses now to have a point.

I can feel my eyebrows forming a V between my eyes, and I reach up to smooth it out. It also offers shelter from their determined gazes. I keep my eyes closed, but there's no blocking the excitement in their voices as they discuss my impending and sudden trip to Boston.

As Nova fills in our parents, my mind wanders. I do like to date monogamously. I like being in a relationship when there are no ulterior motives. Or at least, I used to. A relationship is a luxury I haven't allowed myself since Christine so publicly humiliated me. But Abby isn't Christine. Abby, by all accounts, doesn't even know who I am. As far as I know, she just assumes I'm a rich bastard she met at a wedding. Not the heir to a massive hotel chain. And Abby is who I need to get this deal done with Ross. So, why shouldn't we get to know each other?

My reasons for keeping my distance from her are quickly deteriorating. My willpower for this girl is nonexistent as it is, and with the threat of not landing this deal? Winning her over is the only solution. One I'm more than eager to embark on.

"It's settled then," my father announces happily. "Lochlan is going to get his girl."

"What?" I demand, snapping out of my daydream.

"And we'll all help," he continues.

"No. No way." I glance around, and all thought leaves my head. "What in God's name are you wearing?"

My father stands proudly and twirls in a circle. The smile on his face is happier than my multicolored candy. "They're coming back in style, my boy! Parachute pants. Aren't they fun?"

"Parachute pants, circa MC Hammer?" Not only are they MC Hammer pants, but their abstract print gives me a headache.

"They match your Skittles." Nova laughs under her breath.

"Dad, those are not back in style."

"Yes, they are!" he says indignantly. "Nono, tell him! Tell him they're on the runways in Paris."

My mother gasps. "Oh my God! Are they?"

"I—I'm not sure." Poor Nova can't lie to save her life, and her face is beet red from the effort of holding in her laughter, so I do what I always do. I bail her out.

I laugh at my father with my mother. And ease my sister's guilt about hurting feelings by making it okay.

Ollie Blaine performs some sort of pirouette, joining in on our fun. He's never taken himself too seriously, unlike me. He's free and fun and offers joy everywhere he goes. I'm often envious of him. What must it be like to live life so freely?

Looking around at my family, I shake my head. They're all insane, but they're all mine.

CHAPTER 17

TILLY

Dannery/Cartwright Wedding

"Can you meet me in Boston on Friday?" Colton asks, and guilt has me sinking deeper into my couch. I'll already be in Boston on Friday. I always planned to get my work for The Westbrook Group completed, but I hadn't actually asked permission to work from another city when Phoebe Dannery hired me.

"She'll already be in Boston hiding out from that sexy orgasm on a stick," Mable shouts more loudly than necessary, almost like she wants Colton to hear her through the phone.

Yanking the phone off the coffee table, I take it off speaker and hiss toward the floorboards. "Mind your own business, Mable. Why aren't you at the senior center making cat eyes or whatever it is you do there?"

"Cat eyes is the reason I called in sick today. I'm sipping on my medicine now."

"You shouldn't drink so much," I whisper-yell with my hand over my phone.

"Titty, when you get to be my age and lived what I've lived, you can drink whatever the hell you want."

"Tilly?" Colton's barely concealed laughter has me bringing the phone back to my ear.

"Ah, sorry about that."

"Mable up to her old tricks?"

"I forgot you probably know her," I grumble.

"Till, we've all lived in that building at one point or another, and Mable has lived there since before we were born."

One of the benefits of working for my brother-in-law's brother is getting set up with a really amazing apartment. They're the only reason we can afford this four-bedroom condo so close to Uptown. And it's a fantastic space. With two Jack and Jill bathrooms between the four bedrooms, and a spacious kitchen that opens to the family room, it's truly a dream come true for us. They're definitely taking a loss on the rent, but as Colton explained, it's their prerogative as owners. As members of their family, even distantly by marriage, they wanted Eli and me in a safe building. It didn't take long to convince us. Mable and all.

"She keeps things interesting," I admit.

"So, you'll be in Boston?"

"About that…"

"Tilly, if I'm not in the office, there's no need for you to be. I'm confident you can get your work done anywhere. But as your family, I hope you're letting someone know where you are when you're traveling."

"I am." I feel like I'm being reprimanded, but that's not Colton's style. He's sincerely only interested in making sure I'm safe. "I'm just going for, umm…"

"Your side-hustle you're not ready to tell me about yet."

An embarrassed sigh whooshes out of me. "I'm sorry…"

"Don't be," he interrupts. "I understand it's important to you, Till. Just promise that when you're ready, you'll come to us. We can help or advise or simply tell you that you're amazing, okay?"

I'm an asshole.

"Yeah, thanks, Colton. So, Boston?"

He explains what he'll be doing there and asks for a favor—not as his employee, but as family. He needs a babysitter for Friday night after our meeting. It's a big ask and so out of character that I agree just so I can get a front-row seat to his personal life.

"I'll see you Friday. Thanks again, Tilly."

"No problem. Good luck," I tell him honestly. Colton is a man misunderstood by so many. I hope he's finally found his happy.

* * *

THE OLD NORTH CHURCH sits on a narrow street in Boston's North End. The steeple is visible on the skyline like a magnet calling me closer. That it's the Italian center of the city is evident as you walk down the cobblestone streets early in the morning, even on a Thursday. With windows open wide in nearly every building, you hear the rush of Italian grannies barking orders. Others talk to neighbors through the open windows. And even more are yelling just to be heard over the noise of it all.

It's the ass-crack of dawn, and I'm shuffling down the street, attempting not to let a dress that weighs nearly as much as I do drag on the sidewalk. Phoebe is a sweet girl, but this is definitely the strangest wedding I've ever been to.

Finally, the street curves to reveal the church in its entirety. It stands like a beacon against a clear blue sky. If I had time, I'd be running into these little shops that smell like heaven. My stomach growls, reminding me I haven't eaten since yesterday afternoon, and I'm thankful for the oddities this day will bring.

I'm pretty sure I'll have time to run into that bakery I saw on the corner earlier.

Searching for the church entrance, I find Phoebe poking her head out the door at the top of the church steps. She waves wildly when she notices me, and I pick up my pace.

"I'm so glad you made it," she calls. "Come on, let's get inside before someone sees me, and I'll go over all the details with you." She clutches her stomach as she shuts the door behind us, and that's when I notice her face is a little green.

"Ah, are you okay?"

She shakes her head, swallowing multiple times. "Pregnant," she forces out while breathing heavily through her nose. She reaches into her pocket and pulls out something that looks like candy as she leads me into the underbelly of the church.

"Candied ginger," she says, waving it in the air. "It's supposed to help, but I think this kid likes me about as much as Jonas's family." There's sadness in her voice, and I'm beginning to understand her odd request two weeks ago.

She slowly chews the vile-sounding treat, still exhaling through her nose, reminding me of a beautiful fire-breathing dragon. "So," she says, interrupting my thoughts. "Here's the deal. Jonas's family doesn't think I'm good enough for him. My family doesn't want me marrying a black man."

"Jesus," I blurt, then glance surreptitiously around our surroundings. I did just swear on God's doorstep, after all. "Sorry, that's just—what year are we living in?"

Phoebe is a beautiful redhead with freckles that shimmer like stars across her nose, the epitome of Boston's finest Irish lass.

"Yeah, it's sad, but it is what it is. My parents threatened to take away my trust fund if I didn't call off the wedding. But there's always a workaround." She grins. "I am a lawyer, after all. I read the laws governing my trust. I dissected them. I get it when I turn twenty-five, or when I'm married, unless the executor of the trust changes it first."

"That's why the sneak attack wedding?"

"Yup, it's also why I needed to tell you about the details in person. I wouldn't put it past any of them to monitor my calls. They all think the wedding is tomorrow, but the way this town gossips, it won't take long before my family or his, maybe both, show up. The church is ours all morning, so no one can get in for the ceremony, but…"

"But you need me to leave in the dress to throw off anyone watching." Now, the dress sizing makes sense. I'm a little taller than Phoebe, and if she weren't pregnant, we would probably fit into the same size much more easily. "How far along are you?"

"Almost five months." She places a hand tenderly over her barely-showing belly.

"Five months? Wow! You can hardly tell!"

She gives a wry smile. "My doctor said I'll pop any day now. The first one always takes longer to show."

She genuinely glows. I'm happy for her, but I also feel that niggling of my own biological clock ticking.

I swallow the uncomfortable lump in my throat. "So, tell me what you need me to do."

She smiles in appreciation, and for the first time, I feel like this crazy world I've fallen into makes sense. I'm making a difference, and that's all I ever really wanted. "We'll have the ceremony," she tells me while hanging up the dress bag. "It'll be quick and sweet, and totally us, with only a handful of guests. A couple of my close friends and a couple of Jonas's. As soon as it's over, we'll switch dresses. I'm sure by then, a crowd will be outside waiting. Jonas hired enough security that they won't get in, but things could get ugly."

Her hands shake as she rubs an open palm over her abdomen.

"We've got this, Phoebe. I promise. I'll draw the crowd away from you, and you can slip away to meet Jonas. I'm assuming that's the plan, right? Where are you meeting him?"

"Yes." She nods. "I'm meeting him at the airport. He'll sneak out the back after the ceremony, and I'll go out the front with you." Her grin grows maniacal. "We'll be in the sand and sun before either of our families realize what happened. By the time they show up tomorrow for the ceremony with all their fake friends in tow, we'll already be married, and they can watch a replay of it on the screen that they'll set up at the altar. I'll also have full control of my trust fund, and there won't be a damn thing my father can do about it. Thanks to my cousin, I know he plans to corner me before the ceremony and give me the ultimatum to walk away or have my trust revoked. But tomorrow will be too late."

"No offense, but this makes me really happy I grew up hovering on the poverty line."

"We all have struggles," she says kindly. "Now, let's get ready. I'm getting married in an hour!"

In the scheme of things, this really is the most bizarre wedding I've done for my growing business, but it's also the easiest. At least, that's what I think until I'm walking down the aisle and my skin sizzles with tension.

I'm the only bridesmaid. I don't have anyone to babysit or fires to put out, so I keep telling myself that my senses are hyperfocused for no reason. But then Blaine leans forward, sticking his gorgeous face into my view six pews in front of me.

Is this some kind of sick karmic game? He wasn't at Jenni Carson's wedding last week. But it can't be a coincidence that at a wedding with fewer than twenty guests, he's one of them.

Nova turns next to him and flashes me a mischievous grin. This is her doing, I'm sure of it. Or I could be thinking way too highly of myself, and this really is just a coincidence. Since rich people tend to hang out with other rich people, anything is possible. The closer I get to him, the darker his gaze becomes, and I know we're stuck in a weird version of cat and mouse.

I shake my head as I pass, barely acknowledging him, and almost fall on my face when he grabs the back of my dress. Glancing over my shoulder, I see Phoebe just behind the door laughing at his antics. She obviously knows him, but he just crossed the line with me.

"Let. Go," I hiss.

"Not unless you promise to give me five minutes after the ceremony."

"Let. Go."

"Promise me, Pepper."

My eyes shoot fire, and he drops the gauzy material.

"Five minutes," he repeats, but I move toward my position so Phoebe can be the star of this show.

No matter how hard I try, my gaze involuntarily shifts back to the man who haunts my dreams. I've tried telling myself that we want different things. That we aren't compatible. That it was just a two-night stand. But two nights with the man have seemingly fried my resolve.

Big blue eyes track mine. Blaine shifts to listen to something his sister whispers into his ear, but his eyes never waver from mine. My skin heats under the scrutiny, and as he trails his gaze down my body, I swear I can feel his tongue. My pussy clenches, and I admonish her for her betrayal, but it's no use. Every piece of my soul is drawn to him. Every piece except my head because my brain knows exactly how this ends.

On the couch with multiple pints of Ben & Jerry's ice cream, four boxes of tissues, and me swearing off all men for eternity. Yes, I've been there once or twice, and he has heartache written all over his stupidly handsome face.

He tucks away the phone that rarely leaves his hand, all while keeping his focus entirely on me. It's a heady feeling, being watched by Blaine. Addicting too. But I can't get caught up in this madness.

I have dreams and goals. I have aspirations for a full and happy life. For me, that means marriage.

But what about a little fun along the way, Titty? Freaking Mable has a way of worming herself into my consciousness like cigarette smoke in carpet.

Blaine stands, clapping along with the handful of other guests, and I realize I've missed the entire ceremony. I turn to Phoebe, and my eyes mist with tears for her happiness.

"You ready?" I ask.

She nods, tears spilling onto her cheeks, and we rush out a side door. Jonas stays behind to speak to the guests.

"Thank you for doing this," she says. "I mean it. This isn't the wedding I thought I'd have, but it's exactly what I needed to start the rest of my life on my own terms."

I can't help myself—I need to know. "Are you sad that your dream wedding didn't come to fruition?"

Phoebe stares at me, unblinking, then slowly shakes her head. "No, Abby. I'm not. Dreams are meant to change. We're not stagnant or paper dolls. If the dreams we have as children don't adjust to the changes in our life, they're just that. Dreams. I'm starting my life with the best man I've ever met, on my terms. I don't feel like I missed out on anything. Everyone that's coming to the supposed wedding tomorrow night? They don't know us or care about us. They're friends of our parents, colleagues, social climbers searching for the next big thing. Everyone that matters to us is here. That's my dream, Abby. To be surrounded by love. The rest of it is just stuff that doesn't matter."

Stuff that doesn't matter. God, my heart hurts.

"That's beautiful. I'm so happy I could help," I say honestly as I strip down to my bra and panties. I also realize how much I mean it. The other weddings I've taken on have been about thwarting other people living selfish lives to make sure the bride has the time of her life. Today was about ensuring everything was simply about the couple. Their love. Just as it should be.

Phoebe hands me her wedding gown, and I give her my dress. As we slip into them, we both laugh.

"This is not exactly how I envisioned wearing a wedding dress in a church for the first time," I admit. "But it's perfect, just the same."

I turn so she can help tie the sash we added to cinch the waist a little, and I adjust her skirt. When we're presentable, I open the double doors that lead back to the altar. Blaine's gaze widens as if he's been watching the door since I left. His mouth falls open with an unreadable expression. I stare as his cheeks flush and his left eye twitches.

Phoebe gently nudges my back, forcing me to break the spell. I just need to actively avoid him for the next twenty minutes.

CHAPTER 18

LOCHLAN

*a*bby steps into the sanctuary wearing a white gown that makes her look like a goddess. My heart stops. Time stands still. I can't look away.

"Why is she wearing a wedding dress?" I hiss to my sister when I can finally compose a coherent thought. My chest itches and my neck becomes unbearably hot. There's a lump in my throat. Am I getting sick for the first time in fifteen years?

"Well, actually that's Phoebe's dress, so I'm honestly not sure." Nova tilts her head to get a better look at me. "Are you okay?"

Ignoring her, I scan the small group milling about, trying to pick out anyone who may step up to the altar with her. There's a couple. A group of three women. An older couple sits in the corner. But I can't picture her marrying anyone.

"Is she getting fucking married? Right now?"

Nova steps in front of me. Her sisterly senses could rival Spider-Man. "What's going on here, Loch? I thought you were just hooking up with Abby, but your expression right now? Your tone? That makes me think you see her as more than just a hookup."

I tug on my earlobe, a nervous habit I thought I'd kicked in college, but I'm finding it hard to breathe as panic sets in. "Who could Abby be marrying?" I straighten my vest three times before lifting my gaze to meet my sister's. Sweat builds on my upper lip as I entertain visions of throwing Abby over my shoulder and running out that door.

"Loch?"

I force my gaze to focus on my sister's worried expression, but I have the worst case of cotton mouth, and it's hard to form words.

"Phoebe is wearing Abby's bridesmaid dress. I've heard that the Dannerys don't approve of this wedding, so just let things play out for a minute, okay? If she's getting married, you'll have your chance when the priest asks if anyone here has any objections."

That has a grin slipping through the panic. I can picture Abby's pissed-off face as I charge the altar and take her with me, away from whatever asshole she's standing next to. Hell, I'll stand next to her.

Full. Fucking. Stop.

I need to get my head on straight. I did not just have a fleeting moment where I actually considered standing up with Abby to make her mine legally. *Did I?*

"I so wish I were a mind reader." Nova giggles. "Whatever caveman thoughts are causing that furious, slightly anguished expression, I need to know."

I open my mouth to respond, but no words come because Abby is on the move. She and Phoebe march down the aisle with an unfamiliar man in tow. "Who the fuck is that?" Scanning the small crowd, I find Phoebe's new husband slipping through the back door.

Nova follows my gaze as the three of them step outside into the morning light. My feet are moving, and I can hear Nova laughing behind me. "At least they aren't married." She's happier than she should be at my misery.

"What the hell is going on?"

Outside, I find Abby posing with the man like they were just married. Phoebe smiles politely next to them as a small group talks loudly on the street. I vaguely hear murmurs of "Thank God it wasn't Phoebe!" and "We still have time."

Time for what?

Studying each of their faces in turn, I recognize similar features in Phoebe. Nova's words about Phoebe's family not approving of her relationship ring true in the bitter expressions of these strangers.

I feel completely detached from reality as the church bells ring. Like I'm not actually here, but watching from a distance. My feet are stuck in place as Abby takes the stranger's hand, smiling like a bride, and leads him down the stone steps.

"Did I miss something? Did Abby just get married?"

"It sure looks that way, but we were in there. They...I...I honestly don't know, Loch."

Abby smiles over her shoulder, and our eyes lock. For the briefest of moments, I can read her mind. I hear all her fears, hopes, and dreams. I wonder if I can be everything she needs in that split second.

Then she gives the smallest shrug, tosses a bouquet over her shoulder that Nova catches easily, and steps into a waiting car.

She's gone before I can get to her. Just like our last night together, she left me before I could find our beginning.

I'm left feeling empty and hollow on the streets of Boston. A sadness I'm not accustomed to threatens to unman me. Generally, I'm not a man ruled by emotions or feelings, but here I am with eyes that feel too hot and words that stick in my throat.

Feelings I didn't have, even after the fiasco with Christine, rack my body. With Christine, it was all rage and revenge. With Abby, it's…fuck me. This hurts.

There's a flurry of activity all around me. I'm vaguely aware that Nova has said good-bye to Phoebe, and the street clears. I stand still.

"I'm not sure what's going on, but one thing I'm sure of—Abby is a wedding fixer. She comes in to make sure these weddings go off exactly the way the bride envisions. That will make it much easier to find her," Nova mutters.

"What?" I bark and immediately regret it. I don't raise my voice to Nova. Not ever. Not even when she was ten and used my condoms for balloon animals. "I'm sorry, I didn't mean…"

"She's got you twisted up good. I like that. There's hope for your cold, hibernating heart yet," she teases. Wrapping her arm through mine, she rests her head on my bicep. "We'll find her. I've got connections now, you know?"

She keeps talking, but I'm lost in feelings I have no bloody idea what to do with. I run on facts. And the fact is that Abby keeps slipping away because she thinks I'm not capable of love. *We want different things.* Her sad voice has tattooed itself on my heart.

We do want different things, but fundamentally, they're really quite similar. All I have to do is make her see it my way.

* * *

"I DON'T WANT to interview another assistant, Angie."

"Good. You're not interviewing Penny because I'm going to hire her. I would just like you to meet so you know who she is. Since you'll be traveling for the next three weeks, I'd like her to fly with you to California."

"No. And what do you mean, you're going to hire her? Like a temp?"

"I said what I meant, Lochlan. I'm going to hire her as my

permanent replacement. She's perfect. She's a single mom of three teenage boys. She's professional, and she can handle your crank. Her ex-husband is a bit of a—well, I'll let her tell you her story, but she isn't interested in you in any way other than a paycheck. She's perfect."

"No," I repeat stubbornly. "I never gave you the authority to hire anyone. She'll have to go."

"She'll be on that plane with you. She might even be able to help you with the Ross deal. You know he's family-oriented. He'll never sell to you unless you can align with his ideals." *He'll never sell to me unless I find Abby and make her come with me.*

"Angie," I growl, but the soft click tells me she already hung up. I'm standing in the center of my newly renovated Beacon Hill hotel, staring at my phone while I rage-type Angie's number when a soft, pliant body crashes into me.

The file tucked under my arm drops to the floor, along with my phone and a purse that spills out a second phone. The clumsy culprit nearly falls on her face, but I reach out at the last second and haul her to her feet, only to come face-to-face with the one that I want.

"Pepper?" I ask skeptically. *What the hell are the chances?*

"I... Blaine. Dammit. Are you following me?"

A lopsided grin catches the corner of my lip, and my gaze falls to her feet to see if she'll stomp in place.

"Lochlan?" Angie's voice calls from the floor. In the crash landing, the speakerphone turned on. I hear Angie huff, and what I think sounds like her hanging up the receiver of her office phone again. Silence falls around Abby and me as we stare at each other.

Then her gaze goes hard. If I thought I'd seen her pissed off before, it's nothing compared to this expression.

"Lochlan?" she spits through clenched teeth.

I grin, and strangely my cock twitches. Her anger turns me on with the power of the sun. I offer my hand and watch her body shake with rage. "Lochlan Blaine at your service, Abby. I think the fact that you're here, in my hotel, is the universe's way of telling us we aren't done."

She shoves her little pointer finger into my chest, and I clasp my hand around hers. "We are done because we never started, and now that I know who you are, we never will."

"What does that mean? It's not like I'm a murderer or anything."

"You're Lochlan Blaine." Every syllable in my name causes her eye to twitch, and her anger is reaching nuclear levels. It intrigues me.

"Yes, I am. I have no record. I can be an asshole, but only when it's deserved. Most people would consider me a catch, so please enlighten me. Why do you appear to have it out for me even more now that you know who I am?"

She pulls her hand out of my grasp and glares at me. "Why are you following me? We had a night. Two nights, I mean. Ugh! That's all." Her hands ball into fists at her sides. "You scratched an itch. I'm searching for forever, you want tonight. I can't keep giving you nights, Lochlan." She says my name like it's battery acid that burns her throat. "Just...it was nice to meet you. Unfortunately, I have a feeling we'll be seeing each other again, but only as acquaintances."

She bends down to pick up her things, then she storms off while I'm left wondering if she's crazy. And if she is crazy, why do I want to join the asylum so badly?

I kneel on the floor to scoop up my papers and phone. As I stand, I notice something is off. I tap the phone screen, and I'm delighted to see a photo of Pepper with three girls on a beach. They're each smiling, but it's Pepper that has me entranced.

"Loch, what was that about? I didn't realize you knew Tilly."

My head snaps up at the sound of my friend Colton's voice. "Tilly?" I ask, thoroughly confused. My mind is still spinning from my face off with Abby.

"Yeah, my assistant who just stormed out of here like she wanted to smack you?"

"Huh," is what I say, but my smile grows wide, and my brain is running in circles. So, my Abby is actually Tilly, Colton's assistant. I've heard him talk of her often enough, and when I search the recesses of my brain, her name clicks. Tilly Camden. *Why the fake name?*

She's a fixer. Nova's words ring true.

"How do you know her?" Colton presses, snapping me from my thoughts.

"We've just met a few times." I love Colton. He's probably my best friend, but he doesn't need to know the details. The sooner I get him settled into his suite, the sooner I can go in search of my Tilly.

Tilly. I shake my head. I knew Abby was too plain for her. Game on, Till. Game on!

CHAPTER 19

TILLY

*S*hit. Horse shit. Dog shit. All kinds of shit. I'm in it now. *Lochlan?* He has to be my boss's best friend? Why does the universe hate me?

My meeting with Colton ran two hours longer than I expected, and now I'm scurrying to my room like a rat in Lochlan's hotel, praying to any deity that will listen that I don't run into him again. Colton is expecting me in an hour to babysit, but I'm still shaking. I need a hot shower and a nice, long chat session with the girls.

I enter my room and sigh with relief when the door closes behind me. My shoulders relax until I round the corner and find a package that's not mine on the small desk in the corner.

Unease settles in my gut as I reach for the package. It's large and has my name on a card lying on top of it. Glancing over my shoulder, I confirm the room is empty, then open it. I'm annoyed to see it only says my name in scratchy block letters.

I lift the lid and gasp. It's the shoes I'd eyed in New York. The ones that cost more than my rent and car payment combined.

Lochlan.

I don't dare to touch them. Obviously, I'll need to send them back. But holy geez, are they amazing.

I trace the strappy sandal and snatch my hand back like it shocked me when an unfamiliar sound fills the room. I turn in circles before realizing it's coming from my purse. Reaching in, I pull out a phone I don't recognize and frown. Then I search all the zippers in the bag for mine. I have my work one, but my personal one is nowhere to be found.

"That's what you get for having two phones." I hear Eli's disapproving words in my ear, then the phone I shouldn't have rings again.

Tapping the screen, I'm shocked to find it unlocked. "Who leaves their phone unlocked these days?" I'm caught off guard when I see my number appear on the screen.

Oh, thank God. Someone found my phone. I hurry to accept the call, then immediately wish I hadn't.

"Tilly." Blaine's deep baritone sets off fireworks in my belly. *Not Blaine, Tilly.* He's Lochlan.

"Lochlan." I'm proud my voice comes out even because my insides are hissing like lobsters in a hot bath. "How did you get into my phone?"

"Have dinner with me tonight."

"How are you, Lochlan? I'm fine, thanks for asking."

"Dinner. Tonight. My suite. The penthouse floor. Suite A."

"I can't. I have a date tonight." Gah! *Why am I being such a bitch?*

"Cancel it."

"I can't. I'm really looking forward to spending time with him." I don't mention that *him* refers to a toddler. "I do need my phone back though."

"No."

"No? What do you mean, no?"

"Who is your date with?"

"That's really not any of your concern."

"It is unless you cancel it," he gripes.

"Not happening. So, my phone. I need it back. How did you unlock it?"

"Not happening, but you know what will happen? The entire time you're with dachoobie, you'll be thinking of me. My face between your legs. My cock driving into you. My palm smacking your ass. You'll remember how hard you came every time a word leaves his mouth because all you'll be thinking about is how fucking much you liked swallowing my dick."

Silence.

"I... Hello? Blaine?"

He just hung up on me. My jaw hangs open. Guilt replaces my rage as I realize I never even thanked him for the shoes. Even though I have no plans to keep them, it was very generous and extremely sweet that he remembered the exact shoe I had coveted.

The phone lights up in my hand as text after text arrives. They're all coming from my phone. What the hell?

Opening them, I see he's forwarding pictures to himself. Photos of me and commentary about why he likes them and what he would have done if he were there. Holy mother of mercy. He's seducing me with my own damn pictures.

Me: What are you doing? Get out of my phone!

Lochlan: Cancel your date.

Me: You're insane.

Lochlan: Why do you look sad in this picture?

Lochlan: (picture sent)

My gaze drifts over the selfie I'd taken with my sisters at the beach last summer when Eli saw her dreams come true by opening her first after-school program. I hate that he's the only one to see my real emotion hidden behind a mask of happiness.

Me: I'm not sad.

Lochlan: You're lying. The eyes in that picture are sad. Why?

Me: Didn't anyone ever teach you that calling someone a liar is rude?

Lochlan: Yes. My mum. She's big on formalities.

The phone rings again, and my shoulders drop in resignation as I kick off my shoes and flop onto the bed.

"Yes?"

"I'm sorry I hung up on you." His voice is quiet but still commanding. An apology is not what I expected from him, and I sit upright, wondering if I heard him correctly.

"What?"

A disgruntled growl comes through the speaker, making me smile.

"I said…" He inhales deeply. "That I'm sorry for hanging up on you. I can't seem to control myself around you, Pepper, and I—I mean, Tilly. Why did you tell me your name was Abby? I hate that name, by the way. It's not right for you, but Tilly? I like that name."

"It's, ah, a long story."

"Cancel your date and tell me about it." His voice is strained like he's struggling to compose himself.

"I can't do that, Lochlan."

"Why?" There's a shuffling sound, and I picture him pacing.

"Because I made a commitment, and I follow through on my commitments."

"Commit to me." He sounds frazzled.

"Do you even realize what you just said?"

"I do. I'm not afraid of commitment, no matter what you think. I'm asking you to get to know me. Spend time with me and see for yourself."

"Why, Lochlan?" I blow out a harsh breath like the words are more than I can carry. "New York was, well, it was amazing, but it also made me sad. I'm not someone who can have a no-strings relationship with someone I know there's no future with."

"Please."

He doesn't say anything else. It throws me. I expect him to bark orders, command me to meet him. Force my hand in some way. Instead, he pleads.

"Lochlan." I sigh, glancing around my room to stall for time. "Thank you for the shoes."

"Meet me for breakfast," he counters. "Just breakfast, and we'll talk."

"Did you hear me say thank you?"

"How is nine a.m.? Do you have any allergies?"

"You're infuriating—you realize this, right?"

"Nova tells me daily."

"Did you just roll your eyes, lover? Because I swear I could hear it through the phone."

His deep, throaty chuckle raises goosebumps on my skin. If I'm honest with myself, it scares me that he can affect me so effortlessly.

"Nine a.m., Tilly. My suite. Or I will find you." Just when I think he's about to hang up on me again, he adds, "My IT guy unlocked your phone with a special machine that he has. Don't fuck your date tonight. Good-bye."

And just like that, he's gone. What the hell just happened?

Scrambling from the bed, I grab my MacBook and fumble with the keys until I get FaceTime open to call the girls.

Hadley is the first to accept the call. "Hey! How's Boston?"

I shake my head and hold up a finger. "We need everyone on for this. I'll be right back." I rush to the minibar for ginger ale. Grey Goose sounds good too, but I have to babysit.

Chimes break the silence in my room. They indicate that Eli and Delaney have entered the chat.

"What's going on?" Eli asks. "Where is she?"

"I don't know. She just said she'd be right back."

"Till? Are you okay?" Delaney asks.

Picking up the MacBook, I set it on the table in front of me and see my face for the first time. I'm a little ashen, and if my eyes get any bigger, they may actually fall out of my head.

"Whoa! What happened to you?"

"Blaine," I croak. "He's here. But he's not Blaine, he's Colton's best friend, *Lochlan* Blaine. He has my phone and won't give it back unless I meet him for breakfast. I lied and told him I have a date tonight, and he practically begged me to 'get to know him.'" It comes out in a rush, and my lungs burn with the need for more air. "He doesn't believe in love," I nearly whimper.

"He said that? Those words exactly?"

"I told you about the library and the art pieces he showed me."

"Okay, just to play devil's advocate here…" Hadley's face takes over my screen. "That shows us he doesn't believe in marriage. Maybe his parents are miserable. Maybe he's been married, and it ended badly. There are a lot of reasons people are turned off by the idea of marriage. That doesn't mean they don't believe in love."

"I think he said something similar," I admit.

"Marriage is a deal-breaker for you," Delaney says gently.

My eyes fill with hot tears as I nod my head.

"You like him though." Eli leans into the screen. "You're upset."

"I do like him." The truth hurts. "But the only things I know about him are he's phenomenal in bed and doesn't believe in marriage. I'm twenty-eight years old. I can't waste time with someone that doesn't want the same future. Right?"

"You're twenty-eight, not fifty-eight. Good lord, Till. You act like you have to marry someone tomorrow."

"But spending time with him puts your heart in danger," Delaney guesses.

"Yeah."

"Oh, sis. You've always fallen fast and hard."

"What? I haven't fallen. We've literally had sex. Twice. I didn't even know his name was Lochlan until a few hours ago."

"Till?"

"Ugh, Hadley! You're about to say something I don't like. I can tell by your tone."

My friend gives a knowing look through my computer screen. "How much have you thought about him since New York?"

Every damn day.

I don't admit that though. "A few times, I guess." I can't make eye contact with any of them.

"Bullshit," Eli coughs.

"Life's too short not to have a little fun, Titty." Freaking Mable.

"For once, I agree with our eavesdropping neighbor."

"I'm not eavesdropping. I can't help it if you're all louder than a bull in heat."

Does a bull even go into heat? How would Mable know if it was loud? All four of us have the same curious expressions on our faces. We're probably all silently asking the same questions, but with Mable sometimes it's best to leave some things unanswered.

"Do it," Mable chants.

The three girls nod in agreement.

"Listen." Eli takes control. "I know how important a happily ever after is to you, but you don't always have to focus on forever. Who knows—maybe finding today's happy will change your forever."

"I agree," Hadley says softly. "You're always trying to force yourself into five-year plans. Sometimes I think you forget that you deserve to be happy today too."

"Do you like him?" Delaney asks as she scribbles on something in front of her.

"Are you making a list?"

Her cheeks flush crimson, and it causes her skin to clash with the bright pink sweater she's wearing. "Sometimes it helps to see things more clearly in brightly colored notes." She grins, holding up a large notebook with multicolored paper. "Do you like him?" she asks again.

"I feel something with him."

"Those are orgasms, Titty. Chase them as long as you can." Mable laughs, and I expect to see cigarette smoke rise behind the girls.

"Oh, for fuck's sake, Mable. Put a sock in it for a minute," Eli barks. She acts irritated, but we all know she stops by Mable's apartment every day to see if she needs anything.

Mable's interruption gives me time to put my scrambled thoughts together. "I've never felt quite like this with anyone," I admit. "I don't know how to put it into words. There's a connection. Almost like I can feel when he's close."

Delaney gasps. "It's like every Hallmark movie ever made."

My eyes burn with unshed tears. "But this is real life, Del. He's made it so clear that we want different things. Even if he's perfect." I choke on a lump in my throat because I fear he really might be perfect. "Marriage? That commitment to me from someone? I need that. I…"

Eli interrupts me. "Honey? I get it. We all have daddy issues, and rightly so." I really hope my scowl is fierce enough to break her screen. "Dad was a broken man. And your mom had mental health issues that forced her to leave you."

"No. We had Emory, and…"

"And we essentially grew up orphans, Tilly. There's no getting around that. Sure, Dad was there physically, but we raised ourselves. I know you've viewed this commitment, marriage, as the thing that will force someone to stay. But you know that's not the truth. I think you're putting so much stock in marriage because you're scared. You're scared of being left behind."

Tears overflow in a river down my cheeks. I've been to therapy just as all my sisters have. I know what Eli is saying. I've been told this before, but it's hard to let go of a security blanket you've had for eighteen years.

I don't want to have this conversation anymore. It hurts too much. "H-He bought me shoes."

Hadley and Eli stare at each other off-screen before facing me again, and I hold up a sparkly stiletto.

"Holy shit. Those are amazing."

"He saw me looking at them in New York."

"What do you know about him?" Delaney asks. She's adding sticky notes to the bulletin board beside her. She must be in her bedroom while the other two sit together on the couch.

"He's Colton's best friend, and he owns the Bryer-Blaine chain of hotels." Three mouths drop open. I nod. "Yeah, him."

There's a flurry of activity, and I know they're all googling him in the background of our video chat.

"Holy Moses," Delaney gasps. "Tilly, this is Lochlan Blaine? The one who took you to tremor town in the New York Public Library?"

She presses a button and shares her screen with us. A photo of Lochlan appears. It's an older paparazzi shot of him on a beach, shirtless and wet.

"Th-That's him."

"Hold on. I'm coming up," Mable yells, and Delaney's screen shakes because she's running with her computer under her arm to the family room.

As Delaney settles on the couch between Hadley and Eli, they snap their shared screen shut just as Mable lets herself into our apartment with a key no one gave her and leans over the back of them. She has curlers in her shimmering white hair, bright red lipstick, and a flannel bathrobe, even though it's nearly eighty degrees in Charlotte today.

"I know this is shallow, but Jesus, Till. He might be the

sexiest man I've ever seen in my entire freaking life. Ride this thing out with him. Live for today, not some version of tomorrow you've had since you were ten," Eli says. Her sympathetic expression nearly guts me.

Their faces grow large as they bring the shared screen in for a closer inspection.

An unnamed emotion curls in my gut as four faces plead with me.

"Titty," Mable says, "there are no guarantees in this life. My Johnny and I were supposed to be living out our golden years in Fort Lauderdale right now, but life had other plans for him. We had twenty-two great years, and it tore me into a million pieces when he passed, but I wouldn't trade that time with him for anything. I only regret that I held out on him for so long." She smirks, and my stomach rolls with worry. I really don't think I can handle a sex story from Mable right now. "He asked me out for two years before I finally caved. That's two years I missed out on his god-awful dirty jokes. Two years I missed out on his love. You're not guaranteed a future, but you do have today. Start livin' for today and build a future on the happiness that brings."

"That was…" Eli pauses, confusion clouding her gaze. "That was remarkably normal and good advice, Mable."

Mable flashes her a wink. These two have such a strange camaraderie that they pass off with snark and humor. Everyone is quiet for a moment, each lost in their own thoughts.

"Take a chance, Tilly. What's the worst that can happen?" Delaney asks.

I slowly lift my gaze, fear gripping my soul. "He could break my heart."

CHAPTER 20

LOCHLAN

*I*t took every ounce of self-restraint I possess not to text Tilly incessantly last night, reminding her just how her body responds to me. Instead, I spent the evening going through her phone like a proper stalker.

I stopped myself just short of reading through all her text messages, but the sheer number that has come through in the past twelve hours tells me everything I'd already guessed about Tilly Camden. People love her, and more importantly, they depend on her.

What I wasn't expecting to find was the blog. The damn blog that has haunted my life for the past several months. *Love in the Lobby. She* is the author, and now I'm even more confused about why she's avoided my hotels. A quick check of the guest log confirms she's stayed at my properties plenty of times. Perhaps it's the connection to Colton?

Give her the benefit of doubt, Banny. That's what my father would do, because the deeper I dove into her phone last night, her vision became clear. She isn't out to ruin anyone. If anything, she's trying to make everyone around her better, from the ground up.

The knowledge that it's not Christine behind the growing social blog also eases a tension I hadn't realized was eating me alive. Though I must remain vigilant where she's concerned, especially as the cogs are put into motion that will ruin her.

I also got a glimpse into Tilly's business plan, and it couldn't be more obvious. She's everything Christine will never be because Tilly is honest and good and finds the love in every situation.

Her ideas for The I Do Crew are original and forward-thinking, if not unconventional in a fairy-tale-like way that makes my skin crawl. I now have enough ammunition to force Tilly's hand into helping me. I just can't get my brain to decide on the best course of action because I've never thought about feelings before. But that's what she is forcing me to do. I can't be an asshole and blackmail her into helping me, even if everything in me would do it in a heartbeat to anyone else. The fact that I care about her opinion fucks with every other thought in my head.

I glance at my watch—7:30. Time is moving at a snail's pace. Why the fuck didn't I tell her to meet me at seven? Dropping into the desk chair, I call Angie from the hotel phone.

"Good morning, sunshine." Her sass is extra irritating today.

"Angie, do not put that woman on my plane today. I'll kick her off. Just hire her and be done with it. I'll meet her when I'm back in New York."

"Hire her? Just like that? I really think you should meet with her, Lochlan. She's already in Boston waiting to take off with you."

My head falls to the back of the chair, and I stare at the ceiling. I'm exhausted, but my body is still a live wire of anticipation because Tilly is near. She shouldn't have this much power over me.

"Lochlan?" Angie forces me to focus.

"Do you like her?"

"I do, very much." Exasperation fills the air between us.

"Then hire her. You've never suggested hiring one of them before, so if you believe she is up to the task and not looking for anything but a job, then train her while I'm away."

"What's going on, Lochlan?" Bloody hell. She knows me too well. "Does this have anything to do with your wedding friend?" My gaze rockets to Tilly's phone on the table in front of me. *Nova!*

"When did Nova get there?"

"This morning." Angie hums. "She said you might be taking a few days off. Is that true?"

"No. I'm going to California as planned."

"Is Abby going with you?" Nova shouts into the phone. One of the problems with living in the hotel where I also house my main office is that Nova lives right next door to both.

"No." But even as I say it, a plan begins to form in my head. "And her name isn't Abby. It's Tilly. Tilly Camden. She's Colton's assistant."

I know Colton will be spending an unfortunate amount of time in Vermont for the foreseeable future with his family. Does that mean Tilly will be there too? Or will she be set free to work on her own? Why the hell didn't I ask Colton more questions about her?

I vaguely hear Nova's string of questions, but I ignore them with a smile. Once again, I'm thankful for Angie when she manages to quiet my sister.

Angie tsks getting us back on track. "Ross is a family man, Lochlan. Have you read the dossier on him? He won't work with anyone he doesn't feel aligns with his outlook on business, life, and love."

I practically scoff. "Business has nothing to do with love, or it shouldn't. Just hire the woman, Angie. I have to go." I don't wait for a response. Riled up, I pop out of my seat a second later and adjust the bottom of my vest for the hundredth time.

Tilly *should* go with me to California. Tasting wine, swimming in the ocean. Skinny dipping. Fuck yes to skinny dipping. It's the perfect solution. Ross is a family man, and he's already asked about *Abby* every time I've tried to schedule a meeting with him. But how do I get her to agree?

More importantly, why do I need her to agree with every fiber of my being?

Instead of digging too deep, I start making plans. Tilly Camden is a woman I can't keep, so I'll have my fill of her before she drives me mad. Three weeks. I'll have her for three weeks, then we'll go back to our lives where she resides in the fairy tale, and I'm the dragon in the tower trying to burn it all down.

* * *

AT 9:23 A.M., there's a knock at my door, and it nearly comes off the hinges when I rip it open. Tilly stands in the hall, hands clasped together, and arches a brow at my enthusiasm.

Breathe, Lochlan.

"I didn't think you were going to show." I lean against the doorframe in an attempt to appear casual, but it only lasts a second because I'm unable to control myself when she's near. Reaching for her, I drag her inside the suite.

"Gah! Lochlan! You really need to get a grip. Most people have a personal space bubble, and you keep crossing boundaries."

I release her arm but stay close by as she walks into the penthouse. "You make me insane," I grumble, and I can feel her smile before she shows it.

"I wasn't going to come, but the girls convinced me it would be rude not to show up."

Girls? Who gets her time?

"What girls? And I think I like them." I force a wobbly smile, thankful she's not paying me much attention. She unsettles me. If I'm honest, it's not just my smile that's wobbly when she's nearby.

"My sister and my roommates. Eli, Hadley, and Delaney. They're my tribe."

"Your tribe? Like family?"

She takes a seat at the table set for two, not at all shy about opening the silver serving trays that cover every breakfast item on the menu. "Yeah. I've basically been an orphan since I was a child, so my sisters and friends are who I count on. They're the ones I go to when a sexy stranger demands my time."

A low rumble vibrates inside my chest. "We're not exactly strangers, Tilly."

"Knowing each other sexually is not the same as knowing each other."

"I agree. That's why I have a proposition for you."

A scowl forms on her beautiful face. Shit. That came out wrong. She stands, but I grasp her wrist and pull her to my side before she can escape.

"Not that kind of proposition, you dirty, dirty girl," I growl, close enough to her ear that her scent fills my nostrils. There seems to be a direct link between Tilly and my dick because the second I smell lilacs, he attempts to rise like one of those waving balloon men at car dealerships. My trousers push him back, and I adjust my stance.

"You're lucky I'm starving," she huffs, pulling away and sitting back down.

"I want to get to know you, Tilly."

"To what end, lover?"

The nickname rankles. I know she's using it to put distance between us.

"I'm serious," I bark.

She takes a piece of bacon from the serving tray and places it between her lips. My gaze catches on her mouth. She chews slowly, like she's playing with me, and when I finally break free from her spell, I find she is. Her dark eyes sparkle with naughtiness.

The twinkle vanishes as quickly as it came though, and she looks at her lap. Her shoulders slump forward, appearing weary. I fucking hate it.

"To what end?" she repeats without making eye contact.

"I'm sorry?"

"Get to know me why? I need the happy ending, Lochlan. I need it like the air I breathe. We fundamentally want different things. Getting to know you more can only end in disaster for me."

"I disagree." My heart rate accelerates like I've been sprinting in a marathon. My palms sweat as I grow increasingly uncomfortable. Worry that she'll leave has my mind running blank, and not even tugging on my vest eases the ache in my chest.

"How can you disagree? I want to get married. I want to have children someday. I can't believe I'm having this conversation with someone I haven't even spent an entire day with. Lochlan, this is ludicrous."

"Then spend time with me. We can be friends."

"Lover, even your eyes fuck me from across the room. There's no way we can be just friends."

My body reacts to her sassy lips, but I shake away the lust. "Help me out here, Tilly. Compromise, something." With a start, I recognize the desperation in my own voice. I'm not sure I've ever been desperate for anything in my life.

"I'm Tilly now? What happened to Pepper?"

"You're still peppery, fiery. But I don't know. I like Tilly better. Abby didn't fit." I shrug off my unexpected insecurities.

"I can't explain it, and you're stalling. Get to know me, then decide about where things go."

"You do realize you're basically asking me to be friends with benefits, and I'm telling you right now, I can't do it. I fall too fast. Sleeping with you, even one more time, will cause feelings to grow, and once they start, it's like a forest fire. I can't control it."

My face relaxes even as my chest constricts. I like that she's so open with me. So honest. I could never be that way. Not even with her. It hurts. It's also terrifying because she just put words to the chaos in my head. Feelings—big, scary ones—are taking root for her even though it should be impossible because she's right—we don't know each other, and I don't do feelings.

Perhaps I should just tell her about Christine and why I need this deal so badly. But as I stare at her, I know it's not just the deal. Yes, I want that winery. I want to make Christine's world crumble just like she did to mine, but my need for Tilly nearly outweighs all that hate. Nearly, but not quite.

"I promise to keep my hands to myself." There goes that desperation again.

She casts an unbelieving gaze my way. I'm not even sure I'm capable of keeping my hands off her, but I don't admit that. "Colton will be in Vermont for the foreseeable future, correct?"

"Yes," she draws out while staring at me like I'm trying to trick her. I'm momentarily distracted when she lifts a bite of pancake directly from the serving tray to her lips, and the ungodly amount of syrup she's drenched it in dribbles down her chin.

I move quickly, before she can protest, before I can think better of it, and tip her head to the ceiling. Her startled gaze watches me intently as I lean down to lick the sweetness from her skin. Her throat bobs as she swallows. My thumb runs in small circles on her cheek.

She's too damn beautiful.

"So much for keeping your hands to yourself," she mutters.

I ignore her. "Do you have to go to Vermont as well?" My face is so close to hers that my breath causes a loose strand of hair to flutter around her cheekbones.

She shakes her head but doesn't try to speak.

"Where will you work? Do you have to be in the office?"

"N-No," she stutters. "I'll be working remotely while Colton is on…on sabbatical."

Gotcha.

"So, you can work from anywhere?"

"Yes," she drags out, stalling for time. "But I do have a wedding in Denver next month."

"Here is my proposal, sweet, sweet, Tilly." Her brow raises, and I release her face. I need to step back and put some space between us so I don't utterly fuck this up. "I want you to spend the next three weeks with me in California."

She drops her head into her hands, and I feel her walls go up. When she lifts her face, the floor collapses beneath me. Sadness. Not just sadness, but epic, soul-crushing sadness in her expression has me dropping into the chair opposite her.

I won't let her go. Not like this. This is not the face of the woman I…the woman I what? My mind goes blank. Fear takes hold as she shakes her head.

"I can't. I'm sorry." Her voice is small. She stands suddenly and passes me a large bag I hadn't even noticed.

"What's this?"

"The shoes. I—I can't accept them. They're much too much."

"I don't know what you're talking about," I lie, holding my hands up and making no effort to reach for them. I want to give this woman the world, but I can't admit it. Christine was a master manipulator. I bought her everything her heart desired, but it was never enough. I've never felt so used. Rationally, I know Tilly is nothing like her, but I can't bring myself to acknowledge the gift.

I'm a bloody fucking mess.

Confusion muddles her face, but it's better than sadness. I'll do just about anything to keep from seeing that desolate expression again. It terrifies me. I've never had reactions like this before. Not even with Christine, and she nearly destroyed me.

A tear slips free from the corner of Tilly's eye, and my chest splinters as she flops down into her chair.

Perhaps a stronger man would look the other away. Focus on his goal. But she makes me weak. I can't bear the sadness, the hollow feeling in my chest, or the constant fear that she'll walk away. And it's the only excuse I have for being the giant prick I'm about to be.

"But…"

Forcing my voice to go cold, I stand and turn away from her. I can't be a bastard to her face. "You also confuse my words for a request. I'm not asking you to come to California with me. I'm telling you to come." The air becomes thick with tension as I knew it would, but I cut her off before she can curse me out. "You will come with me. Spend time with me. Get to know me. Or…"

"Or what?" Her voice wavers with a mix of hate and fear, and it settles heavily in my gut. At least I'm no longer the only one feeling fear here.

"Or…" I want to force her hand. I want to be the bastard and take what I want. It's what I do, but when I glance over my shoulder at the expression in her dark brown eyes, I tug roughly at my hair as the fight leaves my body in a whoosh. "I don't understand this connection, Tilly. I don't. But I can't walk away from it, so I'm going to make a deal with you. A deal you'd be a fool to walk away from, and a deal that you have ten minutes to consider."

What are you doing? How do you know you can trust her? Self-preservation screams at me to reconsider this. Not to force her hand into something that will tie her to me and my company, but I don't back down. *She's not Christine.* Of that, I'm sure. I'm also sure if she betrays me, there will be no digging myself out of the dark hole she'll cause.

Her shoulders are hunched around her ears, but I see fire in her expression. She's ready to give me the verbal beatdown of my life.

I stop her in her tracks.

"Spend three weeks in California with me. Help me close a deal out there with the winery. We'll spend every second getting to know each other. The owners want a family man—we'll give off that vibe easily, and if you're still searching for your happily ever after at the end of our time, we'll part ways."

"That's not a deal, Lochlan. The only thing I'll walk away with in that scenario is heartache. What you're really saying is that you want me to choose between you and your ideals for a successful, happy life, and a dream I've had for myself since I was a little girl."

She's so sure she'll fall for me. My brows pinch together, and I have to physically restrain myself from clutching a hand to my chest. A broken heart would destroy her very soul. The truth is, I know I could fall for her too, but not the way she needs. She's putting so much on the line—it's up to me to do the same, even if for very different reasons.

I need her to fulfill my quest for revenge. She needs the fairy tale version of love.

"You don't understand, Lochlan. Being with you meant something to me, even if they were one-night stands. Beyond the walk of shame, I knew what the risks were. Pushing this, spending time with you…"

"You'll get my hotels," I interrupt.

Her jaw drops open, and she stumbles as she jumps to her

feet. I take two quick strides closer in case she faints. I've never seen someone pass out before, but I imagine Tilly is the poster child for it right now. Her heart-shaped face is pale, eyes unblinking. I'm not even sure she's breathing.

A phone buzzes on the table, but I don't know if it's hers or mine, and I really don't care. Tilly's bottom lip lowers and rises like she's testing out her jaw, but nothing else on her moves for the longest time.

"Y-Your hotels? What in God's name are you talking about?"

I don't know, I almost shout. I'm reacting instead of the meticulous planning I usually take with me into negotiations. My methodical arguments go out the window when confronted with the fear of losing her. I take a step back, and with measured breaths that feel like dragon fire through my nostrils, I slowly and carefully lay out my plan.

"If we still want different things at the end of three weeks, I'll walk away. I'll leave you alone." Even when it kills me. Because, let's face it, I will be walking away. She's a means to an end. I can't and won't give her what she needs, but I'm not bastard enough to tether her to me indefinitely for my own gains.

Her eyes dart to my mouth, waiting for the rest of my proposal. "And you'll have exclusive access to my boutique hotels and the winery for your parties and...and weddings." I don't mean to gulp like a bullfrog, but that's what happens. She turns me into an unsteady teenager without even trying.

I search her molten eyes. Does she feel this? Does she know what I'm giving up for this chance? *Does she care?*

"I saw your business plan, Tilly. Or at least the one in progress. I know you have more to offer than being a wedding fixer. Your ideas for expansion, for event planning, are spot on. If you have access to three of the premier venues in New York and California that no one else can secure, you're guaranteed clients, which means…"

"You're padding my business plan. With your hotels, I'll have built-in, top-tier clientele because no one else can offer what I'll be able to."

Her beautiful brain is working overtime behind her fearful eyes.

"But if we want the same thing at the end of three weeks, we both win." Except I know that's not true. Even if I get her in the end, it'll be tainted. For me to win, she'll have to give up her vision for happiness, and I'm not sure I'll be strong enough to stop her.

CHAPTER 21

TILLY

"Why would you do this? Why don't you allow weddings at your hotels? That seems like professional suicide. Why are you willing to hand them over to someone you don't even know?" Questions pour from my lips as I sink back into my chair with a heavy thud.

None of this makes sense. I shove a mini quiche into my mouth to give my brain a second to catch up. I'm almost surprised food and spittle haven't flown from my lips yet.

I've lost all comprehension of basic manners, and I can't even control it. I cram a giant bite of eggs Benedict into my mouth, another question forming before I even remove the fork. "What if you don't close your deal? Will that be my fault? Is that your easy out?" A bite of waffle joins the eggs, and I start cutting into the next dish straight out of the serving tray. "Why are you spending so much energy trying to force my hand?" I swallow hard, and then a piece of cheesy omelet melts behind my lips. "You could sleep with anyone. This doesn't seem very…"

A napkin blocks my vision, and I realize I've been chattering away and hovering over the plates.

Lochlan stands inches away with a bemused smirk on his face.

"I'm a nervous eater, okay? Why did you order so much food? This is…" Heaven? Amazing? "Wasteful," the bitter part of me desperate for control bites out.

He shrugs as if my foul mood and disgusting manners don't faze him. "Three weeks to woo you, Tilly. Three weeks of wineries, the beach, and me. If we realize we're not compatible at the end of our time, I'll fulfill my end of the bargain. I promise."

I wave my fork wildly, and he carefully pulls his arm back to avoid being stabbed. My brain refuses to come up with a reason I can't do this. A reason I shouldn't do this.

"I…" With a frown, I take a deep breath and slow my manic chewing. Suddenly whatever medley of brunch I'm munching on feels like glue, and I'm not sure it will make it down my throat. When I swallow, the food lodges like when you take an Advil without water. It sits there, letting you know it was a stupid decision, but now that it's there, you have no choice but to suck down your own saliva and make it work.

"Do you think you'll ever change your mind about marriage?" I finally manage.

He shakes his head.

"Will you tell me why?"

Lochlan contemplates his answer. I can see his brain working behind shrewd eyes. "Possibly, after we spend some time together. Will you tell me why happiness hinges on a wedding for you?"

"It's not the wedding, lover. It's the marriage and what it means."

He tilts his head, tugging on his earlobe with one hand and adjusting his vest with his other as he watches me. "What does it mean to you?"

"That I'm worth sticking around for. Fighting for," I answer honestly. "I deserve at least that much. Let me ask you this. Would you enter into a business arrangement without a contract? A safety net that protects your assets?"

"Of course not," he huffs. He's handsome when he's agitated. His hands slip into the pockets of his very expensive-looking pants, and he rocks back on his heels. "So, that's what marriage is to you? A contract?"

"Sort of. It's a commitment. A legal one that you choose."

"Commitments come in all forms, Tilly. And even the best contracts have loopholes."

I sigh sadly. He'll never understand. How could he? He has two parents who chose him. Chose to love him. They chose to stay. How do I explain to someone like him that I need someone to choose me? To take the ultimate leap and choose me every day?

I can't. But his offer is also too good to pass up, so I sit back in my chair and try to put my feelings on lockdown. The only way forward is to come at this like a business decision. *He* must stay a business decision.

"Will you put it in writing?"

"Our deal?"

"Yes. I need our terms. I want to know exactly what you're offering. What I'll walk away with." The price for my broken heart.

He nods succinctly. "You're so sure you'll walk away from me."

"I am. I won't have a choice. Choosing you would be giving up on myself. I can't do that." Even if it rips me in two.

He stalks toward me slowly. Awareness prickles my skin. "I'll give you your contract, Tilly. On one condition."

My stubborn streak flares to life, and I lift my chin. "What's that?"

"You promise me that you won't hide yourself from me. I

want to know you. All of you. Give me your everything for the next three weeks."

"You're going to crush me." My words are barely a whisper. They're as fragile as my heart, and he knows it.

"I'm going to make you mine."

I gasp, and he grins.

"Yours until you tire of me, you mean."

He narrows his gaze, and his face goes hard. "I may have a reputation as an asshole, Tilly. But sometimes, reputations are curated to protect the truth. Make your own decisions about me. Don't judge me on other people's assumptions."

"Get to know you," I mutter.

"Yes. Are you in?"

Is it just me or is there a hint of fear in his words? Lifting my gaze, I glare into pools of blue, searching for answers. A slow smile creeps across his face. It troubles me that he can read me before I'm even aware that I've made a decision.

Three weeks. I can survive a friends-with-benefits relationship for three weeks if I keep my eye on the prize. His hotels. My business.

A partnership.

My eyes widen at the realization. Does he know he has ultimately handed me exactly what I've been searching for? Even if the benefits part of this ends, we'll be tied together in business for years to come.

A partnership is exactly what I want in a marriage. A partnership in life.

It's all so confusing. My head starts to pound.

"Stop thinking so hard. We'll draw up the terms on the plane. I'm not looking to stiff you, Till. The truth is, you're right. My blanket embargo on weddings is not good business sense, but it had to be that way. I—I can't handle the details of weddings on a daily basis."

"That's what your event planners are for," I huff.

He flinches, and I rear back to study him, but he puts the mask back in place as quickly as it fell.

"I refuse to work with wedding planners." That's the coldest I've ever heard his voice.

"And yet you're willing to work with me?" I ask cautiously.

His gaze softens as he scans my face. A gentle nod of his head, and I swear I swoon. "That would indicate I'll lose this wager we have going on, Tilly. I never lose. I'll have you and my hotels in three weeks."

Correction. He'll have my broken heart and his hotels. I stab at the food on my plate. This has disaster written all over it. If I win and get his hotels, that means I lost him. My heart skips a beat, confirming my suspicions that it's already attaching itself to this mercurial man.

I nearly jump out of my skin when he leans down to whisper in my ear, "Finish up. We leave in twenty."

"What? I don't have enough...gah! I don't have anything for three weeks. I need to go home first. I—"

He cuts me off with a scorching kiss that leaves me dizzy. "We'll stop in Charlotte so you can collect your things, but this"—he waves his hand between us—"begins now."

"I thought you were going to keep your hands to yourself?"

His wicked grin makes my pussy tingle. "I tried."

He leans against the table and pokes around in a candy bowl. His movements are methodical as he selects the ones he wants. When he removes his hand, I peek over to find it's full of Skittles and raise a brow.

His voice drops and takes on a gravelly tone that grates across my clit like my favorite vibrator. "I like to taste the rainbow."

And now I need new panties.

A dimpled grin peeks through his façade, and he winks. "Your rainbow is still the sweetest though. Let's go, Tilly. We have some stops to make."

CHAPTER 22

TILLY

*W*e arrive at 528 Charter Oak a few hours later. My condo building stands tall and proud against the clear blue sky. A giant navy blue WB emblazons the top of the well-maintained complex.

My sister and her husband Preston used to live in the penthouse, but they moved out a couple of years ago when they decided to start a family. Technically, Eli and I are the only *family* who live in the building now, but Colton says they'll never get rid of it for nostalgic reasons. His parents lived here when they were first starting out, and it was a rite of passage for each brother venturing out on his own.

"I won't be long," I call over my shoulder, then pause halfway out of the car because Lochlan is exiting too. "What are you doing?"

"I'm coming in to help." He shuts his car door and rounds the hood to my side.

"I don't need help. You really don't have to come in."

He smiles, and his eyes dance in the southern light shining off the glossy windows of my building.

"I'm coming in, Tilly." Grabbing my hand, he hauls me toward the door.

Monty stands guard just like he always does. He's an older gentleman who sits on his perch at the top of the stairs, leaning against the building. Most of the time, he's napping under his downturned hat, but today, his smile is bright.

"Welcome home, Miss Tilly. How are you today?"

I soften my voice for his benefit even as I frantically try to remove my palm from Lochlan's grasp. "I'm good, Monty. How are you?"

"Can't complain, Miss Tilly. Can't complain at all. Your girls all went charging in about twenty minutes ago. Looks like you're the last to arrive," he offers helpfully.

A low groan escapes no matter how hard I try to hold it in.

"Problem?" Lochlan asks like he doesn't know they all ran home in the hopes of catching me before we left for California.

"Not for me," I mutter. "They might tear you apart though. Last chance to wait in the car."

He doesn't take the bait. "I can't wait to meet them."

"Of course you can't," I grumble as we push through the double doors and into the atrium.

He glances around but doesn't slow his pace as he marches us toward the elevators. The doors slide open before he can press the call button, and Mable lets out a low whistle.

"Monty said he was a looker, but this is next level, Titty. Next. Level," she wheezes.

"Geez, Mable. Seriously? You're not even dressed. What are you doing in the elevator?"

"Monty called when you pulled up. I had to check this one out for myself." She narrows her already squinty eyes on Lochlan. "So," she says, crossing her arms as we enter the small space. "You can deliver on the orgasms. I'll give ya that. I didn't think Titty would walk straight for a week after New York, but…"

"Mable!" I screech. "What are you doing?"

My words don't even distract her. She just holds up a finger and shushes me. "What kind of game are you playing at here?"

My mouth snaps shut. Mable sounds...pissed. On my behalf. Obviously, she was listening when I called Hadley earlier. She was the only one home at the time, but she listened patiently when I gave her the run down and told her it was a "code Polly."

Code Polly is our version of a disaster warning. It started a few years ago when Delaney babysat for a neighbor and didn't realize the children had filled her pocket with Polly Pockets. Those little fuckers melted all over our dryer, caused a small fire, and ruined her favorite pink jumpsuit.

Lochlan is unfazed by the bathrobe-wearing older woman with a leathery face and a smoker's cough invading his space. He squeezes my hand and flashes her a pleasant smile. "I just want to get to know Tilly. She wasn't going to give me the time of day unless I got creative, so I came up with a mutually beneficial, er, arrangement." He falters only briefly and is saved when the elevator lurches to a stop.

Mable waves her hands dramatically but follows us out of the car and into the hallway. "Sex tapes?"

"Are you asking if I have one or if I watch them?" he replies as if this is an everyday question.

"Both," Mable blurts as I usher him into my apartment. She moves quicker than I anticipate and slips inside with us.

"I do not have a sex tape, but I have watched a few," he admits with absolutely no remorse.

A loud squeak comes from the family room, and I know our audience just got a lot bigger. That was Delaney's uncomfortable sound.

"Ever made one?"

"Jesus, Mable. Enough with the sex tapes," I hiss as we round the corner to find Eli grinning. Delaney is so red you'd think she got locked in a tanning bed, and Hadley is perched halfway to the couch like she can't decide if she'll sit or stand.

"I haven't made a sex tape," he replies mildly.

"Any STDs?"

Hadley drops into the couch with a woosh.

"Not at the moment," he says, glancing around.

"But you've had one?" Mable pushes.

It's the only time she seems to rattle him. "Well, once. It's how I found out an ex was unfaithful. Antibiotics and a messy break-up got rid of both."

The silence hangs in the room like a dark cloud that doesn't know if it should open up and drown us or clear the way for the rainbow trying to peek through.

"Well, that's one way to introduce your new boyfriend."

I'm going to kill my sister. "Eli." I clench my teeth so hard they're likely to crack. "He's not my—"

"Tilly prefers to call me 'lover,' but boyfriend works just fine. I'm Lochlan Blaine," he says easily, crossing the room to offer my sister his hand. I'm forced to move with him because he has my palm in his giant paw with no indication he'll let go any time soon.

"Oh, we know who you are." Eli smirks. "We Googled you."

"As you should, I suppose." The slight frown marring his features turns into a brilliant smile that masks his thoughts when Mable opens her mouth again.

"You believe in love, boy?"

"I love lots of people," he answers evasively.

"It's marriage he's opposed to." It slips from my lips before I can swallow it down.

Delaney squeaks again. It's a high-pitched sound like pinching the end of a balloon and releasing the air slowly. Hadley starts humming, a sure sign she's as distressed as I am. I shoot her a pleading expression, but her gaze is sealed on Lochlan. It is truly unfair how handsome he is.

"You've talked about marriage?" Eli cackles. "Marriage? Already?"

"Only in how it relates to me spending three weeks with him." I don't have to finish. They all know what I'm getting at. Three weeks with this man is putting my heart on the line. Not only putting it on the line, but willingly putting it out there for someone I can have no future with.

"You," Delaney, finding her voice, points to Lochlan. "Sit. Mable? Keep him company." Dragging Hadley from the couch, she grabs my hand on the way by, forcing Lochlan to release me. She doesn't say another word, knowing Eli will follow right behind us, and we don't stop until we reach my room.

Eli scoots around me to open the door, and we all pile in, then scramble onto the bed and stare at each other.

Delaney breaks first. "We need a plan before that man out there chews up your heart and spits it out."

I nod.

"If Mable doesn't rip him a new one first." Eli's eyes dance with mischief.

"Three weeks, Till? With...with him?" Hadley's hands twitch, and it's only a matter of time before she starts pacing.

"What did Colton say?" Delaney asks.

"Nothing. I didn't tell him anything, and neither will any of you." I glare at the girls.

"You really think he's just going to hand over his hotels at the end of this?" Eli asks skeptically even as she jumps from the bed to grab a suitcase and start filling it with all my sexiest underwear.

"Eli! Enough with the thongs."

"You're right. Think Mable still has those edible panties from April Fool's Day?"

"Oh my God. Stop! Everyone, just stop."

"Till?" Turning toward Delaney, I brace myself for the verbal beating I'm sure she wants to give me. "I—I know what you said on the phone. It sounds like a no-brainer. A deal you can't turn down, but..." Her eyes go glassy, and she blinks feverishly. I have no doubt my empathetic friend is imagining herself in my shoes. "But do you think it's worth your heart?"

"I know, deep down, that he isn't going to try to hurt me."

"That's not what I asked," she replies softly.

"I think it has to be. With his hotels in my back pocket, I won't have to rely on anyone to get The I Do Crew going."

"There are so many loose ends though. How do you know he'll follow through with this?" Hadley asks with a shaky voice that matches her hands.

"I just do. I can't explain it, but I do trust him on this." I scan their worried expressions before adding, "And we'll have a contract."

"And Colton would probably kill him if he didn't follow through," Eli points out while poking her head out of my closet. She's holding up four different bikini tops. Her boobs are much bigger than mine, so I'm not sure why she's holding them up to her breasts. As she tosses some into the suitcase, it becomes clear. She's choosing the tiniest ones she can find.

"There's going to be a contract?" Delaney asks, not glancing up from her notebook.

"Yes. We started going over it on the plane. The terms are straightforward." I swallow past the lump working its way up my throat.

"Then we have to ensure this goes the way you want."

"How do you suggest she does that?" Hadley groans, flopping onto her back dramatically.

"You either make him fall in love with you so you get him and the hotel—because let's face it, if he's in love with you, he won't sabotage your burgeoning business."

My eyes roll in my head so hard I'm afraid they'll get stuck.

"Or," Eli prods.

"Or," Delaney drawls, "you make sure he doesn't fall in love with you."

We all turn slowly to gape at her.

"What?" we ask in unison.

"He doesn't believe in marriage. That's one of your goals in life." Delaney turns kind eyes on me. "I don't mean that in a bad way, just that it's an important piece you're not willing to give up, right?"

I nod.

"Then you need to remind both of you how much you love love as often as possible. And weddings. And the happily ever after."

"You want to weaponize her love of love?" Eli nods appreciatively.

"Well," Delaney hedges. "I didn't exactly mean it like that. I just meant…"

"That's exactly what you meant. She's going to Trojan horse him with weddings. Bombard him with love from the inside out. He'll either crumble and see the error of his ways, win-win for Tilly, or he'll run for the hills, which will still be a professional win for Tilly."

"Trojan horse him?" I ask.

"Trojan horse him," they all reply.

"No! I don't want to fiddle your anything." Lochlan's raised voice has us all scrambling from the room.

"Are you packed?" he asks, panic evident when I enter the family room to find Mable lounging on the sofa and him backed up against the wall.

"Mable," Hadley hisses. "Did you ask him to, to…"

"Oh, relax. I did not. I asked him if he liked Fiddle the Bean."

Lochlan narrows his eyes. "You asked if I liked *to* fiddle the bean."

"That two-letter word makes all the difference in that

sentence, Mable, and you know it." I scold. Turning to him, I bite back a grin. "Mable owns a coffeehouse chain called Fiddle the Bean."

His gaze is wild as it darts around the room. Mable definitely put him through his paces, and I can't even feel guilty about it.

"Are you ready to go?" he asks again.

Turning to the girls, Eli rolls a suitcase out behind her. "Anything you don't have you can buy." She winks but I'm not sure I like her expression.

"Done," Lochlan exclaims, grabbing the suitcase in one hand, and me in the other. "Let's go. Nice to meet you, ladies." He lowers his voice and nudges me out the door. "Most of you, anyway."

Lochlan on a mission is like a cyclone, and I'm caught in the eye.

Where the hell is he going to spit me out when this is all said and done?

Outside, he puts my suitcase in the trunk while I settle in the front seat. Suddenly exhausted, I rest my head on the window. When I wake again, we're back on his private plane and Lochlan's gaze covers me like a blanket.

CHAPTER 23

LOCHLAN

*T*illy stirs in the seat across from me. As much as I'd wanted to lay her across my lap, I needed some space after the clusterfuck in her apartment.

"Hi," she says sheepishly.

"Hi." My voice is nearly unrecognizable. There's a warmth to it I'm learning is reserved just for her.

"Sorry. It's been a day."

"It has. Are you hungry?" After watching her stress eat earlier, I'm concerned I didn't prepare the flight staff well enough.

A low groan of protest tells me she's feeling the effects of her champion-esque eating skills. "God, no. I don't think I can eat again for a week." She smiles sheepishly and lifts her gaze. "Or at least until tonight."

"Good to know. I have the contracts if you'd like to look at them. It's all laid out for you. The terms, I think you'll find, are very generous." And they are. I made sure of it. I may not be able to explain the connection between us, but she deserves to be rewarded for making me feel something again. I truly had thought myself a lost cause in that respect.

She nods and takes the folder I hand her with one hand while wiping sleep from her eyes with the other. I watch as she scans each sheet twice. She scribbles notes, asks questions, and finally, sets down her pen. "Did your lawyer put these together?"

"Yes."

"They seem to be very much in my favor."

"Yes."

"Why? You're obviously a savvy businessman. Why wouldn't you ensure you had the upper hand?"

"You're helping me get something I need, Tilly. There isn't a price I wouldn't pay to have this deal succeed. Plus, I get to bask in your sunshine for three weeks. I like that more than you could know."

Her cheeks flush, and I watch in fascination as a hint of it creeps down her neck.

"Can you promise me one thing?" Her voice is small, so unlike her usual self, that I lean forward in my seat.

"I'll try," I answer honestly.

"Promise me you won't hate me at the end of this? Promise me we can be friends, even if it hurts."

I nod. That's the last thing I expected, but it's so her. Kind-hearted to her very core. She closes her eyes, and when they open again, she's regrouped. Grabbing the pen, she scrawls her signature across all the pages with yellow tags sticking out.

It's done. She's mine. For three weeks. I'm going to get my revenge and remember what it feels like to be happy, even if only for a short time.

"Can I ask you something?" I shouldn't, but it's been bothering me since I went through her phone.

"Sure." She pulls her legs up under her in the seat. It's such a relaxed position, so innocent, it does something to me. My heart reacts to the vision of her like a sprinter attempting a marathon. I clutch my chest and know I'm losing all control of myself when she's around.

"Why haven't you written about my hotels? In your blog, I mean." My breath halts in my lungs as I wait for her answer.

She scans my face for a moment. "It didn't seem right. You're Colton's best friend. I try to keep my posts and reviews honest, open, and fair. Sometimes venues don't like the truth of how they treat their employees exposed. I didn't want to put Colton in a bad position if my identity ever came out."

Jealously unfurls in my chest. She did it because, in some way, she cares for Colton. It has nothing to do with me. I know that's ridiculous, but I can't help it.

"I see." Vulnerability creeps out in two little words.

"I have stayed at your hotels before though." I lift a brow to see if she'll continue. "From everything I've gathered, you're a good employer. You raise industry standards for all your competitors. I admire that about you. From housekeeping to the concierge, you're invested in their well-being even if you do actively keep yourself apart from them. Most large chains can't say that."

Pride blooms in my chest. Not because of my work, but from her praise of it. I know I work tirelessly to be the best. Hearing Tilly compliment that hard work is a reward I didn't know I was seeking.

"Thank you. Employee morale is important to me," I say quietly. I'm unable to keep from glaring at the candy bowls to my right. This conversation has me on edge and the urge to make sure the candies are sorted into the correct containers is all-consuming.

A loud song startles me. My phone vibrates as a woman sings, the last word in the lyrics is "lover" before it starts again. I raise a brow at Tilly. I'd had my phone on silent until this flight.

"What did you do?" I ask lightly. My cheek twitches as I attempt to suppress a grin.

"You told me once that you don't listen to music, so I changed your ringtone. Taylor Swift's 'Lover' seemed appropriate." She studies me, smiling, but her eyes are troubled.

"You're right. I don't listen to music. It's distracting, I guess. I'm a singularly focused man." My gaze rakes over her body, and the hairs on my arms stand on end. She's a live wire, all right.

"What about when you were younger?"

I think for a moment. My father loves music. My mother too. It always played at their homes, but I can't remember anything about it. I shrug. "I'm sure it's been around, but it's not like I have a favorite song or anything. I probably wouldn't even be able to name a song that's been popular in my lifetime."

Tilly gasps. "That cannot be true."

"Why not?" The way she stares at me makes my spine tingle, so I reach over to the table at my side. Five tiny candy bowls house my pre-separated treats, and I take my time pulling one from each.

"Skittles? Again?" She's amused. I'm embarrassed. Not many people in my life know about this slightly compulsive habit of mine.

"I like them."

Of course, she doesn't drop it. Standing, she inspects the candy. "You're very…organized."

It's not a question, so I don't reply.

"You like things a certain way."

Again, not a question. Instead, I watch her as she tries to understand my quirks.

"Is it a control thing? You take one of each, but never more? Do you have a favorite?"

"Yes. I take one of each. I like the green ones."

"So, you never just take a handful of green?"

"No."

"Why?"

"Because then I'd be left with a bowl of yellows. And yellows are my least favorite."

"It's about being fair…to the Skittles?"

"It's about taking what you need and not overindulging."

I watch as she moves closer to the table. She reaches in and grabs a few green candies with her gaze on me, but drops them into the red bowl. My eye spasms, but I say nothing. It's just candy. She takes a few oranges and eats them. I make a mental note to add more orange to keep it even.

Then, like a literal kid in a candy store, she darts to the bowls and mixes them all up so much like Nova that I almost laugh. The entire incident takes just a few seconds.

She sits back down with a huge, satisfied smile.

Even though my hands fidget with the need to sort the candy, I have more self-control than that today. *Is she the reason why?*

"So, your flights are silent, then?" she asks as if she didn't just throw a temper tantrum with my candy.

"I'm usually working." My cheek aches with the effort of not following her gaze to the candy bowls.

She plays on her phone, and then a beat starts, stops, and starts again. I lift a brow but say nothing. She stands up and sings along.

"'Good Riddance' by Green Day?" Her arms move in a strange pattern that makes me smile.

"I don't know what that means."

Her eyes widen in shock. "This song doesn't evoke any memories?"

I listen to the words, but they're just that. Words. "No."

"This was my high school graduation song. We marched out of the gym to it."

"That's… Okay."

She changes the music and dances in front of me to something new.

"'Semi-Charmed Life,' Third Eye Blind."

Out of the corner of my eye, I find my flight staff smirking. What is happening?

"This song reminds me of my high school job at the gas station. I probably listened to it a hundred times when we had no customers. That was my mantra. I wanted something else—something more than what I was born into."

She presses a button on her phone, and the volume increases as the nonsense continues. Tilly's arms flail as she spits words like she's rapping about Chinese chickens. The words fly from her mouth so fast I don't understand a single one.

"'One Week' by Barenaked Ladies. My first bonfire party. My friend was in a band and only listened to music of the nineties and it rubbed off on me." Tilly shrugs like she was caught in a memory. "I got so drunk." She laughs, and I feel it in my chest. "I was convinced I knew all the words to this song, but no one remembers all the words. Especially not intoxicated." She twirls as a flight attendant I don't know walks past.

"This song came out when I was in college," the attendant says, smiling fondly at Tilly.

What in the actual hell is happening right now?

The song doesn't finish because she's jumped to a new one again, and a woman's voice echoes eerily. The lyrics are angry, jilted, but Tilly sings right along, her voice a stark contrast to the words.

"Alanis Morrisette's 'You Oughta Know' is the breakup anthem every woman belts out at least once in her lifetime."

"What are you doing?" I'm so confused that laughter escapes as I observe her like a circus animal.

She doesn't answer. Just touches her phone screen. "After

you're done being angry about a breakup, you play The Cranberries' 'I Can't Be With You' to have a good cry."

A sad, heart-wrenching voice filters into the air, and I shiver.

With the next button press, a heavy beat vibrates throughout my plane. Before Tilly can even say anything, my pilot chimes in, "This song played on a loop in my fraternity house for three years."

"'Mo Money Mo Problems' by The Notorious B.I.G.," Tilly supplies.

Tilly's absurdity keeps one chuckle rolling into the next until my side aches. "What is the point of this, Pepper?"

The song changes again. This time they sing about stealing someone's sunshine, and something pounds against my chest. Regardless of what happens, I don't want to be the one to steal Tilly's sunshine.

"The point is, lover, something happened to you. I can tell. There's a reason you believe in love but not marriage. Why you hold yourself to standards that keep you from enjoying life, and if you're not going to tell me, I'll do everything in my power to make you feel alive. You're hearing the words, but you're not feeling them. Music is meant to be heard in a way that feeds your soul. Simply understanding the words is not the same as experiencing the music, and that makes me think you need to learn how to feel again. For the next three weeks, I'm going to overload your senses so when I'm gone, you'll remember how to feel."

"You're going to spend all this time…helping me?"

She crosses her arms over her chest with the brightest smile I've ever seen. "Yup."

"Instead of spending it planning out your future, you're going to spend it getting me to feel something."

"You've got it, lover."

"Why? Why focus on me?" I'm curious, but my heart thunders in my chest with fear too.

"Because, Lochlan. Some people are meant to do great things in life, and some people are meant to help make those things happen. I'm a helper. I've always been a helper, and right now, my mission is to help you be the man I know you are under all that anger."

I stare, shocked and in complete awe. Tilly is so much more than a helper, and she has no idea. This woman is going to change me forever, whether I'm ready for it or not.

CHAPTER 24

TILLY

"*W*hy aren't we staying at one of your hotels, Mr. Moore?" I ask with a smirk after our bags are dropped off and the door closes behind us in the beach house suite of the famous Rosewood Hotel in Montecito, California.

Lochlan stalks toward me with sex in his gaze. Good lord, I have no willpower where he's concerned. "Because, Mrs. Moore, how else am I supposed to keep an eye on the competition?"

"For clarity's sake, you have no objection to pretending to be a married couple? But the real thing is..."

"Not an option," he growls just before capturing my protest with his mouth. It's not fair that he can make my body melt with just a touch of lips. His fingertips cause a riot of sensations as he skims the skin at the top of my waistband.

Pulling back, I blurt, "Trojan horse," and slip away from his grasp.

"Trojan horse?" He chuckles. "Okay, we can talk about protection." He pulls something from his briefcase. "Are you on the pill?"

Trojan horse. He thinks I'm talking about condoms. Freaking Eli.

"You said you were going to keep your hands to yourself."

"Is that what you want?" His gaze travels the length of my body, and I feel it everywhere.

No!

"You laid out the rules," I remind him instead.

"Tilly?" He moves like a panther, his actions smooth and calculated. He doesn't stop until he's inches away from me. I back up against the sliding glass door, and he puts a hand on either side of me.

"Yes?"

"We're renegotiating our terms."

"Tsk, tsk, tsk, Lochlan. We haven't even given our current terms the old-school try yet."

He darts forward, forcing my head to tilt as his lips land on my neck. "Renegotiate with me, sweet Tilly."

"What do you suggest?" I feel his smirk against my skin. His trail of kisses already has my toes curling.

"I suggest that you let me touch..." His fingers ghost up my arms. "Taste." He sucks my earlobe between his teeth. "Experience every inch of you."

"You want to know me sexually."

"I want to know you in every way," he counters. "Say I can have all of you."

My head falls against the door with a thud. Trojan horse, Tilly! Trojan horse him!

"I'll let you have my body if you let me have you." It comes out on a breathy sigh. The heat from his body excites every nerve ending I possess.

"I'm right here."

I shake my head. "All of you."

He pulls back to scan my eyes. "What do you want, Tilly?"

"I want you to give me all of you. My workload is lightening now that things are settling for Colton. I want you to give me your time. Unless it has to do with the winery deal, I want you free to have fun. With me."

"Are you asking me to take a vacation?" His smile is one I haven't seen before. It's light and unguarded. It makes my heart squeeze with the knowledge that something or someone made him so intense. So focused. So determined not to love.

"Er, I guess I am? I mean, I guess I am. Yes. I'd like you to go into vacation mode."

"Vacation mode," he repeats as if testing out the words. "Till, I haven't taken a vacation since college. I'm not sure I know what vacation mode is." He smirks, but it hides something darker.

"Not even with your family?"

He shakes his head.

"A day off?"

His brow raises. "When Nova was sick once and my parents were in the UK. I sat with her until her stomach stopped trying to escape her throat."

I blink at him. Slowly. "You have every resource known to man at your fingertips, and you don't ever take advantage of them?"

"Do you take vacations often?"

"I would if I could afford it, but yes, I do make time for vacations. It's important to reset and regroup sometimes."

He takes my hand and leads me out to the patio that overlooks the water. The view leaves me speechless. We're steps away from the ocean. It's breathtaking.

And then I see the hammock. A freaking private hammock.

I totally squeal like a little girl meeting Cinderella for the first time.

"Ah, what was that?"

I turn to Lochlan. "There's a hammock."

"I see that." His unassuming grin is indulgent. "And hammocks are good?"

"I have wanted a hammock since I was a kid. We didn't have anywhere to put one growing up. Not that we could have afforded one anyway, and now I live in a condo. Not much use for one in the city."

"Well…" He sweeps his arms toward the dark blue fabric swaying in the breeze. "Don't let me keep you. Have at it."

I nearly sprint but catch myself. "We're not done talking. You go change, and then I want you to lie with me."

He stares at me like I just recited the periodic table backward. Glancing down at his suit, he adjusts the bottom of his vest, then returns his gaze to me and shrugs. No man should look that good in a suit.

"What would you like me to change into? A bathing suit?"

"I mean, you can. We are definitely swimming in that later," I say, pointing to the private pool between us and the ocean. "But I want to talk first, so swim trunks or lounge pants."

"Lounge pants?"

"Sweats? Shorts? Comfy cozies? What do you normally wear on weekends?"

He tugs at the top button of his dress shirt. "This. I normally wear this."

"I mean, what do you wear when you're just hanging out at home?"

He stares blankly. "Sometimes I remove the vest."

I have the uncontrollable urge to look over my shoulder to search for a hidden camera because surely he's messing with me. But there's something vulnerable shimmering in his gaze that keeps my attention glued to him.

"What do you sleep in?" I ask.

"My birthday suit."

My hands land on my hips as I regard him. "Did you bring sweatpants?"

He scoffs. "I don't own any."

"Jeans?"

Lochlan shakes his head and undoes another button.

"Do you own jeans?"

"I'm sure I have a pair or two at home."

"Shorts?"

"In my gym bag."

"Lover, are you telling me the only time you're not pressed to perfection is when you're at the gym or sleeping?"

He tugs at his earlobe, and I have to actively work at keeping my smile neutral. "My standard wardrobe is this. I prefer suits with vests, but I'll lose the vest for less formal occasions."

"Uh-huh. Okay. Lose the vest. We're taking a field trip." Pulling my phone from my pocket, I call for an Uber.

"What do you mean? I thought you wanted to talk. And the hammock?"

"We will talk about everything, and I will be spending plenty of time on that hammock. Trust me. But first, we're buying you some loungewear."

His body goes rigid. "I'm not wearing those."

My handsome little snob. "Why? I wear them all the time. They're heaven in cotton form."

"Because I've seen men wear them everywhere from the grocery store to the gym, and they look like slobs."

"I'm not saying you have to wear them out, but at home, here, I want you to be comfortable."

He's shaking his head but following me to the door. "I'm not doing it, Tilly. I draw the line at sweatpants."

I grin sweetly. "Okay, lover. Whatever you say."

CHAPTER 25

LOCHLAN

"*I* think my brain is bleeding."

"Oh, stop being so dramatic," Tilly calls over her shoulder. She's pushing a giant red carriage through a store that accents everything in red bullseyes.

"I cannot believe you've never been to Target before. This is like my happy place."

"Why?" It sounds like a snarl, and I suppose it is. Glancing left to right, I feel like everyone is staring at us, but Tilly marches on, oblivious. "How can one store sell produce and windshield wipers?"

"That's why it's so amazing! It has everything!" The glee in her voice thaws some of my unease. "Here we go. Oh, feel how soft these are." She hands me a pair of navy cotton trousers. "Sweatpants," she says expectantly.

I keep my hands in my pockets, and she rolls her eyes. "Those are baby trackies."

She pauses with a gray pair almost to the carriage. "Baby trackies?"

"Baby jumpers? Trackies? They look like something only an infant should wear."

225

"But have you ever tried them?"

"Sure. When I was a baby."

"Will you try them again?" I'm about to yell, but she adds, "For me?"

"Why is it so important to you?" I grumble, feeling multiple sets of eyes on me.

"Because your comfort should be important to—to someone," she huffs. Without another word, she tosses them into the cart and a few other pairs in various colors. "Do you have T-shirts?" I tug on the collar of my dress shirt so she can see underneath. "Not undershirts. T-shirts."

"No," I mutter, knowing she's about to grab a few more *necessities*.

"I've met Nova. She's so laid back. How did you end up so...formal?"

"That's a great fucking question. My dad is parading around in M.C. Hammer pants, so who the hell knows," I say, throwing my hands in the air in exasperation.

"Have you always been this way?" There's no malice in her tone. She's genuinely curious, and the uncomfortable truth is, I don't remember. Have I always been this way? Tilly turns down another aisle and almost gives me a heart attack with her squeals of joy, but at least it stops the introspection.

"What the bloody hell is wrong with you?"

"It's Sloane's book. Her new one. Right here on a Target shelf. Here." She thrusts her phone at me. "Take some pictures."

I watch as she arranges some books on the shelf, then grabs one and poses with it. It takes me a second to drag my gaze from her shining face to the book in her hand. *The Love We Made* by Sloane Camden. My brow furrows.

"Who's Sloane?"

Tilly beams with pride, and in that moment, I know I'd give my left nut to have her shine like that for me. "My baby sister. You have no idea how hard she's worked to get her books onto bookshelves. It's nearly impossible for a self-published author. Take my picture," she repeats, and I comply.

She's radiant even in the harsh overhead lighting.

"We have to buy this."

"Of course." I grin like a fool as she tosses three copies into the carriage. "You're proud of Sloane."

She pauses in the aisle to peer up at me. "I am. We didn't have much growing up, and it wasn't easy. Our father was an alcoholic. And all our mothers left us."

"All? How many of you are there?"

Her shoulders relax as she talks about her family. "Well, you met Eli. She's the second oldest. Her mom took off when she was almost a year old. Emory, she's the oldest. Her mom passed away when she was three. Then there's Sloane and me. Sloane's mom had cancer. It was fast, but we were old enough to remember her leaving one day and never coming back. We were too young to realize she was sick, though I think Emory suspected it."

She moves through the store again, and I follow. "What about your mom? Where is she?"

I see her body tense even from ten feet behind her. "We lost my mother to mental illness."

The air drags through my lungs like razor blades, and I snatch Tilly's arm to ground myself. "Jesus, Tilly. I—I'm sorry."

She gives one quick nod but doesn't make eye contact. "We're all dealt cards in this life, lover."

She gives me a small smile, and I get the feeling it's for my benefit. Through her pain, she's trying to protect me, and I don't know how to react to that. I lose my chance when she speaks again.

"We play the best hand we can. Sometimes we win, and sometimes we lose. I lost in the parent department, but I know it's not my fault or theirs. Life can be hard and cruel. It can also be beautiful and magical if you let it. My sisters are my rocks.

My friends are my sounding boards. You can't miss something you never had, so I try to be thankful to my parents for giving me life. Thank them for doing the best they could, and never take anything or anyone for granted. We only get one life, Lochlan. That's why we have to make it a good one."

I lace my fingers through hers, but I can't speak through the lump in my throat. Together we steer the carriage toward the self-pay kiosk. I want to say something, anything, to lighten the mood. When she squeezes my hand, I know she's taking comfort as much as she's giving it. That's all she needs from me right now, and emotions I can't name zip through my body like a live current.

Tilly just unloaded her pain. I need to sit with it for a minute and internalize what that means for her.

Magical.

She really does love that word. And now maybe I understand why. It gives her hope. I trip over my own feet when I realize that Tilly Camden is the magic. Moment by moment, she's giving me hope. In life, in her, and in love.

Magical. Bloody fucket magical.

CHAPTER 26

LOCHLAN

"Get out here, Lochlan."

"Not a chance in your magical bloody world," I call through the bedroom door.

There's a pop a half-second before the door bursts open. Leaping from the edge of the bed, I stare at her in frustration. "Did you just pick that lock?"

"You wanted to get to know me, lover? This is me. All of me. I have a lot of talents." She does some kind of wiggle with her fingers that makes me want to suck them. "Lock picking," she continues while still waving her hands, "I owe to Sloane. She could be a little shit when she was a kid. We have three weeks together—you're not going to lock me out on the first day."

Her gaze drops to my crotch, and I watch in satisfaction as her eyes do a triple take. I might feel marginally better if they start to roll like the exorcist, but the hitch in her breath has my cock reaching for her sassy mouth.

"They, well, shit. They look good on you."

"What?" I don't want to snap at her, so I take a deep breath before continuing, but surely she's joking. Baby trackies look good on no one! Even my custom suits were never good enough for Christine.

"Yeah, ah, sweatpants look good on you. Come on. The hammock is waiting for us." She grabs my arm with the intention of guiding me outside.

"I'm not leaving this house in these things." Digging in my heels, I stop her from dragging me from the room.

Her laughter is light and makes me frown. "You think this is funny?" My heart flutters in my chest like it's dancing to her song.

"I think it's funny that you have such an aversion to comfort."

"I most certainly do not." Even as I say it, my spine straightens. "I have a luxury home. A luxury car. A bloody luxury plane, for Christ's sake."

"That you wear three-piece suits in. All the time."

"Yes."

"You're stiff, Lochlan."

"I'm not."

She raises that damn brow to contradict me, and without a zipper to control my cock, he bobs happily. I want this sassy, outspoken goddess like I want my next breath, and it doesn't seem to dissipate the more she frustrates me. If anything, I like her more. The more she pushes, the more I want her. It's all kinds of fucked up.

"Lochlan, what do you put on when you wake up in the morning?"

I cross my arms and feel the cotton baby trackies slip lower on my hips. The way Tilly's eyes smolder when she notices is the only upside of these godforsaken things. When I don't answer, she crosses the room and places her palms on my biceps.

"When you wake up in the morning, what do you put on to roam around your house?"

"I wake up, start the coffee in the butler's pantry of my bedroom, shower, then dress for the day."

"You make coffee in your bedroom?" She tilts her head back, appearing confused.

"Yes."

A sexy V forms between her brows, and I lean down to kiss it. She swats me away.

"Okay, we're getting sidetracked. So, you wake up. Make coffee. Shower and get dressed. In a suit. Every day."

Feeling attacked, I shrug. "I don't always put the jacket on right away."

Tilly fights a smile and loses the battle. But her gaze is kind and sweet, just like the rest of her. I clench my ass cheeks in an attempt at taming the hard-on, but it proves fruitless. She wants me in the damn things, she'll just have to deal with the consequences.

"I'm going to teach you to have fun and relax," she says with authority.

"If you don't step back and stop touching me, I will show you my favorite way of relaxing really soon." My voice is hoarse, and it broadcasts my lack of control around her.

She tilts her head and moves her body closer to mine. My nostrils flare, and my muscles burn with the effort of holding still while being so tense you could bounce quarters off my pecs. Her hands slide up my chest and wrap around my neck. She encourages me to bend at the waist with a gentle tug so her lips land at my ear.

Her quick breath hits the sensitive flesh there as she pants lightly. "Tilly." I groan but don't move to embrace her. If I do, I'll come undone. Instead, I watch in approval as her little body shivers in response to my tone.

"Later, lover. Right now, we need to talk."

My hands fly to her backside, and I grab two handfuls, giving each cheek a rough squeeze. "Then I suggest you move this ass before I penetrate it." The words even shock me. I've never been this demanding with anyone, but apparently, I'm incapable of controlling this side of myself around her.

I don't know if it's a mewl or a squeak that escapes her throat, but she moves faster than I've ever seen her, and I follow in hot pursuit, the baby trackies forgotten until my cock swings around inside them like a giant inflatable balloon marching down the street in a Thanksgiving Day parade.

"How the bloody fucket do men walk in these things?"

Tilly's eyes go wide with mirth as she calls over her shoulder. "I think most men wear underwear, Lochlan."

"That's a hard fucking no." She's sprinting around the bungalow, grabbing things in each hand. I stalk behind her because I can't stop until my hands are on her in some way.

I follow her laughter out onto the patio, and my body relaxes at the sheer joy on her pretty face. She points at the hammock with the book in her hand. "Sit."

I comply and gingerly fold myself into the swing, but I can't relax. The damn thing sways, and I windmill my arms to keep from toppling out the other side. I know she's excited about this thing, but has she ever actually attempted to sit in one?

She hasn't stopped laughing, but at least, for the moment, I'm not in danger of falling on my face.

"Scoot over."

I spread my legs wide to straddle the hammock and place my feet on the ground to keep my balance. "Are you fucking with me?"

She displays her teeth one by one in a slow, sexy smile. Leaning forward, I'm tempted to haul her into me so I can claim her mouth, but she waves with her hands. She's on a mission, and I can't seem to say no to her.

Gingerly, I lift one leg onto the floating bed of doom, then the other. It's like walking on that godforsaken ferry in Rhode Island. I have no control over the way it swings me around. I hear Tilly's laughter, but I know I'll end up face-first on the patio if I glance at her.

"I'll hold it still," she explains while holding the material under me. I get my entire body into the death trap with a heavy sigh. "Now, lie down. Relax."

I cast her an *are you out of your damn mind* expression, but she's watching me with something too close to love in her eyes, and it knocks me for a loop. Literally. I drop my head into the dark blue padding and turn my gaze to the sky.

"Okay, lover. Hold these."

As her supplies land on my belly, I don't get a chance to reply more than an oof. She moves forward, and fear hits fast.

"What are you doing?"

"I'm climbing in with you."

Before I can say anything else, she flops down beside me. We swing wildly, and I grasp for her like a lifeline. I wrap my arms around her and haul her to my chest so that when we hit the ground, she lands on top of me.

But it doesn't happen.

We sway side to side, then just as quickly as we took off, it settles into a slow, gentle rhythm.

"You thought we were going over." She laughs into my chest.

"Is this going to hold the both of us?" I look at the metal hook attached to the end of a braided rope.

"Take a deep breath, Loch. Close your eyes and breathe."

Lifting my head, I stare down into her shimmering brown eyes. In this light, I see flecks of gold that match her tanned skin as her silky brown hair blows in the breeze. Then I do the last thing I expect.

I follow her orders and close my eyes. I breathe deeply. Lilacs and the ocean. Her.

My body relaxes as she gently scrapes her nails through my chest hair. "Are you relaxed?"

I nod on a long exhale, somehow knowing she's watching me closely. "What do you want to talk about, Tilly?"

"We're going to renegotiate."

I crack one eye open, already feeling a smile forming. "Is that so?"

"Yes. You've already proven you can't keep your hands off me, so it only seems fair."

She's right, and I prove it again by slipping my hand under her shirt. My palm rests on her hip, and I run rhythmic circles over her soft skin with the pad of my thumb.

"I see your point. What are your terms?"

She lifts up on her elbow, and my heart skips a beat as our swinging bed of doom rocks. "We're not going to fall." Leaning down, she kisses my chest, right over my heart. Could she feel it jumping around in there? "My terms are simple. If you want to get to know me in every way, spend time with me. Give me your time like you would a, a..."

"Girlfriend," I supply and watch as her brow furrows, but she shakes her head. "I like having a girlfriend, Tilly. Or at least I used to. So, be my girlfriend."

"For the next three weeks?" The uncertainty in her tone makes me tense.

"For three weeks, and then we'll renegotiate, but I have some stipulations."

A scowl forms on her face, and I feel it everywhere. I flash a smile full of emotion as I lean down to kiss her forehead. Thankfully, I'm getting used to the unnatural movement of the death trap we're lying in.

"What?" If she were standing, I have no doubt her hands would be balled on her hips. "What are your new stipulations?"

"I want you bare."

She glares at me, but it quickly morphs into a blank expression. Whatever she thought I was going to say, that wasn't it. I like catching her off guard. I like the way her face transforms, hiding nothing from me. I just like her, I realize. More than I should. I've never asked this of anyone.

Three weeks. I can have her for three weeks. I can't give her marriage, but I can show her—and myself—that I'm capable of love. Of a relationship. Christine may think she ruined me, but staring at Tilly's gentle expression, I want to prove to the world that I can do this. For Tilly, I can do this. And for myself.

"B-Bare?" She hides her face in my side, obstructing my view as she laughs.

"Why is that funny?" I frown. Hooking my finger under her chin, I lift her face to mine. "I can't give you everything, Tilly. But I want you to feel me. Feel what I mean when words aren't enough. Nothing between us."

"You're trying to break my heart, aren't you?"

"No." Her words hurt, and I inhale air that feels too thick to breathe. "No, darling. I'm not. Not ever. I'm not the man who can give you everything you need, but I'm also selfish. I want to give you what I can and hope it'll be enough." I shift to my side to see her better, then immediately wish I hadn't. My body jerks against the movement of the hammock and I tense, waiting for the impact of the ground.

My wild movements shock her momentarily before she flops her arms around my chest. "Lochlan! I promise you won't fall out of this thing. If it were a net one, maybe, but this canvas bed is sturdy. You could roll around on here and be perfectly safe."

"Prove it." The words are a growled dare that light up her eyes, sending lightning straight to my balls.

"How would you like me to do that, lover?"

The last thread of my sanity snaps as I drag her on top of my body, knocking her book and whatever else she had thrown at me earlier to the ground. Her legs straddle my hips, and with no barrier between these fucking baby trackies, my arousal juts toward her opening. She grinds down on me as she positions herself on her knees, and a pained groan escapes from deep within me.

"Ride me."

Tilly's gaze darts around the property. It's private enough, though in all fairness, it is still a resort. I'm not one for public fornication, but I hold my breath as I wait for her response. Will she do it? Won't she? Does she trust me?

I don't even realize how much I want this until she lifts the hem of her skirt over her thighs.

Her intrinsic trust in me, for me, could very well be the end of me.

CHAPTER 27

LOCHLAN

*T*illy hovers over me, slowly inching her skirt up her thighs, when a voice I recognize filters in over the ocean breeze. I don't think. I just react. My hands cover hers, gently easing her skirt over her knees.

The voices get louder. *Fucking Nova.* I bolt upright, my forward motion causing Tilly to shift her weight to the right, and before I can stop it, the hammock shifts. I clutch Tilly to my chest and brace for impact as we tumble to the ground.

We hit with a thud, stars exploding behind my closed eyelids. My balls are on fire, but all the air in my lungs is trapped like a latex balloon is holding it hostage.

"Are you okay?" Tilly's sweet voice cuts through my pain.

"I think you broke my dick," I wheeze.

It takes her a minute, but she finally realizes her knee is crushing my groin.

"Oh. Oh, shit. I'm sorry. Do you need ice?" She runs her hands down the length of me like she's checking for a broken bone.

"Tilly," I bark through clenched teeth. "A boner is not what I need right now."

"Oh, god. Sorry." She pulls her hand away quickly, but we're so tangled up she doesn't know where to put it. She's flailing her arms and legs, trying to untangle us while I attempt to catch my breath.

"Tilly," I plead. She freezes instantly, one of her legs trapped beneath mine. Her face pales when I lift my lower half and my cock gets pressed into her belly.

"Well, at least it isn't broken." She chuckles uncomfortably, and I close my eyes. Moving a hand to the small of her back, I hold her to me as I sit up, ensuring she doesn't topple over. Again. Just as I do, I hear my sister.

"Well, what do we have here?"

Tilly flinches, but I hold her to me.

"We fell out of the hammock, Nova. What are you doing here?"

Slowly, Tilly angles her head and offers Nova a small wave. Only then do I realize I'm smashing her face to my chest. Reluctantly, I release her. She hastily stands and nearly trips over my legs in the process.

I get to my feet easily but have to adjust myself before facing my sister.

"Nova," Tilly says. "It's, ah, so nice to see you. I'm sure you have a lot to talk about. I actually have to check in with Colton. And my sisters. My roommates are probably calling me too, so I should—"

"Tilly." It's a command, and I puff up my chest like a preening stallion when she responds in kind. Grasping her wrist, I entwine our fingers and gently pull her to my side. I lean down so I can whisper in her ear. "Relax." I love my sister, but Tilly will not freak out on me right now and put an end to us before we even begin.

Her shoulders shake with a fortifying breath. When she turns to face Nova again, my confident girl has returned.

Nova stands at the foot of the patio gaping at us. A hint of a smile shows only in the twinkle of her eye. "I'm sorry I interrupted. I mistakenly thought Lochness would be here locked away by himself. I came to push him out of his comfort zone a little." She glances down with an amused expression when she realizes what I'm wearing. "But I see someone much more capable has beat me to it."

Nova's assistant, Sam, rounds the corner then with two large suitcases. "Oh." He frowns when he sees me, but it's gone a split second later.

"Sam," I say in greeting. Turning to Nova, I give her my best *what the fuck* look. She smirks.

"So," Tilly starts, "okay. Are you staying? Here, I mean?" I've never seen her ramble. She's always in control. Squeezing her hand, I try to catch her eye, but she's actively avoiding me.

Nova runs up the steps and, bypassing me completely, wraps Tilly in an embrace. "How did you do it?" she stage-whispers while flashing laughing eyes my way.

"Do what?" I instantly dislike the wobble in Tilly's voice, so I lean down to pry the two women apart.

"Get him to wear those." Nova snorts while pinching the sides of my baby trackies. I swat her away like an annoying gnat that won't bugger off.

"Oh, God. I'm sorry," Tilly's worried gaze cuts me deeply. I don't know what has gotten into her, but I'm going to find out right this second.

"Nova!" I try not to raise my voice, but something has Tilly spinning, and I'm not willing to let her turn this into something it's not. "Stay here for a minute? I need to talk to Tilly."

I don't wait for either of them to respond. When Tilly doesn't immediately move with me, I lean down and toss her over my shoulder.

Nova laughs hysterically, but at least it knocks Tilly out of whatever funk she was in.

"Put me down, Lochlan." She smacks my ass, causing me to

stutter-step. My hand lands on her behind a second later, and I keep moving into the house. "Hey!"

I don't stop until I reach the bedroom. Using my foot, I slam the door shut, then flip her onto the bed. A satisfied smirk appears on my face when she lands with a bounce. She's up on her knees in an instant. Here is my determined spitfire.

"What happened out there?"

"What happened?" she hisses. "What happened?"

"That's what I asked." A full smile slides onto my face as she gets worked up. Her brows draw together, and her hands land on her hips. Right where I want to squeeze. It takes great effort, but I return my gaze to hers.

"What happened is I nearly fucked you out there for the entire world to see. Then we were interrupted by your sister. Your sis-ter!"

"Yes. And?"

"And?" she splutters. "And? And your sister saw us."

I glance down at my appearance, then give Tilly a once-over. What the hell am I missing here?

"Oh, for crying out loud." Tossing her hands into the air, she stares at the ceiling as her nostrils flare. "Not saw us *naked*. She saw us *together*. This—us—is not real. It's a business proposition. I don't want people thinking I slept my way into anything. What will she say when my company starts invading your hotels?"

"This," I grumble, "is us for the next three weeks. The real us. We will handle the rest when the time comes, and my sister will not say anything. I promise you."

Her shoulders droop just before her chin falls to her chest.

"Till?"

"You want a real relationship for three weeks. It's always going to come back to this. There's a time limit because neither of us will compromise."

My hands tug at the baby trackies, and I suddenly wish I had my suit on. I feel too exposed like this.

Tilly, always in tune to my needs, softens her gaze as she slips off the bed. "You don't have to wear these, lover. Not for me. If you're more comfortable in your armor, then that's what you should wear. Go talk to your sister. I'm going to head down to the water's edge to check in with Colton and my sisters."

"Till…"

"We're good." She flashes a practiced smile and a horrifyingly cute thumbs-up. "We have a plan to stick to. I'll be back soon." She's gone before I can stop her. Grabbing one of the T-shirts she purchased at Target, I slip it over my head and go in search of my sister.

She's lounging in the hammock with Sam.

"What the fuck?" I snap.

Nova rolls her eyes, but I swear something sparks in Sam's gaze. "You idiot," she scolds.

My patience is nonexistent. "What now, Nova?"

"First"—she sits up, forcing distance between her and Sam, so I offer my hand to haul her up—"it's Sam. My assistant. *Nothing* is happening." I don't have to look at him to know he flinched at that comment. Before I can delve too deep into my thoughts, she continues. "Secondly, what the hell is going on with you and Tilly? Whatever it is, I love it. I love it so damn much. Don't mess this up."

"It's not what you think."

Sam sits up in the hammock, and I force myself to be cordial. I hired the dickhead, after all. "Sam, could you give us a minute?"

He looks between my sister and me before nodding. "I'll go check on our room."

"Room?" I growl my displeasure.

"Jesus, Lochness. We showed up at the last minute. There

was only one room left. But it's fine. Doesn't look like we'll be staying long anyway."

Nova and I sit in silence as Sam walks down the path. On the horizon, I can see Tilly, and my shoulders relax.

"You like her more than I realized." My sister leans in and shoulder-bumps me.

I tug on my earlobe, and before I can stop myself, my hand reaches for the vest I'm not wearing. Nova grins and shakes her head as she plops down on the top step. I join her, keeping my gaze on Tilly.

"You know, I spoke to her brother-in-law this morning," Nova says.

"Colton?" He may be my friend, but I don't want him anywhere near my sister.

"No, one of the other ones. His wife is the photographer that shot my fashion show a couple of years ago?"

"Halton," I grunt. I don't know him well, but Colton's entire family is made up of good people. "What did he have to say?"

"Well, I mentioned I'd met Tilly." My gaze snaps to hers. "I didn't give anything away. I don't need details about why she uses a fake name at these weddings, or why she's keeping it a secret that she's spending time with you, but it was an interesting conversation."

"Why's that?" I try to keep my tone neutral, but like everything else where Tilly is concerned, I have zero self-control.

"He described her as kind of a wallflower, a huge heart, but someone who helps everyone else shine."

I jerk at the hem of this godforsaken shirt. "She's not a wallflower," I grunt in displeasure. *Do they know her at all?*

"That's what I thought, but Halton's wife agreed. They had the nicest things to say about her, but none of it seemed to fit. Not how she is with you anyway, from the small glimpse I had of you guys together."

"What else did they say?" My neck itches, and my palms prickle. Why didn't I change back into my suit?

"Just that she's a good girl. So are her sisters and friends. But they also said that Tilly is the one they know the least. She's always moving around in the background, getting things done. Making sure everyone is happy."

"She does," I mutter. "But how can they not see she's so much more than that?"

"You know, even in families, we have a role to play, and what's expected of us isn't always who we're meant to be. I think sometimes the best parts of ourselves only blossom when the right person is nurturing them."

"What does that mean?"

Nova tilts her head to study me. "It means, big brother, that sometimes we only become who we're meant to be when we feel safe enough to let the big, scary parts out. Maybe you give her something no one else can. If every other person in her life views her as a wallflower, it must be you giving her the courage to embrace the hidden parts of herself."

"That's ridiculous. I was drawn to her because she was this fiery little thing that didn't take anyone's shit. She didn't become that way because of me."

"Maybe not," she agrees. "But how many people in her real life get to see that side of her?"

Who sees you the way I do, Till?

"It's only temporary," I finally admit.

"I'm not going to get into a war with you over this, Loch. Your view of marriage is skewed. I think it's time to reevaluate your stance on a few things before it ruins your future. Just because you thought something once, doesn't mean it has to stay that way. Stop being so rigid in your thinking."

"Stiff," I grumble.

"What?"

"Tilly said I was...that I was stiff." I pluck at the baby trackies. "She's trying to get me to relax and have fun. She wants to pretend this is a real vacation."

"Well, you are stiff. But you weren't always *so* stiff, and you are kind of on vacation already. Did you tell her that Kitty is covering the office so you can learn all about the winery over the next few weeks?"

"She knows I'm here for the winery, but not about Mum."

"So, you're holding back from her."

"No." She raises her brows. "I'm not. You interrupted us before I could agree to her terms."

"You're compromising?" Nova asks in shock.

"I am capable of compromise. I'm wearing bloody fucket baby trackies."

"Baby trackies?" Nova's laughter makes me smile. "You're wearing sweatpants, Lochness. Everyone wears them."

"They're hideous."

"And yet, here you are."

I shrug as I weigh my words. "It seemed important to her."

"And that's important to you. Why?"

"I—I think she genuinely wants me to be happy."

She nods thoughtfully. "And what she wanted seemed more important than staying in your comfort zone."

I grunt because I don't like where she's leading me. She should have been a damn lawyer, not a fashion designer. "She messed up all my Skittles on the plane." I don't mean to say it, but it slips past my lips anyway.

"I knew I liked her. Did you yell at her? Fix them? Throw them away?"

A wide grin shows off all my teeth. "No."

"Hmm. I think you like her, Loch."

Leaning forward, I place my forearms on my thighs so I can drop my head into my palms. "What if she's trying to change me?"

I don't have to turn my head to know my sister is staring at me. I can feel her contemplating her words, so I wait her out.

"What if she's trying to help you find yourself again?" she finally asks softly. "I know you don't want to hear this, but Christine changed you long before she deceived you. That entire relationship was never about you. It was always about her, what she wanted, and what she could get, but you trusted her. You couldn't see past that blinding love. Has Tilly asked you for anything?"

Pulling at my hair until it almost hurts, I think about Nova's question. "I bought her some shoes, and she tried to return them."

"What else? Has she dropped hints about what she wants or needs? Is there anything about her that screams manipulative?"

"No, not Tilly," I say defensively. "She…" Bloody hell. "She's only asked for my time and keeps trying to take care of me."

"Mm-hm. Who takes care of her?"

Tilly's voice carries ahead of her as she makes her way up the beach. It sounds like she's finishing a call.

"We're temporary, Nono. Just temporary." The words smash against my heart as I watch Tilly's silky hair flow behind her.

"What do you want from her, big brother?"

A sigh that weighs more than I can carry wooshes out on a low groan. "I don't know. I don't think what I want and what I can give her coexist with what she needs."

"Then don't play games with her, Lochlan. That will make you no better than Christine. If you never plan to give her what she needs, let her go."

My gaze is still on Tilly as she walks through the sand. Nova's words make my chest ache, but when Tilly's eyes find mine? Her smile covers my body like the most sensual caress. I can't let her go. Not yet.

I'm so in tune with her that I know something's wrong when she looks back down at the sand. Tilly isn't one to shy away from me, so I'm out of my seat and drifting away from my sister without a second thought. "Everything okay?" I ask, reaching for her hand as soon as she's within arm's reach.

Tilly flashes me a questioning gaze before gracing me with a smile. "Oh, sorry. Yeah. Everything's fine. I was just checking in with my client in Denver." She glances over my shoulder, and I already know my sister is watching us closely. It's confirmed when Tilly offers a shy smile. "Is everything all right with Nova?"

"She's fine. Just being an annoying younger sister checking up on me."

She pulls free from my grasp and places both hands on my cheeks. There's a noticeable shift between us in this moment and my eyes burn. I'm startled to realize tears are forming at their corners. The fear that our end is near causes my knees to buckle and it takes all my strength to remain standing before her.

"I'm glad you have her." She pats my face like you would a small child, then sidesteps me to walk toward my sister. "Sorry about my freak-out earlier. We've been in a little bubble, and I forgot the outside world exists." Her smile is warm and friendly, but it's also sad, and the sledgehammer goes to work on my heart again. "How long are you staying? Do you want to stay for dinner? I'm sure we can get some groceries in that big kitchen we have. I'm a great cook."

"We're on vacation," I bark, then shake my head. Calm the fuck down, Blaine. "Sorry," I mutter. "We're on vacation. You're not cooking anything. We can go out."

"No, no. That's okay. Now that I know Lochness isn't alone, I'm not going to stay. I only flew out here to check on him, but I've got plenty of work to do in New York. I'll be back with Kitty and Dad for the gala in a few weeks."

Tilly's gaze darts to mine. I haven't told her anything about our time here, and I feel like a prick. "They're coming for the winery gala at the end of the month. That's when Ross will make an announcement either way."

She steps to my side, seemingly forgetting about my sister, and pats my chest. My heart squeezes painfully when she straightens out my T-shirt so I don't have to. "We'll get the deal for you, Lochlan. I know it. We'll make a good team."

"Yeah," I force out as my throat attempts to close. "We do make a good team." I close my hand over hers and hold it to my chest. It isn't until Nova clears her throat that we break the trance we're in.

"Geez. Sorry. I—I don't know what's wrong with me. Your brother makes me crazy, I think." Tilly laughs while yanking her hand free, and I feel the loss deep in my bones.

This connection I have with her is so intense. It terrifies and delights me at the same time. I just hope I don't burn to the ground when it comes to an end.

CHAPTER 28

TILLY

"So, you were already planning to be on vacation?" I ask, crossing my arms. "Did you trick me?"

Lochlan's laugh is deep and warm, like dark chocolate melting on my tongue. He doesn't laugh like this nearly enough.

"No, darling." As soon as it's out of his mouth, his cheeks flame, and I can't help but tease a little.

"First Pepper and now darling? Who knew you were so verbally demonstrative?"

"I'm not. Usually. But there's nothing usual about you." His tone indicates he isn't sure how to handle that information, so I let him off the hook.

He's sitting in a patio chair, one knee bouncing while he plucks imaginary lint off the other.

"Lochlan?"

He stares at the ocean, watching the sun start its descent, but he turns instantly when I say his name. "What's the matter?"

Why does he always assume something is wrong? "Nothing's wrong. I was just going to say, I'm sorry I pushed you into wearing those. You really don't have to. I didn't mean anything by it. You look very sexy in your suits. I just wanted to push you a little."

He nods and glances down at the dark gray cotton. "They're not…" He pauses as his face contorts. "They're not terrible."

My laughter eases some of the tension in his shoulders, and I climb back into the hammock. "You can't even say that without grimacing, lover." Folding my hands behind my head, I let the gentle sway soothe my frazzled nerves.

"I like seeing you like that," he admits quietly.

Turning to face him, I wiggle my body to lie on my side. "Like what?" I ask, propping my head up onto my hand.

"Relaxed. Happy."

"It's hard not to be when you're in a hammock at the ocean, lover. So, tell me about your plan. Why are you on a pseudo-vacation for three weeks?"

"There's nothing pseudo about it. Perhaps, before I met you, I would have planned to fill every waking second with meetings, but my mother ran Bryer-Blaine for years without me. She can handle the day-to-day for three weeks. And to answer the second part of your question, I had told Ross that I would be here to learn everything he wanted to teach me about the winery. It turns out, it isn't so much about how wine is made but the people who run it. He's big on family and taking care of his employees."

"But so are you." Okay, I may have researched him even if I never put him in the blog.

"How do you know that?" He leans back in his chair, appearing relaxed for the first time in hours. But his gaze remains intensely focused on me. A reminder that I'm the prey in his chase.

"I know because every time we've stayed at one of your properties, every employee I spoke to, from the kitchen staff to front desk clerks, all loved and respected you. Even if they did fear you a little." His lip quirks, but he remains silent. "You work hard to make sure your staff is a priority, and they recognize that."

He nods thoughtfully, but then his face clouds over.

"Thank you," he eventually offers. "I know there will always be the occasional bad apple, but my parents believed in respecting our employees. It's why Nova and I both worked every job in the hotel as teenagers. You learn to treat people with respect when you're slinging drinks to assholes all night only for them to leave a fifty-cent tip. Or walking in to clean a room and finding shit on the walls and used condoms on the floor." He shudders at the memory.

"I'm impressed."

"So am I." He doesn't take his gaze off me, and his intensity is unnerving, so I glance away.

"What impresses you, Lochlan?"

He moves quickly and is standing over me a second later. Leaning down, he captures my lips, but it's a gentle kiss. It's different, more controlled than I'm used to from him. "You, Tilly. You impress me."

My heart flutters, but I tamp it down. Don't get carried away here, Tilly. Three weeks. Three weeks. Three weeks. That's all we have. Instead of fishing for the information I desperately need, I focus on our time. "What is the plan while we're here?"

He lazily scans my body, causing my toes to curl. "There are two dinners and a gala that I know of. Ross may want to do some tours and some informal get-togethers. He's run his winery as a family business his entire life, but with no heirs to take it over, he's forced to sell. He wants to make sure that the family vibe continues with its new owners." He's quiet for a moment before finishing. "And he likes you."

I'm sure he can read the confusion on my face like a flashing neon sign because he smiles, and I get the oddest sensation that this specific expression is reserved just for me. "Me? What do you mean? How do I know him?"

"You probably don't, but he's Audra's godfather, and she spoke very highly of you. He's who we ran into at her wedding when I was taking you on the tour." His voice drips with sexy innuendo, and my tummy tightens.

"So, you needed me to get this deal done. Not just anyone, but me specifically?"

"Darling, I think I need you for a lot of things."

"You don't sound so happy about that." I try not to hold my breath as I wait for his answer, but I can't expel the air from my lungs no matter how hard I try.

"I am happy, Tilly. I just don't know how to handle it."

"O-kay." My gaze darts to the melting sun on the horizon. The sound of the ocean eases the tension in my shoulders and my anxiety slips away. When he doesn't immediately speak, I force us back on track. "So, a couple of dinners and we're at his beck and call?"

"Pretty much." He shrugs, suddenly appearing so much younger, and I grin.

"Otherwise, we're free to do whatever we want?"

"As long as it includes you naked."

"Lochlan! We're getting to know each other outside of the bedroom too." His hand lands on my ankle, momentarily stunning me into silence.

"Sounds delightful." His eyes twinkle as his hand methodically roams up my leg at a snail's pace.

"Parasailing," I blurt. His hand pauses near my knee. "And a campfire. Fishing. Umm...pedicures. A movie marathon. And... and reading in the hammock."

His hand rises from my leg to pull at his earlobe. It's oddly endearing to see him so confused. "What are you talking about?"

"Dates. Vacation. I mean. Gah! Those are the things I want to do on vacation. With you."

Laughter that warms my heart escapes his lips in a deep, soul-pleasing sound. "Parasailing and a campfire?"

"And pedicures, fishing, movies, and reading."

"All at once?" He's still laughing, but his hand travels up my leg again, making it hard to think.

"No. Not all at once, but…"

His fingers skim the edge of my panties, and thinking goes out the window. My body is on fire, and I need him to keep touching me. Teasing me. Torturing me out of my comfort zone and into this bubble where only he and I exist.

"Wha-What do you want to do on vacation?"

He pauses his forward motion on my leg to stare at me, but he's shaking his head like he misunderstands. "What do I want to do?"

Lifting up onto my elbows, I try to read his expression. "Yes, Lochlan. What do you want to do while we're here?"

"Besides you?" His lip curls. It's almost a smile, but not quite.

I pull my knees together when his hand inches higher. Something in his tone has me on edge. Not with fear, but sadness. "Yes, lover. Besides me."

His cheeks puff out as he releases an exasperated breath, and he scrubs his free hand over his face. "I don't know, Tilly. I want to do whatever you want." I'm already shaking my head, and his eyes go wide. "No? Why not?"

"I have my list, but before we do anything on it, you need to make your own list. Tit for tat."

"Fine," he says like a curse. "Snorkeling. And then I want to do everything on your list. That's what I want. I want you to have fun."

I purse my lips into a tight line, gearing up for a fight, when he interrupts my thoughts before I can argue.

"The sun is almost down," he says out of nowhere.

My head swivels left to right like I just realized we're still outside. Me lounging in the hammock, him hovering above me. "Uh-huh." My breath catches as he ghosts his pointer finger over the cotton of my panties, then slips his fingers under my ass. He's so freaking good at distracting me with his thumb that lands just above my clit. He's cupping my pussy, and it clenches with wanton desire.

Lochlan's hand grips me tighter, and my eyes go wide as he swings me side to side. With hooded eyes, he lowers his mouth to my cheek. "My opinion of this goddamned contraption might have just changed."

He straightens with new determination and lifts my dress with his free hand. He's so tall standing above me. It makes me feel safe and confident in a way I've never felt before. As he slowly strips me naked, I've never felt more seen. Not because I'm before him in a bra and panties. No. I feel seen because he gets a part of me no one has ever bothered to search for.

Why does the man I can't keep have to be the one to break down my walls?

"I'm trying, Tilly. I'm trying so damn hard," he whispers, gently laying kisses around my navel.

Did I speak my fears out loud? Or is he having the same concerns as I am?

"Stop thinking so hard, darling. There will be plenty of time for that later." His teeth nip my hip bone as his fingers slide into the soft band of my thong, yanking it from my body. "Bloody fucket, you smell so damn good. Everywhere. Every fucking where you smell delicious. You smell like..." His words are muffled as he dives into my heat, already slick with arousal, but I swear he said "mine."

You smell like mine.

CHAPTER 29

LOCHLAN

I have to stop saying shit like this. Nova's warning rings in my ears, but try as I might, I just can't quiet the dangerous words buzzing around my head.

What do I want? Why did my chest ache so painfully when Tilly asked me what I wanted? She's cast a spell over me, and I quickly realize the walls I've built around my heart are no match for her.

I had every intention of seducing her slowly tonight. In a bed, for Christ's sake, but with her spread out before me on this floating devil, my intentions are blown to hell.

I drag my hands to the underside of the hammock and hold her to me. With her body steady, I suck her clit into my mouth. The bloody floating bed of doom has its uses, after all.

"Lochlan." Her voice is a hoarse whisper. She's fighting to remain quiet, but I won't have it. I won't be satisfied until this entire resort hears her calling my name. "Fuck me," she whimpers as my tongue flits roughly against her tiny bundle of nerves that vibrates under each ministration. "Please, Lochlan. Now."

My body complies before my brain processes her words,

and I stand in a rush. Hooking my hands under her legs, I spin her so she's sideways across the hammock and grin maniacally. I love this new position. She's at the perfect height for my cock. Her teeth bite down on her lower lip, and I drop my trousers, suddenly oddly at ease with the way the cotton slips free with a gentle tug.

Tilly slips her hand between her legs, reaching for me, but I swat her away. If she touches me now, I won't last. I'm too on edge. Stepping forward, I grab both sides of the hammock and gently rock her into me.

I'm physically incapable of tearing my gaze away from how my cock glides between her lips. With each downstroke, she coats me with her wetness, and a groan starts in my toes, working its way north, vibrating through my veins.

"I don't have a condom on," I warn. If she objects, I'll tear this house down until I find one, but her eyes shine in the waning light. She bites into her bottom lip and gives a nod of consent that shreds my heart.

I blink rapidly as my eyes grow hot with unshed tears. I haven't cried in years, and this woman is reducing me to a blubbering mess with her pussy. I'm losing my damn mind.

"Yes, Lochlan. I want you."

"Bare?" I snarl.

"Yes."

I clench the side of the hammock, and with one forceful tug, I impale her.

"Holy," she moans, unable to finish the sentence as I step forward moving the hammock with me.

"You fit, Tilly." My cock. My life. My heart. "You fit." I know I'm not making any sense as I leverage the motion of the hammock to rock her into me over and over again. She makes me believe in things I've sworn off when we're connected like this. She's dangerous and addicting and so fucking mine.

Reaching down, I pluck her nipple and pinch it. When she

groans in pleasure, I tweak it again harder. Folding my body over hers, I release her nipple just in time to take it into my mouth. I lick and suck the pebbled peak, ratcheting her pleasure as high as I can take her.

"Lochlan."

"Mm-hm."

"Lochlan," she moans again, but this time she twines her fingers into my hair and gives it a hearty tug. Lifting my head, I'm forced to release her nipple. Something in her gaze gives me pause, and I freeze.

My breathing is heavy as I try to keep her in focus, but my body goes rogue when I'm so deep in her.

"I love how you feel inside of me."

Pride fills my chest. A growl worthy of a black bear erupts from me, and I slowly begin to move in her again. She bounces and sways, but I slow down our movements. This needs to last. Pulling out, I grit my teeth. I fucking love the drag of her walls, and when she uses her internal muscles to squeeze the head of my cock, I ram back into her.

"You were made for me," I tell her.

"Yes. Yes. God, Lochlan."

Using my hips to steady the hammock, I drop my thumb to her clit and rub in slow, torturous circles to match the pace I'm setting. Her hips buck against the contact, and she digs her heels into the fabric bed. As my thumb goes to work, she grinds her pussy up and down, taking control and riding me. I stand and watch as this goddess pushes me over every wall I've constructed.

"Made. For. Me," I roar, and she picks up the pace. "Say it."

"Made for you," she hisses.

"Mine." I come in a riot of curses and damn near black out. My cock twitches violently, bringing me back to the present, and my fingertips flick Tilly's clit at an ungodly pace. Back and forth, repeatedly, until her legs shake and her belly quivers.

"Mine," I growl again. "Mine. Come for me, Tilly. Fucking come." My hand is going numb as I strum her like a banjo, and when her eyes go wide, I know I have her. I watch in awe as her pussy spasms around me, milking the last of my orgasm. I'm never going to get enough of this woman, and that thought terrifies the living hell out of me.

I don't trust myself to speak, so I silently lean down and lift her to my chest. Cradling her to my body, I kick off the baby trackies still around my ankles and carry her into the bedroom. The feelings of rightness, of being whole, that I have when she's close like this—those are thoughts for another day. Today, I'll embrace what I have and hope like hell I come out on the other side in one piece.

* * *

"Have you seen this?" Tilly asks as I step off the patio with two bottles of water in my hand.

My smile is more than indulgent. She lounges in yet another hammock, but this one is sturdier and doesn't swing like Tarzan when she moves. At my request, the Rosewood brought it in when they set up the outdoor movie screen.

We still have the one on the patio, and I smile every time I walk by it. To think, only a week ago, I hated the contraption. Things are changing. With me. With us. With my beliefs, though I don't say so out loud.

Yesterday she got stuck in a couple of meetings, and before we knew it, the day had gotten away from us. While she worked, I put plans in motion for the rest of her vacation goals. I hate to admit how happy it made me to do these things for her. But nothing could have prepared me for the sheer gratitude she shows every single time.

"I haven't," I answer sleepily, and she frowns.

"Are you tired?"

My shoulders relax as I move closer. It's happening more often. Or perhaps I'm just noticing it now, but when she's within reach, my body responds in a multitude of ways.

We're still in bathing suits from our earlier swim. Her tanned and toned body is on full display in a sparkling gold two-piece that's decidedly for my eyes only. My hand falls to her ankle when I'm close enough to reach out. The compulsion to touch her is stronger than my willpower, and I take comfort in the contact.

"A little," I admit. "I didn't realize you'd be a fish." I like to tease her. Her reactions to me are magical.

Bloody fucket magical.

"Hey!" she scoffs with mock outrage. "You cannot expect me to be twenty feet from the ocean and not want to live out all my *Little Mermaid* fantasies."

"Darling, you can live out any fantasy you want as long as I get to watch." A yawn sneaks past my defenses. "What are we watching next?" Her movie marathon turned out to be exactly what it sounded like. So far, we've watched three chick flicks where she mouthed ninety percent of the words and cried at every happy ending.

I've spent more time watching her than the bloody screen.

"Your turn to choose. What do you usually watch?"

"Me?"

"Yes, you, lover. Doesn't anyone ever ask what you want? Why is it always such a surprise to you?" She laughs until she turns to face me and reads my expression.

"I'm sure they do," I say to deflect.

Her mouth drops open, and she rolls over to sit up. My gaze follows her body but snags on the table to her side. Room service delivered a plethora of snack items Tilly had requested, and there, on the tray, are my Skittles. All sorted into neat little piles. I can't take my eyes off them. Did she do that? For me?

My brain seizes, trying to remember if anyone has ever done that before.

"Nova?" she asks gently.

"Is my baby sister who I love dearly and have always catered to," I reply on autopilot. My head darts between Tilly and the food tray, but I don't want her to get the wrong idea about Nova. She's as protective of me as...fucket. She's as protective as Tilly is.

"I can tell she loves you very much."

I nod, still lost in my own thoughts. "Did you do this?" I finger one of the brightly colored candies and watch it spin on the hard surface.

"You were getting our drinks." She shrugs like that explains everything.

"And you sorted the candies?"

"I guess. It's how you had them on the plane. And I noticed they were already in candy bowls here too, so I figured it was a big deal to you. I was only trying to help."

"To clarify, you did it for me?" My voice sounds strange, and I don't fault Tilly for appearing uneasy.

"Yes." She sounds calm, but her hands are clasped so tightly in front of her that I can tell I'm freaking her out.

"I..." Pausing to stare at the tray, I rake a hand through my sea-tousled hair. "That was very thoughtful, Till. Thank you. It's such an odd habit. My sister is the only one that pushes me on it, but no one has ever just accepted it."

Relief shows on her face as she smiles and walks to me. She doesn't stop until her arms encircle my waist and her head rests on my chest. My arms wrap around her, anchoring her body to mine.

"It's not about accepting a quirk, Lochlan. It's about accepting you as you are. A stiff, rigid, candy-sorting, pain in the ass with a heart so big, even if he forgets to let people see it."

I squeeze her a little more tightly. "Is that how you see me?"

She lifts her head so her chin rests on my heart. "I think there are many layers to you, lover. I think some of them have been burned so badly that after the scars healed, you forgot to undo the bandages to let the light in again. Have you always liked things, er, so particular?"

Feeling a lengthy chat coming on, I guide her back to her favorite spot on Earth. Well, the safer version anyway. Together, we gingerly climb into the hammock and lie side by side. A low rumble of approval floats through me as she nuzzles her head on my chest.

"I've preferred suits for as long as I can remember. Schedules. Lists. Rules. But no, this level of me-isms is relatively new, I suppose." She doesn't say anything, but she drags her fingers through my chest hair in an oddly soothing rhythm. "I have an ex. It ended badly, but before it did, well? It was a slow progression of awful, is the best way to describe it. We got together when I first took over the hotels. There were a lot of demands on me. On my time, my energy. She became demanding too, in her own way, but I didn't see it."

"Blinded by love? Lover, I'm shocked!" She's teasing, but she has no idea how right she is. "I'm sorry," she says when I don't continue. "What happened?"

"I don't want to talk about her."

Tilly's gaze goes wide with hurt, and I hate myself for doing it, but she recovers so quickly my head spins. "Then tell me about you? What happened with you?"

"Why do you want to know all the gory details?"

Her expression is so open, so honest, I look away for fear I'll be the one to break her. But she surprises me yet again with her response. "Because, Lochlan, it's the gory details that are the bedrock of our souls. They make us who we are, who we want to be. It's in pain that we find our worth. You're capable of love. Of giving and receiving it, if that's what you want.

Forgetting and forgiving old hurts are two very different things. I forgive my parents for being unavailable to me, but I don't forget the pain they caused. I learn from it and keep it from happening again."

"You're very wise, Tilly Camden."

Her teasing smile lights my body on fire. "I know. If only you'd listen to me."

I'm listening, my sweet Pepper. Trust me, I'm listening.

CHAPTER 30

TILLY

"Fishing? For real? On a boat?" My foot taps out an excited beat as Lochlan watches on with a mixture of fear and sheer pleasure in his expression.

"Yes, Tilly. But John Ross and his wife are coming too. He seemed…eager when I told him our plans for the day." He frowns like he's unsure of something.

"Well, there's no quicker way to smoke out a rat than being stuck out on the ocean with no way home."

Lochlan's unexpected laughter fills the cab of the Uber. "What the bloody hell are you talking about?"

"You know." I grin, bumping his shoulder with mine. "We'll be out at sea all day with no escape. If they have any concerns about us as a real couple, it will be easy for them to flesh them out."

His face transforms into a scowl at the realization. "You're right—"

"I am," I cut him off. "But you know what else I'm right about?"

"If you say everything, I will take you over my knee right here."

"Promises, promises," I tease but inch to the other side of the car when his gaze darkens.

"Tilly." It's a warning I don't heed.

"Lover." He reaches for my leg, and I squeak with wide eyes when I catch the driver's gaze in the rearview. I'm laughing uncontrollably as I swat his hand away, but there's joy on his face. Pure joy that makes me burst with contentment.

"Okay. Okay!" Holding up my hands in defense, I wait until he calmly returns his hands to his own lap. "What I was going to say is, we already look like a real couple. No one at the resort has questioned us. That older couple even commented how cute we were at dinner the other night. All we have to do is be us, and we'll be fine."

"Us is real, Tilly. I'm not pretending here." He doesn't make eye contact, instead opting to peer out the window, but I see the disquiet of his furrowed brow and downturned lips. "Are you having a good time?"

My head snaps up, and I slide across the seat to his side. "Lochlan, look at me." His shoulders tense, and his entire body goes stiff, but he does as I ask. "I've had the most amazing time with you here. I mean that with my whole heart. Have I not shown my appreciation?"

"Of course you have. But you don't ask for anything," he huffs.

My brain scrambles, trying to understand his meaning. Angling my head to the side, I watch him and feel my lip hitch like a bad Elvis impersonation while my nose scrunches in disgust. "Ask for anything? What could I possibly need, Lochlan? We spend our days at the beach. You've made reservations or ordered the most amazing meals. You're making every wish I had for this trip come true, and you're giving me the only thing I truly wanted every single day."

He tugs on his right earlobe as his elbow rests against the

door. "I'm not giving you anything. You haven't asked for anything, Tilly."

"But I did. I asked for your time, and you've given it freely."

"It's not like it's a hardship," he grumbles. "You've worn that dress three times now."

His words suck the air from my lungs. They hit harder than a punch to the gut, and I retreat back to my side of the car.

"Fuck. Tilly, I— Goddamn it." He unbuckles, because of course my mercurial, rigid companion would be buckling his seatbelt in the back of an Uber, and drags me into his lap.

He rests his forehead against the side of mine, but I refuse to look at him while I collect my words. Old insecurities about being the poor girl from Camden Crossing threaten any self-preservation I've acquired with age.

"I like this dress, Lochlan." Lifting my chin, I feign confidence. "That was incredibly rude."

"Baby? Tilly? Look at me, please." There's regret in his voice, but there's something else there too. His baritone is shaky, and when he lifts his hand to my cheek, I feel the vulnerability in his touch.

Slowly, I lift my gaze to his, attempting to mask the hurt. It's easier to be mad, but when I find his piercing blue eyes filled with sadness, my mask crumbles.

"I love this dress too. You're breathtaking in everything you wear. I don't care if you wear the same thing every day." I arch a brow and roll my eyes. "Okay, maybe not every day," he concedes.

"Do people always want things from you?" I keep my tone gentle, but his grip tightens on my hip.

"Most people."

Lowering my chin, I wait until his gaze meets mine. "I'm not most people, Lochlan. I don't require things. If I truly need something, I'll find a way to get it on my own. I don't need anyone taking care of me, and I'm not interested in a human ATM."

An angry grunt has me pulling back to fully take him in. His expression curdles my stomach, and a wave of emotion hits me hard in the chest.

"Your ex? She made demands of you." I'm starting to understand this man, and anger furls in my gut at the faceless woman who hurt him so deeply. "She used you and took from you, and you allowed it because you loved her."

Knowing he did love someone that much has my eyes growing damp with unshed tears, but I refuse to allow them to fall.

"I didn't see it happening," he mutters before closing his eyes. When they open again, I can see the war raging within him.

"Because you trusted her, Lochlan. We're programmed to trust those we love, and she took advantage of that. In a perfect world, it would never bite us in the ass. But the world isn't perfect. People aren't perfect. I'm guessing you didn't see it because she worked hard to ensure you didn't. That's on her, not you. Don't let the bad behaviors of others affect your future."

"Trust doesn't come easy to me," he admits quietly.

"Trust is earned. I've learned that the hard way. My default is to trust everyone. Assume everyone is my friend, but I know that many people will be your friend or your partner when it suits them. That's not friendship, and it's definitely not love. The reality is people will generally hang themselves with their true nature if you give them enough rope. It's okay to keep them at arm's length until they've earned your trust, but Loch? Eventually, you have to trust someone, or the loneliness will crush you."

He pulls me into him and buries his face in my neck, whispering words I can't make out. We're silent for a few miles, each lost in thought. The car turns at an intersection, and Lochlan kisses my cheek while one hand rubs circles on my back.

"Thank you," he breathes.

"Can I ask you something?"

He leans back into the seat but pulls me with him. "Anything."

"Is your ex… Is she the reason you'll never get married?"

His hand freezes, and his heartbeat accelerates under my palm. When I glance down, I see his right hand in a fist. I push myself into an upright position so we're face to face. I search his eyes for unspoken truths, but he doesn't answer me. There's a faraway look in his expression, and I get the distinct impression he's lost in a memory.

The car rolls to a stop, and I feel the driver's eyes on us. "Loch?"

Gently, he slides me into the seat next to him as he reaches for his phone.

"Lochlan?"

Dark, cold eyes cut to mine. His words are nearly a hiss. "Something like that, Tilly. I'm done talking about her."

My heart recoils against my ribs, and I swallow painfully. When he opens the door, I school my expression but flinch when he offers me his hand. My entire body shivers when I place my palm in his, and for the first time since we've met, it's not in anticipation of what's to come, but dread.

"You're quite good at this," John Ross exclaims, swinging a large metal hook to catch the white sea bass I've just reeled in.

My cheeks hurt from smiling, and when I peek over my shoulder, I find Lochlan leaning against the side of the boat with an indulgent grin, but also a little green. We found out pretty early on that he wouldn't be baiting any hooks. Who knew my lover would have such a weak stomach for blood and guts?

"I used to fish in the creek near my house growing up. It was one of the only places I ever got to be truly alone."

"Did you go with your dad?" It's a fair question, and you'd think I'd be prepared for it after all this time, but it still catches me off guard.

"Tilly's father wasn't around much," Lochlan interrupts, hesitantly coming closer. "I had no idea when you said you wanted to go fishing that you actually wanted to fish." His chuckle is infectious as he kisses the top of my head.

Turning to Billy, the first mate, I shrug. "Might be time for you to take over." He moves quickly to undo the belt around my waist that helps anchor the rod, and Lochlan growls at the poor kid.

I lift my arms, and wait for Billy to make his adjustments, then turn in place and wrap them around Lochlan's neck. "What did you think I'd do, lover? Lay out on the boat and read?"

He slow blinks, and I realize that's exactly what he thought. Shaking my head, I let the laughter flow freely without any hesitation or self-doubt.

John passes behind us, clapping Lochlan on the shoulder. "The more your woman can surprise you, the happier your life will be. Trust me on this one."

"She surprises me every day," he whispers, leaning in for a chaste kiss. Raising his voice, he calls over his shoulder. "Are you ready for lunch?"

"I'm famished," John's wife, Doreen, coos, lifting her face from the book she's reading.

"You wouldn't tell by looking at her, but my wife is always famished." John laughs sweetly. "Let's get you fed, then." He holds out his hand, and I nearly blush as they exchange a look of lovers.

"You two are very cute together."

"Well, it hasn't always been easy, has it, Dory?"

"Lord, no. We had a rocky start, that's for sure. But we came through it, and now, thirty years later, I spend every day with my best friend."

"You didn't find it hard to work together every day?" I ask as I slip into the cabin behind Doreen.

"Oh, child. It was a nightmare some days." Her shoulders shake with laughter. "Living together, working together? There were weeks when he was the only other person I saw. You learn your likes and dislikes pretty quickly that way, but you also learn what you can tolerate and what you'll learn to love eventually. Life and love are pretty similar, Tilly. They're all about choices. When we found out we couldn't have children, we made the winery our baby. Our blood, sweat, and so many tears went into building it up to what it is today. We're quite proud of that."

"You should be," I say honestly. As soon as we're all seated, a crew member arrives to pour drinks and deliver salads. "Thank you," I whisper as the young girl slides a glass toward me. "Oh my God. What happened to your hand?" A bandage is wrapped haphazardly around her palm and I can tell from here that it's not going to keep her wound clean. Without thinking, I clutch her fingers gently in my palm and turn her hand over.

"Oh, it's nothing. Really. I guess I'm still getting my sea legs. I swayed when the ship rocked and nicked myself with the knife. I'm sorry. I should have bandaged it better."

I'm already out of my seat, dragging the girl behind me.

"Tilly." I pause at Lochlan's command, but he isn't mad. When I turn, he appears concerned.

"Sorry. Sometimes I just jump into action without think-ing," I explain to the group sheepishly. "You go ahead and get started. This cut is pretty deep, and she needs an extra set of hands to wrap it properly. I'll be back soon."

He stares at me, slightly bewildered, and I notice Ross watching him closely. Silently, I nod. "Do you need help?" he finally asks.

"Are you good with first aid, Lochlan?"

"Ah." He shifts uncomfortably in his chair. "No, actually. I fainted the first time Nova got a bloody nose." When he reaches up to pull on his earlobe, I blow him a kiss.

"I'll be right back. You guys start eating. No worries. I've got this. My sister made sure we all knew first aid at a very young age."

Lochlan tilts his head at this information, and I see all the concerns that statement brings play across his face. He takes a step forward, but I hold up a hand to stop him.

"We'll be right back." He's searching my face for something, and I guess he finds it because he nods and slowly lowers himself back to his seat.

Turning to the girl at my side, I ask, "What's your name?"

"Sara. I'm so sorry…"

"No apologies. Accidents happen. Let's just get it cleaned up. Okay?" Her worried gaze bounces between me and the rest of my party. "Don't worry about them. They're more than capable of serving themselves. Trust me, they'll be fine."

Ushering her forward, I lead her toward the rear of the vessel. "It's just that he's so…intense," she finally whispers.

I gape at her. "Who? Lochlan?"

"Mr. Blaine?" She startles, and I know I'll find him at my back if I turn. Warmth spreads throughout my body knowing he couldn't stay away. He's kinder than he gives himself credit for.

"Don't worry about him," I say conspiratorially. "His bark is worse than his bite." I feel more than hear him chuckle behind me. "He's a big teddy bear. His scowling angry persona is simply a defense mechanism." We reach the sink, and I turn her palm over so I can remove the dirty bandage. Sara's gaze is still darting back and forth, so I know Lochlan is nearby.

"If that's true," Sara whispers, "I don't know how you handle his bite. His glare alone has scared off every other crew member. I drew the short stick."

I hear him scoff and can't hold back a giggle as I turn toward him. "That's what you get for eavesdropping, lover."

"I'll take it," he growls. "It's better if they don't get too close. Are you all set?" I don't have time to question what he means because I hear John and Dory calling out.

"Is everyone all right back there?"

"Tilly?"

"We're good," I answer. "Go eat. I'll be there soon."

He answers with an uncomfortable nod, then retreats to the cabin.

"In-tense," Sara mutters.

She doesn't know the half of it.

CHAPTER 31

LOCHLAN

"She's a caretaker," Ross comments as we make our way off the boat.

As a general rule, talking like this makes my head explode with the effort of keeping the skin from crawling off my body. Especially with business associates, because altruism in business does not exist. People are out for themselves, end of story.

But there is something about John Ross that I connect with, so I swallow my practiced curt quip and reply, "She is."

My gaze drifts ahead to where Tilly laughs arm in arm with Doreen.

"Can I be honest with you, Lochlan?" His tone is contrite and gives me pause, but my game face stays firmly in place, my gaze locked on Tilly.

"I prefer it that way."

"I thought you might. I had my reservations about you." My jaw ticks, but otherwise I take great care not to show my irritation. "The truth is, the circle we run in is small, but the talk is plentiful. The gossip surrounding you since your divorce has not shown you in a positive light."

"Gossip is stories created of non-truths by jealous people," I say calmly, even though internally I'm preparing for a battle.

"Are they?" He questions with a hint of humor, and I stop walking. I stand tall with arms hanging rigidly at my sides. It's a stance I've perfected over the years, and it tells everyone within my orbit not to fuck with me. Any passerby would see a confident man. Anyone who causes me to react this way knows differently. They see a man ready to burn you to the ground. I casually flex my hands to release some of the tension building from this conversation. The last thing I need is for John Ross to question my self-control.

"Yes, John. I have no private life for gossips to shred. The life they have access to is my professional one, and I provide for my employees as I would my family. No one messes with my family."

"And Tilly?"

"She's a goddamn saint."

His head turns to watch our women. "Why do you really want my winery, Lochlan?"

Revenge, retaliation, retribution all flash through my mind, but then Tilly's smiling face freezes when she turns back to check on me, and some of the hatred I've been holding onto melts away with her warm expression.

"Are you okay?" she mouths, and all the fight leaves my body.

Yes, I'll still avenge my past, but now there's a new reason, a greater reason for making dreams come true. Tilly. My lip curls even as my breath stalls. I nod once, and she raises her brow, assessing my stance.

"I'm fine." I silently mouth the lie with a smile before she finally believes me and turns back to her partner in crime. They're three glasses of champagne in, and I love how carefree she is in this moment. Tilly settles the rage rotting my soul even from twenty yards away.

John clears his throat, and I snap my attention back to find him watching me closely. Then I remember his question. "Tilly doesn't ask for anything. Not a damn thing, and she deserves more than I can give her."

"Good women usually do."

My shoulders droop to a neutral position as I give him my full attention. "It makes good business sense for my ten-year plan on all my boutique properties. I will rebrand some of the wine to fit each property, but the Ross name will remain."

"But why do you want my property in particular?"

As I stand before this man, my reasons for wanting his winery splinter and become twofold. "Your winery is one of the few remaining with a proven product whose event space still remains untouched, but you have the land for all types of events. Tilly needs to build something of her own, and I want to give her the opportunity."

"You want the winery for Tilly?" He seems genuinely surprised.

"It's not completely altruistic, no. I'm branding my boutique hotels into a once-in-a-lifetime experience. Food, wine, entertainment? They're all part of that experience. You have a proven product. I want your wine in my hotels."

"But," he prods.

"More than anything, I want to give Tilly the world, even if she fights it every step of the way."

"And your ex-wife?"

Bloody fucket. "Obviously, you know she's with Paul Mercer. In business and life." I force my tone to stay neutral, but sweat trickles down my spine at the effort of the nicety. "And I know they lease land on the northern piece of the property for their...endeavors." It is not common knowledge that Paul has mortgaged his entire empire on the success of that venture, so I don't offer it up. "I will not interfere with their ability to sell their product."

"You won't?"

"No. Quality control and vendors will need to go through proper channels for vetting, but I'll have a team that handles… that particular piece of our deal."

"You surprise me, Lochlan. Not many people do." He claps me on the back, and we walk down the dock toward the girls. As soon as we're close enough, I reach out to take Tilly's hand in mine.

Ross pulls Doreen to his side and smiles fondly with a fatherly nod. "Do you two have dinner plans?"

Tilly tips her head back to stare at me in silent question. *Do we?* her eyes ask. She turns back to the Rosses with a smile that sparkles brighter than pixie dust. "I think we're free, but you'll have to forgive me if I pass on the wine. I think I've hit my limit today." She giggles, and I tuck her into my side.

"We can go home," I whisper, not caring if John finds me rude.

Tilly lifts up onto her tiptoes and kisses my cheek. "I'm okay. It'll be fun."

"It's settled," Doreen cheers happily. "You'll come back to the winery with us. Our chef will prepare something casual, so no need to change."

Words are exchanged, but they fly over my head. I'm caught up in the normalcy of the moment. Tilly, so graceful and welcoming as she interacts with my colleague's wife. And John Ross, welcoming us as friends.

Events were never this easy with Christine. She fought to stand out, to be the center of attention. I realize now it could be off-putting for most, and I turned a blind eye to her behavior.

Tilly, on the other hand, goes out of her way to make sure she blends in and that everyone around her is comfortable. She works hard to ensure everyone in her sphere is having fun, and all I can see is her. While she's busy caring for everyone else, my only priority is...her.

"Ready?" Tilly asks with concern.

I'm concerned too, sweet Tilly. So fucking concerned that this is what love feels like, and there might not be a damn thing I can do about it.

* * *

"AUDRA TELLS us you're extraordinary at what you do. She also says you helped her recently with a fundraiser she's hosting. You're very talented. Have you always wanted to go into event planning?" Doreen asks over dinner.

That faraway look covers Tilly's expression, and a warm smile hooks at the corners of my mouth, knowing she's about to use the word magical.

"Gah! I've been planning weddings since I was ten years old. They're just...they're just the most magical day in someone's life. The one day where you can shine so brightly, you can't help but feel the love in every step you take. I can tell you what flowers are in season any time of the year. What songs get the guests dancing. How to keep one bridesmaid from hiding a shoe and thwarting another from dousing everyone in champagne while wearing the most uncomfortable dress that could rival any Halloween costume."

She glows with pride, transforming her from beautiful into the *magical* goddess I know her to be.

"That is oddly specific," John chuckles.

"You wouldn't believe the things that happen behind the scenes at even the most exclusive weddings. The shoe and uncomfortable dress were a recent experience for me." She winks, and I notice how John and Doreen relax around her.

"Well, you've most certainly found your calling, dear. Love looks good on you."

Tilly's fork pauses halfway to her mouth.

When I see it begin to shake, I lean forward and place a hand on her thigh. "It does, doesn't it?" I agree and give Tilly a gentle squeeze.

"It looks good on you too, Lochlan." John's words cause a riot in my chest that I try to ignore as he continues speaking. "When we met last year, you were an angry, bitter young man. I don't know if it's time or Tilly, but if it is her, the influence she has on you is astounding."

"Oh, no. Lochlan has always been amazing," Tilly interrupts, always my defender. "It has nothing to do with me."

Doesn't it though? My inner voice screams.

"I'm sure that's not true, my dear," John insists.

I clear my throat more loudly than necessary. He could expose secrets I'm not ready to face with Tilly just yet. "I'm afraid he's right." I move my hand from her thigh to the back of her chair. "You have softened me with your *magical* ways."

Her eyes crinkle at the corners, and before I can stop myself, I lean in to kiss her temple.

"Your wedding will be the event of the decade." Doreen beams. "And just imagine how beautiful their children will be. Oh my, I'm sorry. Do you even want children? I of all people should know better than to force that question on people."

"Yes," Tilly says as I watch her expression change.

"Dory, they're not even engaged yet. Don't push. Remember how much you hated that when we were dating?"

Tilly deflates under my arm, and she won't look at me.

"Oh, I know, but the wedding planner and the hotelier, John! Can you even imagine that event? It will be gorgeous."

"We'll make a great team. All the events we coordinate together will be amazing." Tilly smiles gracefully.

I know she's alluding to our future working relationship, but the flutter in my chest begs me to make it true personally as well. "We do make a great team," I amend as I attempt to contain the wild thoughts invading my head.

Tilly's head tilts as she takes me in. She's becoming quite adept at reading me, even with a mask in place. It comforts me more than I'm ready to acknowledge.

The evening continues with my attention divided between the *here and now* and the *what-if*s. The chef quickly and gracefully managed a delicious four-course dinner at the drop of a hat. But it's Tilly who holds court for most of the meal, regaling us with tales of bridal baddies and other odd wedding mishaps without ever being overbearing. The Rosses are drawn to her warmth, her kindness, her magic, and I wonder how I've ever survived these dinners without her.

Something Tilly said once rings in my ears like the buzz of a fly you can't catch. *"I need the happily ever after. I deserve the happily ever after, and I won't settle for anything less."*

If I can't give her the happily ever after, I'll lose her. And what will become of me if I do? My heart weeps, and it's the most painful thought I've ever had. The internal war of my past and present collide as Tilly and our companions laugh at her stories of love and lunacy.

Love and lunacy. That's what life is. You're either blinded by love or torn apart by lunacy. How in the hell is there no other choice?

CHAPTER 32

TILLY

"*A*re you sure you're okay?" My voice trembles and I twist my fingers together in my lap waiting for his response.

Lochlan shut down during dinner. Outwardly, he was present. He answered direct questions, he laughed halfheartedly at all the right moments, but there was darkness behind his eyes and an aloofness that told me his mind was somewhere else.

He watches the night sky for a second from the window of the town car Doreen insisted we take before turning toward me. "Yes, darling. I'm good. Everything went so much better than I could have ever expected. I do believe Ross will have a counteroffer any day now."

"Then what's troubling you?"

My phone rings, interrupting the moment. It's almost eight on the West Coast, but it's nearly eleven for everyone in my life. I dig through my large bag and pull it out to find Colton flashing on the screen.

"Shoot. It's Colton on FaceTime. I should answer."

"Don't let me stop you." He smirks.

"You have to remain silent. This"—I wave between us—"is still temporary." Lochlan's expression goes hard, but I cut him off. "I know it doesn't feel that way, but nothing has changed. I can't give up my dreams, and you can't...well, you have your reasons, but I'm not willing to put Colton in the middle of anything or put friendships and familial relationships through undue stress for something that has an expiration date. So please..."

"I won't say anything," he grinds out through clenched teeth.

My eyes close for a long second to gather myself, and if I'm honest, to block out the hurt I saw in Lochlan's expression before angling my body against the door and answering Colton's call.

"I'm getting married," he explodes the second his face fills my screen.

"W-What?"

"I'm getting married. On Saturday." I've never seen Colton so happy before. He's bouncing around his kitchen and speaking so fast that I have a hard time keeping up.

"On Saturday? This Saturday?"

"Yes! Where are you?"

"Ah," I hedge. "I'm in a car. How are you getting married in four days?"

"Everyone has a job to do. It's all taken care of. We're keeping it small, basically just family, so you'll need to get here soon."

"Do you need me to do something?"

His grin is so infectious I nearly laugh out loud. "No, just get here and celebrate with us. I'm trying to get ahold of Lochlan. He'll have to be my best man."

I see Lochlan open his mouth to protest out of the corner of my eye, but I hold up a finger out of Colton's view to silence him.

"Lochlan? He hates weddings. Why not ask one of your brothers? You have about twenty to choose from."

Finally Colton stops moving, and his expression turns serious. "For one, my brothers are acting like assholes, and I refuse to fight with them over this. And two…" He glances away from the screen, and I realize I'm holding my breath. "And two, Loch wasn't always like this. He doesn't like weddings, but he doesn't hate love like he thinks he does. He was burned—"

The phone is ripped from my hand, and Lochlan hangs up without showing his face.

"What the hell?"

"Colton doesn't know what he's talking about," he grumbles. He holds out my phone while staring out the window.

"Then tell me. Tell me why you're like this. You say you believe in love, but not the ultimate gesture of it. Why?"

"Weddings ruin people, Tilly. It ruined my parents time and time again. It ruined them while they were together, but they love and respect each other today as friends because they're divorced. They nearly lost themselves in each of their marriages. That contract? That vow? It broke or damaged a piece of their souls every time. When I—" he stops short, and ice fills my veins. "Text Colton back before he calls again."

This conversation is giving me whiplash.

The car pulls up to the Rosewood, and Lochlan has his door open before the vehicle fully stops. His phone rings once he's standing. I'd bet money it's Colton.

"What?" he barks.

There's silence as he listens, but his gaze finds mine when I step out of the car.

"You don't need me. Have your brother do it."

More silence, then Lochlan's face goes hard.

"Fine. But I will leave right after the ceremony. I have a gala in California that I cannot miss."

"Shit. What time is the wedding?" I hiss.

"What time is the ceremony?" Lochlan asks. "Done. Don't say I never did anything for you." He pockets his phone.

Did he just hang up on his best friend?

"How will we be in Vermont for his wedding and California for the gala? Colton is my boss, but he's also family. I have to be there, Lochlan."

"It's fine. We'll only miss an hour of the gala as long as his bloody wedding goes by quickly."

He might as well have stabbed me through my heart. "Listen, Lochlan." I fist my hands on my hips, prepared for a fight. "If you agreed to stand up with him on his—"

"Magical day?" he cuts in with a sneer.

"Yes," I fume. "If you agreed, you will do everything in your power to make it perfect, or so help me, you will not like the outcome. Do not fuck with me on this."

Lochlan's eyes go dark as lust clouds his expression. "My Pepper returns. Why do you have so much fire for everyone in your life, but then hide yourself behind the smoke?"

"What? Lochlan, I'm serious. Please don't ruin this."

His sigh is heavy enough to knock me over as he closes the gap between us. "I won't."

"Promise me."

"Darling?" That one word commands me to submit to him and holy Moses, do I want to. I stare up at him, barely lifting my face, but I can read every thought in his dark blue irises. "I'm pretty sure I'd give you the world if you only asked."

"But," I gasp. "But," I try again, but no other words come.

"Shh." He entangles his fingers with mine and leads us through the quiet resort toward the ocean and our temporary home. "You make me feel...*things*, Tilly. *Things* I haven't allowed in a very long time."

I don't know how to respond, but I squeeze his palm to let him know I'm listening. He stops us at the entrance to the beach bungalow, and a painful realization slaps me across the face. I've felt safer here, with him, than I've ever felt in my life. Fear of never being enough, never being loved, of being left behind has been so ingrained in my day-to-day since childhood that I didn't even know I felt unsafe until Lochlan Blaine, in all his boss-holery, showed me what it was like to be cared for.

Tears spill onto my cheek, and I quickly brush them aside, hoping he didn't notice.

I should have known better. He catches the last tear and cradles my face in his large palms. "I don't know what I can offer you in the future, Tilly. But I do know if you stay with me, I could love you forever." He shakes his head before I can respond. "But I also know what you need. My views are blurring, but they haven't changed."

I choke back a sob. "I know." And I do. He's allowing fear to guide him instead of love, and it makes me want to hate him a little. But I won't beg him to choose me. He'll break my heart, and I'll have allowed it. I knew that from day one. I chose my professional future over protecting my heart, and now I'll live with the consequences. "Swim with me?"

Lochlan pulls back and scans me head to toe. "Don't hide from me, Tilly. Not me. I know you're hurting, and I know it's my fault. If I knew I could give you what you need and not fear what it would do to us, I'd bend over backward to give it to you."

"But…"

"But I can't take the chance of having your love and then lose you in the eventual downfall."

"My heart hurts for you." This time a sob breaks free.

"Why, Tilly? Why do you allow other people's emotions to affect you like this?"

"Because emotions are what make you feel alive, Lochlan! You've walled yourself off so you don't get hurt, but you're missing out on every single joy life can offer. You live behind a mask of rigid indifference, but that's not what's in here," I say, pounding roughly on his chest. "I know it's not, and if you won't tell me how she hurt you so deeply, I'll never be able to stay. You don't have room for me in your heart so long as you keep it filled with hate for her."

"This isn't about her," he roars.

An overwhelming sadness threatens to crush me. "Isn't it, though? Isn't it all about her?"

"No." He shakes his head violently.

"Until you stop lying to yourself, nothing I say will make a difference. Your heart has endless potential for love. You prove it every day with your employees. With your sister and your parents. Even with Colton, but you're forgetting to love the person who matters most."

"But I just told you. I do love you. Or…"

"No, you said you could love me. It came with a condition. That's not love. And it's not what I was talking about. The person you have to love first is you."

Lochlan stares with a blank expression and misty eyes as I rise onto my tiptoes and kiss his cheek. "It's late," I say quietly. He nods as I ease out of his grip, and it takes every ounce of strength I have to walk inside and prepare for bed.

We move side by side in silence, and when the light clicks off, propelling us into total darkness, I know our end is near.

CHAPTER 33

LOCHLAN

"We have three more days," I plead. Tilly sits like a statue on the edge of the sofa, her hands clasped and eyes downturned. We've barely spoken since last night's disaster, and I'm spiraling because I don't know how to fix this.

An end was eventual, but I thought I had more time. I need more time. More time to prepare. More time with her. More time to force her to stay.

She speaks without looking up. Her hollow words cut like a serrated knife. "You got the preliminary contracts this morning, Lochlan. You're getting your deal. I'll come back for the gala on Saturday with you, but staying here for the next few days will only make things harder in the end. I told you..."

It's the first time her whispered words have choked up all day, and as fucked up as it is, it gives me hope. The monotone robot that came out of her earlier terrified me. It wasn't my Tilly. This emotional goddess is the one I need.

"There's been a connection between us since our very first meeting," she continues. "And I told you..." She swallows loudly, and I move to her side, but she doesn't meet my eyes. "I told you I fall too fast. That feelings would grow like a forest fire. The kindling is catching, lover. Let me go before I go up in flames."

"You knew even then?" I didn't think it was possible, but her shoulders slouch even more, and she seems so fragile. So... broken. Bloody fucket. How did I do this to her?

Her sad smile is more of a grimace when her gaze finally finds mine. "I warned you." She chuckles. The sound is heart-breaking.

"But I feel it too. I..."

"I thought about this all night, Lochlan. When you love, you love with your whole heart, I have no doubt about that. But you can't be in love with anyone until you love yourself, forgive yourself, and let go of whatever hate has your heart locked in a fortress."

Her phone dings, and she glances down, then stands before I'm ready.

"You're leaving?"

"My car is outside. We're parting on good terms, lover. I don't think you even realize all you gave me these past weeks."

"What?" It's hoarse, and my voice cracks with emotion I didn't think possible. "What have I given you?"

"You made me feel seen. And safe. You gave me confidence. You're an extraordinary man, Lochlan. I hope you find your way out of the dark or someone that can lead the way."

But you are. You did! I want to scream, but words stick to the roof of my mouth.

"I'll see you at Colton's wedding, but it's better for everyone if we pretend not to know each other. I'll make an excuse to leave after the ceremony, but everyone will be so busy they won't notice anyway. I'll go with you to the gala. I always honor my commitments, but please don't ask me to stay today." I watch in horror as a tear slips down her face, but she stands quickly.

Everything after that happens in slow motion, like I'm not really part of this scene. She grabs her suitcase. Moves toward the door. Turns the knob. Then, without a backward glance, she's gone. Tilly's gone, and for the first time that I can remember, my suit feels suffocating.

I'm tearing at the vest and the buttons of my shirt as my breath comes in harsh bursts. I'm dizzy by the time I've stripped down, but my breathing only accelerates.

My hands shake as I clutch my chest, crashing roughly onto the sofa so I can place my head between my legs. When that doesn't work, I slip to the floor and lean against the sofa's hard frame. What the hell is happening to me?

Time passes. Five minutes? Five hours? I have no idea. Eventually, I pull myself from the floor and pace the confines of a space that only yesterday offered hope. Now, everywhere I look, I see despair, and it sets fire to the rage roiling in my gut.

I lost myself once, and I won't do it again. Grabbing my MacBook, I'm about to go outside when I realize I'm naked, so I switch directions and head to the bedroom. Stomping like a pissed-off giant is more like it, and when I enter our room, I'm assaulted by the scent of lilacs. My heart threatens to stop as I tear open a drawer, but I pause when my hand lands on a pair of dark blue baby trackies.

"Bloody fucket." I curse under my breath but stab one leg into the garment, then the other and slide them up over my ass. Opening another drawer, I retrieve a shirt and slip it over my head. I'm on the warpath as I head outside, and then I'm forced to pause yet again at the sight of Tilly's hammock before me. Both of them.

I scowl so deeply that the tiny hairs of my dark eyebrows fall into my line of sight, and I march forward. I can't drop as dramatically into the damn thing as I want to for fear the bloody contraption will toss me overboard, but once I'm settled, I prop my head up on some pillows and get to work.

Or try to.

She loves this thing so much—I will figure out why. Placing my MacBook on my chest, I twitch and adjust my body, finally just feigning comfort. My nostrils flare as I huff in an exaggerated attempt to expel the nervous energy flowing through my body.

I don't dwell on the baby trackies. Or the hammock. Or why I need them both to soothe my frazzled nerves. No, instead I focus on the one thing that will bring me happiness. Revenge.

Pressing the green button on the bottom of my screen, I pull up Blake's name and press send. A breeze blows the hammock, and I tense as it shifts. Closing my eyes, I count to five. I will enjoy this. It's just a freaking floating bed of doom.

"Oh, for fuck's sake," I curse and sit up.

"Lochlan?"

Blake's voice startles me, and my body goes right while the floating death trap goes left. My arms windmill as I grab hold of my computer just before the floating fucker dumps me on my face.

"Bloody fucket," I growl, rolling over. Blake's laughter rings out loudly to my right, so I crawl that way and lift the screen to my face as I sit up.

"You look like shit," he barks with a wild grin on his face. "If you're calling to talk about whatever has got your knickers in a knot, you've got the wrong guy."

"There's nothing to talk about, except it's time to move."

His brows lift in sync with his hands, which he clasps behind his head. "Tell me."

"It will happen quickly. I got the preliminary contracts this morning."

"What are you wearing?" he asks as I cross the patio and set the computer down on a table.

I adjust the screen so just my torso and head are in view. "What?"

"What are you wearing?"

Glancing down, I squeeze my eyes shut to keep from rolling them. The T-shirt I pulled over my head is a Tilly special. It's heathered gray with bright yellow lettering that says *Relaxed AF*. I won't address the baby trackies.

"I'm relaxing," I deadpan.

"Since when, Lochlan? I've never seen you in anything but dress pants. Even at summer camp, you wore khakis. What's going on with you?"

"It doesn't matter. It's over now. Can you move on Mercer?"

He glares through the screen of his computer. The old Blake would have pushed. I'm not sure what damaged Blake will do. He's the only person I know who's more broken than me, and I'm sure that's the only reason he lets my attire go.

"I'll call Nate today. Has anything changed with your plans?"

"Like what?"

"You still want them shut down and sold off?"

"Yes. That's the entire point of bringing you in." If he hears the annoyance in my tone, he ignores me. Most people do. Most people, but not Tilly. She'd be right by my side, making sure I was okay. My jaw ticks at the thought.

"And all the events? The weddings? I investigated the venues last week. There are eight high-profile weddings happening during the two months it will take to transfer ownership to a new holder. Then there are a few smaller events—I'm assuming not too many because it will already be post-wedding season. You still want to fuck over all those innocent people?"

"It's not personal, and I'm taking care of the employees," I mutter, but Tilly's face is all I can see. How she glows when she's at these soul-shattering events.

"I know, but…"

"Give them the option to move to my hotels." The words don't taste as bitter coming out of my mouth as I thought they would.

"Loch?"

"Honor their contracts at my hotels. If they don't accept that offer, they'll get a full refund."

"From who?"

"I'll eat the loss."

"Dude, are you feeling okay? Who will manage these events? It's not like it's in your wheelhouse, and without Christine, you'll—"

"Without Christine, I will fucking soar. Tilly Camden's company has exclusive access to my hotels. Forward them her contact information, and she'll take over the second that fucker signs his life away."

"Is Tilly responsible for that shirt?" He smirks.

I scrub a hand over the scruff on my jaw so I don't curse him out. "She was."

"Was?"

"That's what I said."

"Is she also why you look like your heart was put through a wood chipper?"

"I do not."

"Have you looked in the mirror, Loch?"

"I didn't call to talk about my feelings."

"And yet you need to. Why is she in the past?"

"She's a goddamn wedding planner." Blake stares blankly, and I know this asshole will wait me out, so I continue. "Everything is so bloody magical for her. She wants a magical wedding. A magical life. A magical happy ever after."

My face throws an uncharacteristic duh expression when he stays silent, and the dick has the gall to chuckle.

"Most people want a happy life, Lochlan. Does she make you happy?"

"That's beside the point."

"Is it? Because you look fucking miserable right now. Well, more miserable. It hasn't been that long since I saw you last. If someone can get under your skin this quickly, you might want to stop and think about why."

"I know why," I roar. Pushing back from the table, I drop my head into my hands. "I know why," I say with more control.

"Why?" Blake's voice is even but no louder than a hoarse whisper, and I see a glimpse of the sadness he still carries when I lift my gaze to his.

"Because despite my best efforts, she got past my armor without even trying. Because she spends so much time worrying about everyone else, I had no choice but to worry about her. She sure as hell doesn't put herself first. Because even though she hasn't asked for a damn thing, I want to give her the world and I can't. I can't give her the only thing she'll ever ask of someone she loves."

"What's that?" he coaxes gently, but I still want to throttle him.

"A contract. A promise to stay forever."

"You love contracts."

"In business. But I've seen what they do to love."

"You're scared, and you're letting Christine win."

"The fuck I am."

"You allowed Christine to twist your vision in business and versions of what love can and should be into something dark and devastating."

"I saw what it did to my parents."

"Did you? Because when I've seen your parents, I've seen nothing but love. Maybe not in the traditional sense that you need, but it is the purest form of love. It looks different for everyone, Loch. Don't box yourself into a version you've constructed from pain, because you'll only set yourself up for a bitter, lonely future."

"I can't give her what she wants."

"You can't, or you won't?"

"Love, in its purest form, is a choice." Tilly's words blast my eardrums, drowning out whatever Blake is saying.

"I'll ruin her."

"Does she love you?"

My fingers go numb, and I realize my hands are balled into fists. I have the uncontrollable urge to move as a tingling sensation invades my limbs. I need to walk or run. To get away from these feelings clawing at my chest. A sharp pinch startles me into the here and now. My fingertips hold my earlobe painfully as my nails dig into the sensitive skin, and I jerk my hand away.

"We haven't known each other long."

"That's not what I asked."

I blink to ease the tightness around my eyes and my shoulders curl over my chest as if that will protect me from what he's about to say. I can feel the veins in my neck bulging, and I tug at the back of my neck to ease the ache there too.

"Lochlan?"

"She warned me that she'd fall fast," I say through the painful lump that's taken up residence in the back of my throat.

"And you let her." When I don't say anything, he continues. "Perhaps you knew you'd fall fast too? Why are you holding yourself back from being happy? If Shannon were here, there isn't a fucking thing that would keep me from basking in her sunshine. You have a choice, asshole. Not all of us do. Don't fuck it up because you spent too many years tormented by Christine's gaslighting. You have a choice."

His final words are pained and forceful. "You have a fucking choice. Choose it. Choose her. Don't let fear hold you back. If... If someone had given me that advice, maybe Shannon would still be here. Are you really willing to let her go? Allow another man to call her his? Because if you do, what will happen when you see her ten years from now with a family, and you're just a painful memory she tries to suppress? Can you live with that?"

My head is shaking no, but my mind is still at war. No. No, I can't be a memory she hides from. "But what choice do I have?"

"You choose her. Now. Tomorrow. Every day for the rest of your life, you choose her."

"What if she hates me in the end?"

"That's a choice too, Loch. Choose to be the man she deserves every day, and that will never happen. People change as years go by, sure, but choose to change with her. Make her the number one priority in your life every single day, and love will bend and shift with you."

"Will you ever choose love again?" I ask.

Blake's face contorts, and the pain in his expression causes a visceral reaction in my gut.

"I had it. I chose it. I choose to love her memory."

"Would she want you living this way?"

"I'll call you when Kingston Corp. has the signatures. Don't fuck up your life because someone fucked you over." His voice rumbles through the speakers.

"You too, mate."

His screen shifts as he slams it down, hanging up on me.

Bloody hell. Love broke him too. Why the hell would he tell me to choose it when I can see what it's done to him? To my parents? To me?

Because it's a choice, my conscience screams. It's a choice that you have. Blake's was taken from him, and perhaps he's right. If I don't choose it, does that mean Christine is still winning?

CHAPTER 34

TILLY

*C*limbing the steps of 528 Charter Oak feels more like a military drill than coming home. Each step is made with precision because if I don't focus on the mechanics, I'll crumble.

"Miss Tilly, nice to have you home. Where's your fella?" Monty, my doorman, asks as he leans against the building. When I approach the top step, he slides off his stool to open the door for me.

"He was never mine, Monty. Just a work acquaintance," I admit sadly.

"Some work you must do then. Is that why I'm supposed to call this number when you've arrived home safely?" He holds up a blue piece of paper with the Bryer-Blaine logo at the top.

Lochlan.

"He's a good employer, Monty. He's just making sure I made it home safely."

"Is there a reason he wouldn't get a confirmation of your safety directly from you?" he asks with a gentle smile.

"He's a stalker?" I offer playfully.

Monty shakes his head, but his eyes sparkle with humor.

"Nah, I didn't get that vibe from him. My guess is he cares. He cares a lot, and he messed up something big."

Hot tears press at the corners of my eyes. "No, Monty. He didn't mess anything up. He was very honest with his intentions. Are the girls home?"

"Eli went tearing up the stairs about an hour ago like her ass was on fire. The other two have been home all day waiting for you. Should I expect some Chinese food and a Ben & Jerry's delivery?"

Laughter that feels foreign is pulled from my chest. "I think that's a pretty safe bet, yeah. Thanks, Monty."

"No worries, Till. I won't even rat you out to Mable." He winks, and I fling myself at him. Monty has been here much longer than I have, but he's always looked out for us like a father figure standing guard.

He pats my head and gives me a squeeze. "In my experience, Tilly, men like that always find their way home. Just give him time." Pulling out of my embrace, he gives me a serious once-over. "And if he doesn't, I'll kick his ass."

I snort before I can catch myself. "Th-Thanks, Monty," I manage through a hiccup.

"You got it, girly. Now get upstairs. Your girls are waiting for you."

With a fortifying breath, I move on autopilot to the elevator. When I'm standing outside our door, I can hear all three of my roommates pissed off at Lochlan. A sentinel army ready to protect me at all costs, but hearing their disparaging account of Lochlan hurts my heart. He's not a bad man. He's a broken one. That makes this so much more difficult.

I know they'll have left the door unlocked for me, so I turn the knob and step inside. The second I cross the threshold, three sets of eyes find mine. As I drop my bags to the floor, the tears pour free.

Delaney reaches me first and guides me to the sofa.

"I'm going to kill him," Eli swears.

"Is she home?" I hear Mable yell from the floorboards. "That son of a fiddler didn't tell me. Monty! Monty," she yells again before her voice fades off, no doubt giving Monty a piece of her mind.

"Are you okay?" Hadley asks, curling up next to me on the sofa.

"I—I'm fine," I whine, but my head shakes no. A sure sign my head and my heart are at odds.

"What did he do?" Eli snarls.

"Nothing he didn't warn me would happen. He—we just want different things." I'm not sure if they can understand me through my broken sobs, but they all surround me. I feel them even if I can't bear to meet their worried gazes.

"You're home early," Delaney points out gently. "Is he not going to follow through with your deal?"

Now my heart bleeds openly. "No, he is. He already has. He must have started the second I walked out the door."

"Started what?"

"Work. He didn't come after me. He didn't even give me a second thought. He couldn't have." I choke on the painful words. "While I was crying across the country, he was—working. I… As soon as I landed, I got an email from someone named Nate that I needed to prepare for an onslaught of unhappy brides starting in August because their weddings would be turned over to me in a new venue they hadn't chosen. Lochlan's opened not just the hotels we agreed on, but all of them."

"It's the least the asshole can do." Eli harrumphs.

"Please, Eli. That doesn't help. He isn't a bad guy. He's…" I can't finish the sentence. Everything hurts.

"You're still defending him?" Hadley asks patiently.

"He didn't do anything wrong, Hades. He told me from the very beginning what he was capable of. I told him what would happen if I spent time with him, and it did. He never changed our rules. I did."

"You fell in love with him in two weeks?" Eli asks skeptically.

I cast a solemn expression her way. "E, if I'm honest, I think I caught feelings the second time I met him. If I'm truly being honest with myself, I knew he was dangerous after our first encounter because I already felt something I shouldn't. He knows what he can and can't give. I fell for him anyway," I cry. "And…it hurts. It hurts so bad because when his sun shines on me, I feel like I can conquer the world. Then he reiterated his truth, and it was like a dark cloud had drowned out the sun. I feel like I'll never be warm again. He made me feel like I mattered. Like he saw me in a room full of sparkling diamonds. He made me feel special."

"Oh, honey. You are special," Mable rasps behind us, causing us to jump at the sound.

"Jesus, Mable. You scared the shit out of us." Eli scolds, but is already moving to assist Mable with whatever she has in her hands. "What did you bring?"

"Breakup food. Isn't that what you girls do? Y'all were so busy cursing out that boy I didn't hear anyone place an order. So I did it. Ice cream too." She leans down and wraps a bony arm around my shoulders. "You're gonna be just fine, Titty. Just fine."

Meow.

"What was that?" Hadley asks, jumping off the couch.

"Oh, Pussy just followed me up. Nothing to get yourself all riled up over."

"Who?" Eli asks.

Mable points to a feral-looking feline prancing into our living room with its tail raised like royalty. "She just kept following me home from Fiddle the Bean, so I decided to keep her."

"And you named her…Pussy?" Delaney asks hesitantly.

"Yup."

Eli pinches the bridge of her nose, and I know this is my chance to sneak out. They'll be caught up with Mable for at least an hour. With all eyes on Eli, I slip off the sofa and scoot down the hall to my room.

Overwhelming sadness threatens to drag me under as I flop facedown onto my bed. With my head buried in a pillow, grief like I've only read about seeps from my soul and soaks the soft cotton.

Why does it hurt so much to love someone who can never love you back? After a while, I roll onto my back and pull out my phone. I know it won't be long before the girls come find me, but I can't seem to let Lochlan go completely. Not yet.

Scrolling until his name appears on my screen, I don't give myself a chance to back out. I press send and wait with my heart in my throat as it connects. It doesn't cycle through one full ring before he answers.

"Tilly? What's wrong? Are you okay?"

A tearful smile forms on my face. "I'm okay." My voice wobbles, and I curse myself for having no self-control.

"Till. Darling." His heavy breathing has me imagining him pacing the beach house. "I miss you."

"Why did you send a messenger to check on me? You have my number."

"Christ, Tilly." I pull the phone away at his harsh tone.

"This was a mistake. I—I'm sorry. I shouldn't have…"

"Do not hang up this phone," he bellows. "Let me finish." He's silent for a beat, and I swear all the blood in my body rushes to my head. "I wasn't sure you'd want to hear from me, Till. This is unchartered territory for me. And truthfully, the damn song threw me for a loop."

I nearly choke on my own saliva. "Song?"

"The song you changed my ringtone to. I nearly fell out of your bloody floating bed of doom."

"You—you haven't changed the ringtone yet? Wait! What are you doing in the hammock?" I sit up in bed, dragging a pillow to my chest. Clutching it to me, I hope it drowns out the wild beating that's raging like a freight train in my ears.

"I wanted to be close to you. To something that you love, anyway."

"Why?"

"Because the kindling was lit for me too, Till."

My breath is harsh as it drags through my teeth, trying to fill my lungs to drown out the painful beat of my heart.

"I don't know where to go from here," I admit. The words feel like razor blades slicing through my lips.

"Me either. But I know I don't like this, Tilly. Not at all. I had three more days with you."

He's still focused on our ending. There's no talk of an extension. No talk of a future. Just absolute certainty that we end. My heart shatters all over again.

"I'm home. I'm safe," I force out. "I'll see you Saturday."

"Tilly?"

"Good-bye, Lochlan." I end the call and turn off my phone. That was a mistake, but he owns my heart, even if he can't protect it. I'm weak to the pull of him in every way. Through blurry eyes, I notice Delaney leaning on my doorframe.

"Oh, sweetie." She crosses the room with open arms and tears in her eyes. "What happened?"

"He doesn't have room in his heart right now." My body heaves as I cry into my beautiful friend's shoulder.

"I found her," Hadley calls from the doorway.

"You didn't think you could hide forever, did you?" Delaney whispers.

"I couldn't hide from Lochlan. He wouldn't let me. He—he

saw me. All the time. Everywhere. He saw me." An undignified wail escapes, and my words are a mucus-y, slobbery mess.

My bed shifts on either side, and arms wrap me in love. The sound of something scraping across the floor catches our attention, and we all lift our heads to find Mable dragging a chair and plastic bags full of food into the room.

"In my day, we sat in night dresses on the living room floor, but if y'all want to pile into a bed, to each their own. I'll sit down here. I brought the tissues, the chocolate, the wine, and the food. We're all set for a good long while, so you just go ahead and let it out. No judgment from me and Pussy."

As if the cat already knows her name, Pussy waltzes into the room with an air of elegance.

Absurd and unconditional love surrounds me, and I finally break. I cry for not taking Lochlan's words at face value. I cry for the pain that someone has caused him. I cry for being so stupid in love that I allowed my heart to get twisted up in such a short amount of time.

I cry as conversations carry on around me, and eventually I drift off into a fitful, heart-wrenching sleep filled with dreams of promises and happy ever afters that seem to avoid me like the plague.

CHAPTER 35

LOCHLAN

I wake with a start and promptly fall on my ass. The floating bed of doom tried to kill me. Again. There will be a mark on my hip after this fall for sure, but then I remember what woke me. That bloody song. Tilly's text tone, because only Tilly would change the ring and text sounds to two different songs. I scramble to the grass beneath me, searching for my phone. When I finally find it, I stab at the screen, but there's no text.

Lifting myself into a chair, I scroll through the messages, but there isn't one. *Fuck.* Scrubbing the sleep from my eyes, I search my surroundings. I heard the song. I know I did. When continuing to scroll doesn't turn up anything, I turn the phone over as if it will unlock all the mysteries. Eventually, I succumb to the realization that I'm hearing a phantom. The phantom of Tilly. She's invading my days and nights now. With music.

My fingers twitch to the rhythm, and I watch them in shock. I hear the music. I feel the music. My thumb scrolls the screen again, this time searching for the settings. *What is this song that's playing on a loop in my head? Why am I still hearing it?*

I hover over a thumbnail of a man I don't recognize, and my phone comes to life. The name Thomas Rhett flashes, and the words "Things You Do For Love" scroll across my screen. Tapping the picture, the song begins to play, and my throat closes up at the realization that I not only know the words, but I feel them in my chest. My heart thrashes wildly in time with the happy beat.

What would I do? Not for love, but for Tilly? Is that the same thing? Does it matter if I'm doing it for Tilly or for love? Or for the love of Tilly? Can I be the man she needs? Bloody hell, I need a drink.

Images of our time together flood my vision. Tilly in the blue dress. Tilly in the purple dress. Tilly laughing with the security guard at the library. Tilly riding that bloody scooter. On the boat with absolutely no qualms about spearing the bait with an enormous hook. And Tilly in my bed. She's everywhere. Branded on my life like she'll never leave.

I tug on the ends of my hair until my scalp prickles. My ears ring like I'm learning how to hear for the first time, and I drop my phone to cover them, but it isn't enough. It's like Tilly's the notes in the song of my life. I feel her viscerally as if she were here with every strum of the guitar.

The thirty-second snippet stops, and I press the button to play it again. It doesn't last long enough for me to get it out of my system. Why is the damn song so short? Glancing at the time, I call Angie. It's just after two p.m. here—hopefully, she's still in the office.

"You're alive," she answers with a grin in her voice. I'm sure she was expecting me to check in multiple times a day, but it never even crossed my mind with Tilly here.

"How do I get a song on my phone?" I bark. The irony of calling my sixty-year-old assistant for help with technology is not lost on me, but I'm not thinking clearly.

"A song?"

"Yes, Angie. A song. How do I get it to play music? Is there an app or something?" I hear her shuffling papers in the background before it's replaced with silence. "Angie? Do you know or not?"

"My brother—"

"Jesus Christ, Nono. What are you doing in my office?"

"Visiting Kitty. But I'm here to help. My brother, who is notoriously music-adverse, wants music on his phone?"

"Yes," I all but growl.

"Any song in particular?" She's having far too much fun with this.

"Yes."

"Well, you have to tell me so I can help you."

"Just tell me how to get it, and I'll do it myself."

"No can do, big bro! That's not how it works. What song? I'll forward you a playlist." Is she fucking with me? She probably is. Perhaps I should have Googled it.

"'Things You Do For Love,'" I mutter tersely, but the words don't carry across the phone because she laughs.

"What song, Banny?"

"This isn't funny, Nono." My spine tingles, and my eyes ache with the beginning of a headache. "I said, 'Things You Do for Love.'"

"By Thomas Rhett?" If Nova were here, I swear her eyes would be the size of basketballs.

"Yes."

"That's a country song."

"I'm not sure why that matters, but okay?"

"Have you listened to it, Banny? It's kind of…happy? And about love."

To my ultimate shock and horror, I belt out the chorus but my voice cracks on the last note.

"What happened?" my mother asks, panic and fear flooding the phone lines.

"Where's Tilly?" Nova asks. There's an abnormal amount of static on the line, and I picture Nova wresting the phone away from my mother's ear.

"Put it on speaker," my mother demands in the background. Only my mother can use a hysterical tone and still command a room.

"Lochness? Are you okay?"

No. "Yes. Can you help me with this or not?"

"I mean, yeah. There should be a bright red button on your iPhone with a white musical note in the center. Just open that and type in the artist's name or song title, and you'll get an entire list. But Loch, where is Tilly? I'm sure she can—"

"Tilly went home. She'll be here for the gala on Saturday. Give Mum a kiss for me." I hang up before they can say anything else and collapse like my body has been beaten by the King's Army.

Then I search for the musical note.

Lightning bursts in the sky just before the clouds erupt, and God unleashes his fury like he's crying too. Ducking for cover, I run into the house. I'm completely soaked in just the few steps it takes, so I head straight for the bathroom.

It smells like lilacs in here. She's everywhere. I slink down to rest against the edge of the tub and stare at my phone. I long to call her. To hear her voice. To know she's okay. But I can't. Instead, I press play on Thomas Rhett and, for once, allow the sadness to overwhelm me.

* * *

"Do you care?" I belt out at the top of my lungs. At some point in the last three days, I've consumed every song Tilly has ever mentioned, an unnamed number of beers, and as many Skittles as my body can handle. My brain is apparently a sponge for Tilly knowledge because it easily recalls every single fucking word the woman has ever said to me. Including song titles.

So now, as I lie in the empty tub, accompanied by my last remaining package of Skittles, I sing The Cranberries. Tilly was right about them too. This fucking Irish lass has me crying harder than I've ever cried in my life. And I'm not even that upset about it.

I swing my hands like I'm a conductor and drunkenly know without a doubt that I've missed my calling. "I should have been a maestro." Imagining myself in front of an audience has me laughing until my stomach cramps. How did I not know how funny I am?

I lift my phone when a new song comes on—"I Can't Be With You"—and turn the volume up as loud as it will go. I'm cramming a handful of Skittles into my gullet when the bathroom door swings open and Nova walks through.

"Nono!" I sing. "Do you feel this song?"

"What the hell happened here?" she asks with wide eyes as she scans the room. I shrug like a fifteen-year-old but don't follow her line of sight. I know what she'll see. I've dragged it all into the bathroom at some point because I like the way Tilly's music sounds in this room. There's a pizza box from this morning. Or maybe it was last night? More than a few beer cans and at least thirty Skittles wrappers because the butler could only find the snack-sized packs.

"Do you feel it?" I ask again with a grin that hurts my cheeks even as my eyes burn. I have no tears left to shed.

"I certainly hear it," she shouts, spinning in a circle.

"Oh my God! What are you wearing?" my father asks, entering with my mother on his arm.

"Perfect." I suddenly wish the tub was full of water so I could drown myself in something other than Skittles. Opening the wrapper a bit wider, I tip the shiny paper to my lips and dump the remaining candies into my mouth.

Nova comes closer but acts like I'm a wild animal and approaches cautiously. "Did you separate your candies?"

"Nope." I pop the p and chuckle.

"What are you wearing?" my father repeats.

"Baby trackies," I say with a shrug.

"He's relaxed AF." My mother smirks, making air quotes with her fingers.

"Are you drunk?" Nova whispers.

"Drunk on love. Did you know there's a song about it? Drunk in love too."

"Lochness? What have you been drinking?" Nova bends down and holds up a six-pack of beer I never got to.

"Banny?" My mother crosses the room and picks up my phone. She silences it after a few attempts, and The Cranberries play only in my head. "Speak."

"Hello, Mummy. Or is it Mummies?" Closing one eye, I confirm there is only one of her.

She raises an eyebrow and waits me out. I cross my arms and sink lower into the empty tub. All the sugary candy I've consumed coats my throat in a thick slime that makes it hard to swallow.

"Banny, talk to us," my father pleads. He has always worn his heart on his sleeve. Nova clears a path to me, and I watch with amusement as he climbs into the tub and sits on the edge near my feet. "Do you need a hug?" He opens his arms wide, and chaotic laughter bursts from deep in my gut. He's wearing neon orange M.C. Hammer pants and a tight black T-shirt that makes him look like a pumpkin.

Oddly, I think I would like a hug, but I can't bring myself to say so. I only want Tilly.

"Banny? You're wearing a T-shirt with graffiti on it, and it doesn't look like you've showered in days. I don't think I've ever seen you with a beard in your entire life. What in God's name is happening here? Do we need to call a psychiatrist?" My mother's cool composure slips as she worries her perfectly painted lip.

Nova kneels on some towels while she rests her arms on the side of the tub near my head. Her light brown hair is in some sort of knot at the top of her head I want to tug.

"You stink, Lochness. Like wet dog. What the hell happened?"

With a heavy heart, I turn my sad gaze her way. "Love breaks people, Nono. Ruins them. I warned you."

"Banny, that is not true." My mother climbs up onto the counter and primly crosses her legs.

"It is. Look at you and Dad." I burp, and it startles Nova so much she jolts back and lands on her ass. I look at my mother, who is still so formal and poised, even with her son drunk in a tub, and my dark chuckle fills the room. We're a freaking hilarious sight to be seen.

I reach for my now-warm beer through a fit of laughter, loving how the bubbles tickle my nose. "I don't understand any of you."

"Understand what?" my father asks, glancing at Nova, who shrugs.

I let my head fall back against the porcelain with a thud. "Why do you do it? Put yourself through love over and over again to end up with the same heartbreak?"

"Oh, Banny. Love is one of life's greatest joys. Without it, we're all just going through the motions." The words sound funny coming from my slightly uptight mother. Is that how I sound?

"Greatest joys," I echo, testing my voice. Yup. I'm a stiff prick. "I'm a stiff prick." I laugh at myself, then take another drink.

"He's drunk," Nova whispers.

"No. I'm intoxicated," I gloat.

"I'll grab some water and order some food." We're silent as Nova hurries from the room.

"You love Dad, yet you divorced him." I point an accusing finger her way, but my eyes catch on the tip of my nose. I shake my head into focus. "You loved husbands two through seven too." Pausing, I count them on my fingers and drop my beer into my lap. "Oops." I laugh at myself, but my parents remain quiet as I lift the can and place it back on the side table. My gaze stays on the baby trackies that are now soaked in beer. "You were heartbroken every time, Mum. And Dad? Jesus. Dad lost himself completely after Lila died, and he's never been quite the same. You're both broken by love, but you still profess it's amazing. Why?"

My mother's face goes stern, and she slips off the counter to pace the confines of the relatively large bathroom. I'm so much like her.

"I do love your father, Banny. I've always loved him. I will always have love for him, but I've never been in love with him."

My head snaps to her, and it makes me dizzy. "What?"

"The same for me, son." My father smiles fondly at my mother. "We married so our fathers wouldn't lose their legacies. The economy was in a downward spiral at the time. Both our families' hotels were suffering greatly. The best chance either of us had at survival was combining the two. Kitty's father wasn't the best businessman, and my father was more interested in the image than the work, but neither family wanted to give up, so our parents, in a way, arranged for our marriage." I openly gape at my father. "I was never a great businessman either." He winks. "That's why Kitty is and will always be the brains of this operation."

"Don't sell yourself short, Ollie. You and your charisma played a large part in turning our fortunes around."

My head ping-pongs between my parents, their affection

for each other more confusing than ever. "You married for money?"

"Sort of. We'd been friends for years. We promised each other that our friendship would always come first. We'd do what we had to do, but we would always make sure the other was happy."

"We've always loved each other, Banny. And we built our life around that love. It may not be conventional, but it's true," my mother says with a fondness to her tone. "Love isn't finite. There are no steadfast rules for it, trust me. I've tried to find them, but love is fluid. It's different for every person and every situation."

"Your mother is my soul mate, Banny. She's my ride or die, and Lila was the love of my life. Love and how you wield it is a choice, son. Your mother and I chose to love each other as friends."

Turning a scowl on my mother, I shake my head, trying to force something to make sense. "But why do you keep opening your heart, Mum? You've had it broken so many times. Surely, it can't be worth it?"

"Do you love this girl, Banny?"

I glare at my mother.

"Do you?" she prods.

"I don't know if I can."

"It's really very simple. Either you do or you don't." She tuts briskly. "I keep choosing love because there's nothing like that first kiss. That first flutter in your chest. I choose love because I deserve it, and I know I'll find it someday." I shift uncomfortably in the tub as my ass goes numb from being in this position for an unknown number of hours.

She leans against the counter and studies my face. "Love isn't just about the highs in life, Lochlan. It's about how you react to the lows. Who has your back and who will pick you up. Loving someone is the greatest gift you can ever give. It's how you love someone in the quiet moments when no one's looking that matters."

"Is there heartbreak sometimes?" My mother continues. "Sure there is. That's life, and it's going to happen whether you let love in or not. But isn't it better to have someone to share the laughter, the heartache, the crazy ride of life with, even if it's only temporary? I didn't go into any of my marriages thinking about the end. I focused on the beginning, and every single one of them brought me joy in some way. I don't regret that. I don't regret any of them because they each taught me something different about myself. Finding what makes you happy in life is what living is all about."

I still don't understand, but when I lift my gaze, I find my sister staring at me with an odd expression. She enters the room with some water and a sandwich. "Nice shirt," she murmurs with an evil grin. "What's really going on with you?"

"Why do you have to be so damn perceptive?"

"I learned from the best." She nods toward my dad, and I let out a groan. The man sits there with the sunniest disposition. You'd think he was Mr. Fucking Rogers. "Why'd Tilly leave? I thought she was here until the gala?"

"Her forest caught fire."

Nova's expression curls the corners of my lips into a smile. "I'm going to need you to explain that one."

"She caught feelings," my father explains, cracking open a beer.

"Ollie!" my mother gasps. "Is that even cold?"

He takes a large gulp and shivers. "Warm as tea, my dear. Want some?"

"Not very likely."

"Focus, guys. So, she caught feelings, and you didn't?" The way Nova is glaring at me, I know this is about to get bumpy.

"Not exactly. She warned me. She told me coming here

would be a mistake. I'm sure it's in a song. Would you like me to sing it? I'm an excellent singer."

They don't appear to find me funny, which is ridiculous because I'm bloody hilarious.

"Was it a mistake?" my mother asks, finally resting a hip on the edge of the tub next to my father.

Instead of answering, I stare straight into my father's soul. "Do you still miss her?"

"Who? What are you talking about?"

I examine my father as he leans forward. So open and honest. I wonder if it ever gets tiresome.

"Lila."

My father's face contorts, and he taps his forefinger on his chin. I don't dare look at Nova. "Every day of my life," he finally says.

"Do you regret it? Loving her when you only had her for such a short time?"

"God no, boy. The great thing about love is that it goes on. It lives in the memories. I've had the love of two amazing women in my life. They've made me crazy. They've made me cry and scream. They've also given me the best gifts a man could ever ask for. They gave me you and Nono."

"I don't understand you, Dad."

"You don't have to understand me, son. But do you understand this girl?"

I nod, weighing his words.

"Why did you ask about my mom?" Nova whispers.

I stare at her sad eyes for a beat too long. When a tear slips free, I want to throat punch myself. Just because I'm miserable doesn't mean I want my family to be.

"I was just wondering how long this feeling would last," I finally admit with a painful gruffness to my voice.

"So, you do love her?"

"I've only known her for a few months. We've only really gotten to know each other the last two weeks."

"Like my Lila and me," my dad surmises.

"Do you love her?" Nova asks again, handing me a bottle of water.

My gaze bounces to each member of my family before falling back to my sister. "She got me to wear bloody baby trackies." I shrug like that's answer enough.

Nova's eyes sparkle as she regards me with a smile. "You're worried that she's like Christine."

"No. I'm not," I bellow. Unable to make eye contact with anyone, I start tossing Skittles wrappers out of the tub. "She's nothing like Christine."

"Then what are you scared of?" my mother asks with none of her usual primness.

My head throbs, and I close my eyes. How long have I been awake?

"I told you recently that Christine changed you long before she deceived you. Do you remember that?" Nova says.

I nod, but keep my eyes closed and feel her hand take the bottle of water and bring it to my lips. I drink greedily, washing down the Skittle scuz.

"Do you know what I meant by that?" Nova's voice wavers in my ears, but I fight the urge to sleep.

"No," I grunt, forcing one eye open.

"She was playing mind games with you from the day she walked into that hotel, Loch. The very first time I met her, she was diminishing the award you had just received for excellence in hospitality. That's something you worked your ass off to achieve. How do you think Tilly would have responded to that award?"

My head sways as my entire body smiles. "She would have thrown a bloody fantastic party."

I don't have to look to know Nova's smiling. "And what did

Christine say when you told her you were uncomfortable with her 'friendly' flirting with hotel employees?"

"I'll answer that one," my mother hisses. "She told him his emotions were his responsibility."

"What about when she'd come home hours later than she said she'd be?"

Jesus, Nova is really knifing me about this.

"That I always remembered things wrong, or I was making a big deal out of nothing." The words taste as bitter as the bile rising in my throat. "If we're going down this road, let's not forget when she gave me chlamydia and told me it was my fault." My voice is hoarse by the time I get the last word out, and the room sways.

Nova lays a hand on my shoulder, grounding me. The room stops swirling, and I stare up at her.

"Do you see what she was doing, Lochlan? The systematic way she twisted things? You loved her. You loved her hard, and that's the only thing you were ever at fault for. You simply chose the wrong girl. She spent years gaslighting you, and there was nothing we could do about it. We spoke up when we could, but when we did, she tried to turn you away from us."

I reach out, clutching Nova's hand for support. "That never would have happened," I vow.

Three sets of misty eyes land on me. "She was very good at what she did. They both were." My mother's disapproving tone is weary, and my father reaches out to comfort her. "We welcomed her into our home, our family. Nova is the only one who had concerns, and by the time we realized she was right, well, you were moving ahead with the wedding at breakneck speed."

I swallow the bile inching closer to an exit.

"What is it that draws you to Tilly?" my father asks, then encourages me to drink more water with a nudge.

"She's so strong, but no one sees it. She's the support beam of so many structures but never asks for a hand. She takes care of everyone around her effortlessly. She gives herself so completely and freely that it's hard not to…"

"To what?" he gently coaxes.

"To…to fall in love with her. Bloody fucket. I love her." My stomach lurches, and I swat Nova out of the way as a rainbow waterfall erupts from my mouth.

She gasps and jumps away. "Gross, Lochness. Jesus, how many freaking Skittles did you eat?"

"It seems my boy has been existing solely on Skittles and beer." My father chuckles while rubbing my back like I'm a sick child.

"Bloody hell."

"Well, what are you going to do about it, Banny?"

"I'll clean it up, Mother." I force the words out inbetween a dry heave. There's a reason I never drink beer. Christ, it's like the devil himself is trying to evacuate my body.

"Not the vomit. What are you going to do about Tilly?"

My head snaps up, and I swear my eyes roll around my skull like a pinball machine. "She wants a wedding." I see the concern in my mother's gaze. "Not today. I don't think, anyway," I say, rubbing the back of my head. "But that's the only thing she'll ever ask of me. That commitment. The promise to choose her every day."

"Is that something you can do?" Nova whispers.

"Tilly is not Christine," I slur and shake my head. "She's not."

"I know she's not. But do you?"

"Yeah. She…holy fucket. She's the other piece of me. The piece that's gentle and kind and carefree. The piece that sees the world and does everything in her power to make it better. She's the best part of me because she makes me believe those good things even exist. I… What day is it?"

Nova flashes a worried expression to my father, who

answers, "It's Friday. Remember? We were going to have dinner tonight."

I stand and quickly stumble out of the tub, but my toe catches, and I go sprawling across the floor. This might hurt tomorrow, but right now, it's funny as fuck because I narrowly avoided a vomit bath. I roll over with a groan and stare up at my parents' and sister's panic-filled eyes.

"I'm going to Vermont. I'm a best man tomorrow, and I'm going to sprinkle him with love glitter."

My belly hurts from laughing, remembering a text I got yesterday from Colton's brother. They have a wedding surprise for him, and I get to deliver it.

"Did he just say glitter? What the hell is he talking about?" I hear my mother exclaim as Nova and my father drag me into a sitting position.

Nova shrugs beside me. "Er, I mean, Colton has sent him about a hundred glitter bombs in the past." She isn't wrong, and it makes me laugh even more.

"Colton is getting married, and that's where I'll get my Tilly back." Raising my arm like a warrior, I point to the door. "To the plane," I shout in my best Irish brogue, though by the way Nova is staring at me, it probably sounded more like "twoler-poolar." So, I try again. "To. The. Plane?"

"You dump him in the shower. I'll pack his bag." My mother sighs.

My father and sister haul me to my feet.

"I'll call the pilot," Mum says from the hallway.

"You're smiling, aren't you, Mum?" My words get muffled as my father wrestles me out of my shirt. I swat him away like a mosquito when he tries to untie my baby trackies. "I'll do it myself."

He chuckles and moves toward the door. Just before I step into the shower, I hear him say, "He's going to be just fine, Kitty. I knew my boy wasn't immune to love."

Immune to love? That would make a good song for my buddy Thomas Rhett. I should call him! Can you just call a musician? I can. I'm bloody Lochlan Bryer-Blaine!

I whistle as I step into the shower, lighter and full of hope because that's what she does to me. Tilly is my sunshine maker. And my sun is finally ready to shine.

CHAPTER 36

LOCHLAN

"We'll be landing in five minutes, sir," the flight attendant informs me. I can't remember her name, and it makes me smile to know that Tilly would.

"Thank you. What was your name again?" I ask without lifting my head. My gaze hasn't strayed from the ring box I've been spinning between my fingers the entire flight. I should have slept. Christ, I probably should have passed the fuck out, considering I haven't slept in three days. But knowing I'm on my way to Tilly has me keyed up on a high only she can bring me down from.

I feel the woman pause next to me, and her voice is hesitant when she speaks. "Uh, Allie, sir?"

"Thank you, Allie." I tuck that piece of information away to surprise Tilly with later. It shocks me how much I want to please her. "Allie?" I call before she can walk away. "Could you do me a favor on the return flight?"

"Of course. What can I do for you?" Allie is an older woman, but our short conversation has apparently given her confidence and I don't miss her suggestive tone. I level her with a glare that could melt icebergs. "My girlfriend will be returning to California with us." I pause to allow that information to truly sink in. "I'd like to surprise her. Could you play the song 'Unforgettable' by Thomas Rhett when we board the plane?"

"You…you'd like me to play a song? But in the onboard instructions, it says no music. Actually, I believe it says a silent—"

"Allie." I try very hard to keep my tone neutral. "I know what the rider says. Please play the song."

"I'll make sure it's done, sir. Is that all?"

"Yes. Uh, thank you," I add as an afterthought because that's what Tilly would do. Have I really become such an asshole that simple manners are foreign to me? She nods in response and continues down the aisle. I spin the ring box again and recall words spoken only a few hours ago.

"Take it," my mother says, pushing a small box into my hands. "It was your grandmother's."

"Why do you have this?"

"I was going to wear it for the gala, but I think you should keep it with you."

"I'm not going to ask her to marry me today, Mother." Stumbling as I speak, I giggle like a schoolgirl. The beer is still wreaking havoc on my system, and my side aches from my fall. Pointing to the sky, I declare, "We have much to discuss. We'll need to live together first to make sure we're even compatible. Get to know each other, you know? Date, for fuck's sake. I'm only going to tell her that I can commit. To her. For her, I will. I'll choose her every day and every way. That rhymes." A hiccup hits and hurts my chest.

"Take it anyway. At least until you can have something made on your own. Just in case." She grins like she knows something I don't. It makes me frown, and with a massive hangover looming, my head aches at the slightest movement.

"Fine."

She shoves it into my hand, and I slip it into the pocket of my baby trackies.

Because yes, I'm still wearing them. Turns out, Tilly was right to buy them in multiple colors. I'm also wearing another T-shirt. This one says *Calm AF*, and it makes me chuckle. Only Tilly would put me in such things and teach me to enjoy it.

The ring box spins one more time and lands at an angle, begging me to open the royal blue velvet box. When I do, I can't take my eyes off the way the ring sparkles and shines. In the center is a large, princess-cut diamond surrounded by a thin ring of pavé diamonds, almost like they're holding up the center stone out of sheer will. *Just like Tilly.* The pavé diamonds continue around the slim band. As the light hits it, rainbows shoot off in every direction like beautiful sparkling fairies. It's magical.

Tilly is fucking magical.

* * *

"Jesus. What the hell are you wearing?" Colton claps me on the back as he pulls me in for a hug. Before I know what's happening, I get passed around to a bunch of his clones. The only one that gives me any breathing room is his younger brother, Ashton.

"Baby trackies." Glancing around the room, I notice the house is surprisingly homey for my charismatic friend. There are a ton of people I don't recognize, but no sign of my Tilly. Turning back to Colton, I stretch out a pain in my side. I'm probably bruised in more than one place from my fall in the bathroom.

"Please tell me you brought a suit, or I might have to kill you." I hold up a garment bag, and Colton takes it from me. "Today has to be perfect, Loch. Everything." I'm craning my neck to see around him when he finally faces me fully. "Are you hungover?"

"Soon on my way to being, yes. Technically, I'm probably still buzzed."

"You look like shit."

"Stop worrying about me. It's your big day, right?"

Colton takes me by the arm and leads me into an unoccupied corner. "Are you okay?"

"Truthfully?"

Concern crinkles his eyes. Colton Westbrook isn't known as a serious guy, but I think he would probably walk through fire for me right now. "Always. You know that. What's up?" He crosses his big arms over his even bigger chest and gives me his full attention.

"I haven't slept in three days. I've consumed my body weight in beer and chewy candy, but I'm here. For you. I'm not okay. But I will be. I fucked up, and I'm going to fix it. I'm out as soon as the ceremony is over though. I have to make something right."

"You've got it bad. Who's the girl?"

Just then, I catch sight of Tilly. She enters without noticing me and heads straight for a door at the end of the hall. When the door opens, she holds up a box I know well, and I forget how to breathe.

Clearblue. A pregnancy test just like the one Christine used.

My brain attempts the calculations. When the fuck was Tyler's wedding? Two months ago? More? What about Audra's? I can't focus. My vision narrows, and I sway on my feet.

"Loch? Oh, shit. Are you going to pass out? Come on, dude! I fought with my brothers over making you the best man. Don't let me down now!"

"I—I…" I can't swallow. I can't move. With unblinking eyes,

I turn back to Colton. Was this all a trap? Is she like Christine after all?

"Lochlan," Colton's harsh voice causes everyone in the room to turn, including Tilly, who goes ashen.

"I won't let you down," I force out. "I just need a few minutes. I'll be ready in time. I promise."

He searches my eyes and finally nods. Glancing around, he catches Tilly staring at us. "Oh, Tilly. Good. You're here. Can you take Lochlan to the lodge so he can change and get something to eat?"

She's shaking her head no, panic clearly visible as she shoves the now concealed package into the hand reaching through the doorway, but Colton doesn't see her. No one appears to see her.

"Thanks, Till." Colton bumps my shoulder. "Thanks for being here, man. I appreciate it."

I'm left gaping at Tilly, whose entire body shakes as she steps closer. We don't speak as I pick up my suit and follow her out the door. My mind is whirling with activity it can't comprehend.

She leads me down a dirt path, and the lack of sleep must be catching up to me because as she floats through the tall trees with birds chirping overhead, she looks like fucking Snow White.

When we reach a clearing, I can't hold it in anymore. "Is it mine?"

She stops but doesn't turn around to face me. In the span of three seconds, my entire world shifts. I'm transported back to the day Christine told me she was pregnant. The fear. The apprehension I felt. The pure joy. But standing here, staring at the back of Tilly's head, I realize the only joy I felt was for a child that didn't even exist. All the negative feelings associated with that fake pregnancy were because of Christine.

I can't categorize my feelings or emotions fast enough, but

I know with certainty that I want this, with Tilly. I want it all with her. It's because of her that I'm not crumbling right now. But when she turns, my world threatens to tear me apart.

"Is what yours, Lochlan?"

"The baby. Is it mine?" The knot in my shoulders eases as I wait for her answer. I want this. I really want this. "Did you do it on purpose?" *What the fuck, Lochlan?* I hear the words, but that's not even what I wanted to say. I'm tripping over my words, and my feet fare no better in my attempt to get to her, but she retreats with hands raised.

"Is that what you think of me?"

"No. No." It's all I can say. I can't shake the fog settling around my head, and I'm tongue-tied. I reach for her again, but she steps out of my grasp. That's when I see the tears. I'm cocking this all up. Again. Think, asshole. Think. Speak.

"I don't know who hurt you, Lochlan Blaine. I do know that I'm not her. I can't do this with you. Not today. It hurts too much. I'm sorry your heart is so battered you can't let anyone in. I'm sorry I couldn't be the one to reach it. But I don't deserve to pay the price for someone else's horrible actions. I'm not pregnant. That test was for my sister. I keep my promises, Lochlan, I always have. I told you I was on birth control, and I take it religiously."

"Tilly, I'm sorry. No—"

"Me too, lover." Tears stream down her face, and I move to draw her body closer to mine, but she pulls away. "There's the lodge." She points behind her. "I'll meet you after the ceremony. I've already told Eli. If anyone notices I'm gone, she'll cover for me." She turns to head back the way we came.

"Tilly. No. I'm…" My hands fist in my hair. I'm not used to feeling out of control, but the lack of sleep, the looming hangover, and the hurt on my beautiful girl's face have me spiraling.

"You need to hurry," she calls over her shoulder. "The ceremony starts soon." She picks up her pace, and I watch until she's out of sight.

"Fuck," I yell to the sky and am mildly satisfied when the birds scatter overhead.

"Well, that's one way to get your point across. What has yer pants in a tizzy?"

Turning, I find an old lady rocking in a chair on the porch. "Sorry," I call out, slowly moving toward her. "I thought I was alone."

"Mm-hm. Happens a lot 'round here."

Walking forward, I introduce myself. "Again, I apologize. I'm Lochlan Blaine, a friend of Colton's."

The woman scrutinizes me for a full minute before speaking. "I'm Rosa, but everyone calls me GG. This here is my mountain. I've gotta say, you're not what I was expectin'."

I glance over my shoulder. Is she talking to me? "I'm not? What were you expecting?"

"You've got a whole lotta hurt in that heart of yours." I'm still not sure what the hell she's talking about, and my head is starting to pound. "Tilly's a good girl."

"I know," I bark defensively. "I know she is."

"You know? Sometimes people go together like puzzle pieces. They just fit. And sometimes you have to wiggle those little fuckers into place. Tilly? She just fits."

I have no idea why I'm listening to this eighty-year-old granny, but she seems to have some wisdom that I lack and desperately need. "And me?"

"Well, that's up to you. But I suggest you wiggle that little fucker into place and get your girl."

"What little fucker?" Am I really cursing at someone's grandmother right now? What kind of town is this?

Slowly, she stands, and I hurry to her side, afraid she'll topple over. Then she pokes me. Hard. Right above my heart.

"This little fucker. It needs a shakedown to get rid of that bad juju you're carrying around."

My fingers rub away the sting of her bony but scarily strong finger. Rosa turns to face me, her eyes scanning between mine. "You're figurin' it out, aren't ya?"

"I think so." It's also possible that I have no goddamn idea what she's talking about.

The door to my left opens, and another Westbrook brother steps onto the porch. Halton, I think. They all look the same.

"Come on then," Rosa says. "You're lookin' a little green around the gills. I've got the cure for what ails ya."

I take a step to follow her, but Halton cuts in.

"Not a chance, GG. Colton needs Lochlan to stand up with him in twenty minutes." He turns to me with a wicked grin. "The last time she gave me a 'cure,' I blacked out telling the world my woes." He wraps an arm around the old lady's shoulders and helps her down the stairs. "You owe me one." He winks. "I just saved you a boatload of trouble."

The woman cackles, and I wince. Jesus. I'm not going to survive this day.

"Talk to yer girl, lover." My head whips toward her, and she cackles even louder.

"Ignore her, I think." Halton interrupts. "She can't help herself. There's an empty bedroom down the hall to the right. You'd better hurry though. Colton is more jacked up than normal."

I nod and head inside. Oh, Rosa. I am going to talk to Tilly, all right. I'm going to talk, and beg, and then I'm going to commit so fucking hard she'll never get rid of me.

CHAPTER 37

TILLY

"He looks like shit," Eli whispers in my ear. "I mean, he's hot as hell, but he looks like shit."

"Shh," I hiss. I try not to glare at Lochlan, but he's standing right in front of me and hasn't stopped staring since I sat down. Leaning into my sister, I cover my mouth. "He accused me of trying to trap him."

Eli gasps so loudly that our other sister, Emory, stares at us with a concerned expression from her perch at the altar. "He what?" Eli demands in a hushed tone.

I watch as my brother-in-law moves in close to Lochlan. With the scowl of a disapproving dad, his attention volleys between Lochlan and me.

"Look away," I mouth to Lochlan. "You're causing a scene."

"No." He glares back.

"You know, Colton said he smelled like a distillery and was broken up over a girl."

I turn in my seat so fast I nearly knock Eli out of hers. "What?"

"Colton said he's in love."

"Not Lochlan."

My body is an inferno. I can feel him staring at me, but I can't. I just can't allow myself to get sucked back in.

"That's not what Colton is saying."

"Eli? I'm begging you, please stop."

She lifts a brow but finally shrugs. "Okay. But what are you going to do on the flight? You'll be confined on a private plane for like six hours!"

"I don't know," I mutter and, despite myself, look at him once more.

His eyes are full of emotion as he mouths, "I'm not done with you."

The breath stalls in my lungs. It's the exact same thing he said when I saw him in New York. My fingers tingle and my eyes burn.

"Tilly?" Eli grasps my arm, and I realize I'm hyperventilating. Quick, shallow breaths are suffocating me as I drop my hands to my knees. My knuckles turn white, and I know I'll have bruises tomorrow, but I can't unclench my hands. I'm trying desperately not to rock in my seat as a cold sweat blooms on my skin.

My ears whoosh and ring with the sounds that normally calm me. The sounds of my happy place. Sounds that suddenly seem like they're underwater.

"Shit. Come on, sweetie. Let's go." Eli crouches as she stands so she doesn't block the guests behind us and tugs me up.

My gaze shifts to Lochlan, and I know he knows. I see it in his eyes. The way he shifts from left to right, trying to make an escape before the bride and groom, but I shake my head in warning. If he moves, he'll ruin Colton's day, and I can't have that. I also can't stay here.

My body trembles, and I follow my sister down the side of the aisle. The fresh mountain air hangs heavy in my chest.

"Geez, Till. Breathe. Breathe," Eli begs as she hauls me around the side of the barn.

Tears burn down my cheeks, but I can't stop them.

"What is going on, Till? What can I do?" she pleads. My sister pulls me into a hug, and I bury my face in her neck. "Shh, Tilly, shh. Honey, look at yourself. You love him," she whispers. "Like really, really love him."

I pull away and use my fingers to wipe the snot from under my nose before it hits my lips. Then I drag my hand through the grass because I have nowhere else to wipe it. I'm back to being disgusting, and I can't help it.

"Ugh, sis. Gross. If this is what love does to you, count me out. Since when did you turn into a teenage boy?"

I laugh, blowing unladylike bubbles from my mouth before dropping to my knees. Eli falls down beside me, and we shift onto our backs. We lie head to head in the grass and stare at the early afternoon sky.

"There's not even any clouds to look at."

Turning my head, I stare into my sister's eyes while my heart rate slowly returns to something that can almost be considered normal. "What do I do, E?"

"Oh, baby bird. I wish I could chew up the answers and regurgitate them."

"God, E. Talk about being a teenage boy." But her words do the trick because I laugh.

Eli reaches over and gives my hand a squeeze. "You might not like what I have to say."

"Isn't that what sisters are for? You have the unique opportunity to give unsavory information, and I'm obligated to love you forever."

She searches my eyes before rolling onto her side to face me. I do the same, just like when we were kids. "I know you view marriage as a contract. A promise to love you forever, and I understand. I really, really do."

"But?" I hold my breath, waiting for her to drop the hammer on me.

"But sometimes a promise is just that. It's a contract between two people. Even with a piece of paper binding you together, there's no guarantee the other person will keep their promise."

"You think I should give up my dream for him."

"I think you're beautiful and smart and so damn talented. I think I've never seen you fall like this before, and if you walk away, you might regret it for the rest of your life. You're still young, Tilly. Isn't it better to explore these feelings and see where it goes, knowing it might give you a happily ever after even if it looks a little differently than the fairy tale you created when you were ten? I guess the question is, can you be happy with a man you love with your whole heart if you don't have that promise on a piece of paper?"

"I...god, E. I don't know."

The sound of gravel shuffling under hurried steps and someone skidding to a halt has us both lifting our heads. My jaw drops open as Lochlan slides to a stop, but he's off-balance and has to windmill his arms to keep from toppling over.

My three-piece-suit-wearing stiff is as disheveled as I've ever seen him, and it makes me smile.

"I think you do that to him," Eli whispers.

His gaze never leaves mine as he crosses the lawn to where we lie at the side of the barn. When he's close enough to touch, I notice he's looking a little more peaked than earlier.

"Are you okay?"

"Me? Why did you leave? What's wrong? Why couldn't you breathe? Why are you crying?" He spits out question after question, slurring some of the words, but doesn't give me time to answer. His hand is resting strangely on the right side of his abdomen.

Pushing to stand, I really look at him. "Lochlan? Are you okay? You don't look so good."

"I—I haven't slept in a few days, I think."

My brows raise as he sways on his feet, and I rush to his side. Wrapping my arm around his middle, I hold him tight.

"Is he okay?" Eli asks at my other side.

"Have you been drinking?" I ask him.

"Not today."

"Ah, okay. Did you say good-bye to Colton? Should we head to the airport?"

"You're coming?" The shock on his face has my heart softening.

"I told you I would. Should we go? Do you have a car here?"

He shakes his head and pulls out his phone. He presses a couple of buttons and looks at me. "Do you need to say good-bye?"

I glance at Eli, who shrugs. "No, Loch. No one will notice I'm gone until after the party, and if they do, Eli will tell them I wasn't feeling well."

"Bloody fucket, Tilly. What is wrong with everyone? How can they not see you?" He tries to sound stern, but I'm even more convinced now that he's not feeling well.

"Should I get Emory?" Eli whispers.

"The doctor?" he slurs.

Standing this close to him, I need to crane my neck to meet his eyes. "Yeah, my sister. Should we get her or are you…"

"Pepper."

I gasp at the now-familiar nickname that makes my heart ache and drop my gaze, but he continues.

"I haven't slept in many hours. I ate too many Skittles and drank too many beers. I'll sleep on the plane. After we talk."

I turn at the sound of a car coming up the driveway and see an SUV with tinted windows. That must be Lochlan's ride.

"Skittles?" Eli giggles. "Did Mr. Stiffy just say Skittles?"

"Shh. Help us get to the car without anyone seeing."

"Are you kidding? Colton is in heaven. You could have a three-ring circus around you, and no one would notice you."

"I would," Lochlan vows. "I'll always notice her."

My heart squeezes, and Eli pats his arm. "I think you might, big guy. But if you hurt her again, I'll castrate you with a dirty butter knife and then cram it up your very British arse. Hear me?"

Lochlan narrows his eyes, then closes one like he's seeing double. "I hear you," he finally says with a hint of appreciation on his handsome, scowling face.

We get him in the car with a final shove, and I turn to hug Eli.

"He does see you, you know," she says. "Just promise me something?"

I kiss her cheek and head around to the other side of the car. "What's that?"

"Promise me that you'll choose love, regardless of how the future might look. Choose love today so you can be happy tomorrow with no regrets."

I swallow a hockey puck of emotion. "No regrets. Got it. I'll do my best."

"Love you."

"Love you too." I climb into the car and find Lochlan slumped against the door. Leaning forward, I tap the driver on the shoulder. "We're all set."

"Very good, miss." He puts the SUV in drive, and we head down the backside of the mountain toward a future I'm not sure I'll ever be ready for.

CHAPTER 38

TILLY

The ride to the airport is short, and Lochlan barely moves. Even as we turn left onto a dirt road that eventually spits us out on a private, grassy airfield, he sleeps through the bumps and divots that toss me around.

"Lochlan?" I nudge his shoulder, and he flops over into my lap with a groan. I cup his cheek and try again. "Lover? We're here."

He opens groggy, hazy eyes and blinks to bring things into focus. When he finds me, his expression of immense relief is so tangible I swear I could reach out and touch it. "You're here."

"Yeah," I say with a heavy heart full of concern. "We have to get on that plane." I point behind him, and he nods. I swear I feel the effort it takes him to heft his large frame from the car, and I contemplate calling my sister after all.

But when I step from the car, he's holding out a hand for me with the most infectious smile I've ever seen on any person, ever. All thoughts fly from my mind as I draw closer. He's the fisherman in our relationship, and he can reel me in with a single glance.

He moves slowly but of his own accord toward the plane.

He's sweating by the time we reach the stairs though, and I frown when he murmurs, "Up you go."

My protective streak wants to force him up first so I can catch him if he falls, but he motions with his hand, and I obey, thankful when I feel him at my back. I've never been on a plane this small before, and my heart rate picks up as I take the last step.

Then I freeze. Thomas Rhett's "Unforgettable" plays loudly over the sound system, but it's Lochlan's voice that has tremors coursing through my body. He's singing. And singing well, if not a little behind the beat.

"I feel it," he whispers in my ear. "The music. I feel it now."

Slowly, and with purpose, I turn to face him. We're nearly nose to nose with him on the lower step. I notice he's panting, and I take his hand, leading us both to the nearest seat.

"I don't know why everyone else allows you to fade into the background, but you shine for me, Tilly. You are unforgettable." Holy swoon! "I think I'll pass on The Cranberries from now on though. That bloody lady can make a statue cry." He rests his head back with a heavy sigh.

After a beat, he turns his head to me and it's like watching the battery on your cell phone slowly deplete.

"Why don't you sleep?" I suggest. "We can talk when we land."

He lays his hand on his thigh with his palm facing up as we race down the runway. I notice he doesn't reach for me, but it's an olive branch. He's allowing me to make the connection or not, and my heart weeps for this man. Without hesitation, I reach over and place my hand in his. He gives it a squeeze, and his shoulders droop forward.

"Tilly, I…"

So much for talking later. "Lover," I say gently and melt at his expression.

"Say it again," he pleads with his eyes closed.

My shoulders shake with laughter. Such a small thing makes him happy, and I do that for him.

"Lover."

Nodding, he pulls our twined hands up to his lips and places gentle kisses on my knuckles. The last of my reservations fade away and I tell him my truth. "I told you in California that I was leaving because I was catching feelings." Lochlan's foggy eyes flick open and land on mine. "But that wasn't quite true."

He stills, and I feel his heartbeat beneath our clasped hands. "It wasn't?"

I shake my head, gathering the courage of every heroine I've ever cried for in movies, and tell him my truth. "The thing is, somewhere, somehow, those feelings caught fire and steamrolled right over all my intentions."

Lochlan's brow furrows, and he uses his free hand to tug on his earlobe. "What are you saying, Till?"

"I—I'm saying I can't catch feelings because they already caught me. I love you, Lochlan. You're my grumpy, stiff, suit-wearing, anti-wedding, generous, kindhearted future. I need you more than I need my security blanket."

He shakes his head, still tugging on his earlobe. "I don't understand."

"I want you however I can have you, Lochlan. I want you more than I need a piece of paper tying you to me. A promise to love is the contract our hearts will make. You, and you alone, are what will make me happy for the rest of my life. I'm sure of that."

"Tilly," he moans and lowers his free hand to his right side. It's the second time I've seen him clutch at it.

"Are you in pain?"

He shakes his head wildly. "Darling…" His voice is strained. "You're willing to give up your dreams? For me?"

"Dreams change, Lochlan. It isn't a dream anymore if you're not in it."

"I, you…" He adjusts in his seat, and I notice how sallow his skin is. Leaning over, I kiss his cheek. It's a move meant to calm him, but the second my lips touch his skin, I know something's wrong.

"Lochlan?" Raising my hand to his forehead, I hold it to his heated skin. "Baby, you're burning up. You have a fever."

"No. I'm severely hung over and haven't slept in days."

Reaching up, I press the call button, and an attendant arrives at our side a second later. This is more than a hangover, I'm sure of it.

"Do you have a first aid kit? I need something for his fever," I explain.

The woman's eyes go large as she peers between us. "Of course. I'll grab it right away."

"Thank you, Allie." Lochlan smirks but doesn't open his eyes.

"You know her name?"

"You've left quite the mark on me, darling. Your imprint has changed my DNA."

Allie appears with a bottle of Tylenol and a glass of water. I take them from her with a grateful nod and hand Lochlan two pills. When he places them in his mouth, I offer him the water. He drinks it like a man lost in a desert, then hands the glass back to Allie.

"Thank you," we say in unison as she walks away.

"Sleep, lover. We have plenty of time to talk later."

His head barely moves, but I know he's asleep when his grip on my hand loosens. I hold tighter as fear creeps into my heart.

* * *

LOCHLAN STIRS with his head in my lap, but only to wrap his arms tighter around my legs like he's afraid I'll vanish. My concern for him outweighs the uncertainty of our non-relationship. I mindlessly run my fingers through his hair, and he moans softly.

Spread out on a leather couch in the center of the cabin, he's barely moved since we changed planes in New York. Moving him from the tiny five-person vessel that transported us to New York was easy. Rousing him from a deep sleep after landing was nearly impossible and required the help of the pilot and grounds crew.

I had used the fifteen-minute layover to text his sister. She confirmed that he was, in fact, hungover and seriously sleep-deprived, but I can't shake the unease of it being something more.

To my left are the clothes he'd apparently traveled to Vermont in. His baby trackies and *Calm AF* T-shirt. I try not to read too much into that. After all, I word vomited my feelings but cut him off before he could reply. Truthfully, I wasn't prepared for him to tell me we'll always have an expiration date. I probably never will be, so I'll live in this fantasy world for as long as I can.

Allie approaches with Lochlan's tuxedo jacket on a hanger. Luckily, she was able to press it for us and ensure he'll be presentable when we land. Our timeline is tight, and we'll already be arriving late, so I'm doing everything I can to save time.

"We'll be landing soon. Can I get you anything else?" she whispers, then carefully places Lochlan's jacket on a hook beside me.

"No, I think we're fine. Thank you. I need to change though. Do I have enough time?"

She glances up at the clock on the wall next to the cockpit and nods. "If you hurry."

It's no small feat to extract myself from Lochlan. He's an octopus. Every time I get one arm removed, the other clamps down in its place like a weird game of tag. Finally, I shift him onto his side. The low groan that escapes raises my blood pressure to uncomfortable levels, but I ease out of his grip and hurry to the small room at the back of the plane where Allie hung my dress.

It takes me less than ten minutes to change and do a quick refresh of my makeup. The perks of being a bridesmaid baddie are all the lovely dresses I'm acquiring, but I chose the beautiful lavender dress I'd worn in New York. I have no idea if Lochlan will remember it, but it felt symbolic for me to wear it tonight.

I take one last glimpse in the mirror, and when I'm satisfied, I shake my arms like I can force all the nervous energy to fly from my fingertips. Tonight is important for Lochlan and for Bryer-Blaine. I'll play my part. I'll make sure everything goes off without a hitch, and then I'll pray to the goddess of love that my heart will survive whatever comes next.

CHAPTER 39

TILLY

*A*s soon as the door of the plane opens, everything moves at warp speed. Lochlan woke just before we touched down, and while he isn't a hundred percent, his mind seems a little clearer. That's something, at least.

"Are you still having pain in your side?" I ask as we descend the stairs.

"I think I'm off Skittles for life," he calls over his shoulder.

The wind picks up, making it hard to hear, so I lean in closer, inhaling his unique scent. Oranges and ocean breezes. My new aphrodisiac.

"I'm fairly certain my body has become allergic since I ate my weight in them in the tub a few days ago."

My mouth opens, then closes again. There's no way I heard him correctly. I tug on his hand to ask when a flash of golden-brown hair and a shimmering gold dress catch my eye. Lochlan's sister runs toward us as fast as her four-inch heels can carry her. Honestly, her speed in those shoes is impressive.

"Nova?" Lochlan uses his fingertips to rub his eyes like she's a mirage.

"Come on, Lochness. We've got to hurry." She grabs for his

free hand and, with shocking strength, drags both of us toward a waiting car.

"What's wrong?" I ask as she reaches the black limo and opens the door before the driver has even rounded the car.

Nova turns and does a double take as she examines Lochlan for the first time. "Oh my God, are you sick?"

"No." He swats her away and ushers her into the car at the same time as I say, "Yes, he is."

Glower is an expression Lochlan has perfected. If you look up glower in the dictionary, you will see a picture of Lochlan's face as he uses the power of intimidation to force us into the vehicle. Once we're all seated, he undoes the buttons of his vest and absently rubs his side.

"You are sick," Nova gasps, pointing at his vest. I'm thankful for the backup, but there's something in Nova's expression that tells me Lochlan's flu isn't the only thing I need to be worrying about.

"What's going on, Nova? Why is the driver breaking every speed limit right now?"

My skin breaks out in goosebumps. My body is reacting before my mind is even aware of the danger.

"It's Christine," she says nervously. Her pinkie finger lands in her mouth as she attacks the cuticles and avoids Lochlan.

His nostrils flare, and his eyes go cold, hard, and scary as hell. I fight the urge to shrink into the background. If I'm going to stand by his side as a partner, I'll do everything in my power to be the kind of woman who demands respect.

"Who's Christine?" Okay, so outwardly I might be able to fool strangers, but the way my voice quivers is a dead giveaway of my inner turmoil, and Lochlan knows it. Before my next breath, he grabs my leg and pulls me as close to him as I can get. The silky dress I'm wearing allows me to slide across the leather with ease.

"She's his ex—"

337

"My ex," Lochlan interrupts. "Christine is my ex."

"Lochness?" Nova's questioning tone has me wishing I could escape the car. My body is in fight or flight mode, and I have no idea what the battle is.

Lochlan's expression is fierce as he relays a message without words to his sister. "What has she done?"

This time, when he speaks, I do shrink in on myself. I've never heard him so cold. A shiver runs through my body, and I can't control the way my body shakes in response. Lochlan drags our clasped hands into his lap and uses his free hand to run soothing circles over the inside of my wrist. It's an odd sensation to be coddled when the tension in the air is so thick that I fear we'll suffocate on it.

"Nova," Lochlan snaps, and his sister and I jump. I can tell it doesn't happen often by the expression on her face.

Her lip quivers for a moment, then fire dances in her eyes. She squares her shoulders and faces her brother head on.

"Don't you dare kill the messenger, Lochness. I'm here to help you."

The air shifts, and he reaches across the small space to hold her hand. "I know. I'm sorry. What are you helping me with?" He's deflating faster than a balloon on prom night and suddenly, whatever is going on with Christine is not nearly as important to me as he is.

I place my hand on his forehead as you would with a child and shake my head. He still has a fever. "Lochlan, you're sick."

He squeezes my hand but never takes his gaze off Nova. "What is she doing?"

"She's at the g-gala," she stutters, and her gaze darts all around the car like she's nervous about his response before landing back on Lochlan. "She's talking up their wine and how great Ross has been. She's throwing out all these charities they're supposedly helping."

"Bloody fucket," Lochlan curses, and I feel the venom in his words. "She's positioning herself so whoever acquires Ross Wines will look like a predator if they force her out."

Nova nods, but from the way she's biting her lip, I know she hasn't said the worst of it yet. "That's not all." Lochlan stiffens but waits. The car rolls to a stop at the winery steps, and Nova whispers, "She's pregnant. Really pregnant."

No one moves. By the eerie silence, I'm betting no one is breathing either. Lochlan's hand lands on the door handle. "Is that it?" he asks, opening the door. When Nova nods with teary eyes, he gracefully unfolds himself to stand beside the car. He reaches in to help Nova, then me.

"Lochlan?" I ask.

"We stick to the plan, Tilly. Got it?"

No, I want to scream. No, I don't understand any of this. But like the love-sick fool that I am, I agree. "Got it."

Nova and I flank Lochlan on either side. Arm in arm in arm, we enter the great hall, and all heads turn toward us. My skin prickles with the need to flee, but Lochlan pulls me tighter against him as Nova slips away to join their parents.

"Let them see you, Tilly. You have no reason to hide," he murmurs. "You're beautiful, and you're mine." Whether for show or for me, his words have the desired effect. With Lochlan clutching my hand, I play the role of his girl, and it gives me the confidence to hold my head high.

"And here he is, the man of the hour with his lovely girlfriend, Tilly Camden." I recognize the voice as John Ross's, but the spotlight that crosses the room like a shimmering snake and lands directly on us has my mouth going dry. I stand like a deer in headlights as Lochlan uses the back of his hand to wipe his forehead. A reminder that he's not feeling well. But like the leader he is, he propels us farther into the room, toward the podium where I finally see the Rosses.

I realize halfway to the stage that Lochlan intends to lead us up onto it, and I stop moving.

"I have to speak, Tilly."

"Uh-huh."

He drops his gaze to mine, and the hard edge he's had since Nova met us at the airport softens. He pulls me in for a hug and whispers in my ear. "Go find Nova and my parents. I'll meet you after I give my speech."

I hold him tighter, and he winces. "You need to see a doctor."

"I need to make this presentation. Then I need to sleep with you by my side for about a week. I'm fine. Go find Nova, and don't..." He pulls back a few inches to scan my eyes. "Don't talk to anyone you don't know."

There's that painful awareness. The horror music that disturbs your psyche before your conscious brain catches up to the danger, but I can see Lochlan fading fast, so I do as he asks. "Okay. But as soon as you're done, you're going to a doctor."

"Will you play nursemaid?"

Someone near us chuckles, and the room around us comes into stark focus. It's so easy to get lost in the vortex of Lochlan Blaine that I'd completely forgotten we had an audience.

"For as long as you'll have me." I reach up on my tiptoes and kiss his cheek before stepping aside and allowing him into the swarm of people congratulating him and patting his back as he passes.

With all the attention back on the man of the hour, I relax. I'm able to fade into the background and observe. He's like a magnet, drawing all eyes to him. All eyes except for the two that are glaring with poison-filled daggers and headed straight for me.

CHAPTER 40

TILLY

A blond woman waddles toward me with one hand under her enormous belly like she's holding it up and considering using it as a weapon. Her pale blue eyes scream murder as she uses her free hand to propel herself forward like a speed walker at the mall.

Her chest heaves with the effort, and when she gets within a few feet, it's like someone flipped a switch. Gone is the nasty troll ready to behead me, and in her place is an almost contrite, friendly expression.

I immediately know two things about this girl. One, she's Lochlan's ex. And two? She's a narcissistic loony bird who can be trusted as far as a fart flies.

"Hi," she says with sickeningly sweet undertones. "I'm Chrissy. It's so nice to finally meet you."

I begrudgingly hold out my hand to shake hers. "Tilly."

Lochlan's voice rings out over the speakers, and I turn to find his face red as a tomato and his voice a choked staccato. Christine seems to realize her time is limited because she pushes on. "Listen, I'm sure you've heard all the terrible things about me, but I'm certain you're smart enough to realize there are always two sides to every story."

I stand ramrod straight, suddenly pissed off that I don't know anything about this demon hoe except that she is, in fact, a demon hoe. I can feel it in my bones. "What can I do for you, Christine?" Her name has a bit more venom in it than I'd intended, but it does the trick. Her walls go up, and I watch as she changes masks yet again.

"Listen, Tilly, I'm not here to fight with you or Lochlan. He's a great guy, and I hope you two will be very happy together. I just felt the need to warn you. We lost our marriage long before we lost our baby." All the air in the room gets sucked into a vacuum inside my lungs. "It was a terrible loss, and we all felt it." She rubs her belly. "It hasn't been that long. I know we both wanted this baby." She places both hands under her stomach to emphasize her point.

How long? Is this Lochlan's child? My head snaps to his, and I see him struggling, but Christine gets louder, and some of the audience's attention turns to us.

"I blamed him for the loss. I know that wasn't fair, but when we lost our little boy, we were in the middle of a very loud argument. He'd lost control, he was shouting. I was emotional. I begged him to stop, but he just kept going, and then the cramping began."

I don't believe her for a second. I might have, right up until she said he lost control. People like Lochlan don't lose control. They walk away. They gather information. They address things head-on, sure, but never in the way she's making it sound.

"What does this have to do with me?" My gaze strays to her stomach again, and I feel her smirk. She knows I'm questioning whose baby it is.

Where the hell is Nova?

"I want to warn you, woman to woman. It isn't fair of him to string you along when there will be so many changes in the future. I've been the rebound girl before. I don't want that for you."

"You don't even know me," I hiss, attempting to keep my voice low.

Christine just gets louder. "I know he bought the winery to punish me. To try and force my hand to come back to him. But he's abusive, Tilly. Verbally and emotionally. He's a master at manipulation. I can't have that for me or our child."

Our child. There it is again, but there's something in the way she says it that won't allow me to believe her. Or is that wishful thinking on my part?

We have a small crowd around us now. Everyone's turned to listen to her tale, but I know in my heart of hearts it's just that—fiction. A story meant to hurt and punish. I've dealt with mean girls like her before, but now she's going after Lochlan, and I see red.

"He's going to force us to sell. We'll lose everything, and our child and I will be forced to depend on him and his trust fund. Lochlan is out to hurt me, Tilly, and he's using you to do it. Don't you see?" She has tears in her eyes, but I can't stop staring at the hitch in her lip. Like she's enjoying this too much not to smile.

I don't notice that the room is silent until I'm shoved forward when Lochlan stumbles into me. He sways at my side. "That is a bloody fucking lie, you raging lunatic."

He reaches me at the same time as his parents do, and we create a wall facing batshit crazy in human form.

"Tilly, none of that is true. Her husband wouldn't let me through," Nova hisses.

Her husband? What the fuck is going on? I pull out of Lochlan's grasp, not because I don't trust him, but because I don't have all the details and I can't think.

"Tilly?" Lochlan's slurred plea drags my gaze to his just in time to see his eyes glass over as he collapses to the floor.

Someone screams on my right as I sink to my knees beside him. My hands roam his body and I hear someone behind me call 911.

"What's going on, Tilly?" Nova asks at my side. Her father sits across from me as a stranger pushes through, saying she's a nurse.

"Has he been ill? Fever? Any symptoms at all?" The questions come in rapid succession, and I swallow, trying to find words. I glance up at the older woman but catch sight of Christine's smirking face right behind him.

When her gaze lands on mine, I mouth the words of Lochlan's promise. "I'm not done with you." It's a vow, a promise, a warning. And I never break a freaking promise. The hatred for this woman comes from a dark place within my gut that tells me she's pure evil, and I do the only thing I can in this moment.

I love on Lochlan.

Returning my gaze to the nurse, I answer all her questions as Lochlan's parents empty his pockets, searching for medical cards and identification. "He's had a fever. And pain in his side." My hands ghost along my stomach, mimicking his earlier actions to remember which side he was clutching. "On his right side."

"He was vomiting yesterday, but we thought it was from all the candy he ate," Nova interrupts.

"Anything else?" the nurse asks as she checks for a pulse. I watch her expression change when she doesn't get the response she expects and then begins chest compressions.

Oh my God. Chest compressions. "He's been a little confused. Like he's drunk, but not really. Is—Is he going to be okay?" My voice cracks.

"We need to get him to the hospital as soon as possible."

A heavy hand lands on my shoulder and suddenly another stranger is explaining the scene before me. "This is probably just a precaution. Sometimes they start chest compressions when a pulse is weak until they can get more stable care." I feel the color drain from my face as Lochlan groans on the floor.

Probably a precaution. Right now *probably* feels like a four-letter word cursed in a dark alley.

We sit for an eternity as the nurse continues to work on the man I love. Eventually—or within minutes, I'm not sure—a stretcher is wheeled in, and Lochlan is hefted onto it. The nurse relays information over the hum of worried bystanders. "Lower abdomen pain. Fever. Possible…" Her voice fades as fear rings in my ears.

I don't know what any of that means, and my body spasms with worry.

Lochlan's mother grabs my hand and slips a cold metal ring onto my ring finger before ushering me after the EMTs. "Can she go with him? She's the only one who fully knows his symptoms," she pleads with the man in charge.

My gaze drops to the ring she just slid on, and my body moves in slow motion as I take in what I'm seeing.

"Only family members, ma'am," the EMT says.

"She's his fiancée." Kitty turns to me and takes my arm, dragging me outside. "We'll follow right behind. Stay with him as long as you can and tell them everything." Her face is lined with worry, but she takes charge, and I realize how strong a mother's love can make you for the first time in my life. You either rise to the challenge, or you melt into oblivion. I don't want to melt. I want to rise up. I want to be the woman Lochlan sees, so I nod and kick off my shoes.

Another EMT offers me a hand and hauls me into the back of the ambulance. I sit where they direct me and watch the nightmare unfold before me. He's poked and prodded. Tubes added here, needles there, all while we race the clock at mind-numbing speeds down a highway I don't recognize.

Please. Please let him be okay.

CHAPTER 41

LOCHLAN

The incessant beeping is what I notice first. Like a mosquito that buzzes around your ear, waiting for the perfect opportunity to suck you dry. The second thing I notice is how sore and dry my throat is.

I flex my fingers. One hand is held tight, so I crack open one eye, then another. The room is dark, but there's no mistaking the pungent smell of a hospital. Slowly, I turn my head to the left and find my beautiful warrior. Her upper body is hinged over my bed with my hand held closely in hers.

She's breathtaking all the time, but in sleep, without anyone watching, she's an angel. My eyelids grow heavy, and I succumb to sleep, content in the knowledge that Tilly Camden is by my side.

The next time I open my eyes, the sun is low in the sky, but I don't know if it's rising or setting. Tilly still sits vigil at my side, holding my hand in one of hers, and scrolling her phone with the other. She's wearing scrubs. How long has she been here?

I watch as her expressions change. She's focused intently on something, and I see it play out on her face. Anger. Dismay.

Determination. It's all there for the world to see. If only everyone would take the time to see her as I do.

"The world is missing out," I croak and smile when she jumps in her seat.

"Lochlan? Holy Hades. Let me get the nurse."

"Wait," I manage. She pauses halfway out of her chair. "Water." I want to add a *please*, but it's too painful to talk.

She wastes no time, lifting a bottle of water out of her bag and holding it to my lips. I drink like it's my first breath of air and relish the way the cool liquid coats my sore lips and throat.

"The doctor said your throat would hurt for a while from the tube they stuck down there."

I slide my gaze to hers. "How long?"

"Have you been here?" she clarifies, so I nod. "Three days."

"What…"

"Happened? I really think I should get a doctor." I squeeze her hand and shake my head no just as I tip my face closer to the bottle for another drink. "Well, I'm probably going to get this wrong, but from what I understand, it's like appendicitis gone wrong. There was a tear, some yucky stuff tried to leak into your guts, and you got a bad infection. They think your little bender held off the pain you would normally feel with something like this, and that made it so much worse. It all happened so fast. You—You could have died, Lochlan. When you collapsed at the gala, I thought I'd lost you."

She breaks down then, and I move to reach for her and have to stifle an agonizing groan when I twist. It feels like shards of glass are cutting me open. The only thing more painful is watching the sadness in Tilly's expression. For me. She cares so much. It's all there on her face.

She uses her sleeve to wipe her eyes and nose. It's bloody disgusting and simultaneously makes me want to kiss her entire face.

"Don't move," she admonishes. "You had emergency

surgery, and you still have some sort of drain sticking out of your belly to help get rid of the infection. If we hadn't gotten you here..." She breaks off and tugs her hand free so she can press the heel of each hand into her eyes. I almost laugh at the realization that she's physically trying to hold in her tears to protect me, but then I see it.

My ring. My grandmother's ring. On her finger.

"You said yes?" My tone is full of the awe I'm feeling but also sadness that I don't remember the event. My princess who dreams of weddings all day and night deserves the most epic of proposals.

She freezes and slowly, almost comically, lowers her hands. That's when I notice she's shaking her head no.

"You said no?" I lick my lips as panic clutches my chest. She said no? Why is she wearing the ring?

"Oh, god! I'm so sorry. No, Lochlan. You didn't ask." She starts twisting the band like she's in a panic to rip it off.

"Stop." At least I can still make demands.

But she doesn't even pause. "Oh, shit. It's stuck. I'm so sorry. I've been living on coffee and donuts. Then your dad brought Taco Bell last night." She pauses and flashes a devastating smile. "I thought he was too posh for Taco Bell, but that man housed fourteen tacos. Fourteen!"

A mixture of a chuckle and a groan shakes my shoulders but nearly splits my stomach in two. "He loves that shit."

She goes back to manically trying to get the ring off. "Maybe if I soak my hand in some ice?"

"Tilly." She searches for the ice bucket. "Tilly." A grin grabs hold of my entire body when she doesn't stop. "I love you."

The ring pops off and flies across the room, followed quickly by a red-faced Tilly. "Oh my God. Oh my God. Where did it go?" She's on her hands and knees, crawling across the floor, and I can't contain the laughter even though it hurts.

"I'm supposed to be the one down on one knee, darling."

Her chin drops, and she pushes back to rest on her heels. "What?"

"Come here." I lift the arm that doesn't have wires sticking out of it and wave her over.

Very gracefully but very hesitantly, Tilly pushes to her feet and crosses the room. Her eyes flash when she spots the ring and dives to pick it up. When I don't immediately say anything, she starts blabbering with the ring held tightly between her fingers.

"Your mother stuck this on my finger so I could ride to the hospital in the ambulance. Then she made me keep it on so I could stay in here with you. Then your dad told me to keep it on so it didn't get lost. Then Nova made me keep it on in case anyone questioned our relationship. Then…"

"Then I asked you to keep it on." My words are losing power behind them, but they still pack the punch I'd intended.

"What?" she gasps.

"My memory is still a bit fuzzy, but I remember your promise. I remember that you were willing to give up your biggest dream so we could have a chance. I can't tell you how much that means to me. But the problem is, I can't let you do that. Love shouldn't come with restrictions. I know that now. And the truth is, I want you tied to me. I want you to be my decision-maker when I can't do it. I want you to be my partner in life, in love, and in business."

Tilly shakes her head, but I push on with a shaky voice. "I had that ring in my pocket because my parents knew something it took a little longer for me to figure out."

"They did?"

"They did. They knew I was already hopelessly in love with you, and when I could get out of my own way, I'd need to make you mine as soon as humanly possible. So, I'd like you to wear it, but not as an engagement ring. It's my promise to you that one is coming someday soon. When I can do it properly and give you everything your romantic heart has ever desired."

"You want to promise yourself to me? Lochlan, we should talk about this when you're feeling better. There's so much we need to discuss. So much I need to know..."

"I'm sorry, Tilly." My voice is weakening, so I reach for another sip of water. I have to get this all out now, regardless of how hard sleep is trying to drag me under. "I'm sorry you were blindsided by Christine. I'm sorry I didn't tell you I was once married. I don't know what she told you, but I'd like you to hear the truth from me."

She lowers herself back into the chair that sits beside my bed. I can see her intelligent mind processing my words. "When you're feeling better, lover. We can talk about it then."

"No, Tilly. You have to hear this, and I have to tell you."

She leans forward on the bed and cradles my hand in hers. Once again, she's offering me strength. Encouraging without pushing. Loving without asking for anything in return.

"My mother's ex-husband Paul introduced me to Christine. He met her at a convention, so they say, and thought she would be a good fit for the events coordinator position that had suddenly opened up with Bryer-Blaine."

"She's a wedding planner? Like me?"

"She was an events planner, but nothing like you, darling. Nothing at all. Where she saw dollar signs and opportunities, you see love and life. She has no moral compass, and you are literally my guiding light. The similarities between the two of you stop at event planning."

Tilly contemplates my words with her bottom lip caught between her teeth. After a minute of reflection, she squares her shoulders and faces me again, so I continue.

"Things were good between us for a couple of years. Then, just when my mother was retiring and handing over the company, things changed. Christine pushed for things I know

now she never should have known about. She picked fights and spun them around to make me think I'd started it. She would disappear for hours at a time, then tell me to stop hounding her like a stalker."

When I find the courage to face Tilly, I'm met with compassion. My heart nearly explodes with love for this woman, but I know she needs the entire story. "I was going to break up with her when she told me she was pregnant. She had ultrasounds and baby books, but I was confused. I felt like a monster, Tilly. I was overjoyed at the thought of having a baby, but tormented by the fact that I'd be tied to her forever. She didn't even seem to like me most days, so how was I going to get through eighteen years of parenting with her? But I refused to walk away from my child, so I went along with it when she pushed for a quickie wedding."

A river of tears streams down Tilly's face as she listens to my tale. A true empath, she feels my heartache as if it were her own. The difference is that she takes it on willingly, so I don't have to carry the burden alone. I've never met anyone like her, and I'm more determined than ever to keep her by my side.

"Things escalated." I swallow bile that burns my raw throat, but push on. "She was picking fights all the time. I tried to chalk it up to hormones, but we were coming up on five months, and she wasn't showing. Then I went to my physician for a physical and found out I had chlamydia. I've never cheated, Tilly. Never. Not once on anyone. I knew she'd given it to me because we'd both been tested when she moved in."

"Oh, Lochlan," she sobs.

I can't look at her for this next part, so I stare straight ahead at a blank wall as I speak. "I went straight home and asked her about it. She blamed me. Accused me of cheating. She shouted and cried and carried on until I truly thought that I was going crazy. We'd only been married a few months, but at one point, I had to stop and think about it. I questioned myself because she's so good at turning everything around. I know now that she planned it, but suddenly she was on the floor, clutching her stomach. I rushed her to the hospital, but she said she was too hurt by me. She didn't want me in the exam room. When she came out, she was so convincing. I thought I was comforting a grieving woman. What I was doing was comforting a coward who had just weaseled another year out of me to get her claws into what she really wanted. My trust fund."

Memories attack my vision, and my fists clench.

"How did it end?" she finally asks, pulling me from the darkest depths of my consciousness.

I chuckle roughly. "She just handed me divorce papers one day out of the blue. I couldn't sign them fast enough. However, she didn't know that my family had seen through her. I was handed Bryer-Blaine in name only. In every way that mattered, my parents still owned it. She divorced me when she thought she could get half of our empire. She didn't find out until litigation that it wasn't mine to give. She was pissed, and she still worked for me."

"Bloody fucket," Tilly curses with my favorite saying, and the monster I've become slowly recedes. I can feel my heart growing to match her spirit. "That bitch is going down."

"Hold on there, slugger. I'm not done yet. Actually, the worst is yet to come."

"No."

"Yeah. Legally, I had no grounds to fire her. So even though she got half my trust fund, she still came to work every day to poke at me. Then there was this huge, high-profile wedding at the Gramercy."

"Where you live?"

"That's the one. The client used a pseudonym to make sure they weren't outed, and they requested that my family and I attend. We couldn't say no."

Tilly's body trembles as she shakes her head, but she can't know the dark turn this is about to take.

"I sat in the front row between my mother and sister. The couple wanted to walk down the aisle together, which was strange, but celebrities are often eccentric. Everyone who was anyone was in attendance. As the music began to play, we all stood and turned like the good society members we are. My mother saw them first, and my father narrowly caught her before she charged them and caused a scene." Lifting my hand to my ear, I pinch the skin of my earlobe as a reminder that she can't hurt me anymore.

"Christine walked down the aisle—my aisle with my mother's ex-husband on her arm." My voice cracks, and I clear my throat to force the words out. "They got married right in front of us, in our hotel, and stuck us with the bill. With half of New York's elite in attendance and every paparazzo outside, all we could do was sit there and watch the train wreck happen. The knife in my back twisted with every word they spoke, but it was nothing compared to my mother's pain. I'm not a vengeful person, Till, but I can't let them get away with hurting my mother like this."

"Jesus," Tilly chokes out through heavy sobs. "I'm so sorry, Lochlan. I'm so, so sorry."

"Hey. Hey, look at me." When she lifts her head to mine, I kiss her gently. "Don't ever apologize for something you had nothing to do with. Never, okay?"

"How did you find out about the baby?" She winces, but I know she needs the entire truth.

"I found falsified ultrasound pictures in a guest room after she moved out. I guess it didn't matter to her at that point if I knew or not. She'd already gotten what she wanted."

"But we Googled you."

My eyes close for a minute, and when I open them, I find her staring at me with more love than I've ever experienced. "I paid a king's ransom to have it wiped from the internet. They do a sweep every six months."

Tilly shakes her head while she contemplates my words. "That's why you bought the winery?"

"He took everything he owned and everything Christine stole from me and made some bad investments. Everything they have left is tied into a boutique winery. They rent land on the Ross property. Without that and the Ross grapes, they'll lose it all."

As soon as the words are out, exhaustion like I've never experienced slams into me. My mind and body are finally free from the hatred Christine wove, and my soul dances freely as my love for Tilly ignites into something I know will never let me down.

"I'm tired, Till. Please don't leave me."

I feel her lips against my skull. "Never, baby. I'll always stand by you."

CHAPTER 42

TILLY

"*J*esus, Tilly. Is he okay?" Colton asks when I've finally spewed every last detail.

"Why are you involved? What's going on between you two? I knew I should have slugged the dingledick when I had the chance," my brother-in-law, Preston, barks in the background.

"Geez, Colton. You could have told me he was listening."

"Ah, hey, Till? Everyone's here."

A chorus of *hello*s rings out, and I groan. "Awesome." Nothing like spilling other people's secrets to the entire Westbrook group.

"Can you take me off speaker, please?"

There's a click, followed by Preston's muttering before Colton comes back. "Sorry, Till. You didn't really let me get a word in. Otherwise, I would have said something. But don't worry, they all know Lochlan's story."

"You knew?"

"I've been friends with him for years, probably his best friend since he's such an uptight prick sometimes, but he has a

355

good heart under all that British." He laughs to let me know he's joking, at least mostly.

"How could someone do that to them?"

"Christine is a narcissist. Paul? I don't know. They're both just evil, but I want to tell you, if he told you all of this, you're special to him, Tilly. He doesn't open up like this. Ever. We only found out because his father put out an SOS after the wedding fiasco, so my brothers and I all rolled up to his hotel and got him blasted. It took six beers before he'd even say her name." He's quiet for a minute before adding, "How is he?"

"He'll be okay, but it could have been a very different outcome if he'd been alone. I've never been so scared, Colton."

"It's hard to see the one you love hurting and not be able to do anything to fix it." I don't argue his point on love. It's evident to anyone listening at this point. "What do you need, Tilly?"

"I'm so sorry to bother you with this. You should be planning a honeymoon or something."

"No, we wanted to settle in as a family, so we're taking a delayed honeymoon. What do you need, Till?"

"Lochlan had a plan in place. I'm sure Kitty is all over it, but I heard her tell Ollie that Christine refuses to sell to Blake."

"She's a stubborn one, all right. She knows Blake is helping Lochlan."

"I know, Colton. Don't take this the wrong way, but…I want to ruin her. And Paul, but mostly her."

"Whoa. Little Tilly is a hellcat."

"It's not just that. If they don't sell, there's no way they'll be able to afford the events they're hosting next month. That's four weddings. Eight people who will have their special once-in-a-lifetime day ruined."

"Are you ready to tell me about your wedding planning now, Tilly?"

"Ugh!" I scoff. "Did you spy on me?"

"No. But you're working in the circles my family has run in for years. Did you really think we wouldn't recognize you on those wedding websites?"

"Err, I guess not?"

"Just because you hide in plain sight doesn't mean we haven't been watching, Till. You're family, and we take care of family. So, for the final time, what do you need?"

"I need to make Lochlan's plan a reality. He's in no condition to do it, but he won't rest if he thinks there are loose ends. I don't even understand what I'm asking, but you're the only one I could think of that might be able to help."

"We'll be there tonight," Preston growls in the background.

"Colton?"

"What? I can't help it. He's pacing behind me like a caged tiger. But yes. Apparently, *we'll* be there tonight. Hang tight."

"Thank you. Both of you."

"That's what family is for, Till. We've got your back, and it sounds like Lochlan might be joining ranks soon, so we've got his too."

"Oh, no. That's, I mean…"

"See you soon, Tilly."

"Ugh! Thank you. See you soon."

I hang up the phone feeling more confident than I've felt all day, right up until I turn to find Nova leaning against the wall.

"You called in backup?"

I can't tell if she's mad or not, but either way, I go with the truth. "I hate that she hurt him so badly. And I hate even more that she has no regard for anyone but herself. But the truth is, I love your brother. And it kills me to see him like this. I also know him well enough to know that if I don't do something, he'll put his health at risk to see his plan to fruition. If I can do something to keep him in that bed and bring him peace? I'm going to do it."

She regards me for a full, excruciating minute before

breaking into a wide, devilish grin. "I knew I liked you. I'm in. What's the plan?"

Oh, shit. The plan. Right, I need a plan. "First, we keep Lochlan on lockdown, so he has no idea what we're up to. Then we wait for the Westbrooks and hope they know what the hell they're doing."

She laughs and hooks her arm through mine. "Sounds good to me!"

* * *

"WHAT IS ON YOUR FINGER?" Preston bellows the second he walks into the room.

"Geez, man! Put your spidey-sight away for a minute," Colton chides, entering right behind him.

"What is your sister going to say? Have you even told her? What do we even know about this guy?" Preston takes up way too much space in the confines of the hospital conference room we've commandeered for our meeting.

"Okay, papa bear, chill out," Colton says, rolling his eyes. "You've known Lochlan for most of our lives. There's really little you don't know about him."

"Your sister is going to kill me. She'll be pissed that I knew about this before she does. You know that, right? She's been very emotional lately."

I smile because I'm not sure if she's told him yet that she's expecting. "Preston? I'm not engaged. Not really. This was so I could be by Lochlan's side, but when he woke up, he said it's a promise that someday he'll ask."

"He gave you a freaking promise ring?" Preston is even more irate over this news. "A promise ring? Is he fucking twelve?"

"Dude," Colton says. "He's in the hospital, stuck in a bed with a tube sticking out of his gut. It isn't like he could just run to the jeweler and have something made. Plus, you know Lochlan. Even making a promise like that is huge. He's in for the long haul, and you know it."

I've never been more thankful for Colton Westbrook in my life.

"He should have told us his intentions." Preston grunts. Actually grunts, then kicks a chair before sitting down. The man is usually unflappable, so seeing him worked up on my behalf warms my chest.

The door bursts open, and a mountain of a man with a full beard and tattooed arms strolls in. I inch behind Colton, but he just stands there and smiles.

"He lives." Colton laughs. "Blake Kingston, it's good to see you, man."

"If I'd known there was a fucking assembly, I never would have gotten on the damn plane."

"But you're here now, for your friend. It means a lot." Colton leans in and wraps the stranger in a bro hug.

"I'm here. What are we going to do?"

"Well, lucky for us, my brother Ashton is a genius and can do some really scary shit with computers." Colton beams with pride as he tosses a folder onto the table.

Nova reaches it first and flips it open.

"Christine and Paul are con artists. The Bryer-Blaine was their crown jewel, or it was supposed to be. They spent four times the amount of resources working your family than any of the other jobs they've pulled, combined."

Nova collapses into the chair beside Kitty, who's gone pale. Her words a breathy whisper. "I let him in. I…"

"Mrs. Blaine? They're very good at what they do. There's no way you could have known," Preston says gently.

My stomach turns as Colton explains, "They spent an entire year watching you. Targeting you all. It wasn't their first job, but they'd hoped it would be their last. I'm guessing that's why they came at you as hard as they did. Christine meticulously planned it, and Paul is basically her gofer. He's by no means innocent, but she was certainly the brains of their operation."

"How do we stop them?" Kitty asks, but her voice is monotone, and Nova takes her hand.

"Should I get Ollie?" I ask, suddenly regretting having him sit by Lochlan's side.

"No, but thank you," Nova responds. "Just tell us what to do."

"Well." Colton's eyes shine as he turns up the charm. "I don't think there is anything for you to do. The two of us," Blake grunts, and Colton flashes him an award-winning smile. "Excuse me, the three of us—"

"Hey." I cross my arms over my chest.

"Oh, for fuck's sake. We'll all go." Colton grins, and I realize that was the plan all along. "We'll offer them a deal. They wouldn't sell to Blake because of his connection to Loch. They won't even take a meeting with us for the same reason."

I stare at him in confusion as dread settles in my gut. "How will this plan work if they won't even meet with us?"

Colton's eyes dance as he glances around the room. "We have shell companies, well, our brother has shell companies that can't be traced back to The Westbrook Group. We're using one of those. They'll never see us coming."

Nova stares between the two Westbrooks and Blake, then shakes her head. "This is a whole lotta testosterone wrapped up in dollar signs."

Colton and Preston laugh with matching full-body chuckles, and even Blake grunts with a grin.

"We'll offer them a deal, but it won't matter if they take it or not—the FBI will close in as soon as we're done. Our brother has connections that will allow you to say your piece to the con artists, but their fate is already sealed," Preston explains.

"Do you think they're dangerous?" My nerves force me to ask the question.

"We wouldn't let you anywhere near them if we thought for even a second that they'd harm you, Till." Preston commands the room when he speaks. He reminds me of Lochlan in that way.

"It's settled. We'll head to their office first thing in the morning. They're expecting a suit, but it's us they'll get. Hopefully, Blake will keep his tats on display. You're a little scary like this, man." Blake doesn't respond, but I see his lip twitch. "I knew you'd show," Colton adds cockily.

"Fuck off. I'm only here because Loch deserves better than —than what he's been dealt."

"He's not the only one," Colton says gently. He crosses the room and pats Blake on the shoulder.

Blake shrugs him off and opens the door. "Tomorrow," he mutters on his way out.

I'm left staring in awe at this amazing group of people, and I wonder if Lochlan has any idea how much he's loved.

CHAPTER 43

TILLY

*M*y hands shake uncontrollably as we enter a nondescript building in northern California that's owned by Christine and Paul. Nova and Kitty flank me on either side as Colton, Preston, and Blake lead the way. They're a sight to be seen, and I watch with morbid fascination as Christine does a double take in the doorway.

"She looks like she wants to run," Nova singsongs beside me.

"She wouldn't make it far." Kitty has my arm in a death grip, and I wince. When I shrug, she eases up but doesn't let go.

"Paul," Christine hisses. "Get. Out. Here."

That's when I notice her baby belly is nowhere to be seen, and I lose my shit. *That motherfucking-piece-of-shit-phony.* I've never had a violent inclination in my life, but I charge her, ready to rip her apart. Blake snags me around the waist and hauls me up like a barbell onto his shoulder.

"You psychotic piece of shit," I yell. "What the bloody fucket is wrong with you? Who pretends to be pregnant?"

With brass balls the size of Texas, Christine steps forward, completely disregarding the wall of human muscle that surrounds me on either side. "Aren't you cute," she hisses. "Like a mouse. I suppose after me, that's how Lochluster prefers them. I bet you blend in, don't you? Never cause trouble. Always the fixer. Yeah, I know about your little side hustle. It's cute that you're so naïve. I'm sure it suits Lochlan to have someone so…hmm, how should I put this? Plain by his side?"

Preston and Colton step forward, but I stop them. "Put me down, Blake. I won't touch her."

"You promise? Loch told me you were fiery, but I wasn't expecting this."

"He told you about me?"

"Not the time, Till," Colton mutters with amusement at my side.

"Ugh. I promise."

Christine rolls her eyes but retreats to the other side of the room to stand with Paul. It's a silent face-off, one I'm all too happy to break.

"Do you even care about the people you hurt?"

"If you're here to throw a Care Bear at me or some shit, you can just leave. I'm not interested in a therapy session."

"And yet you need one more than anyone I've ever known," Kitty remarks dryly.

"Oh, boo-hoo. Is the old lady sad that her husband didn't love her? That none of her husbands have ever loved her?"

Jesus, this woman is the worst kind of evil. "You're a wicked, disgusting excuse for a human being, you pathetic, giant turd. I'm done with this. Lochlan had a plan, but I'm not as nice as he is. I want to watch you rot, in a cell, for all the crimes you've committed while yielding love like a weapon."

She flinches but recovers quickly. I probably would have missed it if I'd blinked, but the rage shooting from my eyeholes won't allow a blink. Instead, I turn to Kitty for approval. When she nods, I go in for the kill.

"Douglas Candor. Elizabeth Riggles." Paul takes a step back, and Christine's face goes ashen as I list their aliases. "Mike Ridgeport. Should I continue?"

"What do you want?" Paul trips over himself, backing into a corner.

"Shut up, Paul."

"At first, I wanted to make a deal. But now, I just want to watch you go down. I'll find a way to make sure all those people you're screwing over still have the wedding of their dreams, but watching you get an orange jumpsuit will be so much more gratifying than anything I've ever done in my life."

"You have no idea what you're talking about."

"Don't I, though?" I turn to Kitty. "Is there anything you'd like to add before the ball drops?"

"Not to them. But to you, I'd like to say I've never been prouder to have a daughter-in-law in my life. You, my dear girl, are spectacular. Carry on."

Tears burn the corners of my eyes. She called me daughter-in-law.

"Ah, Tilly? Focus." Colton nudges me along.

"Oh, right. What was the code word, Colton?"

"Who let the dogs out?" He laughs. "Nah, it was something much more original and not at all *plain*." He winks, and I watch with delight as Christine darts for the door only to be thwarted by lumberjack Blake.

"Original and not at all wallflower-ish," Nova grins. "Say it, girl."

"Badass bridesmaids bring down the house," I call.

Colton, Preston, and Blake usher us against the wall as the door bursts open, and within seconds, we're swarmed by the FBI.

"Should I be concerned that my boss and brother-in-law have the FBI in their back pockets?"

Colton winks. "Nah, it's not us. Our brother Ashton is the

genius in our family. He's also ex-special ops. We're just the pretty faces with the big muscles."

Blake groans and pushes off the wall. "You all good?" he asks, staring at me like he can see into my soul.

"Yeah, I'm good. Are you going to go see Lochlan?"

"No. I'm going back to my island. I fucking hate peopling."

Colton tackle hugs him. "Don't be a stranger, asshat."

A shriek has us all turning in time to watch Christine get escorted out in handcuffs and chains. I'm shocked to realize it isn't as fun as I thought it would be. My heart actually hurts. Not for her, but for the person she could have been and for what happened in her life that caused her to turn out like this.

"Don't do it, Tilly. Not everyone can be redeemed. Sometimes, you just have to let them go," Kitty says sagely. She wraps me in a hug and kisses my cheek. "I meant what I said. It may not happen today or tomorrow, but my son loves you. You're ours to keep now. Come on, let's get back to the hospital before Lochlan burns the place down looking for you."

"Thank you, Kitty."

"No, thank you, my dear. You brought my son back to the land of the loving, and for that, I'm forever in your debt."

CHAPTER 44

LOCHLAN

*J*ust when I think I've hit the pinnacle of my rage, Colton drops another detail of their outing today.

"Then Blake lifted her up over his shoulder, and she kept clawing away like she was going to rip them limb from limb."

Okay, yes. A large part of me is impressed that Blake left Block Island for me, but that's not overshadowed by the fact that my mother, sister, and the woman I love were put in a potentially dangerous situation I should have handled.

"She never should have been there," I roar and immediately regret it. My raw throat burns in protest, but it adds fuel to my anger.

"Hey." Tilly stands with hands fisted on her deliciously sinful hips and a pissed-off expression on her face. "This was my idea, lover. Mine. I was not about to let that twatsicle get away with what she did to you. If they weren't there, I would have found a way to do it on my own, so you can get those protective, caveman-ish, outdated thoughts right out of your handsome skull."

My body calms, watching Tilly take control. She excels

working in the background, but my girl was born to shine. My neck finally relaxes enough to rest against the pillow, and I smile at my girl, my partner.

I could feel weak in this moment, but watching her, knowing what she did, all I feel is pride. Pride that when I'm down, she steps up, and pride in the knowledge that I will always be there to lift her up when she needs me. Forever.

"Plus, they messed with Kitty. And she…" Every muscle in my body goes tense as Tilly gets choked up. "She said she was proud of me. Like—like a daughter-in-law." She sniffles and glances away.

If my mother were here right now, I'd hug the life right out of her. I haven't told my family about Tilly's history, so she has no idea how much a statement like that would mean to someone like Tilly. But the Westbrooks and I do.

Holding out my hand, I beckon her closer. When I can reach her, I tug her to me and kiss her softly. "Soon, darling. I'll fulfill my promise soon."

Until this moment, I hadn't thought about a timeline. I just assumed we'd go through the motions and let things play out naturally. But watching Tilly, feeling her emotions, I get why it's so important to her. She needs that family, and I'll go to the ends of the Earth to be the one to give it to her.

There's a knock on the door, and John Ross pokes his head in. Bloody fucket. This can't be good.

"We'll get out of your way. We're headed back soon anyway," Colton explains. He leans in for a hug and whispers, "I'm happy for you. Tilly's a great girl. Take care of her. Welcome to our chaos, man! You're part of the family now."

Emotion I'm not accustomed to clogs my throat. "Thanks."

Colton steps back, and Preston's stern face comes into view. He has a smile in place, but his eyes tell a different story. Bending down, he doesn't even try to whisper. "Tilly is my wife's baby sister. If you hurt her, I will ruin you. Their other sisters will rip off your balls and then watch you choke on them. Don't fuck this up."

I know he's deadly serious, but I can't help but laugh because one of her sisters did give me an almost identical warning. "No need to worry, Papa Preston. I'm in for the long haul. What is it you always say, Tilly? Without a hitch? Yeah, we may stumble a little, but our happily ever after will go off without a hitch, I promise you that."

Preston scans my eyes for sincerity. When he finds it, he winks, and it transforms his entire face. "Good. Welcome to the family then."

John Ross steps to the side to let the Westbrooks pass. When the door closes behind them, he casts a questioning expression my way. "I hear you've had quite the scare."

"It could have been worse. But the doctors have the infection under control, and I'll be out of here before you know it. Who knew you didn't actually need your appendix for anything?" I chuckle, but it's not reciprocated, and I tell him what he needs to hear. "Nothing will change with Ross Winery. I promise you that."

"I know," he says solemnly. "Tilly filled in Doreen this morning. That's why I'm here." Tilly squeezes my hand, but panic rises deep in my chest. "Doreen and I had a long talk after she got off the phone with Tilly. I wouldn't have believed Christine's story, not after getting to know you, but I wanted you to know you're not the first businessman to get taken by a con."

He's staring at the floor when he talks, and when he glances up, realization hits. "They got you too. That's how they're operating on your property."

He nods, shame causing his shoulders to slump. "More like blackmail for something I did when I was younger."

Tilly releases my hand and rounds the bed with graceful speed to wrap the older man in a giant hug. "This was not your fault, John Ross. You hear me? We all make mistakes when we're younger. Trust me. I'm never allowed in Shooters again after a bar-top dance gone bad in college. That doesn't mean it's okay to exploit them. Those two preyed on good people. Who knows how many others? I will not stand for you feeling guilty about it for even one more second."

John pats her back affectionately, casting a look of gratitude my way. "Is it true they were arrested?"

Tilly laughs, and it frees my soul. "Handcuffs and chains. I saw it myself. And with the amount of information we gave to the FBI, they'll be locked up for a very long time."

He leans down and kisses Tilly on the cheek. "You're one remarkable lady, you know that? Because of you, Doreen and I are heading into retirement with a clean slate. Nothing chasing us."

"You're free to live out your best happily ever after, John. Send me a postcard?"

He chuckles, and I see the effect Tilly has had on him. He's lighter than he was when he walked in. She is truly magical. "I'll send you a postcard, but something tells me you're in for one hell of a happily ever after yourself."

"She is. I promise." When Tilly turns to me, I wink and mouth, "I'm not done with you."

And truthfully, I don't think I ever will be.

CHAPTER 45

TILLY

Three Months Later

"*H*ey, Titty! Your prince is here," Mable calls up through the floorboards.

"Would you like to come say hello, Mable?" I laugh, shouting back. Because that's what you do with Mable. You yell to each other through the floorboards.

"Already catching him in the elevator," she calls, her voice fading, proving she is trying to reach him before he makes it to my door.

"Is he used to her yet?" Delaney asks with a knowing grin. Her bright pink sweatshirt matches her lip gloss.

"Can you ever get used to Mable?"

She lifts her head from her laptop. "Good question. I'm on year number three of trying. I'll let you know if it happens."

A sharp knock on the door lets me know he's here, and the following three knocks tell me Mable caught him.

Eli emerges from the kitchen and reaches the door first. She swings it open with a flourish. "Stiffy," she teases.

Lochlan leans in for a hug, muttering under his breath. "You know what a stiffy is, yes?"

Eli's grin grows dangerous, but it's Mable that speaks, pushing past them both. "Oh, we know what a stiffy is. We hear you putting it to good use every time you visit." She pats his chest with a mixture of a laugh and a cough.

His face goes red as he stalks forward out of their reach. "I missed you," he groans, dragging me in for a blistering kiss.

I wrap my arms around his neck as my body melts into his. When he releases my lips, I gasp for breath. "I missed you too."

His gaze darts toward the hallway leading to my bedroom, and the heat in his eyes is unmistakable. This is the longest we have been apart since our time in California, and my body longs for his touch.

"Alrighty then," Delaney says. "Before our apartment goes up in flames, we're going to head out for lunch and give y'all a couple hours on your own." She winks, and it always makes me laugh. She's the one person I know who can't wink. No matter how hard she tries, it always looks like someone spit in her eyeball.

"Two hours?" Lochlan murmurs in my ear. "That's not nearly enough. I need you every day. All day. This commuting bullshit is killing me."

We returned from California as a couple, but a new couple who had a lot to work out.

"I was in New York two weeks ago," I remind him as Eli drags Mable from the room with a wave and a thumbs-up. She also makes a crude thrusting motion with her hips, but I ignore her.

"That was fifteen days ago! Three hundred and sixty hours, Till."

"And we've FaceTimed multiple times a day, every day."

His hand glides up my back in a sensual caress. "But I couldn't touch you, darling." He pulls me into him with a sharp tug at my back. "And I need to touch you." Without warning, he scoops me up and charges into my bedroom like a raging bull.

We're both laughing and carefree as he topples us onto the bed. Hovering above me, he's careful not to drop his entire body weight on me. We stare for a long minute, gazes darting eye to eye as we just feel the intimacy of the moment.

"I love you."

His eyes shine with happiness. "I love you too. So much it's driving me bloody insane when you're not with me."

In the past few weeks, he's hinted about me moving to New York permanently. It would make sense since over fifty percent of our events are held there, but I've wanted to give him time to be sure. I never want to force anything on him.

He grins against my neck as he dips down to taste me. "Are you still pissed that Colton fired you?"

Honestly, I was relieved. I was angry, yes, but also relieved that I didn't have to make that decision. I was terrified of having to choose, even though Lochlan had essentially handed me my dream job.

"Yes and no." I pout. "Colton did it because he knew I felt guilty about leaving him high and dry."

"He did it because he wants you to be happy, Till. Are you happy?" His face grows serious.

"I'm happy now that you're here."

Lochlan leans back and grasps my hands. Raising them above my head, he pins me down, and my tummy does that delicious whirly thing only he can cause. He's slowly relaxed with me in his life, but he'll always be dominant in the bedroom. His thumb and forefinger spin the ring I still wear on my left hand. "In all your Pinterest boards for your dream wedding, you never picked out a ring. Why?"

His question catches me off guard, and I shrug. I'd forgotten that he'd gone through my phone so many months ago now. "I guess I wanted that part to be a surprise. I don't wear much jewelry, so I wanted my fiancé to choose something he thought suited me. Something he saw and just knew it was meant for me. It's silly, I guess."

"No, it's not. But you do know what you want, don't you?"

My face flames and contorts into a grimace. I try to break eye contact, but I should know better.

He hooks my chin with a single finger and drags it back to him. "Show me," he demands.

"Lover…"

"Show. Me."

Wiggling my body, I slip out from under him and trudge to my closet, where I retrieve an eighteen-year-old three-ring binder. Heat creeps down my neck, followed by a light sheen of perspiration. Turning toward Lochlan, I hang my head and hand it to him.

Mortification cannot begin to describe my state of mind as he opens the cover with a loving smile that grows with each turn of the page. Before him is the progression of my dream wedding, starting when I was ten years old. As he gets closer to the end, he pauses, and I know he's found the ring I sketched a little over five years ago.

"This is the ring?" Shock is clear in his expression. "Your dream ring?" He's smiling so broadly now I fear his face will split in two.

He closes the binder with a snap that makes me jump, and a second later, he tugs my hands so I'm falling into the bed on top of him. He flips us fast, and he's once again hovering over me. It's my favorite position.

"That's the ring," I say, still unable to meet his eyes.

"When did you draw that?"

I shrug, but he waits for an answer. "Fine. I did it in economics class like five years ago. I hated economics and because I could only afford to go part-time the first two years, I put it off as long as I could."

"And now you're wearing one that's almost exactly like your drawing."

"I actually like the real thing better. I like that the outside diamonds are rounded. I'd probably scratch the hell out of myself if it had sharp edges."

His eyes smile at my answer. His freaking eyes. "I wanted to plan the perfect proposal." I gasp, and he kisses my open lips. "But you didn't have anything about that on your Pinterest board either. Another surprise?"

"Sort of. More like I didn't want a big show. The idea of everyone staring at me makes me break out in hives."

"So something...intimate? Private?" I nod as my heart rate picks up. His fingers twist the band on my ring finger again. "If I were to tell you that I want this to go from a promise ring to an engagement ring, what would you say?"

I swallow loudly, and he smirks. "Um, I don't know. I suppose it would be a spur-of-the-moment decision." Feeling self-conscious, I glance away.

His hips dig into my belly, and I feel his hard shaft. "Tilly?"

"Yes." I laugh and lift my hips to him at the same time.

Releasing one of my hands, he cups my cheek. "I want this to be an engagement ring. Will you marry me? In front of everyone? Give me the promise, the contract, the everything?"

My eyes burn with unshed tears. They spill over when I nod frantically, trying to force words to come. "Yes. Yes, I will."

His lips crash into mine. "And move to New York with me?" I hesitate. Not because I don't want to, but it will mean leaving my sister and friends for the first time in my life. This man has learned to read my mind in a relatively short amount of time. "There will always be a room for the girls, Tilly."

A tiny sob escapes because he knows how much my girls mean to me. He surprises me again, and I worry that I'm actually speaking out loud. "Our family is growing, Till. Your girls are part of that. A big part. I know you wouldn't be you without them, and I'll always support them with and for you."

"Thank you, Lochlan. For everything."

"Is that a yes?"

"Yes. It's a yes to everything."

We speak no more words. Everything else that needs to be said is done with our bodies. Lochlan slips his hands under my T-shirt and lifts it over my head. "You're so bloody sexy," he growls just before his lips cover my nipple through the satin of my bra.

He wastes no time undressing me, or himself, and he enters me slowly. We've had sex in a number of ways and positions. Lochlan is nothing if not adventurous in bed. But like this, eye to eye as he moves in and out of me so slowly my body begs for more, I know I've found my happy.

He uses his body like a key that opens me just for him. His tongue laves and laps at my nipples while his hand reaches below me to tease my ass. We haven't gone all the way there yet, but every time he teases me with his magical fingers or tongue, I nearly beg for it.

My legs start to shake as he slips a finger inside me and rotates it in time with his cock. It's always too much, and not enough, but it always pushes me over the edge.

"Thank you," I cry out. "Thank you for loving me."

He pauses to cup my face. "Tilly, loving you is the easiest thing I've ever done because I know the outcome will always be the same. Loving you is my greatest joy, and I will thank you for that every day of my life."

Tears cling to my cheeks as we move as one. Love is a powerful thing, and it brought me the happiness I've always searched for.

CHAPTER 46

LOCHLAN

Two Months Later

"Honey, I'm home." Tilly's voice rings out through my office door, and my clusterfuck of a day is forgotten. Tossing my pen aside, I close my laptop and rush around my desk to greet her.

"That's the best thing I've heard all day," I say, catching her around the waist in the foyer. Burying my nose in her hair, I breathe in deeply. I love how all the stress of the day vanishes on an exhale.

"Hey," she says softly. "Tough day?"

"Oh, darling. A bloody fucket nightmare." Today was the first meeting with the prosecutors in charge of Christine's case.

"I know it's hard to rehash everything, but just think of all the people you're saving from the same fate. You're doing a good thing, lover."

"I know. The lawyers need me in California next week for the preliminary hearing."

Tilly lifts her phone and pulls up the calendar. "Okay. What day do we need to leave?"

Love I could never have imagined just pours from this woman. "We?"

"I'm not letting you face the twatsicle alone, Lochlan. Plus I think she's a little scared of me now, and that makes me crazy happy."

"Your events?"

"I've hired enough employees for The I Do Crew to run things for a few days. They're truly amazing. Wait until you see them in action."

I regard her fondly. She's built this business from the ground up and refuses my help at every turn. Except for the venue access and the built-in clientele searching for those specific spaces, she's built a remarkable company and has increased reservations at my hotels by twenty percent in three months. I'm in awe of her every day.

"I'm sure they're amazing."

"They really are." Her smile lights up the entire room. "I'm so proud of them, Lochlan. Every event has gone off without a hitch."

"Without a hitch? That could be your slogan!"

"Hmm, it should be. Maybe I'll start a new blog with it."

When she partnered with me, she shut down her blog. She didn't want to be accused of favoritism, but I know she misses the community she'd built. "You should. People love you, Tilly. And no one knows more about weddings than you. Speaking of which, can we set a date now?"

She giggles and walks past me into our home. "There isn't any rush, lover. We've made the promise. That's all I need."

The irony of this conversation is not lost on me, but Jesus, I need that piece of paper. I want her to be mine in every way, and my inner caveman grunts wildly every time she puts it off.

"Tilly?" My tone is harsh, but I scrub my face with my palm to make sure my expression stays neutral. "Set a date. I want a date. I don't want to wait anymore. Never in a million years did

I think I'd desire that legal bond tying us together, but I do. I require it more than my next breath."

"Lochlan, are you sure?"

"For fuck's sake, woman. Yes! Yes, I'm sure. Please, please set a date."

"Well, it just so happens I have May twenty-eighth blocked out at the winery next year."

"You do? For what?"

"In case a certain mercurial man decided a legal contract was something he really did want."

My eyes go wide with incredulity. "You've been testing me?" I move toward her with panther-like precision.

"No. I've been giving you time and not pushing."

"Push, darling. Always push," I growl before hauling her off the floor in a bear hug that leaves her feet dangling at my shins.

"There will be a lot to do. A lot of parties, plans..."

"The only thing I care about is that we say I do. The rest is just details."

"Oh, but lover, the details make the day!" She glows with happiness, and for the first time in my life, I truly believe in magic.

EPILOGUE

LOCHLAN

Washington/O'Malley Wedding

"You have to stop running, Tilly. Seriously, what are we even doing here?"

"I told you, Sybil is a friend I made a long time ago in the bathroom of a bar." She shrugs like that's an explanation.

Pulling at my T-shirt, I jog to keep up with her. "But you haven't seen this woman in how many years?"

"I don't know. Two maybe? But we text all the time." Tilly comes to a quick stop at a bungalow on the beach and knocks. I stand behind her, trying to understand why she's in such a hurry.

The door sweeps open, and squeals I was not prepared for have me stepping back.

"OMG!" the small woman shrieks again as Tilly leans in for an embrace.

"It's so good to see you." I hear the emotion in Tilly's voice and smile. She really does feel with her whole heart.

"Are you kidding? I wouldn't be here if it weren't for you."

The woman lifts her gaze to me, and I give an awkward wave. "Is this your husband?" she stage-whispers.

Tilly glances over her shoulder and smiles. "Yep, he's mine. Lochlan, this is Sybil. Sybil, meet Lochlan."

Sybil's eyes shine with tears as she stares at me. "I hope you know how special your wife is. She literally gave me the courage to walk away from an engagement I knew in my heart of hearts was all wrong. It's because of her I was free to meet Connor, and I've never been happier."

"I'm so happy for you," Tilly interrupts before I can respond. "I'm just popping in to tell you my friend Hadley is on her way. She'll be my other bridesmaid wrangler. Between the two of us, we'll keep your mother and stepmother from ruining your day."

Sybil had called with a last-minute emergency, and Tilly was unable to pull any of The I Do Crew from other jobs, so Hadley stepped in.

Another squeal has me shrinking back.

"You are the absolute best."

"Right back at you! I'm going to meet Hades now. We'll be back in the morning to kick things off."

The two women exchange another hug, then Tilly's hand is in mine, and I feel her relax. "She seems to be one of the many who attribute their happiness to you, my beautiful wife."

In true Tilly form, she waves me off. "Nah. Her ex was cheating with her best friend. I just gave her perspective when she needed it. She would have figured it out on her own—I was just the catalyst."

My spine stiffens like it always does now at the mention of a cheater. "What happened to him?"

She peers up at me through long lashes with a quizzical expression. "Sybil's ex?"

I nod. "And her friend?"

"Oh, they got what they deserved." She smiles up at me, and

I wait expectantly. I need the bad guys to get their comeuppance.

"Which is?"

"Her friend and her ex got together right after Sybil broke things off. They eloped, and within a year, they were both cheating on each other. But there's this weird law in North Carolina. If a spouse is caught cheating, the harmed party can sue the person they cheated with. Her friend and her ex both got sued and are paying out the nose for their indiscretions. Quite literally." Tilly laughs, and my shoulders relax.

"Is that really a law?"

"Yup." She goes onto her tiptoes and places a gentle kiss on my lips.

We stand arm in arm, waiting for Hadley's car. We were expecting a taxi, so we both do a double take when she climbs out of a Tesla with a man I don't recognize and a giant dog.

"Who is that?" I ask.

"I have no idea, but look at the smile on Hadley's face. I'd say she and mystery man have hit it off."

Tilly releases my hand and speed walks to meet her friend. I hang back and try to size up the stranger who now has his hand on the small of Hadley's back.

"Who is this?" I bark, catching them all off guard. I've become very protective of all Tilly's friends, but Hadley especially because she always seems so scared.

"Lochlan, you scared the crap out of me," Hadley says with a hand over her heart. She walks to me and gives me an awkward hug. "Ah, well, this is my new friend, Noah."

Tilly stares between them. "I thought you were taking the bus to Florida?"

I tried like hell to get her on the plane with us, but she refuses to fly. Or drive. There is actually a lot she won't do. Tilly explained it's leftover fear from losing her parents years ago. It makes me that much more protective.

"How new?" I growl.

"Lochlan."

Glancing over, Tilly tells me to be nice with her eyes, but I don't heed her advice.

"Ha, ha, ha. Funny story, actually. There was a giant tornado in Georgia, and the bus couldn't get through. I had to get an Airbnb."

"And?" Tilly elbows me in the gut, but I barely flinch as I glare at *Noah*.

Hadley's voice shakes as she continues. "Well, I accidentally booked a shared Airbnb."

"We both did," Noah smiles, and I narrow my eyes. He steps forward and offers his hand. I don't take it, and he awkwardly pulls it back. "I appreciate that you're protective of Hadley, but I'm not here to ruin anything."

"What are you here for then?"

Hadley squeaks, and I feel like an ass for making her uncomfortable. But someone has to watch out for her.

"Believe it or not, this guy here is Jimmy Chew."

I glare at him, then the dog he has on a leash, waiting for an explanation, but it's Tilly who speaks. "Connor's dog, Jimmy Chew? You're the best man?"

"In the flesh." He smiles and offers his outstretched hand to Tilly.

Tilly has a mischievous expression on her face that I know means trouble. "You two booked a shared Airbnb in Georgia, that you were stuck in for four days, and randomly happen to be coming to the same wedding. In Florida?"

"Er, crazy coincidence, huh?" Hadley pushes her glasses up high on her nose, and Noah takes her hand. I recognize the moment she relaxes, and I see him in a different light. I've never seen Hadley quite like she is right now, and obviously, by Tilly's shocked expression, she hasn't either.

"Some people would call it a coincidence. I'm calling it fate.

Karma is repaying me for the good deed of watching out for Sybil in that bar bathroom, and destiny is now smiling on us all these days, I think." Tilly shines with her magical happiness like a sunbeam.

Hadley looks up at Noah with stars in her eyes and a happy, content expression on her face. "Maybe."

Tilly's grin is so broad that I swear I can see all her teeth. So much freaking smiling, it makes my scowl deepen even as Tilly pushes forward with her plan. "Well, come on, you two. I'll show you to your rooms. Or should it be room?"

"Tilly," I warn, "don't push."

"Um," Hadley hedges, turning an uncomfortable shade of red.

"Why don't you give us both rooms, and we'll figure it out later," Noah suggests. I'm still not sure I like the guy, but when Hadley smiles, I give in and follow them all to the front desk.

I don't miss the fact that Tilly arranged for their rooms to be next door to each other, but I bite my tongue as we drop them off.

We walk back to our bungalow in comfortable silence. When we cross the threshold, I wrap her in an embrace and feel her body deflate. She's exhausted. "How about if I run you a bath?"

"That would be amazing. Thank you." She reaches up on her toes to kiss me. Tilly still doesn't want gifts, I've realized. She wants my time and my love, but she doesn't seem to realize they are hers for the taking, so every time I do the smallest thing, she responds like I've just given her the world.

It doesn't take long to fill the giant tub, but when I go in search of Tilly, I find her passed out in the hammock. The beach and a hammock are still her favorite places, but I go about putting cushions under her anyway. She's only four months along, but I'm not taking the chance of her falling out of the floating bed of doom. Not even if I have grown fond of the damn things.

When I'm confident she's safe, I pull a chair over. Sitting down next to her, I take in our surroundings and notice the piles of M&Ms on the small table to her left. After the bathtub incident, I haven't been able to eat Skittles again. But, shortly after Tilly moved to New York, I found small bowls of M&Ms all over the house, all sorted by colors, and she's done it everywhere we go ever since.

Every time I think I can't love her any more than I do, she does something like this and rips my heart wide open so it can grow even more.

My life is so much different than how I envisioned it just a few short years ago. Remembering the hatred that was rotting me from the inside out is always hard. It's also a reminder of Tilly's giant heart.

She is the only one who could have pulled me from the dark. She's truly the better part of me, the magical part. My hand rests on her ankle, and I rub her soft skin with the pad of my thumb.

"My sweet, sweet Tilly." Her eyelids flutter but don't open. "I love all your bloody fucket magical ways, my amazing angel."

"I love you too," she mumbles automatically. Even in sleep, she loves me, and happy contentment washes over my entire body.

It's true that love changes a person. I will be forever grateful that Tilly Camden Blaine changed my DNA the day she entered my life. And I wouldn't have it any other way.

EXTENDED EPILOGUE

TILLY

Myers/Parker Wedding

"Put the hairspray down," I plead with an outraged bridesmaid. My Creamsicle-colored dress made of an obscene amount of tulle sticks to my hands every time I move. "And you—I swear to all that's holy, if you dump that bucket of ice on anyone in this suite, I'll send you a bill that will make your head spin."

Both bridesmaids lower their weapons, and I breathe a sigh of relief. I don't participate in babysitting the baddies as often as I once did. Coordinating events at so many properties leaves little time, even with an events manager at each location. But this wedding required my expertise.

A third marriage for both the bride and groom meant a lot of adult children were gaining a family they didn't ask for, and these two newly minted stepsisters are the reason I'm here today.

We almost got by without a hitch, but with less than twenty minutes to go before the reception ends, one stepsister called the other a "cunty-cow." And here we are.

A knock at the door has all heads turning, and everyone

straightens when Lochlan walks in. Seeing me standing with arms spread wide like I'm defending the Queen herself, he narrows his gaze.

"This is why I didn't want you doing this," he grumbles. "I swear, if you ladies are upsetting my very pregnant wife, you will not like my wrath."

He's joking, of course. Mostly. But I'm thankful for the backup. Peanut seems to have dropped low in my belly, and the pressure he's causing is making my back ache.

The bridesmaids gape at Lochlan but don't say anything.

"Okay, I think we're done here—right, ladies? Time to go to your corners and cool off until brunch tomorrow. Come back at this with clear heads and an understanding that your parents' happiness is what matters this weekend. Not whatever power trip you have going on. Got it?"

One lady nods, the other storms off, but at least the end of this evening is in sight.

When we're left alone in the bridal suite, Lochlan scans me from head to toe. He has been overly protective the last few weeks, and today is no exception. "Are you done now?"

I scan the room and shrug. "Yeah. The I Do crew can handle the rest." I haven't even finished the sentence before he scoops down and lifts me off my feet.

The second I'm pressed against his chest, I feel a gush and his eyes go wide.

"Did you?" he sputters. "Was that? What do?"

"Breathe, Lochlan. Yes, I think that was my water breaking."

With me in his arms, he runs directly to the front desk. The attendant stares with a worried expression as he bumbles his way through an explanation. "Call a car. Tell my dad. Hospital."

Jason, a new hire, nods with the telephone to his ear. A few minutes later, Kitty, Ollie, and Nova burst out of the elevator just as we're walking out the door to a waiting car.

"We'll meet you there," Ollie shouts. I glance over Lochlan's shoulder and laugh. Ollie comes barreling out of the hotel wearing denim capris and a very tight T-shirt. His fashion sense is always the star of the show.

Lochlan sets me in the car, and my stomach cramps. Oh, shit.

"What? What's going on?"

I practice the breathing we learned in our birthing class as a contraction hits, and he goes pale. When the pain subsides, I realize Lochlan is breathing in time with me. I don't even get to smile about it before another one strikes, and I squeeze his hand to balance the pain.

"Hurry up," he barks at the driver, but it doesn't really matter. The contractions roll on, one right after another, and by the time we get to the hospital, I think I might pass out.

"She doesn't look right," Lochlan tells the nurse, but I barely hear him.

"She's having a baby. Happens all the time, sir."

Another contraction hits, and I know our little guy is ready to make his appearance this time.

* * *

Lochlan

Tilly sleeps with Jackson on her chest. Who knew nursing would wipe them both out? I can't look away. Our families have come and gone, and I sit beside them with the early evening light filtering in over them. They look like angels. My angels.

Love is a funny thing. Before Tilly, I was sure I'd never love again. After Tilly, I thought I wouldn't be able to love anyone more. Now she's given me Jackson Bryer Blaine, and my heart just continues to grow.

"He's amazing, isn't he?" she whispers.

I lift my gaze from his little head to find her watching me. I've never felt such all-consuming emotion before, and I can only nod.

"Are you okay?"

My shoulders shake with silent laughter. "That's supposed to be my question to you."

"Well, we knew what I was getting into. You're the one who had to handle the blood and guts and—"

I hold up a hand to stop her. "I'm proud of myself for not fainting, but I'd rather not relive the gory details. Only the perfect ones."

"He is pretty perfect," she says through a yawn.

"So are you, Tilly." I lean forward to take her hand. "You surprise me every single day." She tilts her head in question. "You teach me new ways to love and live, and just when I think I have it all figured out, you show me it's possible to love in even greater ways. I don't know what I did to deserve you, but I'll spend my life thanking God, lady luck, and karma for you."

"You're pretty amazing yourself."

Her eyes drift closed, and I take Jackson into my arms. When she startles, I place a hand on her shoulder. "Sleep, darling. I've got him." She nods sleepily, and a soft snore follows.

With Jackson in my arms, I walk to the window over-looking our city. "Your mum is a bright light, Jackson. I hope you'll always know that. She taught me to feel when I thought I was empty. She taught me compassion when I thought I was too broken to care. She taught me to love, buddy. It's the greatest gift I've ever received because it also brought me you."

He coos, and a tiny fist makes its way into his mouth. I'm in awe of every single thing about him—like his little eyes that look like his mother's. I sing the first few lines of Cat Stevens's "Father and Son" because that's something Tilly's given to me too. A love for music that you feel in every part of your soul.

And of all the things I could hope for my little man, the only thing I truly want for him is to find love. To be happy. And to find the partner that will make him a better man.

I'm a better man because of Tilly. I know that to be true. I feel it, and I'll never take it for granted. My life, my love, my heart, expands with our family, and I've never felt more whole in my entire life.

ACKNOWLEDGMENTS

There are always so many people to thank when I finally finish a book. It's a process that takes many eyes, many ears, many hugs, and so much patience. I never pretend that I do it all myself because the reality is, that's not possible for me. It takes a village. So, these are my people:

My husband and my children. Thank you for bending, for your patience, and for your unconditional love you've always given me. We've had to pivot as a family so I can make these stories happen, and I couldn't do anything without your LUV and support. I'm not me without you.

Rhon, my fabulous PA who listens to my months of tears, rage-typing, fears, and anxiety attacks, and never makes me feel bad about my process. There is so much that you do behind the scenes to keep me afloat, and I'd definitely sink without you. XO.

Marie & Carissa, thank you for always helping us keep The Luv Club the kindest place on Facebook. I appreciate your time and support more than you could ever know. XO.

My Beta & Sensitivity readers, thank you for helping make this book something I can be proud of. Your input and insight ensure my stories flow correctly and that my characters are true, kind, and authentic versions of themselves.

My Street & ARC teams, thank you for luving my stories and for your never-ending support. Readers are finding my books and The Luv Club because of you. XO.

The Luv Club, you are truly the best group of people. Social media can be daunting. It takes time and a lot of effort to keep it all going, but with you, it feels like coming home. Thank you for all your support and for helping us make the world a little kinder, one group at a time. LUVS!

Beth, my medical proofer, my longtime friend, my always-give-it-to-me-straight friend. Thank you for your honesty, your friendship, and for always being unafraid to tell me to get my head out of my ass. You're the best. XO.

Joyce, just thank you. Thank you for being a sounding board. For being one of my biggest supporters, and for being the voice of reason when things go nuts. I "Care Bear" the heck out of you. XO.

"A.A.A." friends. Thank you for being a safe space to vent, cry, chat, laugh, and sometimes just not feel quite so alone. You help keep me sane in the insanity of this crazy business and I luv you all for that. XOXO.

TWSS, thank you for taking a chance on me and for all the support you give. I am forever thankful for your guidance, your encouragement, and for your all-around awesomeness. I'm beyond thankful for all that you do.

Kari March, thank you for the phenomenal cover design. You took my ideas and gave them the perfect visual representation.

Jessica Snyder, editor extraordinaire. Thank you for making my words sparkle and shine!

Emily, thank you for proofing my book with fresh eyes to make sure it's the best it can be!

GET TO KNOW AVERY!

I'm a New-England girl born and raised, but now I live in North Carolina with my husband, our four kids, and two dogs.

I write sweet, sexy, small-town contemporary romance because I'm a romantic at heart. My stories are of friendship and trust, heartbreak, and redemption. I try to bring my characters to life and make you feel every emotion I pour onto the page.

I've always been a fan of the happily ever after and the stories that make them, and now I get to write a soul mate for us all. My heroines have sass, my heroes have steam, and together they create the stories you won't want to put down.

Want to hang out with me more? I'm in The Luv Club every day sharing my chaos, my crazy, my life. Pop in to say hi, meet the other luvables, and stay a while. It's the happiest, kindest group on the internet and I'd LUV to see you there!

ALSO BY AVERY MAXWELL

The Westbrooks: Broken Hearts Series:

Book 1- Cross My Heart

Book 2- The Beat of My Heart

Book 3- Saving His Heart

Book 4- Romancing His Heart

The Westbrooks: Family Ties Series:

Book .5- One Little Heartbreak- A Westbrook Novella

Book 1- One Little Mistake

Book 2- One Little Lie

Book 3- One Little Kiss

Book 4- One Little Secret (Coming Soon)

"Nah, I didn't get that vibe from him. My guess is he cares. He cares a lot, and he messed up something big."

Hot tears press at the corners of my eyes. "No, Monty. He didn't mess anything up. He was very honest with his intentions. Are the girls home?"

"Eli went tearing up the stairs about an hour ago like her ass was on fire. The other two have been home all day waiting for you. Should I expect some Chinese food and a Ben & Jerry's delivery?"

Laughter that feels foreign is pulled from my chest. "I think that's a pretty safe bet, yeah. Thanks, Monty."

"No worries, Till. I won't even rat you out to Mable." He winks, and I fling myself at him. Monty has been here much longer than I have, but he's always looked out for us like a father figure standing guard.

He pats my head and gives me a squeeze. "In my experience, Tilly, men like that always find their way home. Just give him time." Pulling out of my embrace, he gives me a serious once-over. "And if he doesn't, I'll kick his ass."

I snort before I can catch myself. "Th-Thanks, Monty," I manage through a hiccup.

"You got it, girly. Now get upstairs. Your girls are waiting for you."

With a fortifying breath, I move on autopilot to the elevator. When I'm standing outside our door, I can hear all three of my roommates pissed off at Lochlan. A sentinel army ready to protect me at all costs, but hearing their disparaging account of Lochlan hurts my heart. He's not a bad man. He's a broken one. That makes this so much more difficult.

I know they'll have left the door unlocked for me, so I turn the knob and step inside. The second I cross the threshold, three sets of eyes find mine. As I drop my bags to the floor, the tears pour free.

Delaney reaches me first and guides me to the sofa.